THE NORTHERN WASTES

THE REALM RIFT SAGA: 3

JAMES T KELLY

Skerry Books Ltd

www.skerrybooks.co.uk

ISBN: 978-1-910599-24-2

For Phoebe.

DON'T MISS OUT ON EXCLUSIVE OFFERS AND EARLY ACCESS TO NEW BOOKS

Join my readers' group today for updates, freebies, and offers on new books! Head to **jamestkelly.com/readersgroup** to sign up!

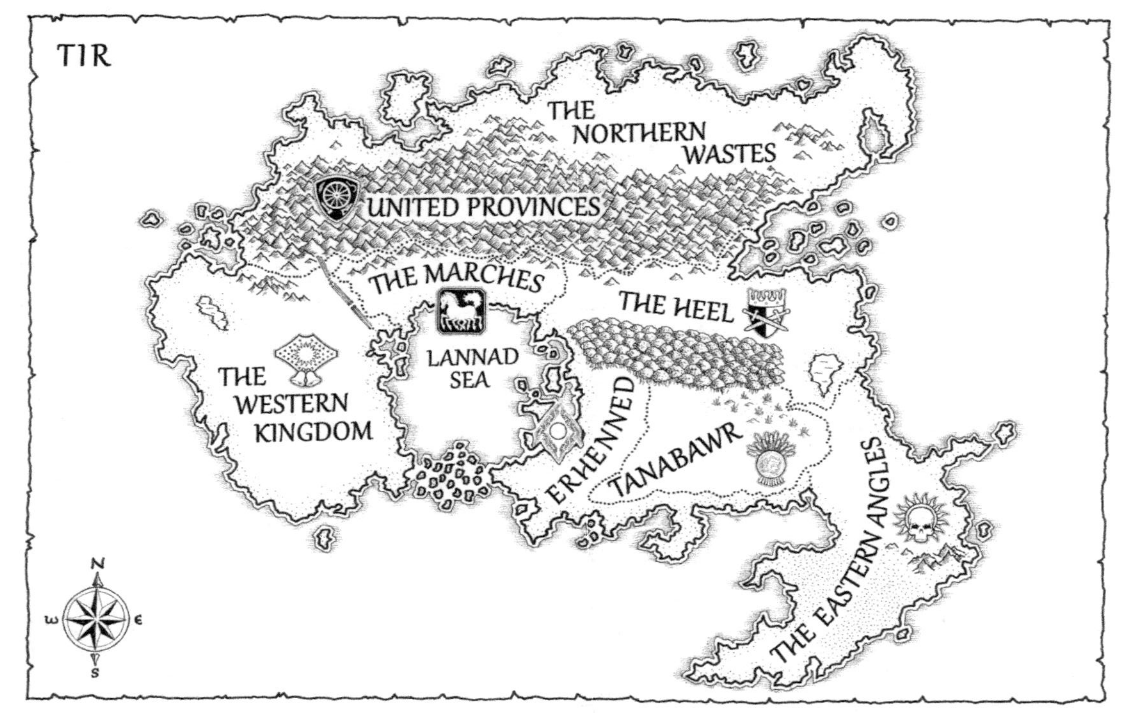
TIR
THE NORTHERN WASTES
UNITED PROVINCES
THE MARCHES
THE HEEL
LANNAD SEA
THE WESTERN KINGDOM
ERHENNED
TANABAWR
THE EASTERN ANGLES
N
W
E
S

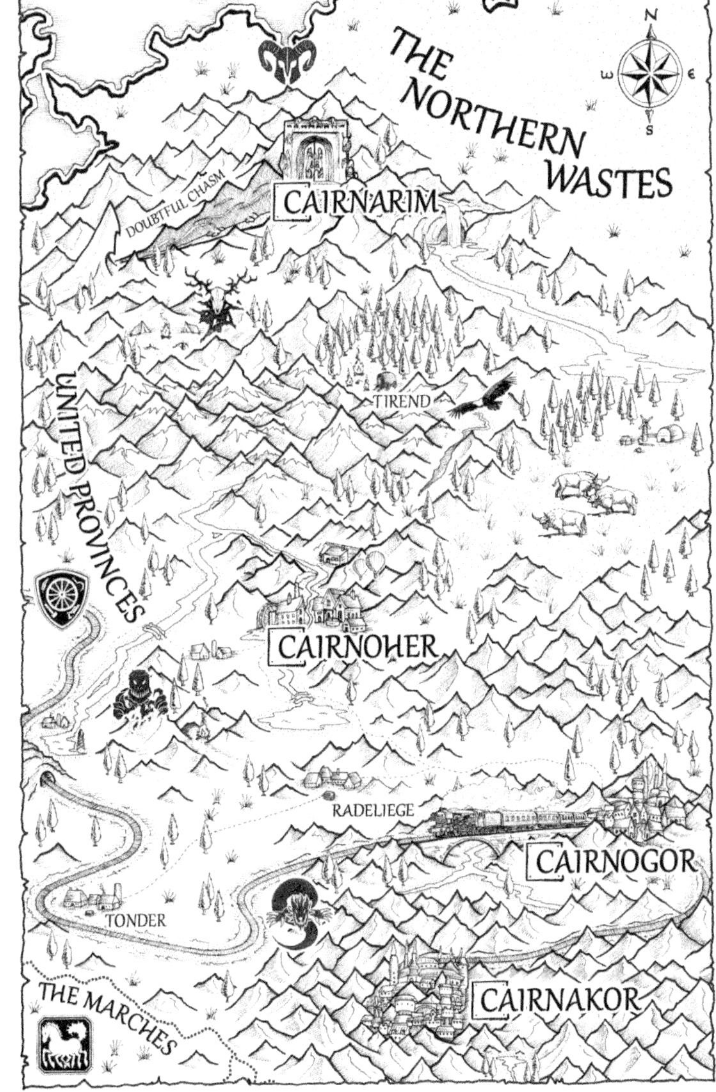

N
W
E
S
THE NORTHERN WASTES
CAIRNARIM
DOUBTFUL CHASM
TIREND
UNITED PROVINCES
CAIRNOHER
RADELIEGE
CAIRNOGOR
TONDER
CAIRNAKOR
THE MARCHES

CHAPTER 1

THE MAELSTROM of magic was worse than being inside the monoliths. It felt to Thomas Rymour that the whirling magics were scratching and tearing at everyone's very thoughts, pooling them, blending them to the point where it was hard to tell whose thought was whose. Who felt that this would be the end of them, that he had killed them all? Perhaps that was Six. All Tom knew was that this would have been easy if his sprite wasn't trapped in a jar. No, that wasn't his thought, it was Dank's. Dank who strained against the world, trying to take them all to Faerie without his link to the fay.

But Tom knew, without a doubt, that it was he that marvelled at the beautiful little life he had discovered: the little girl that Katharine carried inside her. The how and when didn't seem important. Just the marvel of it. He quested towards the child, swimming through the pool of thoughts and fears to her alone.

She was panicking, a nameless, wordless, formless fear of the chaos around her. Shush, he told her. Shush. It will be okay.

She wrapped her feelings around that thought so hard Tom thought he might cry out. So tiny. So helpless. It unmanned him in a moment, filling him with a terror he'd never felt before.

Someone needed to keep this little life safe from sickness, hurtful words, cruel looks, from every man who would look her way. And who was he? Just Thomas Rymour. He couldn't be enough for her.

But he shielded her from the fear that stripped every ounce of courage he had, and instead conjured for her every good feeling and thought he could imagine. He wrapped her in every little pleasure he could think of. A soft blanket, a held hand, a beautiful warm morning, laughter and smiles and dancing and running for the sheer pleasure of running under warm sunlight.

And a promise. I will do anything to keep you safe. No matter what, I will protect you.

Then the maelstrom was gone and he was on his back, staring up into a blurry twilight sky, cheeks warm and wet.

"Tom?"

He blinked, pushed fresh tears down the side of his head. Tried to lift himself. His body ached. Exhaustion. Pain. And loneliness. He couldn't sense the child any more. Couldn't wrap her in comfort or protection against any distress.

"Tom, what happened?" Gravinn asked, trying her best to lift him. She looked pale, sick. So did the others. But they all looked at him, concerned and worried.

Except Katharine. He couldn't read her expression. "We have to hurry," she said.

Yes. That little girl would need a home. And clothes. Money, for food and toys. She would need teaching too.

"We tried to get us as close as we could." Dank wiped his mouth. The sour tang of vomit was in the air. "To Emyr."

Oh. Suddenly their daring raid to rescue wounded King Emyr from Faerie didn't seem so important.

But they were all waiting on him. "Right." Tom hauled himself to his feet, wiped the tears from his face. Stared at Dank until he took the lead.

The boy had done well. They were in the barrows, the low, undulating hills that surrounded Emyr's resting place. The fay didn't much like the barrows, so they were mostly deserted. But Tom knew that, even if there were no eyes to see them, they were discovered all the same. The fay had a deep link to their realm. The fay would know they were here.

He'd once worried about merely requesting entry. Now he had broken down the door. Maev would never forgive that.

The clearing was empty. Emyr lay on his white stone bier as always. But Ankou, the hooded fay who tended to the old king, was nowhere to be seen.

Ankou never left Emyr's side. Ever. Tom didn't know what this meant, but he was sure it wasn't good. He rushed to the bier, touched Emyr's hand. Did the old king seem older than last time? Did his wound bleed less? Emyr's eyes fluttered open and there was peace in them for just a moment before the pain came rushing back to him. He took a breath through gritted teeth before his gaze fell on Tom.

"I thought you left, son?" he asked. So tired, and in so much pain that Tom's resolve faltered. Who was Thomas Rymour to decide that it was time for Emyr to return, to fight the fay and protect the people of Tir again?

But who else was there, if not Emyr?

"We did," Tom said. "We came back."

"So soon?"

"My king, there's no time to explain. I'm sorry." And Tom put an arm under Emyr's head, around his shoulders, and lifted him. Fresh blood oozed from the wound in his stomach and he cried out.

"What are you doing?"

"Taking you back to Tir."

"No." He pushed weakly at Tom. "I'll die."

"The dwarfs can heal you."

"No." He shook his head with the violent panic of a man who thought he was facing his final moments. "They can't."

"They can." Tom realised what he had said, and added, "I can't lie, remember? So, if I can say it, it must be true."

That stilled Emyr's protests and he sat dumb as Tom lifted his legs over the edge of the bier. The others crowded around them and Tom looked for Dank. "Ready?" The boy nodded and Tom turned to Gravinn. "Where do we go?"

But before the dwarf could speak, another voice said, "There is nowhere we cannot find you, little Tom."

Too late. Of course it was. The others turned, parted, and Tom saw Melwas stood at the entrance to the clearing. Tall, handsome, proud Melwas, king of the winter fay, wearing a furious smirk and cruel, black armour. Attended by Herne. Followed by two Faerie hounds, foul, ugly things, skinless and slathering beasts with enormous fangs. They stood as tall as Melwas' waist, their flayed flesh leaving blood on the grass as they followed their master. Tom had seen them eviscerate aurochs in seconds, their jaws powerful enough to snap a man's limb from his body as easily as plucking a leaf from a tree. And while Herne was smaller, he was no less dangerous, muscles bunching beneath filthy skin and eyes glowing red and murderous within his hart-skull head. Tom felt his guts twist and freeze with fear. Had he led them all to their deaths?

"We must admire your spirit, little Tom." Melwas stepped into the clearing, stalked by his horrific retinue. "We had not imagined it of you. To be so bold, so rebellious." Melwas stopped and gave them all a flawless grin. "To show so little fear in the face of our wrath."

Don't show him how scared you are, Tom told himself. Don't give him the satisfaction. "You used me."

Melwas clapped his hands together and tipped his head, a condescending gesture. "Bravo, little Tom. We did."

"You used me to help you terrorise Tir."

"You seemed to enjoy it."

"I was wrong."

Melwas opened a hand, palm up, as he said, "Right." Opened the other hand and said, "Wrong." Then he flicked his wrists, dismissing the ideas with a careless flourish. "Mortal concerns, little Tom. Such things bore us. You must know us poorly if you think we care for them."

"No. I know you don't care."

"We should go," hissed Six. "Dank, take us away."

But the boy was pale and stiff as a corpse. The only part of him that moved were his eyes, tracking Melwas around the clearing, tracking the hounds at his heels.

"Of course, you know we would have had our way, little Tom. Had you failed us, we would have found another mortal to play our game. Him." Melwas pointed at Six. At Draig. "Or him. Or perhaps we would have finally healed Emyr and sent him back. Now that would have been a true challenge." Melwas grinned. "To convince the legendary King of Tir to break the monoliths and help us make Tir and Faerie as one."

Tom couldn't tell if it was the pain or Melwas' words that made Emyr shudder. They had to leave. But Tom couldn't help but ask, "As one?"

"As one," Melwas confirmed, petting a hound at his heel, admiring the blood that the flayed flesh left on his fingers. "No more doorways, no more Circles or barriers. Just one playground for our people." It made no sense. How could you take two places and make them into one? But Melwas seemed certain as he said, "Imagine it, little Tom. The great castles felled, the stone used to build mighty thrones for us and our queen. The little cities remade into glorious arenas. And those mortals that do not fight and die for our pleasure will instead turn their toil to building great amusements for us."

It made Tom's stomach churn to think of it. He could picture lines of men, women and children queuing to work and bleed and die just to alleviate the boredom of the fay. He couldn't let that be the world Katharine's child grew up in. "I'll stop you."

"Will you, little Tom?" Melwas gave him a pitying smile. "Or will you stand aside at our queen's command like a good little pet?" He lifted a finger to Gravinn and said, "If Mab wished it, would you watch our hounds chase down and devour this little one?" His attention shifted to Dank. "If she told you it would make her happy, would you hold the sharp objects and the burning brands while we tortured him for an aeon?" His gaze fell on Katharine and he grinned. "And would you scrape and bow while our queen exercised her little jealousies on this one?"

Jealousies that would likely mean eternal misery and torment. And what would Mab do when she discovered Katharine was with child? "No."

"No?" Melwas tossed his head and laughed, a hearty chuckle that turned to a growl in a heartbeat. "No?" His eyes were dark and furious as he spoke through gritted teeth. "Always have you defied us, little Tom, always have your bows been too shallow, always has your heart belonged to this one." Melwas jerked his head at Emyr. "But we will change that. We will hurt you, little Tom. We will show you pain you thought impossible to live through." The Faerie King advanced, fingers clenching as if he imagined crushing something of Tom's. Then he smiled, his voice light and empty of all fury and violence. "Then we will stop, and bring you wine and bread, and you will begin to hope that maybe the pain is no more." A dark delight crept into the fay's eyes. "But again we will start hurting you. Again we will stop, again you will hope, again we will hurt you. Over. And over. And over. And one day, many centuries from now, we will stop for good. And you will be so grateful, little Tom." Melwas was close now. Too close. Tom had to tip his head back to meet his eye, and the fay lifted a hand, brushed the back of his fingers across Tom's upturned cheek, and murmured, like a lover, "You will swear yourself to us, because we made the pain stop at last. You will love us, little Tom. We will make sure of that."

I will not break. That's what Tom wanted to say. I will not break for you. But Melwas had eternity to torture him. Who knew what centuries of torment could do to a man?

Tom swallowed. Forget the threats. Get Katharine and the child beyond Melwas' reach. Every other concern could wait for another day. But his voice betrayed him, shaking as he said, "Emyr is my king."

"For now." Melwas sighed a satisfied sigh. "But when we are done with you, a cripple will never compare to our majesty." And he turned his head to smirk at the old king.

Melwas was quick. Tom knew that. But he was cocky, too. He thought he had won. So he was slow to react. Slow to see Tom push Emyr aside and draw Caledyr. Slow to see Tom thrust the blade toward his chest. Too slow to twist aside and avoid the blade that slipped through his armour like butter and skewered his shoulder with ease.

It took Tom a moment to realise that everything had changed. Melwas was roaring a wordless roar. The ground was shaking and rain was lashing down on them. Tom looked up into dark clouds that had obscured the twilight sky in an instant. Rain in Faerie. He had seen light showers before. The fay would revel in them, dance in puddles, huddle under shelter and watch their realm shimmer under a hundred thousand miniature prisms, emerge to gaze at rainbows made of colours unseen in the mortal realm. But this was something new. This was a storm. There were no storms in Faerie. Not ever.

Melwas dropped to one knee, Caledyr still buried in his shoulder, and the ground shook. Tom looked down, drenched to the skin already, hair slicked to his forehead.

Tom twisted the sword.

Lightning flashed and forked across the sky.

He realised he could end this right here. Right now.

"I wasn't sure this would work." Tom had to shout over the noise of rumbling ground and driving rain. Melwas rolled his eyes to meet Tom's. But they were empty things. Tom couldn't be sure the fay understood him. The Faerie King reached for Tom, fingers grasping for a hold, but Tom twisted the blade again.

The hounds whimpered with a shared pain. They were hunkered to the ground, slinking back, slinking away.

Herne was gone.

"But I couldn't understand why you'd hidden the sword. Why you demanded I bring it back to you." Tom's breath was fogging, the air grown chill. Melwas moaned and Tom leaned closer, twisted the sword again. "It's because it can hurt you. Can it kill you, Melwas? Could I end you right now?" He wanted to. After so many years of dodging the fay's wrath, after months of being manipulated. It would feel good.

"Tom!" Katharine screamed and he risked a glance. She was huddled with the others, waving him towards them. "We have to leave!"

He looked back at Melwas. Felt his fingers twitch around the grip, felt his arms full of anticipation. He felt himself on the edge, ready to pull the sword free and then swing it through the fay's neck.

The ground shook again and he almost lost his balance.

"Tom, we have to leave." Dank was in the centre of the huddle. Everyone had a hand on him. "Faerie isn't safe. You're hurting it."

Hurting Faerie. Because he was hurting Melwas. Tom nodded. He'd always wondered if the fay and their realm were one and the same. "Then I can end this now," he said. He could put an end to years of blind servitude. He'd never be a Faerie puppet again. And Katharine could raise her little girl in peace. Yes. This was how it should end.

"Not with us inside Faerie. We're not safe here," Dank cried to him over the storm.

"Then go." Let them escape. It would be worth dying here to protect them. "Take everyone to safety."

They shouted at him, all of them, tried to reason with him. But he knew the rightness of what he did. He knew it now. He had always said the fay were dangerous. Not because they were immortal. Not because they were good or evil; they were neither. The fay were dangerous because they didn't care who they hurt, who they killed, who they manipulated or tortured. They would do whatever entertained them, and the mortal cost wouldn't even occur to them. But Tom could stop them. Here. Now. Let all of Faerie come down around him. As long as it came down on them too.

"You kill your queen." Melwas' groan was almost inaudible over the rain and the roar.

Yes. It would kill her. And he would never see that little girl born. His resolve faltered. He had made her a promise. I will keep you safe.

Perhaps destroying Faerie would be how he fulfilled his promise.

He felt hands on his shoulders and arms, Katharine slapping at him, pulling him. "Go," he told her.

"No." Her efforts jostled him and twisted Caledyr, eliciting dead moans from Melwas. The fay had given up fighting, hanging limp from the sword. It was strange to see him so still. So empty of his strange, malicious drive. "I'm not going to let you do this," she said.

"You'll be safe," Tom replied. "Both of you." He shifted his feet. Readied himself for the swing. Would it end with Melwas? Or would he need to kill Mab too?

"Don't leave me alone."

"You're strong," he told her. He didn't dare look at her. Didn't dare test his resolve that way. "If anyone can raise her, it's you."

"She needs her father," she replied. "And I need you too."

So. He was the father. He tried to steel himself for the final blow, but he already knew that he'd made his decision. He wouldn't abandon his daughter.

"It would be easier if I didn't know." He wasn't sure why he said it aloud. Perhaps he needed Katharine to know why his resolve had failed. Perhaps he needed Melwas to know.

He pulled Caledyr free, and Melwas groaned and collapsed. The grass at their feet had grown black and dry, the rain pounding it into dust.

"Let's go," he told himself. Katharine took his hand and led him to the others. Tom couldn't help but glance back at the Faerie King, who lay on his back and stared unseeing up at the rain that never fell in Faerie. Couldn't help but enjoy a moment of dark pride that he, Thomas Rymour, had brought Melwas to his knees.

He let Katharine place his hand on Dank's outstretched arm.

"To Cairnakor," Gravinn said.

There was no simple tug. It was a struggle, as if Dank was lifting a mountain by himself, climbing a waterfall, staring unblinking at the sun. Tom felt the battle in the very heart of himself, thrashed against the magic that wrapped around them like a malicious, suffocating sheet. Again they were all as one, like individual inks poured into the same bowl, mixing their fears and loneliness together.

And that tiny new life. That little impossibility. Tom reached for it without thinking, sheltered it in warmth and promises against the storm of magic, against the tidal wave of thoughts and identities.

He felt her settle, put a thumb in her mouth. His daughter. He could laugh. Or cry. Maybe both. His daughter.

I will look after you, he whispered. I won't let anyone hurt you, he promised.

And he felt Katharine's relief at his words.

They were thrown into Tir, crashing to the ground. Old injuries awoke and Tom tasted grass. The world was spinning and lurching and he felt very certain he would be sick. He curled into a ball for a moment, taking deep breaths. Deep, cool breaths. But there was a smell of burning in the air that made him feel worse. He opened his eyes, shut them against the spinning, forced them open again and made himself meet the dark gaze of the man standing over him.

"You're here," Tom said, swallowing the bile that threatened to follow his words, staggering to his feet and leaning on his knees. If he'd felt tired before, now he was beyond exhaustion. It was oddly freeing. He felt he could walk for days, if only because he couldn't feel worse for it. He straightened his back and said, "I won't ask how you got here."

"Because you know I don't remember." Ambrose stood still as stone, robes stiff with mud and filth, face shadowed by a wide-brimmed hat. His hair and beard, both a dirty grey, were long and unwashed, and his skin was leathery and wrinkled with impossible age. Yet he did not lean on his simple wooden staff. He didn't shift or seek a place to sit like many old men. He just stood, impossibly still. Like a statue made flesh. Tom wasn't even sure if he was breathing.

The sorcerer's lips twisted in a smile. "It's good to see you again, Tom." His smile didn't touch his eyes, which remained two pits with just a hint of light. Nothing but an ember, the tiniest spark, trapped deep within the dark.

The present faded and Tom saw himself sat in darkness, no sun or moon or stars to light the cold, dead world he found himself in. "You lost Caledyr," someone said.

A groan from Emyr swept aside the foresight. "My king," Tom said, rushing to his side and lifting him to his feet. "We need to get you to a healer."

"I can't do it." Emyr words pleaded for relief, his hands pale and shaking and covered in blood.

"Just a little farther," Tom promised him.

But Emyr's legs were weak, his steps stumbling. Tendons and veins stood out in his neck like they would burst. "I can't."

"Just a little farther." But it was no good. There was no way Emyr could walk anywhere. Tom looked at Draig, still sat in the grass. "Help me carry him."

Ambrose stilled any response Draig would have offered. "Not you," the old sorcerer told Tom. "Draig and Six."

"Why?" But Tom knew why; Ambrose's dark stare was resting on Caledyr. "Gravinn, lead the way." Tom relinquished his grip on Emyr and drew the sword, the blade singing in his grip.

"A moment," Gravinn begged, pale and curled around her belly.

"We don't have a moment. We need a place filled with iron, and we need a healer." Emyr groaned, and Tom added, "Now."

But the word was barely past his lips when the back of his neck began to tingle and the air began to hum. Magic. He turned, and the air behind him seemed to thicken, like a wisp of a shadow that drew its fellows to it, growing larger and darker, growing legs and arms and solidifying into pale skin and a cruel smile.

Queen Mab. Stood in Tir, dressed in a tapestry of mismatched clothing and adorned with strange jewels and trinkets. A parody of a Pathfinder. Even her hair was bound in a tail just like Katharine's. But where Katharine's outfit spoke to her journeys to foreign lands, Mab's was designed to accentuate her figure, stretched over her skin, baring her midriff, drawing the eye to a generous cleavage. She was beautiful as ever, and her eyes danced with promise.

Tom hefted Caledyr, placed his feet where the sword told him to, and tried to ignore how his traitorous heart danced.

Her smile grew wider and she ducked her chin. When she spoke it was with a coquettish air. "Surely you do not think to use that against us, our Tom?"

Her manner was all wrong. Just moments ago he had brought her king to his knees. He had violated Faerie, he had threatened to pull it all down. And Queen Mab smiled at him.

"What do you want?" he asked.

Her smile faded and her manner cooled. "Is that any way to address your queen?"

The others were still, silent, barely breathing. "Go," he told them. "Gravinn, take them where they need to go."

"We have not dismissed them," Mab said.

"Your audience is with me," Tom replied. He told the others, "Go," once more and, when Mab bristled, he said, softer, "Let them go. I'll sheathe the sword. We can talk."

"No, Tom," Katharine said. Tom risked a glance over his shoulder and saw her stood with her hand on her belly and reproach in her eyes.

"I'll catch up," he told her.

"It seems you are always racing to catch up," Mab said. And to Katharine she added, "You'll have your hands full with two of them."

Katharine made no attempt to hide her disgust. "Don't take

too much time with this thing," she told him, and turned and walked away.

Mab traced a long nail across her own jawline and down her elegant neck. "We have flayed mortals alive for less," she mused.

"You have forgiven more," Tom reminded her.

"Is that what you ask, our Tom?" Mab let out a throaty laugh. "Do you want to return to our bosom and be told that all is forgiven?"

Tom tried not to look at her bosom as he asked, "Would you offer forgiveness if I asked for it?"

Mab looked him up and down and quirked an eyebrow at him. "Would it amuse us to do so?" she mused. Tom tried not to imagine a passionate embrace, her rough touch, the taste of her skin. A rush of blood brought warmth to his face and she raised her eyebrows. "It seems it would amuse you," she added.

Fight.

The sword was right. Mab might be all seductive wiles, but she was as dangerous as any other fay. And she might be only a diversion to separate him and the sword from the others. So he said, "Leave the others be."

She stepped closer and looked over his shoulder. "Dank has opened our doors to mortals, and Draig forgot his oath to stop you." She shrugged and brushed at something on his shoulder. "But no matter. That isn't why we are here."

He could smell her. Jasmine and rich, dark earth. "Why are you here?"

She pushed her body against his, sliding her hand across his shoulders and murmuring into his ear, "To warn you, sweet Thomas. Our Thomas," she claimed him. "You did great harm to our king. That will not come without consequences."

She had her hand in his hair and sighed satisfaction and desire. This was not the kind of torment he had imagined. "I will bear them willingly, if you spare the others."

"You will bear them, willingly or no," she warned him as another hand snaked around into the small of his back. "You will bear whatever we decide you will."

He felt her smile against his cheek. She had hold of him. Entirely. She could pull him back into Faerie in an instant. Part of him thrilled at the thought. Another part was disgusted that he had let her entrap him without a single protest.

As if sensing his conflict she tightened her embrace, waking old pain in the wound he'd taken from an Erhenni fighter. An Erhenni who had died so he could free Tir from the Western Kingdom. From oppression and suffering.

"Release me," he told her.

A moment of silence. When she spoke, her words were breathy. "Do you really want us to?"

But it was all a lie. Nothing more than an act. Nothing like the blood and sacrifice he had witnessed and suffered. Nothing like the promise of birth to come. "Release me," he said again. She stepped back and gazed into his eyes, trying to find something. Let her look. "Melwas threatened me and mine," he told her. "I hurt him to protect them. If you want me to apologise, Your Majesty, I must disappoint you. Because I'll do the same to any fay who tries to hurt them."

"Even us?" She sounded distracted, as if she was barely listening. Still looking for something in his gaze.

"It would pain me to do so." That was true, as much as he didn't want it to be. "But, yes. Even you."

A slow smile spread across her face. "Such fire, Thomas. A fire that would make any maiden weak in her knees." She placed a finger beneath his chin, and made a satisfied sound that somehow seemed to promise more than mere satisfaction. "Go," she purred. "Protect you and yours." She brushed a thumb over his lips. "Hurt the fay we send after you, if you can. Show us this new fire." She released him and stepped back. Her abrupt dismissal stilled his tongue and, despite himself, he bowed his head.

"Don't spoil it," she told him, and he looked up to see her form softening, like her flesh was smoke being plucked at by the faintest wind. "Do not raise our expectations, Thomas, only to disappoint us. You will like that even less than our king's wrath."

And then she faded into nothing, and he was stood alone on the hill.

CHAPTER 2

"WHAT DID THAT CREATURE WANT?" Katharine demanded when Tom rejoined the others.

"I'm not sure." His thoughts still felt foggy, as if her scent had crept in and muddled his mind. Perhaps it had. "But I'm not sure I made anything better."

"Please, Tom," Six grunted. He was waddling backwards along the white gravel road with Emyr's feet in his hands while Draig had his arms hooked under the old king's armpits. "Such a shocking revelation might make me drop him."

The sarcasm made Tom blink and he drew breath to bite back. But, before he could, Dank asked, "Are they coming for us?"

The boy's obvious fear deflated Tom's anger and he nodded. "They are."

"Then does any of this matter?"

The fay were immortal. They wouldn't be stopped. Yes, they had Caledyr. But one blade could not keep the whole of Faerie at bay.

But what could he say? Nothing but, "Yes." Dank didn't believe him. That much was clear. But Tom reached out to

Katharine, who wouldn't look at him but was listening intently, and brushed a finger across the back of her hand. "Nothing matters more."

Her lips quirked with the effort of hiding a smile. And Ambrose said, "We have time." The old sorcerer didn't look at anyone as he spoke. He stared at and through the road at his feet, shuffling along and leaning on his staff as if it was the only thing keeping him upright. "Two days."

"Is that true?" Dank asked.

"You know who Ambrose is," Tom told him.

"I don't," Gravinn called over her shoulder.

"Your people called me by a different name," Ambrose replied. "Melled."

That stopped Gravinn in her tracks, and Six grunted. "By all means, let's stop and stare at the old man. Emyr gets lighter with every step."

Gravinn started walking again, but kept looking back over her shoulder. "The Thunder King's advisor?" she asked. "You live too?"

"In a way," Ambrose replied.

"Do you have to tell the truth like Tom?"

"No. I don't."

"But you trust him?" That question she directed at Tom, and for a moment he wasn't sure how to answer. The old man lies. That's what Nimuë had said. But Ambrose had given him the Call, the one that had saved them from Gerwyn's rat pits. And Gravinn had it right; Ambrose had been Emyr's most trusted adviser. Tom trusted Emyr. Did that mean he trusted Ambrose?

"I believe him," he said. It was the truest answer he could offer, but it seemed to settle the matter for Gravinn; her eyes turned back to the path ahead.

"Nimuë called him a liar," Six grunted.

"Ah." Ambrose's lips twisted into a smile. "Nimuë."

"She also said he was a Faerie treasure."

Yes. She had. An odd term to use. Was Ambrose a creature of Faerie now? Was this another of their elaborate games?

"Nimuë only remained Nimuë because of a Faerie boon," Ambrose told them. "In exchange, the fay told her to watch over me. And over Caledyr. The fay were under the impression that both could be kept. They were wrong."

The sword grew larger in Tom's mind for just a moment, like a giant turning in its sleep.

"The stories say you were infatuated with Nimuë," Tom said.

"I am." His smile grew sadder. "Until my end."

"She was in thrall to the fay," Six's voice was strained. "You were in thrall to her. Oen's blood, are we there yet?"

"You don't trust me," Ambrose said.

"You're a quick one."

"On the contrary." Ambrose nodded to his shuffling gait as if his neck didn't twist the way it ought to. "But Tom can attest to this: being infatuated with someone doesn't mean you are their creature."

All eyes turned to Tom. None of them seemed reassured, and Tom felt his cheeks warm.

"You and I," Ambrose said, and turned his gaze away to the horizon. "You and I, Tom. We do what we have to do."

No-one spoke until they reached the city.

Cairnakor was a sprawling, cramped creature. The buildings were either close and tall, or squat and teetering on mountain-sides. They jostled for space with great chimneys that belched dark smoke into the thick, stinking fog that settled in the streets.

The mountains clambered up from amongst the press and the stench to claw at the sky, as if trying to climb away from the miasma, but the swarm of the city kept them from the blue skies with its thick smog.

There was no wall, no gate, no solid beginning to Cairnakor. Homes began to appear alongside the road, which became stone paving worn smooth by use, and the fog became denser until they could barely see three foot ahead. The air felt thick and unhealthy, still and quiet in the early morning, though the streets were far from deserted; the alleyways were filled with dwarfs lying under rags or blankets. Tom had seen beggars in every town he'd visited, but never so many in one place. What was wrong in Cairnakor that so many were without homes?

And how could they sleep with all this smoke? It rose out of the chimneys before sinking back into the fog that clogged the streets, making Tom cough and gag. The smell was unlike anything he'd smelt before. Something was burning, or had burnt, but there was no wind to toss away the stench. Tom glanced at Emyr's wound. Didn't dwarfs know that bad smells carried disease?

"You get used to it," Katharine told him, and he felt a stab of guilt. Why hadn't his first thought been of her and the child?

"I'm not sure I want to," he replied, and lowered his voice to add, "We should leave as soon as possible."

"Don't start fussing over me," she told him, but her smile told him she was pleased.

Gravinn lead them down a wide road filled with abandoned carts and rough sleepers before taking them down a narrower path. The buildings on this street had huge glass windows behind which were arrayed a bewildering variety of goods and wares. Bakeries proudly displayed huge platters and trays soon to be filled with warm breads and pastries, and grocers showed off pyramids of apples and mounds of carrots. Tom's stomach growled and he tried to remember when he'd last eaten. But Gravinn passed them all and stopped in front of another shop. Tom couldn't read the sign, but the window told him everything he needed to know. Saws and hammers, knives and cogs and instruments of iron stared out at them through the glass. The fay would think twice about entering this place. Tom lifted his hand and hammered on the wooden door as hard as he could.

The sound echoed down the empty street. No dwarf or creature stirred. He hammered again.

This time there were rustlings and mutterings behind them. Tom whirled, brandishing Caledyr, but it was only a vagrant in the alley opposite. The dwarf emerged from underneath sheets of paper and blinked sleepily at them. He was, if not well-groomed, then certainly tidier than most rough sleepers Tom had encountered. He was clean and his clothes, while by no means rich, were sturdy and well made. His hair was bound into an uneven tail and his face bore equally uneven stubble, as if he had cut both without a mirror. He offered them a smile filled with yellowed teeth. "You can hammer until you wake the four giants themselves," he said. "But the proprietor of that particular establishment will not open the door until he decides to open his shop. All you will gain is trouble for others."

How did this dwarf know that? Or was this simply a prelude to a request for money? Or food? Tom opened his mouth to offer an excuse, but Katharine stepped forward without hesitation and said, "Good dwarf, trouble has come to us." The ease with which she spoke to him left Tom feeling embarrassed. "We need the help of those inside." And she gestured to Emyr, whom Six and Draig had laid down on the street.

The vagrant paled and muttered something in dwarfish. It was only when Katharine replied in the same tongue that he dragged his gaze away and offered her a weak smile and a question.

"He does," she replied. "But we need to take both cirgeon and patient in there." She gestured to the smith.

"Whyever for?"

"It would take a long time to explain."

The vagrant nodded, finishing her thought with, "And he doesn't have time for the telling." He cast his eyes over them all, weighing them, balancing a decision in his eyes. But when his gaze fell on the sword in Tom's hand, his eyes grew wide and he breathed something in dwarfish.

"Part of our tale," Katharine promised him.

And at that the vagrant sprang to his feet and rushed past them. "This way," he hissed. "Quickly." He dashed into a narrow alley beside the smith that was swathed in shadow and gloom. The dwarf seemed unfazed, stopping halfway down and knocking on a door that was out of sight. His knock was little more than a tap, and the only indication that the door had opened was the whispers, the vagrant's insistent, the unseen party behind the door incredulous. The dwarf waved them forward, and Tom was too dazed and confused to disobey. A moment later, he found himself staring down at another dwarf blocking the doorway who was dark in both appearance and countenance. Short, overweight, the guardian of the door glowered up at him from under bushy eyebrows that matched the hair on his head, cheeks, and upper lip. "Apologies, master human," he said a swaggering accent that often dropped the harder letters and sounds from words. "Kunnustenn's made you promises that ain't within my power and authority to grant. Good day."

"We have a wounded man who needs urgent help."

"Then I reckon you should take him to a cirgeon."

"We need to take him inside."

"What you need and what will happen are two very different things."

"Jarnstenn!" Kunnustenn stabbed a finger perilously close to Caledyr's edge. "Look at it."

"A sword."

"*The* sword."

Jarnstenn shook his head. "It's a good replica, no doubt."

"I don't think so."

"I'm a smith, Kun." He grinned. "I could make you one in an afternoon."

"I'm a historian, Jarn. I'd know the difference." Kunnustenn took an angry breath. "Let them in, or I'll stay out here tonight."

Jarnstenn glared at the other dwarf for a moment. "Suit yourself."

The door closed with a bang that echoed down the narrow alley.

Whatever was happening here, it was clearly done. And they had wasted time that Emyr didn't have. "We need to find somewhere else, Gravinn," Tom called as he began to walk away.

"A moment," Kunnustenn called.

"Time is not on our side," Tom replied. "Thank you for your efforts."

But Kunnustenn only pointed at the door. And, just a moment later, it opened again. "Get inside," Jarnstenn growled.

Tom didn't hesitate. "Everyone inside. Emyr first." He stood aside to allow Six and Draig to pass with Emyr between them. "Gravinn, you and I will fetch the cirgeon."

"I'll go with you," said Katharine.

Tom just shook his head. "Stay close to Ambrose." He wasn't sure what made him say it. A whisper of a hint of a foresight, perhaps. No time to ponder it now. When she didn't move, he added, "Go."

She went, but with a scowl. But she went, and that was all that mattered. "We'll have to hurry," he said to Gravinn.

"It isn't far," she told him, but she set off at a trot, and Tom ran after her.

The sun was still struggling against the stinking fog. Unable to burn it away, it managing only a scattered, ethereal light as they ran through the city. The streets remained empty, the world still muffled and quiet. Tom wanted to ask Gravinn about the fog, about the homeless gathered in the alleys, but his lungs were already burning and his feet were heavy.

"Sheathe the sword," she told him.

"What?" His mind felt dull. Was it the smoke or fatigue?

"The sword." She was looking over her shoulder at him, frantically waving her hands. "Put it away!"

He obeyed, his bouncing step making it difficult to slide the blade home, and panted, "Why?"

"Coppers."

The road opened out into a cramped square, filled with a few short, skinny trees imprisoned within tiny patches of fenced dirt. Token attempts at greenery, though they looked brown and wilted. Nevertheless, stone benches were arranged to face them as if they were something to look at, and two dwarfs sat on one of those benches, glowering at Tom and Gravinn as they dashed across the square. They weren't armed, and they seemed to wear no uniform. But they had the unmistakable air of those with authority.

Tom waited until they'd left the square to ask, "Were they guards?"

"Of a sort," Gravinn replied. "The constabulary certainly guard the pockets of the wealthy."

Hired swords, perhaps, without the swords? He opened his mouth to ask, but Gravinn had stopped. She leant on her knees and pointed at a shop window. "Here," she said.

Tom couldn't read the sign, but he could understand the display in the window, saws and a skeleton and a diagram of the dwarf body. Panting, he lifted a hand to hammer on the door.

"The bell." Gravinn pointed at a length of rope hanging by the door. "This is a civilised part of town."

Tom tugged the rope. The streets were so quiet he could hear the sound of a bell ringing inside.

But that was the only sound. No-one came to the door. No-one even stirred.

He rang again. And again. It was only when he'd rung a fourth time that a window opened above them and a dwarf leant out, red-faced and cursing at them. When he saw Tom, he swore again and growled, "What the blazes do you want at this hour?"

"One of our party is wounded." Gravinn's call was weak and gasping. Why was she pushing herself so hard? What ties did she have to Emyr, or any of them? "Only a dwarf of your skill can save his life," she added.

But the dwarf at the window seemed unimpressed. "Do you know what time it is?" he asked. There wasn't a hair anywhere on his head, but he rubbed his chin as if he expected to find some. "Cirgeons need their breakfast too. A civilised dwarf would wait until a more civilised time."

Why were they talking about the time and breaking fast? "He's dying," Tom said.

"They're all dying," the dwarf replied.

"We have coin," Gravinn added.

"They don't all have that." The dwarf eyed them, and Tom waited for him to leap into action, to fetch his tools and herbs and come dashing back with them through the city. But he just nodded. "Very well. Come back in one half of an hour. If he still lives, I will practise my craft on him."

The window was closed before Tom could finish saying, "He needs you now!" and there was no answer save the silence of the street. There was no rough sleeper to show them a secret entrance. No alley hiding a side door. Just an indifference that made Tom's chest tight with rage.

Fight.

Yes, he thought. I think I will.

"I'm sorry," Gravinn said. "Dwarfs of medicine are like any other. Their shops open and close at appointed times."

"And the dwarfs that get hurt outside of those hours?" he asked as he examined the shop window. The panes of glass were small, held in a grid by black iron. Gravinn said nothing, and spoke volumes with her silence.

Caledyr slid through the iron like it wasn't even there.

"What are you doing?" Gravinn asked. But he didn't want to hear her objections. She'd find out soon enough. The glass creaked as he cut through more iron, some panes cracked and splintered. Finally he'd cut through enough iron to kick once, twice, three times and a section of glass and iron crashed into the shop beyond.

The sound was deafening in the early morning quiet. There was no doubt it had been heard. But there was no time for subtlety. He clambered through the gap he'd cut, avoiding sharp metal and broken glass until he stood in the cirgeon's shop.

This room had been all about display. Shelves on the walls bore skulls and bones and tools and jars with pieces of entrail floating in them. A table near the wall was covered with papers. The ceiling was low, forcing him to bend his back, and even then his head brushed the wooden beams above. This was not where the cirgeon did his work. Perhaps that was in a back room. He didn't have time to explore; running footsteps announced company before it arrived.

The dwarf wore a white apron over her cheap clothes, both stained by bloody work. Her mouth gaped and a cheap, slender cigar fell from her lips to the floor. She lifted her hands to cover her mouth as she shook her head and moaned something in dwarfish.

"Don't be afraid," Tom told her. "But a man is dying. I won't be turned from your door while he needs your help."

She lowered her hands, but her gaze never left the sword.

"You have nothing to fear," he told her, but thumping footsteps and bellowing anger drowned out Tom's voice.

"What is the meaning of this?" the cirgeon roared, but his fury died as soon as he saw Tom's drawn sword.

"My friend is dying." Tom kept his tone calm, even, and unthreatening. "You will come with me, right now, and you will do your best to heal him. You will be paid well, and compensated for the damage I have caused." He couldn't help but add, "And perhaps you will think twice about ignoring a dying man in favour of your breakfast."

"You can't do this," the cirgeon protested.

"We'll find out." Tom nodded to the rooms out of sight. "Fetch your things. He has a serious gut wound. He's lost a lot of blood."

"I won't." His protests were weak. "You can't make me."

Tom didn't want to injure or wound the dwarf. But there was no possibility of letting him be; he had to heal Emyr. So Tom said, "Are you sure you want to test an armed man who has broken into your shop?"

The cirgeon quailed. But it was the other dwarf who broke the silence. She took a deep breath, straightened and said to the cirgeon, "I will fetch your things, Master Dorstenn." She left the room with a quiet dignity that was beyond her master.

"You work for him, now, do you?" he called after her, trying to muster outrage. But it came out weak and feeble. "Dorstenn won't be bullied by brigands and barbarians."

"As I said," Tom reminded him, "You will be paid well."

"Humans think everything can be bought. But there is more to this world than money."

"Such as saving a good man's life?"

Dorstenn sagged. But he was still unconvinced. Would he save Emyr's life under duress? Or would he waste time by resisting, and lose Emyr's life in the process?

So Tom tried a different tack. "Save his life," he said. "Take enough to repair your window and fill your pockets. Tell the tale of how you were cool and calm in the face of an armed madman who dared you to save a king's life."

A light flashed in the cirgeon's eyes, quickly replaced with scepticism. "A king?" he asked. "Surely not King Idris?"

"He isn't the only king in Tir."

Dorstenn snorted. "Name another."

"You'll meet him soon enough." Would that intrigue the dwarf? Or would he dismiss Tom as a madman? But the dwarf's gaze was already growing distant, and Tom guessed he was imagining how he would tell his story, how other dwarfs would crowd around him in a tavern and gaze up at him as he told his heroic tale of adventure. Dorstenn's lips quirked in a smile, quickly stifled as he drew himself up and painted an expression of stern authority on his face. "You will pay for the damage you have caused," he commanded. "And I will expect a kingly fee."

Already promised, but Tom knew this was part of the tale Dorstenn was telling himself. "Anything you ask. Only help my friend."

"Coppers," Gravinn hissed. She hadn't climbed into the shop, but stood outside, looking as casual as possible.

"Don't call to them," Tom warned Dorstenn. "It would be a dull end to your tale."

He wanted to call out, Tom could tell. But he also wanted the adulation and praise that would come of bearing this adventure alone. So he nodded, lips thin. "They would only delay us," he said. "I will not risk a monarch's life by incurring the delay of the authorities."

"A noble deed," Tom said, and saw Dorstenn adding to his own story in his mind.

The other dwarf came back with two heavy leather bags, so full they could barely be closed. "I am ready," she said.

"Then let us go, Mennvinn," Dorstenn said. "Lead the way, madman."

"Tom," he replied, sliding Caledyr into its sheathe. "I can take those," he said to Mennvinn, who only bobbed her head, wide-eyed. She dashed ahead and opened the door just in time for the two coppers to walk past, staring goggle-eyed at the smashed window.

"What occurred here?" asked one of them in a serious voice.

Dorstenn glanced up at Tom, and for a moment seemed ready to blurt it all out. But his gaze dropped to the sword and he straightened. "No time, Inspector. I have a life to save." And he invited Tom to lead on with a gesture.

The coppers called after them but made no effort to pursue. Tom led them at a gentle jog, well aware that the length of his stride was twice theirs. Nevertheless, Gravinn caught up with him, and soon took the lead, taking them back to the smith. Tom tried not to imagine the worst, that Emyr would be still and cold, his life bled away onto the smith's floor and all their hopes leeched away with it. He had to live. All of Tir needed him to live. Tom needed him to live.

Raised voices could be heard within the smith. A sudden wave of dizziness struck Tom as they reached the door and his hammering was weak and feeble. It was Six who answered. "Thank Oen you're here," he murmured. "We're one word away from murder in here."

The shop itself was deserted, the voices rising up from a set of stairs leading down into a cellar that was filled with iron in various states, piles of unworked bars stacked alongside finished articles. Emyr was stretched out on a wooden pallet balanced on two anvils, lying still and whiter than Mab. Was he dead? Tom didn't dare move or breathe until he saw Emyr's chest rise and fall in the most shallow of breaths.

"Dorstenn," he said. "Your patient. Do whatever you must."

"No," bellowed a dwarf. This one was older than the others, bald and wrinkled, his dirty grey beard so long it almost touched his knees. It seemed somewhat impractical for a smith. "No-one else is to come in here. Get out," he roared, flailing a hammer in each hand as he stalked towards them. "Get out!"

Caledyr was enough to halt his charge, the point perilously close to his chest, the edge slicing hairs from his beard that fluttered to the stone floor. He stepped back, and back again as Tom advanced, clearing the way for Dorstenn and Mennvinn. "Enough," Tom told the older dwarf. "I have had enough of people telling me what I can and cannot do to save my king."

The older dwarf's eyes were wide, his anger blunted, and he nodded, the action brushing more hairs against Caledyr's edge.

Another wave of dizziness struck Tom, and the effort to remain standing was almost too much. He blinked, slowly, and took a deep, shaky breath. "You own this place?" he asked. The dwarf nodded. "You are angry that we have forced our way in, taken over and turned it into a healing house?" The dwarf nodded again. "I understand. I apologise for the disruption. We will pay you well. But I will not let you do anything that puts my friend's life in danger. Do you understand that?"

The dwarf nodded. Slowly. "Are we prisoners?" His question was both surly and edged with fear.

"No." Tom lowered the sword. The dwarf didn't move. "You may go, if you wish."

"I'll stay." As the fear of immediate danger faded, the smith's anger grew more confident. "But not down here. Too crowded."

He was right. Emyr's temporary bier took up most of the cellar. The others had tried to squeeze themselves into what spaces they could find, but there was little room for Dorstenn and Mennvinn to work. "Perhaps some of us should move upstairs."

"Not all of you," Dorstenn said. "You stay, and you too." He nodded at Tom and Katharine.

"Why?"

"We need some of your blood. He's lost a lot."

"You can take what you need from me," Tom replied. "But not her."

"Tom," Katharine began. There was reprimand in her voice, but she knew he was right and said no more.

So he turned to the old smith and said, "Master dwarf, please place my friends where it would be convenient."

"Out of my establishment would be convenient," the dwarf growled, but he waved them forward. "Upstairs with you."

"Gravinn, you know the city," Tom said. "Take Draig and find us some food."

"I know the city," Katharine said.

"I need you to stay here."

"Maybe I need to do something."

He was too tired to argue. Whatever reserves he'd been burning had left him, and now he felt tired and cold and weak. "Talk to the owner. Perhaps we can buy some iron blades from him," he suggested. "And get some rest."

It wasn't the task she wanted. But she nodded and followed the others up the stairs.

Ambrose's voice made Tom jump. "What will you do in two days?" The old sorcerer stood in a corner of the cellar, unmoved by the request to leave, wreathed in shadow and as still as the metal and stone around him. But he looked stronger down here. More human.

"We'll run." Tom sheathed the sword and found a space where he could sit. The stone was warm and the relief in his limbs was instant. "The fay know we're here. We can't hide from them, but we can make it harder for them to find us."

"What kind of foe is defeated by running from it?"

He was falling asleep. He should get up, make sure the others were settled, that Katharine was okay, that Dorstenn didn't need him to fetch anything that would help save Emyr's life. But he just said, "The slow kind."

Ambrose's laugh was wrong, like it hadn't been used in many years and rust had stiffened the joints and dulled the edge. "You won't win this war by running."

War. No, Tom wouldn't win any wars. But, "Emyr won a war."

"This isn't his story."

He'd open his eyes in a moment. Just a moment. "He'll know what to do."

"He won't." Ambrose's voice was soft, like a father speaking to their child as he slept. "But you will."

Tom dreamt of Glastyn. The two of them were sat at a small table, each with a glass of wine in their hands.

"This is your final moment," Glastyn was saying, and then Tom was in the dark and the cold. Glastyn was gone, and someone was crying. He was holding Katharine's hand, but her hand was slack in his. "Be strong, just for a little while," he begged her. "Come back. Please."

Then something had hold of Tom's arm and was pulling him and he woke with a start and an incoherent cry, snatching back his arm and reaching for Caledyr.

"Peace, sir." A dwarf, who was she? The memory came back slowly. Mennvinn. Dorstenn's assistant. "I didn't mean to startle you."

"Then you should have woken me gently." He sounded surly even to his own ears. But what way was that to wake someone?

"Your friend," she reminded him, and he felt guilty. He'd slept while Emyr's life hung in the balance. "He needs blood."

He nodded. "Very well." He took a deeper breath, tried to clear the fog of sleep from his thoughts. "What do you need me to do?"

"Sit here." She lead him to a pile of iron slates. "Roll up the sleeve on the arm you favour least."

He did as he was told and she tied a length of cloth tightly around his upper arm. Dorstenn was muttering to himself, his hands full of strange tools that poked in and out of Emyr's gut. "This," Dorstenn muttered as he worked, "is quite the mess."

The words blew on an ember of anger Tom had thought himself too tired to feel. "That mess is my king."

"Indeed." There was a greedy look in Dorstenn's eyes. "May I ask how he procured such an injury?"

"In battle."

"Battle? Curious." He grunted as he reached deep into Emyr's gut, looking at the ceiling as he felt for something. "Your friend picked his opponents well."

"What do you mean?" Tom asked as Mennvinn brought over a glass jar and some thin tubes.

"I mean only that this wound looks worse than it truly is." He grunted, satisfied, and withdrew his bloody hand. "The blade that cut him was sharp, but it left every major organ unscathed. Whoever wrought this wound wanted to cause pain and immobility; not death."

Melwas had hounded Emyr throughout his reign, made every effort to steal his queen, harried his kingdom from coast to coast, before finally fighting him to a stand-still and gutting him on the battlefield. The idea that Melwas hadn't wanted Emyr to die made little sense.

But then why had the Melwas allowed Emyr into Faerie, if he hadn't wanted him to live?

It was all too complicated.

"Hold still," Mennvinn told him, and interrupted his thoughts by pushing a needle into his arm.

Fight?

No, he told the sword. But he'd jumped and Mennvinn had stepped back. "My apologies," she said. She waited a moment, watching him as if he were a wild horse or angry dog. She didn't move until he nodded, and then she swiftly connected the needle to the glass jar with a thin tube and began to turn a handle that caused his life blood to ooze down the tube and into the jar.

"How sick will I become?" he asked. He felt a coward for asking it while Emyr lay on the brink of death. But he had to know how strong he would, or wouldn't, be.

"We won't take too much," Menvinn replied. She didn't stop turning the handle but watched the tube and the jar and the needle in his arm; she didn't make eye contact. "You might feel a little tired. Nothing worse."

"But my elements." Now she looked up at him, a frown on her face. "The elements of the body. The humours," he explained. "Fire, water, earth, air and void."

She gave him an indulgent smile, like he was a child. "What about them?"

"They won't be balanced." It was what had made him sick when he left Faerie. An imbalance in the elements of the body.

"Don't worry," she told him. "You won't get sick. I promise."

He wanted to believe her. But she was laughing at his concerns. It made him question what she knew about healing.

But he was too tired to argue. Perhaps he would get sick. But Emyr would live. And Tom knew he could rely on Six to make sure Katharine and her child were safe. So he closed his eyes and let Mennvinn drain his life blood, and listened to Dorstenn mutter to himself in dwarfish.

Finally Menvinn said something in the same language, stopped turning the handle, and slipped the needle from his arm. Blood began to pool in the crook of his elbow and she gave him a piece of cloth and said, "Hold that there." She wheeled the trolley over to Emyr's side, connected a different tube to the wounded king and worked a different handle, encouraging the blood into his arm instead.

"What do we do?" Tom asked.

"You can go," Menvinn said. "But not far. In case we need more blood."

"Eat something," Dorstenn added. "Drink fluids. Nothing strong."

And then they turned all their attention to Emyr. Tom was dismissed. If he had been tired before, now he felt like his limbs were made of straw, ready to fold beneath him in a moment. Did he feel emptier? Hollow, like a husk? The thought itched at the back of his mind, so he stilled it by putting a finger to his wrist. His blood moved beneath his skin. He pushed himself to his feet, turned to Ambrose, still stood in his corner.

"Go," he told Tom. "I need neither food nor rest."

Tom believed him and that gave him a chill. What had the old sorcerer done to himself? But Tom shook his head. "Come," he told him. At his questioning look, Tom just shook his head again. So much talking. He was tired of so much talking. "Come," he repeated.

Ambrose stared at him for a long moment before beginning his shuffling step, winding through the cellar towards the stairs, which were narrow and shallow; climbing them left Tom's legs aching more than they should.

The shop upstairs was as cramped as the cellar, each room filled with people trying to find a space amongst the wares. Katharine was in earnest conversation with the owner, and Tom went to her first.

"Are you well?" he asked.

She smiled up at him; while the dwarf sat on a stool, she was sat on the floor with her back to the wall and her legs awkwardly spread and bent. Her Western shawl covered her belly, but her posture told Tom she was probably showing by now. How long had she carried this child in silence?

Not silence, he realised. Six was nearby, in heated conversation with the dwarf called Jarnstenn. But, despite how excited the pair were about the device they were talking about, Six cast a glance towards Katharine every now and then.

He knew. Six knew that Katharine was pregnant and hadn't said a word. Tom wasn't sure if he was proud of Six for keeping her secret, or angry with them both for keeping that secret from him.

Fight?

"Tired." Katharine's response brought him back to the moment and away from Caledyr's question. Priorities.

"Here." He offered his hand, which she took with a frown before making a sound of protest as he lifted her to her feet. "You shouldn't be sitting on the floor. Master dwarf, is there anywhere more comfortable she could rest?"

He looked put out, and said something in dwarfish to her. She responded and he stood up and walked away. "He's not happy," Katharine told him. "If we weren't promising him so much money, he'd have called the constabulary by now."

"Is it going to be a problem?"

She took a deep breath and sighed it out. He didn't like how she had to crouch beneath these low ceilings. "He might decide the money isn't worth the trouble."

Tom sighed too. He'd hoped they could rest here for a time. But why shouldn't the dwarf be upset? Strangers had occupied his shop, taken his livelihood prisoner with promise of money, yet he had no coin in his hand.

"What's our plan?" Katharine asked him.

"I don't know," he admitted. He looked at the shawl veiling her belly. "I had an idea. Now everything's changed."

"We should get everyone together and figure out our next steps."

"No," he murmured. They were already stood close, hunkered underneath the dwarfish ceiling, but he closed the gap and touched her elbow. "We need our own plan now."

She smiled. It was a kind smile, but she was laughing at him. "Are you planning to whisk me away, Thomas Rymour?"

Was that so funny? "Maybe."

She put a hand over his. "How far will we get after what you did in Faerie?"

He knew how the fay thought. They preferred the towns and cities, filled with the mortals on whom they loved to play their pranks. So he would find somewhere remote, somewhere isolated where he and Katharine could live in peace.

And what sort of life would that be for their daughter? Always afraid of people. Never seeing anything but whatever hut or cave they cowered in.

What kind of foe is defeated by running from it?

"You said we would stop the fay," Katharine reminded him. "That's the only way we can keep her safe." She still smiled. But she was scared. Terrified.

He touched her cheek. "I'll do anything," he promised her. "I'll stand between you and any harm."

Her gaze flicked, just for a moment, to the sword at his hip.

He'd hurt her for that sword. It had wormed its way into his thoughts. He had told her that he'd stop carrying it, but it still sat on his hip.

"I'll give it to Emyr," he told her. But she bit her lip, torn between some private decision. Of course. She'd seen what it had done to Melwas. She'd want that kind of weapon nearby. "You take it," he told her, releasing her hand and reaching for the scabbard.

"No." Her response was quick and sharp. "No," she said again, with less of an edge. "Just don't let it think for you."

The sword will think for you, Nimue had said. And the old man lies.

But Tom knew he needed both Ambrose and the sword to find a way out of this. Because Katharine was right. They couldn't run. They had to fight. So he turned to Six, who was watching the two of them intently. "Fetch the others," Tom told him. "We need to make a plan."

CHAPTER 3

THE LARGEST ROOM was at the front of the shop, and the old smith went red in the face when he found Tom and Draig clearing the great table in the middle of the room. Katharine said something in dwarfish that sent him stamping up the stairs, leaving everyone hunkered in a circle around the cleared table.

Dank was the first to speak. "They'll come for us." He was blunt and afraid. Tom could see their doom in his eyes. "They won't stop looking, they won't get tired or bored. They'll roast us over fires and flay our bodies and pull us apart and we won't die because nothing dies in Faerie so they'll put us back together and start all over again and again and again."

He ran out of breath and no-one filled the silence.

"He's right," Tom said.

More silence.

"Well," said Six. "I certainly feel motivated."

"It's important that everyone understands," Tom told him. "We can't hide. We can't run. Our only option is to fight."

Fight.

"Couldn't we live out our days in a nice iron bunker?" Six asked.

"Iron only hurts them," Dank replied. "They'll suffer the pain if they want something enough." His eyes were wide, like a panicked rabbit's. Time to dial back the doom and gloom.

"We have Caledyr," Tom reminded them.

"It won't be enough," Dank replied.

"No. It won't," he agreed. "So tell us about the glarn."

Dank blinked. "The glarn?" His tone was careful, controlled, giving nothing away.

But Tom was too tired to play games. "You've been lying to us all, Dank. And the fay have promised you pain and torture in return. Do you really want to keep lying for them?"

Dank lowered his gaze. "You know what they would have done to us if we hadn't done as they asked."

How long had the boy been bonded to the fay, how many times had they used him, pushed and pulled him like a plaything. Tom could imagine what that was like. For a moment, he felt Mab's embrace on the hill. "You can be free of them," he told Dank, and maybe told himself too.

Dank wanted to speak. But he was too afraid. And perhaps with good reason. He had shared a mind with the fay. He knew exactly what they would do to someone who revealed their secrets.

So it was Ambrose who said, "Everything hinges on the glarn." He drew a deep, shuddering breath, as if it would be his last. "It is your only hope for success."

"What are they?" Tom asked.

"The elements given form," Ambrose replied. "Fire. Water. Earth. Air."

"Where do we find them?" Six asked.

"You have one." Ambrose's gaze fell on Caledyr. "Water."

"How is Caledyr being water?" Draig asked.

The sound of excited whispering came from outside the room.

"It came from water. To water it will return." Ambrose spoke as if he was reciting something.

It didn't convince many faces. But it was Six who asked, "What are the others?"

"There is one in the mountains," Ambrose replied. "Orlannu. The trap."

"Sounds ominous," Six said.

The whispering grew to murmuring.

"And the rest?" Tom asked.

Ambrose's gaze fell and he seemed to shrink a little within his robes. "I don't know."

The silence was ruined by the unseen discussion growing in volume.

"You don't know." Six's words were an inch from hopelessness, and Tom hated how they echoed with something inside himself.

"Can we stop the fay with two?" Tom asked. "Will Caledyr and Orlannu be enough?"

"No," said Dank. He was slouched, his shoulders slumped, resigned to his fate. "You need all four glarn. That much we know."

All four. And with all of Ambrose's wisdom, they knew of two. "Do you know what the other two are, Dank?" Tom asked.

"You think the fay would tell us?"

It was a fair point.

"Is this madness," Draig said. "Do you ask us to find two objects in the whole of Tir. Could they be anywhere!"

"He's right," Tom said. He looked at Katharine as he added, "I can't believe this is our only hope of escaping the fay."

"Yet you must believe it," Ambrose said. He caught Tom's eye with his dark gaze and said, "You will."

The words had a weight that settled in the room. They felt like a burden on Tom's shoulders. "You've foreseen it," he said. It wasn't a question. But Ambrose nodded once. So. There was no discussion. That, at least, was a relief. It would happen.

Katharine's hand would grow weaker in his.

No. He wouldn't allow it.

"It isn't enough," he told Ambrose. "You can't ask me to hang everything on such a slim hope."

"I do not ask."

He was offering them so little. Tom had expected more. He had expected someone with perfect foresight to offer more certainty. More hope. "Will we succeed?" he asked.

Ambrose was very still as he said, "I do not know."

Which could mean only one thing. It wasn't the first time Tom had looked at someone and known they would die. But this was different. He felt detached from it, too worried about Katharine and the child she carried to properly feel the certainty of Ambrose's death. Instead, he could only think about how Ambrose's fate meant that their own was just as uncertain, and he felt ashamed of that even as he feared for Katharine.

Her hand would grow weaker in his.

"Can you at least tell us where to start?" Six asked.

"I can. But I do not."

"Then why did you come here?" Tom snapped."Why come all this way if you aren't going to help us?"

It was cruel. To answer the revelation of Ambrose's death with harsh words. And Tom knew he wasn't angry. He was scared. If Katharine died, the child would die too.

But if Ambrose felt any sting from Tom's words, he didn't show it. He just blinked once and said, "It is Kunnustenn who tells you."

Kunnustenn? It was only when a dwarf popped his head into the room that Tom even remembered the vagrant. He was followed by the other dwarf, Jarnstenn, who pushed

Kunnustenn back and said, "No, no. He ain't getting into your malarkey."

"But Jarn! Caledyr. Orlannu. Don't you see? It's all true."

"True as my breeches are made of gold, Kun." Jarnstenn placed himself in Kunnustenn's path, ushering him out of the room. "Don't be getting seduced by tall tales."

"It's true," Tom said.

Jarnsten's voice dripped with sarcasm as he said, "And I'm Sir Rimestenn of Tir, pleased to meet you." But Kunnustenn said nothing. He wanted to believe. Tom could see it in his eyes.

"My name is Thomas Rymour," he told them. "Does that mean anything to you?"

"Not a thing," Jarnstenn said.

But Kunnustenn nodded. "The stories say that Thomas Rymour was stolen into Faerie by a peskie for telling a lie. It took him a hundred years to find a way back, and since then he never again dare spoke a lie in case the peskies came for him again."

"Not even my little niece would believe that," Jarnstenn said. "Not even children believe in peskies."

"They're real," Tom said.

"Bit handy that peskies can't be seen or heard, ain't it?"

"Believe me, Jarnstenn," Tom replied, and he put every ounce of sincerity into each word as he could manage. "They are very real. And if you can help us, please. Please help us."

Jarnstenn glared at Tom. "There's no evidence. Nothing to see or hear or touch."

"That's why you have to believe." Kunnustenn's words were tentative and he made no eye contact.

"All I need to believe in is my work, my roof, and my belly." He slapped it with the palm of his hand. "Don't have to believe in Faerie tales or listen to a bedlamite." With that he stalked out of the room.

But Kunnustenn stayed. He watched the other dwarf go,

shook his head and wrung his hands. "You'll have to forgive Jarnstenn," he told them, staring at the floor. "He isn't a dwarf of faith. He believes only his senses." He shrugged. "I've studied histories all my life. They agree too much on certain things. Including the glarn. And the peskies."

"Fay," Tom said. "They call themselves fay."

"Fay." Kunnustenn nodded. "The term is known to me. From older texts." He lifted his gaze to Caledyr. "Those texts have another name for that sword."

Another name? "What is it?"

"Ymellith."

The sword stirred, as if the thoughts Tom had felt had been nothing but mumbles in its sleep, and Tom couldn't help but shiver.

"Dead-bane," Kunnustenn added.

Dead-bane. Tom could feel a puzzle unfurling in his mind, but it was too frightening to consider. He pushed it to one side. "What do those texts say about the glarn?" he asked. "Do they say where we can find them?"

Kunnustenn shrugged. "Orlannu is easy," he told them. "Everyone knows that's one of the names for Rimestenn's treasure."

"Rimestenn's treasure," Tom repeated. Kunnustenn said the words as if such a thing was well-known.

"It's a legend specific to the Provinces," Katharine said. "Rimestenn took something dear to Emyr and hid it inside his city."

"Rimestenn has a city?" Tom had never heard of one before.

"So the stories say. It doesn't appear on any map," Katharine replied.

"Because Rimestenn hid it," Kunnustenn said. "We think it most likely he buried it, somewhere in the Northern Wastes."

"Here." Gravinn rolled a map out over the table and pointed

to an area north of the Provinces. Empty. Barren. Nothing but mountains.

Tom heard Katharine draw a deep breath and he cast a glance at her. She gazed at the map as if its presence pained her. What had happened to the maps she'd left behind in Cairnalyr? He reached out and brushed a finger against the back of her hand and she buried her pain.

"A hidden city is a common myth," Six pointed out.

"Oh yes," Kunnustenn agreed. He was looking at the map now. "But none of them had a road attached to them too."

"The Forgotten Road?" Gravinn asked and, when Kunnustenn nodded, she gave a small shake of her head. "The Forgotten Road is a myth too."

Katharine stepped forward and laid her fingers on the map and drew a breath, as if drawing strength from it. "I've heard of the Forgotten Road," she murmured. "They say it led north, out of Cairnajorr," she said.

"Cairnimor, actually," Gravinn countered. "If we're going to be wrong, we might as well be right." Katharine's shoulders tightened, but she said nothing even as Gravinn added, "Hundreds of Pathfinders have tried to find it and failed. It isn't there."

"That's because the road is gone now," Kunnustenn said. "Sir Rimestenn had it broken up and the stone carried away."

"I've never heard that." Gravinn's tone made it clear: if she hadn't heard it, it wasn't true.

Kunnustenn shrugged. "I read it in *Gellvinn's Thirty-Two Marvels of the Provinces*."

"What's that?"

"It's a book." Katharine couldn't take her eyes from the map, tracing rivers and roads with her fingertips. Gravinn's glare went unseen. "Gellvinn gathered stories. Each year she put them in a book."

"Stories won't find an imaginary road."

Before the conversation could devolve into argument, Tom asked, "So the road will take us to Cairnarim. What will we find when we get there?"

"A ruin," Kunnustenn told them. "A city of the dead. A paradise where Taranau waits to return. Countless stories have been wrapped around that place like a shroud, hiding the truth beneath it."

Katharine nodded. "I was told it didn't even exist," she said. "That instead of a city, Rimestenn built a temple to some dark magics."

Gravinn snorted. "Another Faerie tale. Rimestenn was the finest of Taranau's knights." Her expression made her contempt clear. "He would never betray his vows."

"It's not for me to judge the world. Just record it."

"A Pathfinder isn't a gossip." Gravinn smirked and glanced at Tom, as if to share the joke. "We record the truth, not the fiction."

Was she calling Katharine a gossip? And did she expect him to agree with her, to laugh at Katharine and belittle her? Tom just shook his head at her and watched the smirk wither and die on the dwarf's face.

Six spoke into the silence. "Truth or fiction, it seems to me that we don't know where to look for a road that might not exist, to take us to a place that might not even be there." He invited contradiction with raised eyebrows and, when none came, added, "Does anyone else think this is an impossible task?"

Six was right. It seemed impossible. But Tom shook his head. "Ambrose says we look for the glarn." There was no escaping it. No sense in questioning it. It would happen.

Six narrowed his eyes. "Are you really going to drag her across Tir on a fool's quest?"

"I've crossed Tir a dozen times." Katharine's words were cold, her expression closed.

"You can't do it in this condition."

"Can't I?" The chill was turning into hot anger. Six didn't seem to see the fires he was stoking.

"Katharine can decide for herself," Tom said, trying to avert the argument, but instead her blazing glare turned on him.

"I can speak for myself."

Tom offered instant surrender, raising his hands and taking a step back, knocking a shelf and sending something clattering to the ground. Jarnstenn reappeared in an instant, grumbling and tidying and berating. Tom paid him no mind. Just stared at Katharine, glaring back at him, angry and fiery and beautiful. Tom tried not to think of his dream, his foresight, tried not to feel her hand grow weaker in his.

Would she take the child with her when she died?

Her fury changed to uncertainty and question. She saw the fear in his eyes, and it froze the words on her lips. She didn't want to ask a question and hear his answer. As Brega had said, saying it made it so.

"We can choose a different path." Six said it softly, as if he was soothing a wild horse. "We don't have to do what these foresights demand."

Six was wrong. Tom knew all of his foresights had come to pass. And he knew Ambrose remembered the things to come. To say they could do something else was like saying they could change what they had done yesterday. But even as he shook his head, he found a terrible, impossible thought behind all others: he had to do it. He had to change what would happen. He knew it was impossible. But he had to do it anyway. He would keep Katharine alive because he had no other choice.

Countless possibilities unfurled in his mind. Take Katharine and ride away. Ride south. Ride to the Eastern Angles; Neirin would protect them. Ride anywhere but towards Cairnarim. If he didn't look for the glarn, if he broke that foresight, then perhaps he could break this one too.

But the fay would never stop hunting them. No. He had to find the glarn. To stop the fay once and for all. To protect Katharine and their child.

The conversation had begun anew while he thought, and he glanced over at Katharine. She was talking with Gravinn, but her body was tense. She sensed something was wrong. Should he tell her? How could he? How could he tell her that he saw her die somewhere cold and dark, a somewhere that seemed likely to be found in a place called the Northern Wastes?

He couldn't. He couldn't tell her. He just had to protect her.

His eyes stung and he blinked away the threat of tears, took a deep breath to clear out his thoughts. They lingered like flies on carrion. But he tried not to think them.

Kunnustenn was talking about the Forgotten Road. "Gellvin wrote that the road went out of Cairnoher."

"So we have three possibilities," Katharine said, pointing them out on the map. "Cairnoher. Cairnajorr, from the story I heard. And Cairnimor, as Gravinn suggests."

"Sir Herstenn, Sir Jorrstenn, and Sir Moorstenn," Kunnustenn said. "The Engineer, the Smith, and the Storm."

"All three cities have access to the north." Katharine tapped Cairnajorr with a finger. "They called Jorrstenn 'the Smith'. Perhaps someone Rimestenn could have called on to help build whatever it was he built out there?"

Tom let the discussion sweep away his fears for a moment and said, "Moorstenn was a warrior, through and through." Emyr had told him stories of how the dwarf had little knack for anything but violence. "Not much use for building."

"But he was rich," Gravinn said. "He had mountains of gold."

"And little use for it," Tom added. Because once he had his favourite armour, his favourite shield, and his favourite weapons, there was little Moorstenn wanted but food, women and battles.

"So he could afford to pay for Rimestenn's road." Katharine peered at the map. "And Cairnimor is served by a river from the north. Roads are often built alongside rivers. It makes materials easier to transport."

"No road could follow the river Dor," Gravinn told her, as if she was a foolish child. "It cuts through a ravine before going underground."

Katharine ignored the tone, acknowledged only the words. "Not helpful at all," she agreed. "What's at the other end of the ravine?" she asked Gravinn.

"I don't know." The dwarf avoided eye contact. "I didn't draw that map."

No. It had been drawn by Gravinn's old, elfish master. Who had been felled by Tom's hand.

Treachery.

Yes. The elf had threatened to reveal them. Had treated Gravinn poorly, too. But had the only answer been to cut him down and steal his life's work?

To that, the sword was silent.

Katharine had shifted her attentions to the third city. "Herstenn." She tapped a finger against Carinoher, gazing through the paper as if she could see into the city itself. "I've been there."

"So have I," Gravinn said, as if there was some form of competition. "There isn't much to see."

"No," Katharine agreed. "A small, unremarkable place. Hardly befitting a knight they called the Engineer."

"Herstenn lit the way for innovation," Jarnstenn countered, still fiddling with whatever Tom had knocked over. "He designed many marvels. Unveiled the secrets of anatomy, alchemy, built great devices and engines."

"So why isn't his city more impressive?" Katharine asked.

Jarnstenn squirmed. He had faced this question before. "Herstenn wasn't a builder," he mumbled.

"Nor was Jorrstenn."

"There are suggestions that Herstenn neglected his city in favour of a great undertaking in his last years," Kunnustenn told them. "Just stories and rumours."

"Stories and rumours," Katharine mused. She tapped the map again. "There's a section of the city wall that doesn't quite match the rest of it. And there's a tavern sat in front of it." She looked at Gravinn. "Do you know it?"

She frowned, dredging up the memory. "The Gatehouse." And a moment later realisation dawned on her face.

"The Gatehouse." Katharine grinned. She traced a finger up the map, north from Cairnoher. "There's a clean path north here. A river to follow. An old quarry here for the stone." She looked up at Tom. "This is it."

"You're sure?" Tom peered at the map. He didn't see a clean path. Just mountains.

"As sure as we can be." She looked to Gravinn, waiting for the contradiction. But the dwarf looked excited. Tom could see her already drawing the new map in her mind.

They had a destination. Or, at the least, a beginning. And there wasn't a fay around to hear their plan. "We should leave soon," Tom said. "Tomorrow, if possible. Gravinn, start buying supplies. There's no knowing how long our path will be from Cairnoher, so get as much as you can." To Katharine he said, "Has the smith agreed to sell us weapons?"

"We haven't agreed on a price."

"Let's get an agreement out of him." And to Jarnstenn and Kunnustenn he said, "Thank you for your help."

Kunnustenn's response was quiet, but it shocked them all. "I'm coming with you."

Jarnstenn snorted. "Like Taranau's wrath, you are."

"This is my chance, Jarn. In years to come, they'll be studying *Kunnustenn's Accounting of Rimestenn's Treasure*." He gave everyone a shy smile as he blushed. "Or something like that."

"You can write that here," Jarnstenn countered. "Where you're safe."

"I live on the streets."

"I keep you fed, don't I?" He took the other dwarf's hands in his. "Give you coin for the baths? Give you a bed?" He shrugged and added. "When I can."

"I need to be more than that, Jarn." Kunnustenn sounded bitter, as if something had been taken from him. "If I stay here, I'll be a vagrant until I die, or the coppers will catch me and send me to die in the workhouse."

"Go with him and they'll find you dead by the roadside in a week."

Kunnustenn's only response was an exasperated noise, so Jarnstenn stepped closer. "Don't leave me," he said, gruff to hide the need, carefully avoiding everyone's gaze. All of a sudden they were witness to a far more intimate conversation, and it left Tom feeling uncomfortable.

"What can we look forward to here, Jarn?" Kunnustenn pried free a hand and put it against Jarnstenn's cheek. "Only a lifetime of hard labour for someone else's pocket. But if we two find Cairnarim? We'll be known. It will open doors for both of us. We can be more than what we are."

Jarnstenn was still staring at Kunnustenn's hand in his. "Maybe I don't care about none of that. Long as you're here."

Tom couldn't help but reach out and take Katharine's hand. A simple life with the person that mattered. It seemed so easy and so impossible at the same time

"Maybe I want more for you," Kunnustenn said. "Maybe I want you to be seen as the master smith you are, to have money and comfort and respect." He touched his forehead to Jarnstenn's. "Maybe I want to give you all the world."

Jarnstenn sighed out through his nose and the room was still. Tom squeezed Katharine's hand. All he had given her was heartache and a horde of immortal creatures at her back. He had lost her maps. He had caused her pain.

But she squeezed his hand back.

"Fine." Jarnstenn muttered. "You'll be the death of me."

Kunnustenn smiled. "And you're my ray of sunshine."

"You'd be easier to handle if you were stone." Jarnstenn patted his hand and said to Tom, "I'll speak to the gaffer about giving us a discount on a few pieces." The dwarf winked. "He'll be in a good mood once he realises I won't be in his hair no more."

"Iron arrows." Ambrose didn't seem to be speaking to anyone in particular, and Tom could see it unnerved Jarnstenn.

"Yeah, I can get you some arrows with iron heads," he said. "Steel would be better, though."

"Iron arrows," Ambrose repeated. "And a bow. Big enough for him." He pointed at Six.

"I can find a bow," Gravinn said.

"Good," Jarnstenn replied. "Because I can't."

Everyone stared at Ambrose, but he made no move to explain.

"So," Six said into silence that had grown thick and uncomfortable. "Tomorrow."

"We can't let the fay find us," Tom replied.

"No," the elf agreed. "But can Emyr be moved so soon?"

"Absolutely not." Dorstenn dried his hands on a rag while Mennvinn washed tools and instruments in a sink in the corner. "He is to lie here, unmolested, for seven days. Then he may be permitted to stand, perhaps even take a few steps to this sink. But that is as far as he must go for another seven days. Then he may attempt the stairs. Carefully. But he must not lift anything, nor venture beyond these walls, for thirty days."

"Thirty days?" Tom shook his head. "We can't stay here for thirty days."

"You are under no such restriction." Dorstenn finished drying his hands and dropped the rag on the floor. Mennvinn paused in her work to pick it up. "Nevertheless, he must remain."

"Tom's right." Emyr's voice was thick and slurred, his eyes barely open. "We're not safe here."

"What's wrong with him?" Tom asked.

"We gave him laudanum." Mennvinn said, and Dorstenn glared at the interruption. "It stops him from feeling pain."

"No, it doesn't." But the old king's voice was empty of the tightness it had held before.

Dorstenn spoke as if he hadn't been interrupted. "Your friend will live. If he follows my instructions as I have laid them out." He raised his eyebrows. "You promised money? A kingly sum for healing your king?"

Tom opened his mouth to argue. But the dwarf had done his job. So he nodded. "But tell us what we should do if we need to move him."

Dorstenn shrugged. "My advice would be to purchase a plot and commission a headstone." And with that he began to climb the stairs out of the cellar. "My assistant will take my fee."

The cirgeon seemed so cold. So detached from the painful reality his patient lived in. Emyr had been drugged and stitched up, and the dwarf was already leaving. There was more to healing than the body. "Wait," Tom called after him. "What do we do when this laudanum wears off?"

"Speak to my assistant," was the response, and then he was gone.

"Give him a drop of it when the pain returns. No more, no matter how much he begs." Mennvinn didn't look up from her work. She spoke in a dull, flat monotone, as if reciting a script that was well-rehearsed. "And you'll have to give him some preventives, to avoid corruption. These are extra costs, but all to the good of your friend. We have seen excellent results with Crowfoot's Remedy, and can particularly recommend it."

Tom just nodded, eyeing up the walls. Brick, but perhaps they could be lined with iron, the stairs barricaded with the same. They could take watches, keep Caledyr close at all times. Then when Emyr was healed enough, escape. Through a Faerie siege? "It won't work," he told himself. He had brought Emyr back to Tir for nothing. The weight of that knowledge was too heavy and it pushed him to a seat on the ground. He felt a rush of emotion, a sense of uselessness, that threatened to burst forth in tears. No, he told himself. You're just tired. Things are not so bad.

Fight.

The only advice the sword ever had.

Rest.

Was it goading him?

Mennvinn made a noise in the back of her throat. "Dorstenn is set in his ways," she murmured, as if imparting a great secret. "He is not willing to accept new thinking. Thirty days of rest is a very old way of thinking."

Tom took a breath and marshalled himself before lifting his head. "Are you saying we can leave?"

Mennvinn kept washing. "I'm saying he should stand within

a few days, walk a little. Immobility will only stiffen his flesh and bones."

"So we can move him?"

Mennvinn sighed again and her work stopped. "At great risk," she said. "His stitches may break, and he will undoubtedly need the care of a cirgeon again. But, yes. You could move him, if you must."

"We must."

"Then expect to find another cirgeon." She began washing again. "And buy extra laudanum."

"Come with us." Emyr's voice was so soft that at first Tom assumed she hadn't heard him.

But her hands slowed. "I could write notes, for the next cirgeon." Her words were tentative, as if she was testing the room.

Emyr drew a long breath and sighed it out. "Come with us."

She shook her head. "Care on the road is good idea," she said. "You should talk to my master about hiring his services."

"No. You."

Why was he so adamant? Had Ambrose told him something? Or was it an effect of the medicine? But Tom wouldn't interrupt. Having a healer in their party could be useful. Especially if Katharine gave birth. Or fell ill.

And hadn't he foreseen this? Months ago, he'd foreseen a dwarf talking to him about a cirgeon. He closed his eyes, tried to draw back the foresight. Was it Mennvinn? Yes, it was. It was her in the cold, dark place, her face serious, understanding, her posture defeated. Giving him bad news.

He opened his eyes and ignored the twisting in his stomach. "My king requests that you journey with us," he said, making it formal.

Her hands stilled and she wiped them on her bloodied apron

as she turned to face them. She squinted at Tom, at Caledyr, before her gaze fell on Emyr. "You call this man a king. We heard snatches of your conversation down here," she told Tom. "Caledyr and Orlannu and Rimestenn." She met Tom's eye. "Is this Taranau?"

The dwarfish name for Emyr. Tom nodded.

"Truly?" When Tom nodded again, she shook her head. "I don't believe it." But she wanted to. Tom could see the yearning in her eyes. She crossed the room to Emyr's side and raised her hands as if to place them on his skin. "He will return to Tir in its hour of need." Her words were those spoken from an old memory.

She seemed to hover on the brink of a decision. On the brink of faith. Should he say something, to nudge her into believing them? Or was it more important to remain silent, to let her come by herself to the faith she needed?

"It's just a Faerie tale." Her words were almost a whisper. "Taranau died centuries ago."

Emyr's dreamy words were almost as soft as Mennvinn's whispers. "Not dead," he said. "Just waiting. Waiting to be what I needed to be."

She drew a deep breath, pulled her hands from where they hovered over his flesh, not out of dread, but out of reverence. He had touched on something. Her breath came shallow but slow. She was afraid to believe, but she was so close. She needed the smallest nudge.

"Each of us needs someone to see our potential," Emyr said. "The rest we can do ourselves. If they see us." And he turned his head, gazing at Mennvinn from beneath heavy lids.

The air was still. Tom realised he was holding his breath. Emyr gazed at Mennvinn. Mennvinn stared right back at Emyr. Trying to convince herself he was just another man under her master's knife. Coming to her decision. Trying not to believe.

Emyr reached out. It cost him, and he made no attempt to

hide that. Mennvinn shied away, but didn't stop him from laying a hand on her arm. She twitched at the touch.

"I need the you that you hide inside." It was all he said. Then he closed his eyes, and let her place his arm back by his side.

Tom didn't dare speak, breathe, even move. Emyr appeared to sleep. And Mennvinn reached her decision.

"Someone must watch him at all times." Mennvinn's voice was so soft that it took Tom a moment to realise she was speaking to him. "I will return soon."

She left in silence, without her tools or tonics. Tom let out the breath he had been holding. She had decided to believe. And it hadn't been in their journey or in the fay, or their purpose of stopping them that had convinced her. It had been Emyr. Somehow he had earned her loyalty in the space of moments. Tom wouldn't have believed it if he hadn't see it for himself.

"Everyone wants something," Emyr murmured, not quite as asleep as Tom had thought. "Recognition. Reward. Adventure." He sighed and his words thickened as true sleep wrapped him in its embrace. "Everyone wants something."

Tom woke as Katharine sat down beside him on a bench against the wall. He smiled at her, then remembered he'd been watching Emyr. He'd nodded off. Did Emyr still live? But she shushed him.

"It's fine," she murmured as she settled beside him. "Ambrose is watching him."

True enough, Ambrose stood vigil at Emyr's side, staring unblinking at his king's face.

Katharine slipped her hand into his. "You were muttering in your sleep."

Tom nodded. He'd been dreaming. Of Jarnstenn at a fire. Of Emyr saying, "He was my friend," and Tom saying, "I don't think he's anyone's friend anymore."

He'd dreamt of Katharine's hand growing weaker in his own.

"Dreams," he told her. "Bad ones."

She nodded. She was afraid to ask. He was afraid that she would. So he filled the silence. "How are you?"

"Tired," she admitted. "Hungry."

"We should find a bed for you to rest in." He pushed the vestiges of sleep from his thoughts and stood. She didn't relinquish her grip on his hand, but nor did she follow him to her feet. "Come," he told her.

"I'm fine here," she replied. "Sit with me."

"It's cold down here."

"It's fine."

He tugged her hand. "Come," he said again. "You need rest."

"I'm not sick, Tom." Her words had a keener edge to them. "I carry a child."

He gave in and sat back down. She held his hand in a firm grip, as if afraid he would let go. "Our child," he said. Katharine only nodded. The air seemed to grow thick and heavy with responsibility. And with all the things unsaid. There were more questions that she was too afraid to ask. Questions he could answer. "Before I was taken to Faerie, I wasn't a good husband to Elaine. And I wasn't a good father to Degor," he admitted, and it stung to say the words aloud. "Over the years I've told myself that his life was better for my leaving. But it would have been better if I had stayed, and been the father he'd deserved." He took a deep breath. How much had Degor hated him? Had the boy grown past his absent father? Had he found someone to love, had children of his own? All the questions Tom had been afraid to ask and now he was desperate to know the answers. "I abandoned him. I don't want to do the same to our daughter."

She weighed her response carefully. "So it's a girl?"

It wasn't the response he'd been hoping for. But he nodded. "I felt it in the maelstrom."

"I wasn't sure if I'd imagined that," she said. She looked down at her belly and laid a hand across it. "Our daughter." Two words that carried such joy and fear and uncertainty.

"How long have you known?" he asked, spoiling the moment.

She didn't meet his eye. "I was afraid to tell you."

Why? Because he'd been intent on his mission to topple Idris? Because he was infatuated with Maev? Because Caledyr had been pushing its thoughts into his own?

Because she didn't want to keep it?

"You once told me that being a housewife wasn't for you," he said. He chose his words carefully; they'd had a blazing row when she'd said that.

"It isn't," she replied, fire burning in her eyes, daring him to question that. "I'm a Pathfinder. It's what I am."

"Where does a child fit into that?"

His question echoed with the twin that lived in her own doubts; he could tell by the way she squared her shoulders, propped up her defiance. "She wouldn't be the first child raised on the road."

"Is that any life for a little girl?"

"Do you think my life is unsuitable for a girl?"

This was dangerous territory. And hardly the most pressing of problems before them. First he had to keep the two of them alive. Then he could worry about raising their daughter. So he shook his head. "She's going to have to get used to the road; it's a long way to Cairnarim."

She relaxed and her grip on his hand relaxed too. "It is." She took a deep breath and rushed into her next words, getting them out before she could think twice. "I won't be like Elaine, Tom, I won't turn a blind eye while you lie with other," she paused, "women. So you need to decide. And once you've decided, that's it. If you're not the man we deserve, we'll go." She took a deep breath and forced herself to meet his eye. "So decide. Are we more important than her?"

The question stung. And it scared him. And the maelstrom of emotions made him ask himself the same question. If Maev came to him, told him all was forgiven, that the fay had given up their plan to return to Tir and she begged him to come back to her, what would he say?

Maev had manipulated him. Tested him to see how loyal a dog he was. How could he ever step into her embrace again?

But he had let her hold him on the hill outside Cairnakor. A dark, fearful place inside told him he would accept her offer.

Katharine was holding in her fear and anger and pain, but he could see glimpses of it behind her firm stare. Always tough, always strong. Stronger than he was. And, without thought, he smiled and lifted her hand to his lips. This was real. This was right. Unbidden, he recalled a night many moons ago, a night spent hand-in-hand when he'd pondered if he was making the wrong choice.

"Remember when we hid in that pit together?" When they'd fled Duke Regent, his men on their tail. Katharine just nodded, refusing to let even confusion show. "I should have run away with you."

He watched her mapping out how events would have unfolded. No Caledyr. No rat pits. No campaign of terror in the Kingdom, no fight in the valley of dragons.

"No." She shook her head. "We needed to free the dragons." But she smiled. "Better that we run away now. To Cairnarim, perhaps?"

Tom nodded and gave her a smile in return. "To Cairnarim." However far that may be. And then onwards, to find two more glarn. How long was their path between here and the last glarn? And would they fail before they had walked it? Ambrose didn't know. Ambrose who had spent decades looking for the glarn and had failed. Would they still be looking for them when their daughter was born? When she started walking, talking? Would she be a woman grown and still looking for them? Tom felt a sudden urge to stand, to run, to dash to Cairnarim right now, anything to avoid the possibility that his daughter would know a moment of fear at the hands of the fay.

Katharine squeezed his hand. "We'll be fine," she told him.

He looked down at her hand in his and tried not to think of how, one day, he would feel her grip grow weak. Unless he could break from his foresight, and change what was to come.

The obvious answer came to mind, and he knew that it would make him a liar and make him despised in her eyes. He met her eye and saw her fear, but also her confidence. She felt sure they could do this.

"Whatever happens from here," he said, "please remember that everything I do is for you and our daughter."

She nodded with a broad smile.

"Everything," he repeated. "Even the things you don't like."

Her smile faltered but she nodded all the same. She wanted to ask a question, but it went unspoken. Too much unsaid. He wished he could unburden himself, share this terrible truth with her. But what kind of man would he be, to tell an expectant mother that she would die? No. He couldn't be that cruel.

"I trust you," she said. He could tell it was hard for her to do so. Hard to forget all the wrongs and the arguments and the hurts. Which is why it cut so deep that she could say it to him, given what he planned to do.

Given that he planned to leave her behind.

CHAPTER 4

THE NEXT FEW hours were a whirl of activity for some, and a chance to rest for others. Gravinn came and went constantly, overseeing deliveries of clothing, supplies, and food; the last was gratefully received, and everyone had stopped to enjoy the slabs of dark bread, heavily buttered and filled with warm, greasy bacon.

Jarnstenn had taken over negotiations with his master, commandeering weapons as well as other bizarre contraptions that he swore might be useful. He enlisted Six as his assistant, but if the elf bristled at being ordered to carry one thing and fetch another, he didn't show it.

Katharine and Kunnustenn had retreated to a corner, putting together her instincts and his clues and snippets over Gravinn's purloined map. Tom would have sent Gravinn to sit with them, to ensure that someone other than Katharine knew where they were going. But only Draig and Dank were available, and he didn't trust them. So he told them to find what rest they could, while he sat with Katharine and Kunnustenn and tried to absorb as much as possible.

It wasn't easy. Gravinn insisted on reporting back to him on a regular basis, showing off what she had obtained and why. So he found himself nodding and praising her for a wise decision on which firestarters she had bought, or which tents she suggested she procure, or arbitrating in a debate between her and Jarnstenn about which daggers would be better. He had no knowledge of any of this, and it wearied him. He began to daydream that Emyr would stride up out of the cellar, magically healed, to take command of everything and let Tom rest.

But that wasn't going to happen. And, somehow, he was going to have to command them all. He was going to have to make them travel onwards when he left Katharine behind.

Should he leave her here? She knew the city, and they already knew a cirgeon who could care for her when she went into labour. But it was a big city, and the fay were drawn to such places. So many people in one place provided plenty of opportunity for mischief.

So, not here. Somewhere else. He tried to focus on Katharine's plan, tried to follow her path north. She'd already mentioned something about a railroad, which would take them to another city. She was plotting a path that took them past dozens of towns and villages. Perhaps one of them, smaller, out of the way, less likely to attract Faerie attention?

And what if they found her? How would she defend herself?

They were talking about something else now. A pass, some canyon that was referenced in one of Kunnustenn's books. Iron nails, he couldn't follow their conversation and nod at Gravinn's latest purchase and figure out where and how to leave Katharine. Not all at once.

The sun set and Gravinn continued to bustle to and fro, bringing back more food for everyone and blankets, which were quickly laid out for sleep. Tom found a space in the cellar for himself and Katharine, who nodded off in moments. But Tom found himself lying beside her, staring at the strange and disturbing shadows cast onto the rough stone ceiling by the candlelight.

No-one would let him leave her behind. They wouldn't understand.

But he couldn't tell them. How could he tell them what he wouldn't tell her?

Six wouldn't stand for it. He'd go back for her.

And Katharine would only follow them. Even if she didn't already know the path they would take, she'd still find them.

If he left her, he would be abandoning her. He might never see her again, or his daughter.

If he left her, she would live. They both would.

They would hate him.

They would be alive.

It seemed there were no good choices. So he lay there, and worried, and tried not to wonder how many nights he had left of listening to Katharine breathe.

He was woken by sounds from above, and stole up the stairs to see the dwarfs awake already, carting crates and bags and great stoppered clay jugs out to a wagon waiting outside.

"We'll be ready once it's loaded," Gravinn told him. "We're leaving plenty of room."

Tom offered to help but she waved him away. "We have a system," she told him, and both Jarnstenn and Kunnustenn made sounds of agreement. With nothing else to do, Tom went back downstairs and let himself doze off.

It felt like moments later that footsteps woke him, and he

looked up to see Mennvinn on the stairs. “It’s done,” she said, voice pitched high by fear and nerves. “I’m coming with you.”

“Good,” Tom replied. He blinked away sleep, his mind fuzzy. “I’m very grateful.”

Mennvinn just nodded, her uncertainty plain. He wasn’t as good at this as Emyr. He rose from his blankets and Katharine stirred. What would Emyr say? “I fear we will have need of your skills on this journey.”

Mennvinn gestured to Katharine. “With two Pathfinders? They can treat scrapes and scratches.”

“I see the things to come. We’ll suffer more than scrapes and scratches.”

Her eyes widened. He was scaring her. So he nodded at Emyr. “And he needs you.” That settled her a little. “He chose you.”

That was better. She ducked her head and smiled. “They say the wagon is ready for him.”

He smiled back at her. “Good.” He spied Draig yawning in a corner. “Help me?” he asked.

The Easterner said nothing, just stood and lifted his end when Tom asked him to, carried the old king in silence, and still didn’t say a word as they manoeuvred him out of the smith’s front door and into the street, which was now dominated by Gravinn’s wagon. It was a strange thing, the wooden frame hard and treated against the elements, the cloth stretched over it tough and unyielding. The whole thing felt at once huge and yet also compact, and it was so full of supplies Tom wondered if Gravinn thought they’d be travelling for a year.

He hoped they wouldn’t be.

“Thank you,” he said to Draig.

Draig just nodded, arms folded, face closed. What was he so angry about? But, he realised, the last time the two of them had spoken, it had been at the top of Cairnagwyn, and they’d been bearing swords. Tom had left Draig in the merrow city. Draig had tried to stop Tom breaking the monoliths. It felt like months ago, but it had been just a day or two.

But so much was different now.

"Am I coming with you."

Tom nodded. He didn't like the idea of leaving Draig at their backs anyway. "Why?"

"To help prevent the doom you unleashed."

The elf was expecting him to argue. But there was nothing to argue with. In weakening the monoliths, Tom had helped open the door for the fay. So Tom nodded. "Good." And left Draig standing by the wagon, uncertainty warring with his scowl.

There was little to prepare. The dwarfs had loaded everything they thought was needed, either into the wagon or onto the horses Gravinn had also procured, small, wiry things that looked like they needed a good meal. So they rose, mounted their steeds, and all looked to Tom.

The horse was skittish beneath him and he turned to Katharine. "What is our path?"

"We take the railroad to Cairnajorr," she replied. "Then we'll ride for Cairnoher."

Gravinn made a noise of exasperation. "Why wasn't I consulted?"

"You were shopping."

"I was getting supplies."

"For a journey you didn't yet understand."

"Is it a problem?" Tom asked, trying to interrupt the brewing argument.

Gravinn scowled before grumbling, "It will cost more to load the wagon onto the engine."

"That won't be a problem." Nierin had granted them a promissory that would cover any cost. Tom waved everyone forward. "Let's go."

The streets of Cairnakor mirrored the mountains it had been built upon, filled with uphill slogs and downhill plods. As the city awoke, the vagrants vanished like fog burnt away by the rising sun, and the streets filled with dwarfs of two kinds, as if the city was populated with two entirely different peoples. Half seemed cut from Jarnstenn's cloth, speaking with his accent, smoking cheap cigars and wearing cheap clothing or leather aprons in various shades of dirty brown. The other half wore much richer attire, all in deep blacks and dazzling whites, festooned with jewels at neck and wrist and finger. They walked with canes or parasols, smoked from pipes, and spoke with Gravinn's precise accent, often making loud demands of their poorer fellows that were met without question.

Perhaps that was why Tom found it unsettling that Six had adopted their style. Though he was dressed for the road, his clothes shone in black and white, and he wore a waistcoat embroidered in fanciful patterns and gloves of pure black. At Tom's look, he said, "Why shouldn't I put Neirin's money to good use?"

"I didn't say you shouldn't."

Six nodded and looked ahead. "We performed Neirin a service. It's only right we should be paid for it."

"Only right."

Six relaxed and gave Tom a grin. Perhaps he thought Tom had agreed. "Besides, the dwarfs have some remarkable artefacts." He tugged his horse closer and pulled a small metal box from his pocket. "Look." He opened it, held it out so Tom could see that inside there was a metal needle under glass, swinging around inside. "When I was a boy I was shown a trick. You rub a piece of metal on a magnet, place it in water, and it will always point north."

"Why?"

"No-one knows. My teachers called it the Mysterious

Needle." Six closed it up. "Here they call it a compass and sell it alongside common knifes and such. I thought Katharine might like it."

Six bought her gifts. What had the father of her child bought her? He glanced ahead, watched her riding with Kunnustenn and Jarnstenn, who regaled her with some tale. They shared the telling with ease, never interrupting or talking over the other. What they had was reviled by many, and yet they made it look easy.

Of course, there was no child involved. No child that had been kept a secret for weeks or months.

"She wanted to tell you." Six's words were soft, gentle, but they still felt like a rebuke.

"So you knew."

The elf had the grace to look embarrassed. He nodded his head.

"How long have you known?"

Six shrugged. "She had to tell someone."

"She could have told me."

"Could she?" Six skewered him with a sharp look. The old wounds weren't forgotten. "You seemed to care more for the sword you still carry."

Tom felt his jaw clench and a sharp retort steam up within. But the elf spoke the truth. So he sighed and said, "I wish she could have told me."

"She's scared." As if that was Tom's fault.

"Did she think I would hurt her?"

"She knew you would." Six turned away. Did he straighten? Ride taller in the saddle? "You'll get her hopes up. And then you'll disappoint her. It's what you do."

Six's words echoed uncomfortably with Mab's. Don't disappoint me, she'd said. Show me a fire to make me weak in the knees. He pushed the memory away. "You're so sure?"

Six turned back. Sad, pitying. "What will you do when Queen Maev summons you, Tom?"

Would she? Her words had felt full of promise. A promise he didn't want to be tempted by.

Six continued, "Katharine thinks you feel something for her. But we all know you belong to Maev."

I don't, Tom wanted to say. I don't belong to Maev. But the words wouldn't pass his lips. What had Duke Ria called him? A pet. A Faerie pet.

Is that what Ria had told Katharine, when they had spoken together on the Harbour?

If Maev called, would he go to her?

"Talk to her," Six said.

"What do I say?"

The elf made a frustrated sound. "If you're going to hurt her again, do it quickly and do it gently."

Tom shook his head. "I don't want to hurt her." At the head of the column, Katharine laughed at something Jarnstenn said. Turned to Kunnustenn and asked him something, laughed again at the answer. She deserved to be looked after. Protected. He wouldn't be the one to hurt her.

"Then don't. It's that simple."

"No." Because even if he didn't hurt her, something else would. Something else would leave her bleeding in a dark place, where her hand grew weak in his own. "No, it isn't."

"Why not?" Six was getting angry again.

Because she would die. And their child would die too. He couldn't lose his little girl, not before he'd even met her. The thought tightened his chest and his head bowed under the weight of it. "Don't."

"Why not?" Six asked. "For Oen's sake, Tom, I'm sick of seeing her like this. She worries, she cries, she's scared. Do something."

"I can't."

"Why not?"

"I can't lose her."

Those words hung heavier and smelt fouler than the fog around them. Six's face went slack, an accusatory finger limp in the air. "You've had a foresight?"

Tom just nodded.

"And she dies?"

He shrugged. "She's bleeding. A lot. Mennvinn tells me there's nothing more she can do. Katharine's hand grows weak in mine." He'd expected that the burden would ease once he'd shared it. But instead it grew heavy and cold within him. As if he'd given form to a nightmare, made it real by speaking its name. Just as Brega had warned him: he made things happen by foreseeing them.

Six let his hand drift to his side and he looked ahead, watching Katharine ride. "How long have you known?"

It felt like he'd lived with this foresight all his life. But, "Since we left. Since Cairnagan."

Six peered at Tom as if he'd spoken in dwarfish. "All this time?"

Tom nodded.

"Does she know?" the elf asked.

"Of course not."

"Why not?"

"What good would it do?"

"We could try to change it."

Tom sighed. "I want to." Desperately. More than anything. But, "I've warned travellers of a fatal storm, and something would force their hands to travel all the same. I've foreseen riots, only for them to be caused by the same soldiers Regent sent to quell them." Six opened his mouth to speak but Tom shook his head. "I'm scared that I'll try to change this, and all I'll do is upset Katharine. I'll hurt her, and it will happen all the same."

Six's expression softened and he nodded. When he spoke again, his tone was gentler, and all the more brutal for it. "That doesn't mean we shouldn't try."

"I want to, Six. I do."

The elf lifted his chin. "Then try," he said. Flicked the reins and rode ahead to join Katharine and the dwarfs. Leaving Tom dejected and alone. Six made it sound so easy. As if all Tom had to do was want a thing for it to come to pass.

But he thought of that little life that lived inside Katharine, how scared it had been as they passed between Tir and Faerie and back again. Six was right. It might not be easy, but Tom had to keep his daughter safe. There was no choice, no trying. He would break the future for her. He had to.

He pulled back on his reins, drew a nervous breath and returned the nod Gravinn gave him as she drove the wagon past him. Only Draig rode behind the wagon, and Tom felt like the Easterner knew what he had planned as he called for Mennvinn. But Draig said nothing, and the dwarf poked her head out through the back of the wagon a moment later, a thin cigar hanging from her lips. "Do you have anything to make someone sleep?" he asked her.

She frowned. "Why?"

"Katharine, the human Pathfinder?" He waited until she nodded. "She needs to sleep." It was the only way he could leave her behind. "She carries a child."

Mennvinn's frown grew deeper. "I would certainly recommend rest, but to give her substances? It is an unnecessary risk to the child."

Risk. He recoiled from the word. But what was the alternative? The risk was far greater if Katharine died. "How great a risk?"

The dwarf made an unhappy sound. "Small. But still a risk."

Tom nodded. "I'll take it."

Mennvinn shook her head but disappeared back into the wagon. Tom was painfully aware that Draig was watching him; he refused to meet the Easterner's eye. Mennvinn emerged a moment later with a small, dark bottle. "Soak it into a cloth and let her breathe in the fumes. Not too much," she warned as Tom took the bottle and slipped it into a pocket.

"Thank you." he told her. She disappeared back into the wagon, and Tom flicked the reins, manoeuvring past the wagon and away from Draig's questioning look.

The fog seemed to grow thicker as the morning passed, and a burning smell joined the general stench. When the road poured down a steep hillside, Tom saw that the new stink was coming from their destination. A scar on the landscape, the railroad cut through the city, leaving rubble, wood, and ruined walls where it had torn through buildings and homes. Lairing at one end was an enormous beast of shining black metal and belching smoke, a great evil wagon that housed a fire within, ready to haul the carriages and pallets attached to its rear. Hundreds of people bustled around it, bringing coal to the machine and loading it with goods. It gave Tom the sense of a religious idol, demanding to be waited on by its followers and stepping on them whenever it willed.

He didn't like it.

But Katharine was excited. "Isn't it incredible?" she called back to him. "It wasn't finished when I was last in the Provinces." Tom would have thought that was a blessing, but she grinned at the prospect of climbing aboard it. The excitement and bustle and noise grew as they descended, dwarfs talking and shouting and laughing, making great crashes and bangs as they loaded the carriages and pallets with goods and people. The crowds were too thick. Even mounted, Tom felt the press of people, like there wasn't enough air to for them all.

"And we're going to get inside it?" he asked.

"Don't worry." Jarnstenn looked excited, and Tom noticed his fingers were clenching and unclenching around his reins, like he was itching to get his hands on the machine. "It's safe as houses."

Whatever that meant. Tom couldn't put his finger on why he felt uneasy about this thing. Fear of the unknown, perhaps? But what was wrong with horses? "We could ride north just as easily."

"Takes longer," Jarnstenn countered. "A horse needs resting. An engine will run as long as there's coal and water. And it's faster."

Faster?

"Horse at a gallop can go maybe thirty miles in the hour," Jarnstenn continued. "Engine can easily go fifty. Maybe sixty at a push."

Twice as fast as a galloping horse. Inside a box. Hauled by a metallic beast filled with fire. "Horses seem fast enough for me," he muttered, but no-one was listening.

They came to the clearing, which Jarnstenn called a station, and was little more than an open area of plain dirt and a few planks to create a walkway for those who didn't want to get their boots dirty. The noise was deafening up close. Not only the hustle and bustle, but the engine itself. No more than a great cylinder lying on its side, covered in rivets and gauges and taps, with wheels as tall as a dwarf. Steam curled out of a chimney rising from the top or occasionally spat from between its wheels; the thing huffed and hissed like an unholy imitation of a dragon in wood and metal. It seemed impatient. Ready to fly. Twice as fast as a horse.

Katharine was trying to buy their way onto a carriage from a dwarf in a leather apron, but he didn't speak the human tongue.

When Katharine stumbled over the dwarfish, Gravinn interrupted, taking over the conversation with no grace, no subtlety, and Katharine scowled at her for it.

"You really wanted to ride in that?" Tom asked, more as a way of distracting her.

"Of course," she snapped. Then she sighed and her brow relaxed. "You're worried."

"I am." A thought had begun to ring in his mind, the sound of metal screaming. If a horse fell at a gallop, the rider could die. If an engine fell at twice the speed, what would happen then?

"It's safe," she told him. Her smile was forced. Her eyes still wary. "Trust me."

He couldn't stop being worried about it. But he could nod and ask her, "How are you feeling?"

She shrugged. "Tired. Hungry."

"I'll get you something."

"It's okay," she said quickly. Why didn't she want him to help?

She was hunched in the saddle, and he could see now that her Western shawl wasn't enough to hide her swelling belly. She searched his eyes, as if she could scry her future in them. But a door opens both ways; Tom could see her hunting for a sign he would disappoint her. Just as Six said he would.

Perhaps the elf was right. Because Tom was going to let her down. To protect her.

He opened his mouth to suggest they find somewhere to sit, to rest for a moment. Somewhere he could rent a room, lie her down, and use Mennvinn's medicine to put her to sleep, so they could leave her behind. But he couldn't say the words. He sat on his horse, mouth open, unable to break her trust. Not again.

And then Gravinn was bustling around them, urging them to dismount, leading their horses up a ramp, organising a team of dwarfs to push their wagon up into a carriage where it was lashed down with straps. What was that for? Would they have to be lashed down too?

"They're only to keep the wagon secure," Gravinn assured him. And when Tom turned around, Six was helping Katharine into another carriage. Giving him a pointed look as he did so. That was Tom's place. To look after the mother of his child.

And just like that, his opportunity was missed. He couldn't decide if he was relieved or angry with himself.

"Gonna stare at it all day or get on?" Jarnstenn asked.

Tom just nodded, touched Caledyr and climbed onto the train.

The carriage was long, cramped, the ceiling just as low as every other in this city, and a narrow gangway cut between cramped wooden benches with soft red cushions.

"How long are we in here for?" He sat on a bench but it forced his knees up to his chest.

"It's a fourteen hour journey to Cairnajorr," Gravinn told him.

Fourteen hours. He couldn't stay in here for fourteen hours. He couldn't.

A groan cut through his rising panic and he saw Draig and Dank struggling to get Emyr on board. They used a blanket to lift him, much as Tom and Neirin had carried Brega, and with a shrug Draig lowered the old king to the floor. There was no room on a bench. Where else could they put him?

"We can't leave him there for fourteen hours," Tom growled. He told everyone to hand over their blankets and began to fold them and lay them further down the aisle. "Lay him here."

"No." Emyr's protests were feeble but they moved him anyway, before covering him in another blanket and putting more under his head. Tom wiped the sheen of sweat from Emyr's face, knowing it was nothing to do with the temperature.

"Can you give him anything for the pain?" he asked Menvinn.

The dwarf settled herself next to Emyr as best she could; there was no more room in the aisle so she climbed over a bench to sit by his head, her little case next to her. She pulled out a small bottle and said, "Give him two drops. No more."

Two drops of anything didn't seem enough but Tom obeyed, letting two tiny pearls of milky fluid drip into Emyr's too-eager mouth. It pained Tom to see him like this. Had it been a mistake, to bring him back to Tir? He seemed to suffer more now than he ever did.

"It will be a long road to recovery," Menvinn confirmed. "But don't worry."

The old king's eyes were pinched shut and his brow pulled a hundred lines into existence, making him look old and beaten. "All I can do is worry," Tom replied. "There's nothing else I can do for him."

"That's why I'm here." Menvinn gave him a strong smile, one that seemed to reach inside him and touch his concern. He couldn't help but smile back. None of his worries were gone. But they were easier to live with in that moment. He looked up at Ambrose, sat on a bench by himself, watching them all.

"Does he get better?" Tom asked him.

"He will," Menvinn said, but Tom needed to hear it from Ambrose. He needed the certainty.

"He will stand and walk and fight," he replied.

"So he survives," he said, trying to turn the old man's dead, hollow words into the reassurance he sought.

"That all depends on you." Ambrose closed his eyes. He was so pale, so thin and wasted, he could be dead.

Tom watched Emyr's breathing relax and slow until he began to snore. He slept through the jolting start of the train, the screaming whistle as they began to move, and the horrendous, rapid pant of the engine over the screeching wheels beneath them. Tom wondered if Mennvinn could be persuaded to spare a few drops of something for himself, but he said nothing. Just gripped the top of the bench in front of him and tried not to think about it. Any of it.

The railroad wound its way between the hills and mountains of the Provinces, sometimes rolling over grand bridges that spanned great valleys, other times plunging through the slopes into dark, echoing tunnels, into the noisy earth itself. They stopped occasionally in towns where goods and people were loaded and unloaded. Tom would gaze out of the window and try to spot a fay staring back. But he never did. Soon the sun was set and they travelled under a pregnant moon and a clear sky, the stars above joined by the flickering, distant lights of farmhouses and villages scattered across the mountainsides. The carriage grew colder as the moon rose but it couldn't affect Tom's ability to rest; the sheer, relentless drive of the engine beneath his feet was too frightening. No-one else seemed to mind; their entire party seemed to be sleeping peacefully.

Tom placed a blanket over Katharine, who snored ever so gently to herself, and stood. His legs cramped and his back ached from being bent almost double. Emyr blocked the aisle towards the head of the carriage, so Tom walked to the rear. He wondered if he should check on the wagon and the horses, but his stomach turned at the thought of stepping across to the next carriage and seeing the ground flying by beneath. Besides, what could he do if it needed doing? If the wagon had come loose, it would likely crush him before he could do anything. And how do you calm a horse in an unsteady, enclosed space? Either they were fine or they weren't. So he stood by the door, watching the world fly past at speeds he could never have imagined. The industry of dwarfs.

"Can not you sleep?" Draig had ghosted up behind him,

head ducked and shoulders hunched, shrouded in a blanket. He kept his distance and his voice low, one hand on an empty bench to counter the swaying of the carriage. Tom had a sudden vision of Draig pushing him through the door, and wished he hadn't left Caledyr in his seat.

"No." He took a step further into the carriage, kept his hands free and tried to balance with just his feet.

"Make strange do these dwarfs." Draig waved a hand to encompass the carriage. "No elf would build this thing."

Was he trying to make conversation? Or lull Tom into a sense of safety? With so much to worry about, he didn't need to be guessing at Draig's motives. Perhaps it would be easier to make peace with the elf. After all, Draig had been a friend, had comforted him after he had killed a man, had shown him how to handle a sword.

Had fought him to a standstill, had given them up to Gerwyn. Had left them in rat pits. "Why are you here, Draig?"

"Why ask you for medicine from the healer?" Draig's expression betrayed no emotion in the dark.

"I won't say."

Draig just nodded. "Have you no trust in me. Just as have I none in you."

The words pricked Tom's anger, though he knew there was no benefit to it. "So you followed us here because you don't trust me?"

Draig tapped his chest. "Broke I an oath for Tir. Not Angles, not Kingdom, not fay or dwarfs. Does my loyalty lie with Tir."

"You think mine doesn't."

"Freed you dragons. Freed you fay. Did you embrace Mab on that hill."

Tom felt his cheeks grow hot. "I stabbed Melwas."

"But not her."

No. Not her. His chest tightened and his breath quickened.

How dare Draig stand there with doubts and talk of loyalty as if he hadn't cast them into rat pits?

But he wasn't angry with Draig. He was angry with himself. The elf was right: he should have stabbed Mab just as he'd stabbed Melwas.

Draig nodded. "Think I that you want to stop the fay," he said. "Fear I that she will stay your hand."

Tom feared it too.

"Some people don't deserve our love," Draig said, repeating the words he'd said in Faerie. Tom had known that the elf was right. Yet he still hadn't lifted his hand against Mab. Was he incapable of doing so? Or was he just afraid?

"I want to stop the fay," he told Draig. "I want Katharine and our child to be safe."

"You will kill Mab?" Draig asked.

Could he? Could he cut her down? He couldn't touch Caledyr for the strength to say 'yes'. So he reached for the memory of the thoughts he'd shared with his daughter. He would protect her. So, if Mab threatened her, he would kill the Faerie Queen. He would. He could.

He opened his mouth to say so.

The world lurched, throwing Tom against the elf and sending them both tumbling to the floor as a sickening scream rent the air. The carriage shuddered and jolted and spun, people were thrown from their seats, bags and cases tumbled onto their heads. Tom could barely hear the cries and panic over the sound of metal wailing, bending, snapping.

"What happens?" he heard Draig cry.

Tom pulled himself to his feet. Their journey had stopped and engine was silenced. But the carriage juddered and shook, hanging at a strange angle. "Everyone out!" he bellowed, climbing over seats towards Katharine. "Get out now!"

He reached Katharine, looked her over. There was no blood,

no obvious injury. She was okay. They would get out. They would be safe. He took her hand and drew strength from her touch.

The carriage shook again, a savage jerk that knocked Tom from his feet. Then all movements, all sounds stopped, and in its place a great breath was drawn followed by a mournful roar. A roar like a reverse wolf's howl, that pitched high and fell, ending on furious melancholy.

Mester Stoorworm.

CHAPTER 5

"Move move move." They had to get out. The sounds of rending metal and splintering wood had started again and Tom knew with absolute certainty that the monstrous fay was ripping his way through the carriages. Inside, there was no room to fight, no possibility of escape. Outside, they had a chance, to flee or to hide. He pulled at Katharine, shouted to Six and Draig to carry Emyr, to the dwarfs to run. Ambrose remained seated, watching them as if they were all very curious.

"Ambrose, get out," Tom called to him but didn't wait, half-ushering, half-pushing Katharine to the door, forcing it open. The carriage shook again and Tom leaned past her and peered out. Mester Stoorworm was tearing at the neighbouring carriage with his mouth, worrying it like a dog with a bone. The fay was strong, his arms powerful enough to break a man in two, his mighty teeth sharp enough to sever limbs, and his scaly, snake-like body could keep pace with a horse. They couldn't fight him, couldn't outrun him. But there was a pile of boulders nearby. They could hide. Tom pointed them out to Katharine and she nodded.

Stoorworm shook the neighbouring carriage and the floor

thrashed beneath their feet. Then the fay paused, tipped his head back to admire his work, and Tom whispered to Katharine, "Go."

She lowered herself to the ground as quietly as she could. Tom felt sure the fay would hear her. But Stoorworm kept chewing at the metal in his mouth, and Katharine crept away into the dark.

The carriage shook again and Tom almost fell out. There was a cry from inside and he looked back to see Six and Draig had lost their footing, dropped Emyr.

The shaking stopped.

Mester Stoorworm peered at their carriage. He had heard them.

Tom's limbs filled with dread and froze, his mind utterly blank with fear, as the fay raised a claw and plunged it into the carriage roof.

The wood splintered, metal bent, talons poked through and scrabbled in the air, one tearing Dank's shoulder, another catching Mennvinn's cloak and lifting her into the air. Everyone dropped to the floor, forcing themselves flat or into nooks and crannies to avoid the fay's sharp grip. Finding no spoils, the hand closed and pulled. Tom saw Kunnustenn reach for Mennvinn, take her flailing hand, hold her and keep her as Mester Stoorworm hauled on the roof, peeling it away, failing to notice the dwarf he almost took or the torn cloak flapping in his hand. Instead he peered through the rent roof, his muzzle open in a dog-like grin.

His gaze fell on Emyr and he purred, "You." But Stoorworm made no effort to attack, no move to retreat. Just basked in the sight of the old king. Everyone was silent and still. The only sound was a deafening, thundering heartbeat.

No. That was Tom's own. And the world wasn't quiet. The

dwarfs were shouting, panicking. They couldn't see the fay. They didn't know what was happening.

Then the fay tossed aside a piece of the roof and began to clamber into the carriage, reaching for Emyr with his claws.

Tom's feet were moving before he could think. "Stoorworm!" he bellowed, snatching up the sword and pulling it free as best he could in cramped quarters. The fay stopped, saw the sword, and his eyes grew wide in fear. He snatched at Emyr, trying to haul him out of the carriage. Emyr howled as claws pierced his skin and tried to pry himself free.

"Hold him," Tom cried, scrambled into a bench and flailing at Emyr's ankles. Six and Draig jumped for the old king, but Stoorworm had another hand on Emyr's belt and was using his tail to pull himself from the carriage along with his prize. The fay had already won. He had Emyr. He would take him back to Faerie. It was over.

Take the fight to the enemy.

The sword was right. They were trapped in here, rats in a cage. Stoorworm had the advantage. So Tom struck the pommel against a window, once, twice, then the glass broke and he kicked it away, clambered through the small opening, ignored the hot streaks of wet pain it opened in his scalp, his hands and legs. He tumbled to the ground into the cold night, dragged himself to his feet. Stoorworm's tail was hanging from the side of the carriage and all it took was a few staggering steps, a clumsy swing, and Caledyr rent a deep gash through Stoorworm's flesh.

The fay howled. It was so full of pain, hurt, mourning, that Tom felt his chest tighten for the fay. Then the tail flicked across his arm, parting cloth and skin and knocking him to the ground. Tom could hear a relieved cry from inside the carriage; they had Emyr. Stoorworm reared out of the carriage, collapsing on the ground, eyes rolling until they found Tom.

He had expected words. Protests, outrage, disbelief, vows of vengeance. But Stoorworm uttered no words. Instead he growled. Barked. And Tom watched the gash in the fay's flesh close and heal in just seconds.

As the fay reared upright, flexing its arms, Tom knew he should be afraid. But he was staring at Stoorworm's tail. There was no sign he had been injured. No scratch, no blood. Nothing. It was as if the wound had never been taken. He had felt Faerie shake under his very feet and seen Melwas mindless in agony and thought he had bought them all days, weeks of time while the fay recovered. But he had probably bought nothing at all. Only a death sentence.

Stoorworm lunged, not with his hands but with his maw. Tom slashed blindly, caught Stoorworm's nose and the fay yelped, retreated, slithered down the hillside and circled Tom. Hunted him. Tom clambered to his feet. He was outmatched here. The fay could heal its hurts in moments. But just one blow could end Tom.

High ground.

Yes, he had the high ground. But it wasn't much consolation.

The fay struck like a snake, a rapid dart forward. Tom swung with the sword, wild and unfocused, letting himself fall as he did so. Stoorworm's mighty jaw snapped shut on the air where he had stood, the click echoing on the hills, and Caledyr slipped through the fay's chin. There was no blood. Nothing at all but parted flesh. Tom rolled, came to one knee. But Stoorworm was quicker. He slammed a fist into Tom's chest. Tom flew and, a moment later, his head cracked against the rim of a wheel. The world went numb and dark for a moment, every thought and feeling knocked out of him. Then Stoorworm had Tom's arm in one hand, his throat in another, pinning him against the carriage. He couldn't move and he couldn't breathe.

Fight.

It was the only thought in his mind and it wasn't his. But his arm was trapped, and Stoorworm's scaly hand was pressed too tight against his throat. The only fight Tom could muster was the fight for air. Stoorworm slavered above, chest like a bellows, his jaw gaping open, teeth sharp, tongue almost beckoning him in.

Fight.

But he couldn't.

There was a yell from above and Tom fell to the ground. Grass and dirt on his face. Soil and stone in his hands. Air in his chest. Stoorworm had dropped him. He was free.

Fight.

Yes. Fight. He gulped at the air, hauling on it. He reached out for the sword, flailing, finding it. It gave him strength he didn't have, letting him borrow its will in place of his own. He lurched to his feet. Stoorworm was thrashing, rolling on the ground, fighting with something on his back. Trying to shake it off.

Distracted. Attack.

A few staggering steps and he was knocked over by Stoorworm's flailing tail. He landed on his back, a rock stabbed at his spine and he groaned.

Get up.

Again he surrendered himself to the sword and it pushed him up, guided his steps. He dodged another lash of the fay's tail. Stepped forward. Stoorworm yelped and thrashed onto his back again.

Tom stepped forward and plunged Caledyr into his chest.

Stoorworm's scream ripped through the air and through his mind, vibrating with magic and with the pain of a thousand voices. The fay's body stiffened in agony and panic and shock and Tom took the chance to pull the blade free and plunge it through the roof of the fay's open maw.

Stoorworm fell silent and his limbs and tail flopped to the ground. Tom let go of Caledyr, leaving it in its new scabbard, and all of the blade's strength left him in a moment. He staggered back, lost his balance, fell. Stared up into the night. A beautiful clear night, the moon heavy and expecting, the stars out in force, and silent. Utterly silent. He closed his eyes.

"Tom?"

He opened his eyes. He hadn't slept. He knew that. He had just stopped, only for a moment. He looked up and saw Gravinn stood over him, fear on her face.

"Is everyone safe?" he asked her.

She nodded and her fear receded. "I think so." She held out her hand and Tom had no desire to take it. Just to lie there. Maybe sleep. But he thought of Katharine and the baby and he reached up and let the dwarf pull him into a sitting position. He looked over at the Stoorworm's body.

"Is it dead?" Gravinn asked.

"No." He touched her elbow and asked, "Would you find Katharine for me? Please?"

She gave him a stiff nod and waddled off. Stoorworm stared blindly into the sky, Caledyr's pommel shining between his teeth. Tom felt a moment of guilt for what he had done. The fay had been gentle and kind once and now he had a sword through his skull. He had attacked first, true. But no doubt it was on instruction from Melwas. He was doing his duty.

Duty done.

The thought was weak, as if the sword was distracted or busy. But it was right. Tom had done his duty too.

The body twitched.

Tom was on his feet in a moment. Was Stoorworm healing? What would Tom do if he rose again? Distract him. Let the others escape. Let Katharine get to safety.

Stoorworm jerked and said, "Help to me, please."

No. It wasn't Stoorworm. It was someone trapped underneath him. Whoever had jumped onto the fay's back and saved Tom's life.

"Draig." The Easterner was pinned by Stoorworm's body, too heavy for one person to lift. But the elf asked, not for help or thanks, but, "Is everyone well?"

Tom nodded. "I think so." It seemed like days ago since they had said they didn't trust each other. Now it felt petulant to have said so. He put hands under Stoorworm's arm, lifted. The fay was heavy. And while Draig scrabbled out from under the dead weight, Tom kept a careful eye on Caledyr. If it slipped, or fell out, Stoorworm would heal. Tom had no doubts about that.

"Thank you," Draig said. He was on his feet, though he looked ready to lie down again.

Tom let Stoorworm drop, watched the sword shake in his maw. "We should move," he said. How long would it be before more fay arrived?

"I agree."

But if he took the sword, Stoorworm would heal.

"I need Emyr," Tom said. "Or Dank. Or Ambrose."

Draig nodded and began to climb up towards the wrecked train.

"Thank you," Tom added.

Draig offered a smile, and it was so like the old Draig that Tom smiled too, pleased for a moment to see the elf he had known, before the memory of Gerwyn and the rat pits soured Tom's goodwill. Maybe it was petulant to feel this way after the elf had saved his life.

But the past hadn't changed.

The dark hillside blurred into a tent, shaking under a roaring wind. He was knelt beside Ambrose and the old man said, "What you remember today is not what you will remember tomorrow."

The question of Stoorworm had no apparent answer, so they circled around it. They had checked each other for injuries, discussed the state of their supplies, rescued the wagon and horses from their mercifully unmolested carriage. Mennvinn had asked if she should see to other travellers, and Tom had warned that other fay might come, bringing the conversation back to Stoorworm again.

"He will heal as soon as the sword is removed," Dank told them. They had all gathered around the immobile fay, speaking in hushed voices as if he was sleeping, or they were attending a bizarre funeral. "It will only take him a minute or two."

"That's not enough time," Six said. "We'd barely be over the next hill."

"Never mind that we don't know where we're going," Gravinn pointed out. She was applying a foul-smelling unguent to a nasty cut on Mennvinn's head, who smoked one of her cheap, slender cigars with shaking hands.

"We know." Katharine sat close to Tom; he hadn't let her stray far from his side since Gravinn had fetched her back. He needed to know that she was here and safe. That their daughter was safe. "Our path is to Cairnoher."

"And you know the path from here to there?" Gravinn's scepticism was plain.

"I don't know it," she replied. "But I can find it."

"Travellers get lost in these mountains."

"I won't." Katharine's tone made it clear that the matter was settled, but Gravinn was drawing breath.

So Tom stopped the argument before it could start. "I suggest we go across country," he said. "Avoid cities and towns."

"That will be a hard journey in this terrain." Katharine shifted often, trying different positions, but anyone could see she was uncomfortable.

"Can you manage?"

All traces of discomfort vanished when she lifted her chin and said, "Of course." But then she shifted, rolling onto her side. She was in no state for a hard journey.

"Perhaps we should find somewhere safe for you," Tom said.

"I'm fine." Her tone warned him away from that idea. But Tom knew he was right. The road was no place for her.

"There are safe places," Gravinn said a little too quickly. "I know of towns where you might be hidden until your child arrives."

The air grew quiet and still. Katharine looked at Tom, waiting for him to say no, we won't leave Katharine behind. But Tom knew he would have to ask Gravinn about these safe places later. So he said nothing, and he felt Katharine cool towards him, and he wished he could just walk away with her and leave all this behind.

"Towns aren't safe," Dank explained. "They're full of people, and people are entertainment to the fay. We'll have to avoid them if we want to travel unseen."

"There are plenty of caves in these mountains," Gravinn suggested.

"I'm not hiding anywhere," Katharine snapped.

"I'm up for hiding," Jarnstenn said. He had an arm around

Kunnustenn, who was huddled against something more than the cold. "You can keep us company."

Katharine smiled at that.

"Are we going to be assaulted by invisible creatures very often?" Menvinn asked. Wisps of smoke from her cigar laced the air with a thick, sweet smell. Of course. How much more frightening must the attack have been without the Second Sight?

"It's very likely," Tom told her.

Mennvinn nodded. "That kind of fear isn't good for a woman bearing child."

"But can we really leave someone behind?" Six said, gazing at Tom and daring him to say yes.

Katharine said nothing, watching Tom, like he was a dog that might bite. He wanted to say yes, they could and they should. But even if he could persuade her, would Jarnstenn then decide to stay behind as well? And Kunnustenn and Mennvinn? They needed the dwarfs to heal Emyr and find Cairnarim. No. They couldn't discuss this in case the wrong people tried to stay behind.

"We journey together." He would figure out how to leave Katharine, just Katharine, somewhere safe. But he felt like the worst liar when she squeezed his hand.

"So it is across the country we go." Draig pointed a finger to Stoorworm. "What is it we do about that?"

And so they had circled back to Stoorworm again. Dank had no answers. Emyr had no answers. Ambrose had no answers. Either they left the sword behind, and left with it any hope of defeating any fay that came for them, or they tried to take it and Stoorworm began his attack anew.

"Cut its head off." Six looked disgusted, like the fay's body was manure he had stepped in. "I'd like to see it heal from that."

It made sense, but Dank was shaking his head. "It won't

work unless you could do it in one swing," he said. And Stoorworm's neck was as thick as Draig was broad.

"Can't we just leg it?" Jarnstenn asked.

Now it was Tom's turn to shake his head. "He'll catch us," he said. "We'd need to stop him from chasing us." They needed a distraction. "Mount up," he told them, and waited while they climbed onto houses and readied the wagon without question.

"Ride north," he told Katharine, and pressed Caledyr's scabbard into her hands. "I'm going to give you the sword. Hold it for me."

He tried to step away but Katharine reached down and took hold of his wrist. "You're coming with us," she told him. Her grip and her tone would brook no argument.

"I'll find you." He gave her his best smile, one he didn't feel, and placed his other hand on hers. "I'll come back."

"She needs you."

Did she know how much she unmanned him in that moment? How she washed away his will, his strength to do this thing? For a moment he was afraid to meet her eye, for fear he would mount up and ride away with her, hide in the hills and live out their lives away from everyone and everything?

But Katharine was right. Their little girl did need him. She needed him to do what was necessary to keep her safe.

He took a steadying breath and said, "Of everyone here, I can persuade Stoorworm not to follow us." He met her gaze. He could tell she didn't like it. But she knew he was right. "I need to do this to keep you safe."

"Come back," she told him. "Or I'll hunt you down."

She was serious, and Tom felt a rush of affection that burst forth in a grin. "I will." He squeezed her hand. "Go," he told the others, and nodded in silent approval as Six disobeyed, staying by Katharine's side while the others followed the wagon north.

"I don't need looking after," she told the elf.

"Who said anything about looking after you?" he replied. "I'm sticking close to whoever's carrying the sword."

He was fooling no-one. "Thank you," Tom said.

Six nodded, but his expression was stern when he said, "Do you really think you can persuade that thing?"

"I hope so." Tom turned to look at the fay's prone form, staring blindly up at the stars. "Stoorworm obeyed me when we were in the Kingdom. Maybe there's a little loyalty left in him." The bruises on Tom's neck suggested the truth might be otherwise.

"You stabbed him in the mouth," Six said.

True. If the fay held a grudge, staying behind might well be akin to digging his own grave. Or worse. "I'll need to give him a reason for keeping us alive." Tom looked north, spotted that the wagon was almost over the hill. "Be ready," he warned them as he released Katharine's hand and stepped over to Stoorworm.

He felt Caledyr's distracted insistence as he got closer. Stay, it told him. Fight. And almost he wanted to. Stoorworm had endangered Katharine and their unborn child. For a moment he felt the old anger, the urge to tear the enemy to shreds, to best them and bring them to their knees and end them.

Kill the enemy.

But the sword was just a sword. It didn't understand. So he took a breath, and another. Calm. Calmness of the soul until death.

He reached up and took hold of the hilt. Caledyr's thoughts surged against his own.

Fight. Kill the enemy. Stay.

The father and the prayers, and fasting and charities, and calmness of the soul until death.

He pulled the sword free, leapt back, waited for Stoorworm to spring to life.

The fay didn't move.

"Go!" he cried, and dashed back up the hill. Katharine held out the scabbard, Tom slid Caledyr home with a hiss, and he waved them on as he stepped back and bid them again, "Go."

Six whipped his reins and tugged Katharine's horse into a gallop too. "Come back to us," she called as she raced away.

He could make no such promise. So he just murmured, "Be safe," as he watched her go.

Stoorworm's groan turned Tom's head.

"You tried to kill us." The fay spoke with a slur, rolling onto his elbows like a drunkard. His tail twitched and flicked as if trying to remember how to move.

"I tried to stop you." Tom countered. Emyr's black bones he was tired. He felt a sudden urge to lie down and sleep. Focus. Fight, as the sword would say. "You tried to kill me."

"Kill you?" Stoorworm reached out for a rock, wrapped his claws around it and hauled himself a little more upright. He held his head in the other paw, like he had a headache. "No." He opened one eye, peering out from between fingers. "We want to hurt you first. King Melwas has promised us we can play lots of games before you die."

Tom had to make his case. Quickly. The twitching tail was less spasmodic, stronger. Stoorworm pushed himself upright, though he still leant on the rock. "I didn't want to hurt you," Tom said. "And I don't think you want to hurt me now."

"We do." Stoorworm let go of his head and his lip twitched in a snarl. He clenched his claws at Tom. "We really do."

"But won't it be more fun to see what I do next?"

That gave the fay pause. "What do you mean?"

"You know what we're looking for, don't you?"

The fay nodded. Gingerly.

"You know it better than I do."

Another nod.

"But we both know it will be a hard road. Challenging. That it might be too much for me."

"How do you know that if you don't know what you're looking for?"

Because he had seen Katharine dying in a dark tunnel. He couldn't imagine how he could continue after that. "Because nothing about this journey has been easy."

Stoorworm grinned. Tom couldn't help but notice how sharp his teeth were. "Yes. That's right. But everyone says the Forgotten Road is dangerous. You might get hurt. Or die. And then we can't play games."

"You can take me to Faerie before I die." Though the thought of being snatched away from Katharine made his stomach tighten. "And won't it be fun to watch me struggle?"

Stoorworm leant back on his tail, stared into his hands as if an answer was written there. "More fun than games?"

"You can play games after, can't you?"

Stoorworm's delighted grin was all the more frightening for its lack of malice. "Oh, yes!"

"So you'll let us go?"

Stoorworm's smile turned to a troubled frown. "You hold one of us in a cage." He lowered himself to the ground, slithered closer with each word. "And you hurt King Melwas." The fay's muzzle nudged Tom's belly, its breath hot on his thighs. "That's not very nice." A moment, a simple snap, and the fay could snip off his legs or chew through his gut. But Tom had faced down a dragon. He could stand his ground.

A fay was much more dangerous than a dragon.

"You want to hurt us." Stoorworm sounded like an upset child, and all the more threatening for it. "Why do you want to hurt us?"

Time for the final card. "Do you think I could hurt her?" he asked. "Do you think I could cause Maev pain?"

"You hurt King Melwas"

"Melwas and I aren't always friends," Tom replied. "But everyone in Faerie knows Maev and I are friends, don't they?"

Stoorworm's brow furrowed and he tipped his head to one side. He might have looked funny if Tom wasn't so worried about his teeth. "I don't know what you're saying."

"I'm trying to say this journey might be a waste of time." What if it was? No, don't think of that.

"So you'll find the glarn but not use them?"

"Is it so hard to imagine that my devotion to Maev might stay my hand?" It wasn't that he had a truth to avoid. It was that he was scared to speak in case he confirmed a truth he didn't want to hear.

Stoorworm growled deep in his throat. "It's like a test."

Tom nodded. "In the end, I may suffer and struggle, to your amusement, and still bend the knee to the queen."

The air was still. Stoorworm didn't move. Tom scarcely dared breathe. If the fay didn't believe this, he had no further ideas, no tricks or counter-arguments. He was lucky he didn't face Puck. The master of wordplay would have interrogated him more thoroughly.

Stoorworm raised his snout, enough to leave Tom staring into his teeth. "You put a sword in our mouth." The meaning was clear: you hurt me, and I want to hurt you. Now.

"I am mortal," Tom replied, trying not to imagine Stoorworm snipping off his head. "You are not."

"We don't want to wait."

"No." How far had the others travelled? Would it be far enough? "But you'd have time to think of even better games, wouldn't you?"

Stoorworm said nothing. Was he thinking? Relenting? Readying for attack?

Then Stoorworm huffed and Tom failed to hold his ground,

taking an involuntary step back. He tried not to show his revulsion; the fay's breath was foul, like old meat dried under the sun.

Then the fay shrank back, sitting on his coiled tail. "Go away." He looked glum, upset to have been persuaded out of what he wanted.

There was nothing to be gained from the last word, no sense in giving the fay a chance to change his mind. No dignity to be thought of, no honour in pleasantries. So Tom ran.

He had no horse, no cloak and the only idea he had as to where to find the others was the direction they had ridden off in. It had to be that way. If he'd been taken or killed, any provisions he'd had would be lost to the others. And if he'd been told their path, it was knowledge the fay could have tortured from him. But it made for a difficult morning. He ran into the hills, keeping to the easiest and widest path under the logic that the wagon couldn't negotiate difficult terrain. But he was cold and tired. He hadn't slept, hadn't eaten or had water in hours. After a time, when his throat and lungs burned with the cold mountain air, he stopped running. Instead he tucked his hands into his armpits and carried on at a stagger. At first he had kept an eye over his shoulder, in case Stoorworm changed his mind. But when the sun rose to its zenith it became clear he had let Tom go.

The only thing following Tom was his own doubts.

He hadn't admitted to anything. But he could feel the unspoken truth inside him, somewhere, lurking like a sickness. Despite it all, despite knowing what the fay intended, what they would do to the people of Tir, what they had done to him, his heart still quickened at the thought of Maev. He tried to imagine doing to her what he had done to Melwas and couldn't picture it.

Tom couldn't believe he would pass that test.

But he didn't have to. Why else had he brought Emyr back to Tir? All he needed to do was make sure Emyr healed. Then, once Emyr was strong enough to carry Caledyr, the King of Tir would defeat the fay. Not Thomas Rymour.

The world around him faded. "It's why you brought me here, isn't it?" Emyr was stood in a dark tunnel, while roaring and clamour crashed against the great wooden door. "So I could finally sacrifice myself for Tir."

The foresight faded and Tom felt his guts twist. Yes. That was why he had brought Emyr back. To do what he didn't have the stomach for.

When he came to a fork in his path he stopped and stared. Both paths were wide and somewhat flat. Neither showed signs of passage. It was entirely possible the others hadn't even come this way. He needed to climb that hill and see what he could spy. But, before that, he thought he might sit for a moment. Sit against the hillside. Lie back. Close his eyes, just for a moment.

He dreamt of a cage. Cold iron bars. Brick walls. Darkness. No light. No soft space. Not even the scurry of vermin for company. Just long, lonely nights.

"You couldn't betray us." It was still dark. But somewhere else. And Maev's voice was darker than it ought to be, full of hard edges. Like Maev was doing an impression of Mab. Or Mab an impression of Maev. "You wounded our subjects. Gutted our king. But you will not lift a hand against your queen. Not even if your world depends on it."

"No," Tom said. "I won't."

He was damp and cold when he woke. Fog, thick and wet. The moisture was too close, reminded him too much of the rat pit. He shouldn't have slept. He'd lose his way. He stretched, feeling his back crack and his shoulders click and pop. A shiver ran across his skin. He'd foreseen himself telling Maev he wouldn't betray her. So he hadn't misled Stoorworm. He would fail, at the end.

Perhaps the fog was a blessing. If he couldn't find the others, he couldn't let them down. Couldn't let Katharine down. She had the sword. She had Six to look after her, and Emyr. Ambrose and Dank to guide her. What could he offer now?

Perhaps he should walk away and let them be. Perhaps they'd be safer without him.

Fight.

The thought was so faint he wondered if he imagined it. Yes, fight. Fight for her. Fight for his daughter. He wanted to. He wanted it to be his hand that kept her safe. But he would fail. He knew he would. After all these years, after learning the fay's plans, their manipulations, their lies, he still couldn't turn his back on Maev. He was sick. A pet, Ria had called him. A liar and a coward.

He took a few steps back the way he had come.

Fight.

Yes. He would fight. He would take the hard road. Away. He would leave them.

Don't leave. That was what Katharine had said. And he had made a promise to his daughter: I will keep you safe. Perhaps she would be safe if he walked away. But that's what he'd told himself about Degor. And he'd been wrong.

He cursed his heart for joy as he realised he couldn't leave. Turned around and walked forward into the fog, following the siren call of the sword.

CHAPTER 6

FOLLOWING the sword was like following a voice in the mist. At times he thought he was walking towards it, only for it to grow fainter in his mind. He had to double back, or take a sudden turn. The terrain would grow rough and he would have to climb around, waiting for the moment the sword grew too faint to hear. But as the day began to darken, the sword grew stronger. They must have stopped. So Tom kept up a constant, plodding pace until finally the fog began to glow ahead. A fire.

They had set up camp in a scattering of rock, the wagon stopped as close as possible, the horses tied together near a patch of thick grass. They'd set up tents, squat pyramids that put Tom in mind of the tombs of the Western Kingdom. Only Six was awake, perched on a tall stone and wrapped in a blanket, keeping watch by the light of the small fire.

"You found us." The elf's voice was soft and full of surprise.

"I did." Tom couldn't help but feel glad of it. It had been a lonely day. He had grown too used to company.

Six didn't move from his perch. "I wasn't sure you'd manage." There was reproach in his tone.

"I could hear the sword."

"You worried her."

"I know," Tom said. "It had to be done."

"I know."

"Is she well?"

Six's expression was hooded in shadow but Tom could tell the elf approved of his concern. "Well enough, with all things considered." He nodded towards a tent. "She went to sleep early."

Tom felt a stab of guilt. She should be enjoying comfort and rest, not this cold trek through the mountains. "And everyone else?"

"Tired. Scared. The dwarfs don't really understand." He spoke as if they were children still. "Gravinn says we're still miles from Cairnoher."

Cairnoher. A small, unimpressive town according to Katharine. Somewhere the fay might not think to look. Perhaps Katharine could be safe there?

But Stoorworm had found them just hours after they'd left Cairnakor.

Tom shook his head. "We can decide our path in the morning," he said. "I need some rest."

"Sleep." Six pointed to Katharine's tent.

Tom wanted to sleep there for a day, but he knew he had to ask, "Who shares the watch?"

"Just Draig." Six shrugged. "Who else can see the fay coming?"

Katharine. No, she needed her sleep. Ambrose. But there was so much missing from the old man, and he was slow to react. Emyr needed rest. And there remained a fog of distrust around Dank. He was of the fay, after all.

And what was Thomas Rymour?

"You've walked a long road, Tom," Six said. "Sleep. You can take a watch tomorrow."

"We have both walked long roads."

Six's nod was slow. "How did you persuade the fay to let us go?"

Six's doubt echoed with one inside himself. "I appealed to their love of entertainment," he replied. "I pointed out they could catch and torture us now, or they could wait, and first watch us suffer on this journey."

"And then catch and torture us."

Tom shrugged.

"So you have delayed the execution."

"Something like that."

Six peered at Tom. "Anything else?"

Tom wanted to give the elf an angry denial. But how could he, after everyone had seen Mab embrace him without objection? "I suspect the fay will dog our heels."

Six just nodded. "Unsurprising."

Tom nodded too and stared at Katharine's tent. "We're all in danger." He'd persuaded Mester Stoorworm. But what was to stop other fay from slaughtering them in the night? Or worse. "She's in danger." Was she in more danger by his side, or if he left her somewhere without Caledyr to protect her? But if he didn't leave her, his foresight would come to pass. "I don't know what to do," he admitted.

"Do right by her," Six said. As if it was obvious. As if it was easy.

"Easier said than done."

"No, Tom." Six didn't snap or raise his voice. Just looked at him like he was weary of having this conversation. "It is easy. You stay by her. You look after her. You be the man she deserves."

"And what if looking after her means leaving her?"

"It doesn't," Six said. "Not ever." He shook his head. "Not ever."

"Then you tell me how we break the foresight."

"Was that your plan?" The elf's eyes grew cold. "Abandon her to save her?"

"The foresight can't come to pass if we're not together."

"Do you really think she would be so readily abandoned?"

No. Of course not. But what else could he do?

Six stood up, blanket slipping from his shoulders and revealing his fancy new clothes beneath it. "You can't solve every problem by running from it, Tom." He looked down his nose with his best Western sneer. "I thought you had learnt that by now."

Tom tried to think of a retort. But he remembered a similar moment in Faerie, when Six had asked him, 'When was the last time you took the hard road?' And Tom had lashed out, even though the elf had been right. So instead he took a breath and echoed other words Six had said to him. "What would Oen do?"

He'd hoped Six would see the effort he was making, smile, soften. But the imperious air wasn't so easily dismantled. "He'd be loyal, he'd be honest, and he'd save her life." With that, Six stalked away from the fire. "Take the next watch."

Tom felt like he should be angry to have his peace offering rebuffed. He could even feel Caledyr stirring from where it lay on Six's lookout point. But the elf was right. Emyr would find a way to do it all.

But he wasn't Emyr.

"Would you protect her?" he asked as Six was about to step into his tent. "If I failed. Would you look after her?"

The fire wasn't large and so most of Six's disappointment was in shadow. "Of course I would," he replied before he disappeared into his tent.

Tom clambered up onto the rock Six had been sat on. He

had no blanket and the fire was too far from his vantage point to provide much warmth, so he hugged himself against the cold. He had a sense he would feel better if he picked up Caledyr, but he left it where it lay. He could feel its suggestion to rest, and he had plans to make.

He wasn't Emyr. He couldn't do it all. But Six would look after Katharine. So he had to think of a way to leave them both behind.

The night passed without incident, and their safety rose with the sun: a Faerie raid would be far more frightening at night, so the fay would not forgo such entertainment by appearing in daylight hours instead. But the others had been more deeply shaken by the attack. Those who could see the fay had never seen them so violent, so ferocious. Those who couldn't see them were still coming to terms with being attacked by an invisible enemy. So they rose early and broke camp without breaking fast. But as they began to mount their wiry little horses, Ambrose ushered Tom toward the wagon.

"We ride with Emyr today," the old man told him.

Tom looked across the camp and saw Six helping Katharine onto her horse. Rearranging her saddle bags for her. Taking care of her. Tom couldn't help but feel a pang of guilt, jealousy, and regret.

"You ride with us," Ambrose repeated. Boxing him in with the things to come. Trapping him with foresight.

Tom admitted defeat. "Fine." He ceded his mount to Mennvinn, who looked distinctly unhappy at being dismissed.

"Call me the moment he needs anything," she demanded, and Tom nodded.

"I won't hesitate," he promised, then turned to Katharine. "You know our path?"

Katharine gave him a curt nod. She was visibly uncomfortable. She'd woken tired and sullen and they hadn't spoken much. "Of course."

"Would you take the lead? Six, ride with her?" Tom asked, and the pair both gave him a cold look. It felt like a return to an old pattern, the pair of them aligned against him in anger. He sighed as they rode ahead, and then the wagon began to move and he had to climb up into it or be left behind.

It was cramped inside, filled with trunks and crates and sacks. There was barely room for Emyr to lie flat, cushioned and heavily blanketed. Ambrose sat on a trunk, leaving Tom to sit on a sack of potatoes. He'd had more uncomfortable seats, but not many.

The first thing Emyr said was, "Get me out of these blankets, son."

The wagon shook and shuddered as they rode, making every moment on the feet a perilous one, but Tom managed to tug back the layers of blanket without falling. Emyr sighed as the cool air kissed his bare chest. "She keeps me wrapped up like an old man. I can't breathe under it all." He spoke with barely-contained frustration, nearly all traces of his drug-induced slur gone. Whatever Mennvinn was giving him, she was clearly giving him less of it.

"She's looking after you." Tom tried not to make it sound like a reprimand, but Emyr gave him a sharp glance all the same.

"I know that," he snapped. Then he sighed again and said, "I'm sorry, son. I've been cooped up in here for too long."

"A day?"

"Too long," Emyr affirmed.

The cirgeon's work was still a nasty gash of puckered, stitched skin mottled blue and black.

"My liege." Ambrose's voice was as warm as Tom had ever heard it. Did the old man looked pained? Sad to see his king so?

"Ambrose."

"We were talking about the glarn." As if Tom and Emyr had abandoned a conversation and wandered off on a tangent. Well, perhaps to Ambrose they had; he remembered a conversation they hadn't started yet.

"Were we?" Emyr asked with a smile. But Ambrose said nothing. Just stared at Tom, waiting for him to speak.

"Do you know where we're headed, my king?" Tom asked.

"Mennvinn told me. Cairnoher. You think Herstenn helped Rimestenn to hide Orlannu."

"What do you think?" If Emyr had different ideas, now was the time to hear it.

"It makes sense to me." The wagon jolted and Emyr hissed, everything growing taut for a moment before he relaxed. "Giant's bones, I can't remember a time when I didn't hurt."

"Shall I fetch Mennvinn?" Tom asked.

"No." He sighed and relaxed. "She deserves a rest." He looked up at Ambrose and said, "I never was a good patient, was I?"

But, of course, Ambrose couldn't remember. So the old man just stared at him, at a loss, and Tom spoke to spare him the discomfort. "So our path takes us to Orlannu. But there are two other glarn."

Emyr shrugged his eyebrows. "So Ambrose says."

"Four glarn," Ambrose said. "Four elements."

"Five elements," Tom corrected.

"Four." Ambrose shook his head. "I do not hold with this modern thinking."

Modern. Mennvinn had dismissed the idea of elements altogether.

"The fifth," Ambrose continued, "which you call void, is nothing more than the four elements together. Like a prism. You pour in light, and it splits into colours. It is the same, in reverse. You pour in the four elements and it combines into the energies we call magic."

"So you think we are all made of magic?"

Ambrose shook his head. "No. But we talk of that another time." And the conversation was dismissed. "Four elements. Four glarn."

"We know about two," Tom said. "What of the other two?"

"My knights hunted for them for years," Emyr said. "We never found them. We never even found a hint of them."

His words were cold and heavy. With all the resources of his kingdom, Emyr had found two. "Have the fay destroyed them?"

Ambrose shook his head. "No."

"You know that?"

"I do."

"But you don't know what they are or how to find them?"

Ambrose just blinked.

"So we don't know what we're looking for or where to find them." Tom shook head. Six was right. This was impossible. "Do we at least know what they do?"

"Once a person has all four, they need to take them to Cairnauran." Emyr sounded like he was on more certain ground. "We think they'll complete the network of monoliths and turn the fay out of Tir."

"Complete them?" It didn't make sense. Were there half-formed monoliths scattered across Tir? Tom hadn't felt any when he'd broken the Western magics. Of course, he hadn't really known what he was doing. "Are you saying they'll make new monoliths?"

"No. But there are some missing. Uran didn't manage to finish them in time."

"Who's Uran?"

"A king before they had kings. He raised the monoliths to force the fay out of Tir. But he died before he could finish them." The wagon jumped and Emyr's breath caught in his throat. When he next spoke, his voice was tight and his words clipped. "The monoliths were a wall that was missing bricks, and the fay could enter through the gaps."

"Faerie Circles."

"Exactly." Emyr closed his eyes for a moment and took some slow, deep breaths.

"So the glarn will stop the holes. But how?"

Emyr only shook his head. It was Ambrose who replied. "That is uncertain."

Too much uncertainty. Too many questions. Tom sighed and put his face in his hands, rubbed his face as if he could rub away his pessimism. "I'm trying, my king. But you're asking me to balance my daughter's safety on the slimmest of hopes."

"I understand," Emyr replied. "All too well. I was a father too."

To a son who had broken his kingdom. Tom could hear the old king's pain and disappointment, could understand it. But it couldn't compare. "They'll take her," Tom said. "They won't care how young she is. They'll take her, hurt her." His breath caught in his throat, unexpected terror forming a lump which words could not pass. He gulped at air and blinked back tears.

"That is why we must succeed, son." Emyr reached out, took his hand and squeezed with surprising strength, words burning with old anger, pain, regret and resolve. "You will succeed where I failed."

There was something terrible in Emyr's eyes that stopped Tom from looking away. "You're a king. I'm just me."

Faith. It was faith in Emyr's eyes. "You will do this. I know it."

For a moment the spell held Tom and he could feel something rising, brave resolve burning through him, finding an echo in Caledyr, in Emyr. Tom would fight, he would march through pain and cold and hardship, he would upend Tir to find the glarn, stop the fay, save his daughter. He could do this. He could.

And then the wagon bounced and Emyr let go of his hand, crying out in pain. And, in a moment, he was just a wounded old man again, and Tom was just a liar and a coward once more. He'd only been lying to himself. The truth was that he was afraid. He was terrified.

Emyr's breath was quick and shallow, hissing through his teeth. Tom scrambled to the rear of the wagon, called out for Mennvinn, and she came and told him which bottle to administer and how much, and soon Emyr slept, snoring, brow ever so slightly furrowed. Small. Old. Mortal.

"Do not ask too much of him." Ambrose hunched as if he felt Emyr's pain too. He had his staff over his knees and held it with both hands as if it were a raft and he was a man overboard. "You were in Faerie a hundred years, were you not? How do you feel, now you have returned?"

"Old and tired."

"Think how he must feel after a thousand years."

Ancient and exhausted. Tom had expected the strong, vital king of legend. But Emyr was old and hurt and wounded. He'd lost a wife, two sons, his kingdom, his knights, his people, his dream of a united Tir. All gone. And through it all, the fay still dogged his steps.

"I wish I could remember if he always snored." Ambrose's voice sounded tense, as if he was lifting heavy weights above his head. "I wish I had understood the price when I was asked to pay it."

Tom thought of Elaine and Degor and just nodded. "Sometimes I would sit with him while he slept, when I was in Faerie. Just to be near another person. He snored then, too."

"You brought him here because you think he'll save Tir." Ambrose shook his head. He stared blindly through the floor of the wagon. "But you're wrong. He won't save them."

Won't save them. He would fail? Was this all folly? "So the fay will win?"

"I didn't say that."

Riddles. Always the man spoke in riddles. "Am I doing the right thing?" He tried not to think of what he planned to do to Katharine.

"Not yet." Did Ambrose know? If he did, he gave no sign. Or advice. "But you will learn to."

"How?" But the how wasn't important. "What am I doing wrong?"

Ambrose's lips twitched, as if he was trying to remember how to smile. "Emyr spoke of the monoliths as a wall. You are trying to put each brick in the place you think it should be, whether it fits or no."

More riddles. "So I should stop trying?"

"No. You should start being the brick you're looking for."

Be a brick. Is this the kind of wisdom and counsel he'd offered King Emyr? "I don't understand."

"I know." There was resignation, like they'd had this conversation a dozen times already. Perhaps they would do. Perhaps he remembered a dozen conversations to come. "Here." And he pulled a twig from out of his sleeve, like the tricks of the hedge magicians. Tom took it, stared at it, expecting it to do something.

But it was just a twig. Hard, rough, uneven.

"Do you know what magic is Tom?" When Tom shook his head, Ambrose explained, "It's undoing. When something is pulled apart, the energy of what it was is released. That is what magic is. And that is why the easiest magic to perform is destructive. Magic begets magic."

"Um." He couldn't see how this related to what he had to do. "I see."

"You don't. But you will need to." Ambrose's fingers twitched around his staff. "Feel the twig. The four elements are in all things. Fire, water, earth, and air. They are all in that twig. Someone with training can reach in, unbalance them and force one of the others to the fore. Break the twig into earth. Draw out the water. Let the fire run rampant."

Odd to think there were four elements inside this tiny stick. All rolling around together in harmony. But of course that was true of all things. Even people.

"Draw out the fire," Ambrose told him. "Come back to me when you have."

"What?" Him? He was no sorcerer. But the old man was staring at him now. Glaring at him with those dark eyes.

"Reach into it. As you did with the monolith. Explore it. Find the elements. Unbalance them."

"I don't know how."

"That is why I am teaching you."

Teaching? This was teaching? "Why?"

"Because I do." Ambrose didn't know why. And it was galling not to know. And saddening. He did it only because he had foreseen it. Following a path he didn't understand without even the hope that things would turn out well in the end.

The empathy buried Tom's confusion and frustration. He just nodded and said, "Is this how I become the brick?" Possibly the strangest question he'd ever asked.

"It is."

Tom spent the next few days staring at a maddening twig. About the length of his thumb, not quite straight, bark so dark it was almost black, with tiny light streaks on it. The wood inside was pale, still soft and fragrant.

And Tom could feel nothing inside it.

No fire, no water, no earth or air. It was a twig. Tom couldn't change that. He wasn't a sorcerer, and by the end of the third day Tom was ready to cast the cursed thing to the wind.

Katharine led them north along a smooth, meandering route that wound through the hillsides and mountains. Everyone had feared another Faerie attack, so only those with the Second Sight took watches each night. But the weather swiftly turned from clear skies and chill winds to thick clouds and driving snow, and Tom watched the others' concerns turn inwards to their physical discomfort.

So although they had gone unmolested for three full days, they were miserable when they spotted the lights of a village at the bottom of the hill.

"Radeliege," Gravinn named it. "It isn't much, but they'll have warm beds, a roof, and a fire."

"Just one of those things would be divine," Kunnustenn said.

"I'll quite happily take all three," Six replied. "With a hot meal to boot."

It sounded perfect. And yet, "We can't," Dank told them.

"Why not?" Katharine sounded exhausted.

"Where there are people, there are fay." It sounded like the last thing he wanted to say.

"Tom?" She looked at him, begging him with her eyes to disagree.

But the boy was right. "People are their greatest source of entertainment."

"So it's not safe?" Six asked.

Safe. Tom remembered how Mester Stoorworm's claws had twitched with the urge to hurt him. The baleful hate in Melwas' eyes. Mab's promise that she would send more fay after them. Would anywhere ever be safe again? "Probably not."

"Probably?"

But Tom refused to be baited. He was just as wet and cold and impatient. "We'll send someone to the village for supplies," he said. "The rest of us will find shelter. A good fire and some dry clothes will make everything seem better."

'We can go," Jarnstenn blurted.

"Fine."

"What about me?" Gravinn asked.

But Tom shook his head. "You're known to the fay. Jarnstenn and Kunnustenn will fare better."

She scowled at that but didn't question him. "Shall I find shelter?"

"Yes." Tom smiled at the thought of a fire. A big, roaring fire. "What we need is a cave."

It was Katharine who found their resting place in the end. Gravinn had started directing them back up the mountain, but it soon became clear that she was guessing. She would stop their progress, scan the hillside, change their path. But she had none of the confidence Tom had seen in Katharine, and when she had them turn back for the third time, Tom had asked if she needed help.

"Of course not." She'd lifted her chin but her eyes were full of uncertainty. "I'm a Pathfinder."

"You're a Pathfinder's apprentice." Katharine had given her a cruel smile and added, "Let me show you how it's done."

"I have maps," Gravinn had spat back, but Katharine took the lead and found a cave within minutes, cramped but deep. Tom left Draig and Dank securing the wagon and tying the horses while he and Six carried Emyr inside. There was barely enough room to stand and the ground was uneven. But it would be easily defended and it kept them out of the horrid weather.

"Good work, Katharine," Six said.

Gravinn huffed, already working on a fire at the back of the cave. "It was I that led us this way."

Tom waited for Katharine to snap back, but her earlier cruelty was gone. She didn't even acknowledge the dwarf. She just sank down into a little hollow and closed her eyes.

They laid Emyr on the flattest surface they could find and Mennvinn spent a few minutes fussing over him, tucking blankets around him and putting cushions beneath his head. "Enough, Mennvinn." Emyr waved her away. "I'm as comfortable as I'll ever be."

She nodded and walked away, whispering to Tom as she passed, "He tires of me."

"Rest a while. You're doing good work," he whispered back. "I'm very grateful."

She seemed to take strength from that, squaring her shoulders and heading back out to the wagon. Tom knelt beside Emyr as best he could.

"Is there anything you need, my king?"

The man's eyes were closed as he said, "A younger body."

"I'm not sure I can help you with that."

That opened the other man's eyes and he stared at Tom for a moment before saying, "You're not as old as you think, Tom."

So everyone always said. But Tom knew how he felt. "I suspect the same is true of you."

Emyr shrugged his eyebrows and closed his eyes again. "Perhaps."

"Tom." Six was carrying in some bags and glowering at him. When Tom didn't reply, the elf jerked his head towards Katharine. Was she asleep already? "You might see to her comfort?" Six hissed.

Tom had let her lie on hard rock with no cushion, no blanket. He felt a flush of embarrassment, and then one of anger. What made Six think he was in a place to question him? "My king is wounded," he said. Surely it was important to see to Emyr's comfort, to ensure he was healing properly?

But Six dropped his bags and said only, "She is carrying your child," before heading back out to the wagon.

"He's right." Emyr muttered.

"My king?"

"I have a healer to look after me. Katharine needs you to look after her."

"I told Mennvinn to rest."

"Why?"

"She says you tire of her."

Emyr took a deep breath, winced, let it out. "I tire of being an invalid. Not of her."

"Tell her that." Only when Emyr's eyes blinked open did Tom realise how blunt he had been. "My king," he added.

"I will." His smile was one of pleasant surprise. "Now go to Katharine."

She was fast asleep already. Mouth agape, making tiny snoring sounds, but beautiful all the same. Tom watched her for just a moment. Gravinn's fire was growing nicely, casting a warm glow across the cave and across Katharine's face. He brushed a finger against her cheek, possessed by a sudden need to touch her. To feel the reality of her. She was here. She was carrying their daughter.

She stirred, frowned, said in a small voice, "Are you well?"

He smiled. "Let's get you out of those wet clothes."

She just nodded in sleepy silence, let him rummage for fresh and dry clothes. He placed a gentle hand on her swollen belly, her skin goosebumping. Then he dressed her, wrapped her in a blanket, put more blankets beneath her and rolled up some under her head. "Thank you," she mumbled before falling asleep again.

Draig was tying the last of the horses to a solitary stalagmite by the mouth of the cave. "Heat and light," the elf said with a grin, pointing to the fire. "We are all like moths."

The elf was right. Who else might be attracted by that fire? Tom stepped outside, where heavy clouds darkened the sky and snow was beginning to fall again. The light was less by the entrance, but still visible.

"You worry," Draig said.

"I do," he replied. "Maybe a fire is a mistake. Someone else might see it."

"There is no-one." Draig pointed at the world. Bare mountains, covered in ice and snow. Not another living thing to be seen. But that didn't mean there wasn't something watching them from out of sight.

"I wish we could bring in the wagon."

"It will not fit." Draig shrugged. "Worry you not, it will be here by morning."

Tom felt the sword twitch. Did it sense something? He strained to peer through the encroaching darkness. But it was still and quiet. Here, at least. "Someone should have gone with Jarnstenn and Kunnustenn," he muttered.

"Are you wet, and tired and cold." Draig placed a hand on his shoulder. Tom felt himself shrink a little under that touch.

Despite his best efforts, he still wasn't ready to trust Draig. But the elf didn't react. He only said, "Change and sleep and sit by the fire. See you then things in a different light."

Tom shivered. Yes. That would make him feel better. And all of a sudden he felt too tired not to let Draig act like a friend. He let himself be led away from his worries, to the light and the warmth inside the cave.

He woke with a start. Danger. Something had woken him. He sat up in silence, drew Caledyr without a sound. The fire had burnt low. Everyone else was still sleeping. Only one figure sat by the mouth of the cave, wrapped against the cold. Draig. But he was still. Untroubled by any sound. Perhaps it had been a dream?

No. There it was again. A sigh. Wistful or sad, he couldn't tell. Was it Draig? No. The sound felt too big for the elf. Tom got to his feet, stepped over sleeping bodies and picked his way across the uneven rock to Draig's side.

"Did you hear that?" Tom asked.

"Just the wind," the elf replied.

But the air was still. The snow had stopped. There was only cloud above, and night sky peeking through where it could.

And a sigh.

Tom felt a chill run over him that was nothing to do with the cold. "I'm going to check it out."

"Nothing is there."

"I'll make sure." He stepped out of the cave, feet crunching too loudly; the cold had made an icy crust of the soft snow. Maybe this was a mistake. Anyone would be able to hear him coming. Whatever was making that noise would know where to run from. Or in which direction to hunt.

"Tom, there is no danger," Draig hissed after him. But Tom carried on climbing the mountainside. Why? Maybe it was the wind after all. And even if it wasn't, what threat did a sigh pose?

But he kept climbing. There was nothing to hear save his footsteps. Nothing to see except mountains and stars and his fogging breath. Nothing to feel save the cold, biting at his skin, seeping through his clothes. He stopped, listened to the silence. Draig was right. There was nothing out here.

North.

Caledyr's thought made Tom start. Was there something to the north? Tom turned his head, uncertain which direction he faced. But then he felt it. Not a presence. But a difference in the air. Sharper. But the difference was so slight he probably wouldn't have noticed if it wasn't for the sword. It was like a breeze that went unnoticed until someone else pointed it out.

There was magic in the north. A lot, to be felt at such a distance.

"And what are you planning to do with that?"

Tom whirled, slipped in the snow, almost lost his balance. The speaker was behind him, a gangly, shaggy figure. Taller even than Midhir yet with none of his grace, she was covered in dirty white fur that flared at wrist, ankle, hip and neck. Her head was too wide, ending in comically flapping ears. She leaned forward on her knuckles and he still had to look up at her.

"Gwyllion." He hefted the sword, feeling its eagerness to strike now and strike fast. Tom knew he stood little chance to talking his way out of an attack. Not again. But if he struck first, he would be the aggressor. Better to not give the fay an excuse.

But still the sword urged him to fight.

"Well met, Thomas Rymour." Gwyllion had an ugly, savage

voice. So unlike her fairer face, Eyllion, who had a singing voice that could bring you to tears of joy.

"Well met."

"You attacked our king."

Straight to it then. "I did. He threatened my friends." He cast a quick glance to the left and right. Tried to edge himself into a better position.

"Yet you live."

"Melwas appears to will it so."

But any hopes Tom might have had that Gwyllion would let him go were crushed by a low growl. "No," she huffed, a great puff of steam escaping into the night. "You raised your hand against our king. We cannot allow you to live to see another morn."

CHAPTER 7

DELAY.

The sword was right. Gwyllion had the higher ground and he had poor footing. "How did you find us?" Tom asked.

"We looked. And there you were."

"Have you been following us?"

She bared yellow, uneven teeth. "We have better things to do."

Gwyllion spent most of the winter months ranging across mountains, threatening the odd traveller and eating the odd sheep or goat. Hardly the most important of duties.

But not everything had to be duty and purpose.

"So Melwas didn't send you?"

"No." She grinned. "But think how pleased he will be when we bring you to him." At this she stood to her full height, towering over him, and flexed her iron claws. imposed as punishment for some forgotten crime. Sharp to cause pain to Melwas' foes. Iron to cause pain to Gwyllion.

"You know this sword can hurt you."

"As if we do not already know pain." She held out a hand, flexed her claws.

"And what if I dismembered you?" he asked. Stoorworm had been too big. But Gwyllion was slender. He could cut through her limbs without issue. "Would that unmake you? As Fenoderee was unmade?"

Gwyllion grew still and huffed again. He was right. If he could stop her for long enough, he could slice her to pieces. And then she'd have to wait to be remade. But then she grinned and reached out with one long, gangly arm, placing it in the snow. "You will have to get to me first." She was showing off her reach. Well beyond his own. She could keep him at bay with ease.

"So you mean to take me to Melwas?"

"You and your friends."

Tom nodded. "Very well." The sword was quiet, considering. But he would never gain a better footing. Surprise would have to be his ally. Calmness of the soul until death. "I wish it hadn't come to this."

He swung Caledyr in an overhead chop, seeking to sever fingers. But Gwyllion was quick. She snatched her hand back with a shriek, before leaping forward and slapping a hand at him. Tom raised the sword, skewered her palm before it knocked him down into the snow.

Gwyllion didn't make a sound. She pulled her hand back, Caledyr slid free, and Tom watched the wound heal even as fingers closed around his ankles and lifted him into the air. Iron claws pinched the flesh at his ankle.

She was right. Pain was nothing to her.

He tried to chop off the hand holding him but she dropped him, he sliced through air, hit the snow with a cold crunch.

Up.

Caledyr prompted his feet to move before he could think, and he was on his feet in time to see Gwyllion sweep her claws at him.

Down.

He dove for the ground, her hand clipping him but no more.

Inside.

He stumbled up again, the snow collapsing under his weight, tried to rush inside her reach. But he'd only made it a few steps before she backhanded him, knocking him onto his back.

Up.

He rolled to his front, got his feet under him only for Gwyllion to send him sprawling.

Up.

He spat snow from his mouth as he stood again, whirling, sword held ready. He jabbed towards her, seeking to make her hesitate. It didn't work. She feinted with one hand, bowled him over with the other.

Up.

Give it a rest, he told the sword. His fingers were numb. He was on his hands and knees, breathing hard and fast, lungs burning with cold night air. But before he could stand, he felt a hand close around his leg and lift him up again. He dangled for a moment, the world swinging, and then his view was filled with her face.

"Maybe we should just eat you." She laughed to herself. "Melwas will thank us all the same."

"I don't think I'll taste very good."

"No." Gwyllion huffed. "A hundred years old. We prefer a younger meal."

She grinned at her own joke and Tom swung, cutting her across the face with the sword. She let out a cry and dropped him. This time he landed on something hard, his back bending around a rock buried under the snow. No time to worry about that. Gwyllion had a hand to her face. He surged forward, under her flailing arms, cutting at her legs and ankles. She staggered back, swung at him blindly. He ducked one blow, sliced at her ankle, ducked another swing, stabbed at her foot. Then her hand clipped his shoulder and knocked him over.

Don't rest. Don't stop.

But it was too easy to take a couple of breaths, close his eyes. Not against the pain; he was too cold to feel that. But against the effort. The effort of getting up again and again and again.

"Damn you, Thomas Rymour." Get up. Don't let her collect herself. Don't let her gain the upper hand. He let out a single, harsh laugh. Upper hand. That's all she had. He pushed himself up. He couldn't feel his hands anymore. He'd drop the sword soon. He should have put on gloves. Gwyllion was stood still, hand still against her face. He must have cut deep.

Forward.

He let the sword guide his feet, lift his arms. She had a hand outstretched as if to ward him off. The blade lopped off a finger with ease and she screamed, snatched her hand back, retreated.

"End this." His breath burned in his throat. "We don't need to fight."

"You think we will let you get away with this?" She bared her face to clutch at her wounded hand, her lip and nose already stitching together as she spoke. "You attack our king and expect to live?"

She was fanatical. Devoted. To a king who had cursed her with iron claws. With constant pain and agony. There was no reasoning with such a creature.

Off-balance, Caledyr told him.

Yes. She was. "Very well," he said. "Then let me leave you with this. After all, you've grown used to the taste of iron, surely?"

He mimed throwing something at her and she shrieked and covered her face. Hidden from her sight, Tom relied on fear as much as the sword to push him forward. Push him through the snow, duck beneath her legs, and swing with all his might at the small of her knee.

Gwyllion's leg buckled.

Tom threw himself against her.

She fell.

Tom watched her tumble down the mountain. She fell end over end before a rocky outcrop launched her out from the mountain and into free fall. She fell in silence. The only sound was his own ragged breathing.

"Luck was with you." Dank told him.

"I know." Tom wanted to sit closer to the fire and yet he didn't. The returning warmth in his fingertips was glorious, but new aches and pains were woken by the heat as well.

And he had new appreciation for Emyr's impatience with Mennvinn's care. "Hold still," she told him. She was poking at his back. When he hissed, she shushed him.

Draig had been quiet when Tom had returned, seeking to wake only Mennvinn, but Six had woken too. "So she didn't attack the cave?" the Westerner asked.

"No." Tom had opened up the cut on his side as well, the one Draig had inflicted in Cairnagwyn. Mennvinn had muttered something about the stitching and was threading a needle. "She was outside."

"But she had found us."

"I think so."

"But Draig, you didn't hear anything."

The elf shook his head. "No." He was holding a lantern up to better help Mennvinn see her work. “Only to Tom was there sound.”

“I heard it,” Tom said.

“Odd that Draig didn’t.”

It was odd. But, “We know the fay can’t be seen or heard by everyone.”

“Draig has the Second Sight.”

Which was true. “Maybe they’ve taken it away.”

“Can they do that?”

He’d never seen it happen. But there were a lot of things he hadn’t seen in Faerie. He looked over at Dank, frowning in his sleep. “I don’t know.”

Six sighed through his nose. “Perhaps you should have stayed here.”

“She might have come to the cave.”

“We could have fought her off together.”

“Caledyr is the only weapon we have that can stop the fay.”

Six made a dissatisfied noise. “We’ve brought plenty of iron.”

Mennvinn stabbed a needle into Tom’s side and he cried out. “Don’t fuss,” she told him as she began to draw the thread through his flesh.

“How do you think Gwyllion found us?” Six asked.

“I don’t know,” Tom admitted. “Perhaps a fay saw them in the tavern?”

Apparently Jarnstenn had felt he deserved an ale for his efforts. They’d procured the supplies and spent an hour or so in the village tavern. Now he and Kunnustenn snored gently together by the fire.

“Perhaps.” Six sounded unconvinced. “But why not attack the cave? Why stand on a hilltop and wait for you?”

“What are you saying?”

“That perhaps the fay hadn’t found us. Perhaps this Gwyllion was simply passing by until you ran into her.”

"You think it was a coincidence?"

Six shrugged. "It's possible." But he didn't seem certain at all.

"It seems unlikely," Tom said. Mennvinn tugged her thread, tying knots. Eirwen's grace. He felt like every inch of him was cut or bruised or somehow damaged. "Hunted by the fay and we happen to bump into one?"

"You were the one doing the bumping," Six corrected him. "If you had stayed in the cave, perhaps she would have walked on by."

So the elf was blaming him. Tom shook his head. "I think it's more likely I caught her before she had a chance to attack us all."

But Six wasn't convinced. "Let's see what the others think."

"In the morning." Tom wouldn't see Katharine woken. She hadn't moved, not since she'd first laid down, and she still looked tired.

When he looked back to Six, the elf's expression had softened. "In the morning," he agreed.

"Rest you all now," Draig told them, and Six and Mennvinn didn't need persuading to return to their respective corners. "You too, Tom."

But Tom shook his head. "I'll take a watch," he said. "Six can relieve me before morning."

"Lucky me," Six muttered.

"Need you rest."

Tom gave the Easterner a smile. "So do you."

Draig looked unconvinced, but the thought of sleeping by a fire was too much to resist. "Wake me, if you are tired."

"I will."

He waited until everyone's breath came soft and even before reaching into his saddlebags. Out came the jar, swaddled in blankets, and Tom huddled by the cave entrance, hunkered over the wad, and pulled aside the cloth.

His face was bathed in unearthly light and the sprite said something in a voice too small to hear. Tom held the jar closer.

"They won't forgive you for keeping us in this cage."

He'd already known it, but the confirmation still cut him deeply. "You're hunting us," he replied. "You're trying to hurt us."

"You hurt our king."

"You used me."

"What did you expect?"

The sprite's words stunned him into silence. He'd watched the fay toy with mortals for seven years. Why had he expected them to treat him any differently?

"How did Gwyllion find us?"

"Will you release us if we tell you?"

And trade uncertainty for sure knowledge that the fay would find them? "No."

"Then why should we answer your questions?"

He had no power here. As ever, with the fay, he was at their mercy. Frustration boiled out of him before he could stop it. "Tell me," he growled and shook the jar.

"You can't hurt us."

But he could. He had Caledyr. And, he recalled, he had a piece of the stone from Ambrose's prison. The same stone that made the monoliths. That pushed back magic. He set down the jar and reached into his pocket, found the fragment with his fingertips.

The merest brush tugged his mind from the moment and he found himself drowning in the world. Brega was stood in a room filled with light as Puck said, "We can help each other." Western soldiers were trying to build a barricade inside Cairnalyr and cursing as fay, invisible to their eyes, undid their work while human soldiers pounded on the door.

Tom jerked his hand away, panting as if he'd been running. It had been just like standing atop the central monolith in Cairnagwyn. How could such a tiny stone have the same effect on him? He shuddered. He'd almost failed to find his way back last time. What if he'd lost his way this time, and Katharine had found him drooling and mindless?

He wrapped the stone in a rag before touching it again, though there remained a dead chill beneath the cloth. The sprite shied away as he held it up to the glass jar.

"What will this do to you?" he asked.

The sprite shook its head and said something inaudible. Tom slipped the stone back into his pocket and said, "I'll put it in with you, if you don't tell me what I want to know."

He lifted the jar to his ear and the sprite said, "She'll never forgive you."

No. Perhaps not. "How did Gwyllion find us?"

"It was a coincidence," he told them all.

Tom's eyes burned with a lack of sleep, his back ached, and the freshly stitched cut in his side throbbed. The sprite's words still haunted him, though he hadn't expected Maev to forgive him anyway. But he'd eaten hot goat meat, unusual but tasty, watched the sun rise, and seen the clouds skip away to reveal a clear, blue sky. It had cured a lot of ills for Tom, and he felt reassured that the fay weren't actively hunting them.

But Six didn't seem pleased that Tom was agreeing with him. "How can you be so sure?"

Because Dank's sprite told me. "Gwyllion is a solitary fay. After Calgraef she disappears into mountains to hunt and terrorise innocents." It was odd to say such words with a smile. But it meant safety. "It was just bad luck she found us."

"Or that you found her."

Yes. As the elf had said, Gwyllion might have passed them by.

"And the truth is," Six continued, "they know where we are now, even if they didn't before. Even if last night was a coincidence."

"Isn't that what you think?" Tom asked.

"I'm not sure what happened last night." Six folded his arms, stared at Tom as if trying to see through him. "It seems strange to me that you seem so certain this morning."

"You do seem very sure she wasn't sent," Dank said. Was he suspicious? Perhaps. He hadn't been allowed to see his sprite since they'd captured it in Cairnagwyn. How would he react if he discovered that Tom had spoken to it? Would he be angry? Jealous? Upset?

"Six made a convincing argument last night," Tom replied. "And Gwyllion is a solitary fay, isn't she?"

Dank nodded. "Usually."

"Not always?" Six asked.

"Not always."

"So Tom is guessing?"

Dank squinted at Tom. "We suppose so."

Six shook his head. "We can't base anything on guesswork," he proclaimed. He drained his cup of snow water, shook the last few drops free. "It's not safe."

It wasn't safe anywhere. Tom looked over at Katharine, eating strip after strip of goat meat. Elaine hadn't been able to keep anything down when she had been with child, but Katharine had an appetite to rival Jenny Greenteeth. "Six is right," Tom said. "Even if Gwyllion didn't mean to find us, she did. We need to keep moving." He stood, spoke to them all. "Carry iron at all times. Keep each other safe. That's our biggest concern."

"No." The cave lent Ambrose's hollow voice an unnatural echo. "Our only concern is finding the glarn."

"I don't want to see anyone hurt," Tom told him.

"But you will."

Everyone's gaze turned on Ambrose, all wondering which of them the old sorcerer thought would be injured. So Tom said, "That's enough, Ambrose."

"Why?"

"Because you're upsetting people."

Ambrose levelled a deep and dark stare on Tom. "There are evil days ahead of us, Sir Tom. Full of evil deeds. My only concern is surviving to do what must be done.

"I don't care about their feelings at all."

"Please, my king, will you tell him to stop?" Tom was riding in the wagon with Emyr and Ambrose again. They had broken camp in quiet unease and Tom could see a number of them wondering if they shouldn't turn back. "We have enough to think of without Ambrose's dire warnings of pain and suffering."

"I know." It was all Ambrose kept saying. But he said it without conviction, like he was reading from a book.

"Then please don't do it."

"I cannot do otherwise," Ambrose replied. "This you know."

"Then you know I will ask you again."

"Just as I know you will stop asking soon."

"Please. Both of you." Emyr was sat up that day. Though he was clearly still in pain, he seemed to be forcing himself to sit, as if he was convincing himself that he was healing. "Please don't squabble."

"My king, he keeps telling us all that bad times are ahead, that we're unprepared, that we'll be hurt and killed." Surely Emyr had to see how bad that was? Emyr, the leader of men. The man who had rallied to his cause everyone he met. "It confuses and upsets the others."

"And you, Tom?"

"Yes, it upsets me too."

"Why?"

"Because we face a task not all of us believe is possible. It doesn't help if someone's calling it impossible and refusing to help."

"Is that true, Ambrose?"

"No, my liege. I have never called our task impossible. And I help in the only way I can."

Emyr's gaze fell on Tom. "Is this true, Tom?"

He opened his mouth to disagree. But he couldn't. So it must be so. And, Tom supposed, it was. Ambrose remembered what was to come. How many times had Tom felt shackled by his foresights, going through motions he had already seen? And that was how Ambrose lived every moment. How could he change his actions if he'd already taken them?

Emyr took a deep breath. "It is difficult to be around Ambrose. I'm sure he'd be the first to agree."

But Ambrose said nothing. And Tom wondered how it had felt to wait a thousand years, knowing his king would call him difficult.

"You will have to manage him," Emyr added. "And the others. It's part of being a leader."

"I'm not a leader," Tom said.

"They follow you, don't they?"

"Ambrose follows you."

"Ambrose follows himself. He always has." Emyr gave his friend a fond smile that wasn't returned, and Emyr's expression faltered a moment later. "Though he is not the man I knew."

"He is still your friend."

"Is he?" Emyr shook his head. "He had such a sense of humour. Childish, really. He knows many arts, and he used them to play tricks and pranks on people. Once he fashioned a powder and scattered it on Emoddir's seat so it created a coloured mist whenever he broke wind." Tom could barely imagine Ambrose smiling, let alone playing such a childish prank. "He was my closest advisor, my fool and my friend. Now I'm not sure he is any of those things."

Tom waited for Ambrose to inject. To persuade Emyr otherwise. To say anything. But he was silent, and it seemed cruel to say such things as if he wasn't there. "That seems unfair," Tom said, but Emyr waved him away.

"He won't remember any of this."

"No," Tom agreed. "But he's remembered it for a thousand years." Tom gestured to the old sorcerer, who stared at nothing. "And suggesting he isn't your friend seems like poor thanks for waiting all that time in order to help you again." Emyr gazed at Tom with surprise and awe, and Tom remembered just who he was speaking to. "My king," he added, and lowered his gaze.

For a time, the only sound was the creaking wheels of the wagon beneath them. Tom began to wonder if he'd offended Emyr.

But the old king sighed and said, "You're right." Tom looked up to see Emyr reach across and place a hand over Ambrose's. "Forgive me. You are my friend. And I am yours. Always."

Ambrose lifted his gaze to Emyr's and, for a moment, he seemed unburdened by the weight of his years. "Thank you. This moment has seen me through many a dark time."

The hurt in Emyr's eyes spoiled his smile. "I am sorry that you have suffered."

"No more than you."

"So much more." Emyr turned to Tom. "Thank you, son. You show me the error of my ways."

Tom bowed his head. "If I can serve in any way."

But Emyr snorted. "Serve?" He waved a bitter hand over the wound he had covered with a blanket. "I am a broken old man, son. My time is past. This time belongs to you now."

Tom shook his head with a grin. "I fear I'll be a poor substitute for King Emyr of Tir."

But Emyr was sombre and serious. "When you came to Faerie you were a boy. Now you are a man. You are capable of far more than you think."

His gaze seemed to penetrate past layers and pretense and Tom felt his plan exposed and the thought of admitting to his king that he was going to abandon Katharine and his child tightened his chest and his palms grew sweaty. He bowed his head under the weight of what he had to do and said, "I fear I am not what you think."

"You're right." Emyr spoke so casually that his words brought Tom's head up again. Emyr added, "I see in you the same potential as my son. And I will not see that squandered again."

Cairnoher was at once like and unlike Cairnakor. The streets were paved, the buildings cramped, the air thick. But it was so much smaller. There was less bustle, fewer people, and while certain thoroughfares were packed, there were plenty of streets that were empty. But, though it seemed like a smaller version of Cairnakor, its skyline was broken by many more wonders. Huge wheels planted along the river's edge were turned by the rushing water. Great balloons hung in the air, some tethered to the ground or to rooftops, others drifting in the wind, bound for other cities. Jarnstenn said they were powered by hot air, but Tom couldn't see how a little air could keep something that big aloft. It had to be some sort of magic, although the air felt still in that place. Like there was a monolith nearby.

But before Tom or Dank could say that it would be dangerous to enter the town, the decision had already been made. "This is the last town before we enter the Northern Wastes," Katharine told them all.

"You mean our last chance for a warm bed and a roof over our heads," Jarnstenn replied.

"Exactly." And Katharine had turned to Tom when she added, "I don't know about anyone else, but I'm not passing that up. And if the fay want to come between me and a hot bath, let them see what happens."

Tom stared at the town, feeling his desire to make Katharine happy at odds with his desire to see her safe, both overshadowed by a deepening guilt at what he had to do. But it was a selfish desire to make her smile, for her to be happy with him one last time, that spurred him to say, "Very well."

Dank wasn't happy about it. But once Gravinn found them a tavern with beds enough for all of them and plenty of strong dwarfish beer on tap, it wasn't long before everyone was smiling and relaxed.

Except Tom.

Katharine had nothing to drink, but she had the slow, dopey air of heavy fatigue when he took her up to their room.

"What's wrong?" she mumbled as she climbed into bed.

She was too good at reading him. And he couldn't lie, if she cornered him. "Nothing that can't wait until morning," he told her. And she accepted it without question, pulled him into bed and put his arm around her. His hand rested on her belly, feeling the little movements of their unborn daughter, sometimes no more than a tiny shift within, sometimes a sharp little kick. Each one felt impossible, like she was here before she was here. Like she was reaching out for him.

Each little movement seemed to cry out to him: don't leave.

I have to. You won't survive with me.

They didn't speak. Didn't need to. They were enveloped in a bubble, a sort of sleepy tranquility. Despite everything going on, everything they faced, somehow Katharine had created a little slice of bliss.

A bliss that Tom's guilt prevented him from enjoying. He realised that he had no experience of little girls. Yes, children were all the same when they were babies. But when they were older? He'd have no idea what to do with her. What if she didn't like him? What if she didn't love him?

Then he remembered he was never going to meet her, and the pain was so sharp he clenched his jaw.

"Shh." Katharine sounded half-asleep and very comfortable.

"I didn't say anything," he whispered.

"You were worrying."

How could she tell? "I suppose that's what I do now."

"It is." She took a deep breath, let it out in a sigh. A contented sigh? Or had he broken the bubble. "You worry all the time now."

"There's a lot to worry about."

"Everything will be fine." She placed a hand on top of his. The baby kicked.

Nothing was fine. The fay had taken his first life from him. Now he had a chance at a second, and the fay were going to take it away again.

No. He couldn't blame the fay. He was the one abandoning his daughter.

"Ssh."

"Sorry."

She patted his hand. "I like that you worry. It means you care." She was right. He did care. "But you worry too much. Sleep."

She drifted off minutes later. Tom couldn't. The knowledge of what he had to do was too heavy to sleep under. How would he do it? Use Mennvinn's medicine on Katharine first. Lure Six to the room, use it on him. Tell the others the two of them had ridden ahead. No, that would involve a lie. That Katharine was ill? Also a lie. That she couldn't ride, and Six would stay behind and look after her. Yes. That would be true. But what if someone suggested they wait until she was better? Too much could go wrong.

And if it went right, he'd never meet his daughter.

Rest.

That was easy for the sword to say. But how could he rest, knowing what he had to do?

Rest.

Help me.

Rest.

Words spoken by Emyr and Six blurred and mixed and haunted his dreams. The same potential as my son. Be loyal, be honest, and save her life.

He woke with a guilty start from a vision of Katharine stood over him, his plans laid bare. But she slept on, and he watched her as consciousness crept back to him.

He wanted to live up to Emyr's expectations. He wanted to be loyal and honest with Katharine. But he would fail. He had foreseen it. Better to fail her now, so she could live.

He had to do this. He didn't want to. But what else could he do?

He was doing it for his daughter.

He rose without zest or vigour, limbs heavy around a hollow core, as if his defeat had scooped out every spark of life and left cold resignation in its wake. The little bottle Mennvinn had given him was hidden in his shirt and he fished it out, stared at it as if it was the source of all his woes. *Soak a rag in it*, she'd said. *Let her breathe the fumes.*

What if the fay came looking for them? Mab could guess they were headed here. It wouldn't be safe.

Katharine and Six could hide. Let the fay pass. He was just trying to find an excuse. He was being a coward.

Katharine would hate him, and his daughter too. They'd both despise him.

But they would live.

His shoulders slumped, as if his heart had shrivelled and the rest of him folded around the void it left behind. His eyes warmed with the threat of tears.

Katharine's sleepy voice made him jump. "Is it time to get up?"

He hid the bottle behind his back. Quick, a lie. No. The truth. "I need to relieve myself." Well. A truth. He stepped out of the room, ducking through the low doorway and closing the door before she could ask any more questions.

His heart was hammering. Why was he so afraid? Because he didn't want her to know. He didn't want to see the hurt and betrayal in her eyes. Easier if he never had to see that. Easier if he could slip away like a coward.

Funny how he felt like a coward no matter what he did.

He jumped at Six's voice. "What are you doing?" the elf

asked and, when Tom floundered for an answer, added, "What's that?"

Tom lifted the bottle. "Medicine." This was solid ground. "Mennvinn gave it to me. For Katharine."

"Why?" The low ceiling forced Six to contort into a bizarre stoop. Somehow it made the elf's size seem threatening rather than comical.

"It will help her sleep."

"She hasn't said anything about trouble sleeping."

"Does she tell you everything?"

"Has she said something to you?"

It was the perfect trap; there was no truth Tom could turn to.

"Unless you were planning to force her into sleep before we left?" Six asked.

He was found out. It was all going wrong. "You could stay with her," he said. Six had to see, he had to understand this was the only way. "Please. You can keep her safe."

Six shook his head. "Stop, Tom."

"I'm trying to save her life."

"I said stop," Six growled. "Stand beside her, Tom, just once. Stop running away and calling it bravery."

Running? "This might be the hardest thing I've ever done."

"Then you haven't done anything," Six snapped. "Other than running from your problems."

All of Tom's muscles were tense with the need to do something, but what could he do? If he now failed to persuade Six to stay, no-one would stop Katharine from following them once they left. "If she's not with me, my foresight can't come to pass."

"And is this the only answer?" Six asked, stepping closer. "Is there nothing else in your foresight you could try to change?"

Details, subtleties. This would be certain. "This is the easiest."

Six nodded. "Exactly. Easy. Why do the difficult thing, the

decent thing, when you can take the easy path and hurt her. Again." Six's lip curled and he said, "Abandoning her is a coward's answer."

A coward. He was a coward. And a liar. The tension tightened into anger and he snapped, "Don't." He stabbed a finger at the elf, who stood there and judged him, as if this impossible choice wasn't boiling within him, too big to contain, too much for him to fix. "Don't you dare."

Six slapped his hand away. "I dare, Tom. I dare you to do something. Anything."

Tom wasn't wearing the sword, but he could feel its thoughts, its constant desire to fight. His fists clenched and he wondered if he would hit the sanctimonious, condescending elf. "I'm trying!" His voice was raised but he couldn't help himself. "I don't want to lose either of them." But every choice seemed doomed to failure, every path led to her hand growing weaker in his. The corridor vanished, just for a moment, long enough to show Tom a great crack in the the world and him trapped within, impassable sheer stone on either side. The foresight faded, but Tom was still trapped. "I don't know what to do," he admitted.

Six seemed unmoved. "Leave her here and you'll lose them anyway."

Tom thought of Katharine waking up to find herself alone. Left behind. Abandoned. She would hate him, and she would follow them, and nothing would change, she would still die, their daughter would still die. He squeezed his eyes tight against the image of her hand in his, held in a cry of frustration. He couldn't let this foresight come to pass, but he couldn't stop it either. He was powerless.

"Help me." The words bubbled out of him, frustration crumbled into despair, and whatever resolve had been keeping him upright failed. He rested his forehead on Six's stooped shoulder, and all the pressure and guilt and fear burst into a sob. “I have to save them.”

Six was stiff, unmoving. His voice was hard when he said, “Promise you won’t abandon her.”

“I promise.”

“I’ll help you.”

“Thank you.”

Six placed a hand on Tom’s back. “For her.”

“For her.”

CHAPTER 8

The tavern seemed empty and cold in the light of morning, despite the flurry of activity. Jarnstenn stood on a chair in the middle of it all, directing, pointing, demanding. It was only a small room, but there was still plenty of space for dwarfs to rush in and out carrying meats, breads, and casks. The ceiling was higher here, but the room was still designed for shorter heads, leaving humans and elfs stooping. The old owner spoke in dwarfish to youngsters, who leapt to their instructions with the urgency of an expected reward, and Gravinn marched about and issued her own orders. It was chaos, and only the dwarfs seemed to thrive in it.

"Hard tack and dried meats," Gravinn demanded. "We can soften them in soups. No fruit, it will only freeze."

"Beer," Jarnstenn pointed at barrels in a corner. "And whiskey too. That'll keep us warm."

"Or leave us frozen in a drunken stupor."

"If you can't handle your drink, milady, don't drink it."

Tom would have left the dwarfs to their preparations, but they both deferred to him, and he was forced to agree or encourage as he imagined Emyr might. He tried not to think of the old king's words: the same potential as his son. The son that shattered a kingdom with one rash, ill-conceived decision.

His feelings of doubt and inadequacy weren't helped by Six. The elf hadn't left his side that morning and, while it rankled, Tom didn't dare say anything for fear that Six would tell Katharine about his plan to abandon her. Besides, he needed the elf. He needed someone to help him find a way out of that terrible foresight.

Katharine sat on a small crate of tea that Mennvinn had requested. She was eating, again, finishing off the heavily salted cold pork from the prior night's dinner. An oasis of calm and potential amongst the madness. "Do you need anything?" Tom asked her.

"I could eat another pig."

Tom caught a young dwarf as he dashed past and said, "Please fetch us some more pork."

The dwarf bobbed his head and scampered off. "I don't need it," Katharine said.

"Then you can eat it later." Tom gave her a smile that felt hollow and fake. "Whatever you need, I shall do my best to give it to you."

Katharine returned his smile and took his hand, her fingers still greasy from the meat. "I would find you. You know that, don't you?"

He froze. She'd heard. She'd heard him talking to Six, heard his plan to leave her behind.

"I know you worry," she said. No signs of hate or anger. Yet. "But plenty of children are born on the road. I'm coming with you. If you haven't already thought about leaving me behind, you will. And you know I'll find you, and you'll regret it."

Tom waited for Six to say something. But the elf remained silent, and Tom just nodded.

Katharine patted his hand and said, "Good." She sat back

and sighed like she was sat on the softest divan in Tanabawr, not a rough, wooden tea crate in a tavern. "That's settled then."

He opened his mouth to apologise. But he knew she didn't want to hear that. So instead he said, "I want to keep you safe."

"Thank you." She smiled but didn't open her eyes. She looked so tired. He should find her somewhere more comfortable to sit. Instead he was about to put her on a scrawny horse and lead her into a frozen wasteland.

She shouldn't be travelling. Not in her condition.

"Don't," she murmured. She didn't even open her eyes.

"Don't what?"

"Don't pity me." Then she did open her eyes. Her tired, sad, determined eyes. "I'm going. That's the end of the discussion."

"You're uncomfortable."

"I am."

"You can't ride."

"Not really."

"It isn't safe."

"Not at all."

"And yet you would still come with us?"

"You're going."

"I am."

She shrugged. Looked aside, as if she didn't want to see his face when she said, "Your place is with me. So if you're going, I have to go too."

She seemed so small, so vulnerable. And he had made her that way. He had forced her to follow him, because he wouldn't stay. He tipped his head, sought her eyes with his. "She won't be safe until the fay have been stopped."

"I know." She met his gaze, struggled with something for a moment. "I just wish-" But she stopped, took a breath, let it out in a sigh.

"What do you wish?"

She shook her head, a tiny, scared gesture.

"You can tell me," Tom said.

She hesitated. Drew breath.

"We're ready." Jarnstenn bustled in, pointing a finger to the crate Katharine sat on. "I'm afraid we're going to need that."

She stood, stepped aside from the bustling dwarfs that came to lift the crate away. They took the moment with them.

When they left Cairnoher, it was Katharine who rode in the wagon. She raised little protest, which in itself was enough of a sign to let her take Emyr's place. Emyr himself, on the other hand, grinned like a fool. He had to be lifted onto horseback and he was sweating by the time he was seated. But he didn't acknowledge the glittering pain that showed in his eyes, nor suffer Mennvinn's doubts and protests.

"I ride," he said. Like it was a great victory. He took a deep, careful breath, tipped his face up to the weak, ineffective sun. He was wrapped in furs, his hair and beard shaggy and wild. He almost looked a bearman from the old stories.

"Would you like to carry your sword, my king?" Tom touched the pommel, ignored the thought from Caledyr: do not give me up.

"Not my sword, son," Emyr replied. He patted a simple iron affair that was sheathed and strapped to the saddle. "This will serve me well enough."

Part of Tom was glad for the refusal. But he felt obliged to say, "It might make you feel stronger."

"It might." Emyr raised his eyebrows at Tom. "But at what cost?"

He couldn't argue with that. And when he took his hand away from Caledyr's pommel, he did his best to ignore the sword's satisfaction.

It was easy to forget the blade, though, in favour of the pleasure of seeing Emyr ride. Tom had only ever seen the man on his back, bleeding and weary. And while he was still deathly pale, and slow and careful in his movements, he sat astride a horse with such obvious pleasure that it was infectious. Emyr waved to children as they rode through the city, exclaimed at stalls or shop fronts, pointed at the great balloons with a child's glee, took deep breaths as if the air was clear and crisp and clean.

The road continued out of the city, winding its way west, but Gravinn urged them away from it as soon as they were out of the city and led their party north. Scratchy grass that seemed to grow out of spite and stubbornness undulated ahead of them, before the ground rose sharply into great mountains, peaks lost in the clouds, grey and white monoliths of rock and snow. Tom remembered all the foresights he'd had where he'd been numb with cold and felt a shiver.

Did Katharine's death wait for her in those mountains?

Tom had thought they'd be up a mountain peak by nightfall, but Gravinn turned them away from every climb she could. Some were forced upon them, but where there was a chance to descend, she took it. It made Tom feel like they kept doubling back, losing a chance at making progress by climbing down what they had just begun to climb. By the end of the day he felt more tired than he should have, and in the mood to be left alone.

So it felt inevitable that Ambrose shuffled over and said, "We speak."

Tom sighed. The sun had long set. He was hungry. He was tired. In no mood for cryptic conversations, and he needed to get

Katharine from the wagon and settled before he could rest. "A moment."

He waited for Ambrose to argue. But the old man just nodded, and waited. Tom was almost too surprised to nod and walk away.

"I'm so glad we've stopped." Katharine was already clambering to her feet. "Another hour in here and I'd have lost my mind."

Tom took her arm and her weight, almost losing his balance as she hauled herself up. "It's been a long day," he admitted. He helped her navigate around crates and chests, clamber down the steps at the back of the wagon.

"You're tired," she said.

"Not as tired as you are, I'm sure."

"You've been tired since the attack on the train."

Had he? He hadn't felt any more or less tired.

"Something's weighing on you."

Be loyal and honest and save her life.

"Don't worry about me," he told her. "You have to focus on the baby."

"I can focus on two things at once." She smiled the moment her feet touched the ground. As if she drew strength from the world. "I am a woman, after all."

"And a very fine one at that." That made her smile even more, and Tom smiled to have made her smile. "Let's get you some food."

"I could eat a horse."

"Perhaps we should have brought a spare."

She elbowed him and he grinned, taking pleasure in how she leant on him as he led her to a spot near the fire Gravinn was building. He gave her a slice of the strangely pale bread they'd bought, covered in butter and jam. It wasn't long until

Gravinn was cooking bacon, and he made sure that Katharine had the first slices.

"I can take care of myself," she said. But it was a half-hearted protest.

"Would you like me to stop?" He held a slice of bacon in mid-air, opened his mouth and made to eat it.

She snatched it from his fingers with a grin.

Mennvinn was tutting over Emyr's stitches, poking and prodding at him as he laid back and stared up at the night sky with a dreamy smile on his face; she'd given him something for the pain he had denied all day. Now he sighed as if contented and said, "All we need is one of Rimestenn's songs." He sounded like there wasn't a care in all of Tir that could ruin his peace. "You always liked his songs, Ambrose. Especially the ribald ones."

Ambrose stood away from the fire, silent, staring at Emyr as if pained.

"Do you remember when you put an enchantment on his voice? He tried to sing 'The Maiden of Seamouth', in that big, deep voice of his, but he sounded like a girl of four summers?" Emyr grinned. Was the legendary King Emyr of Tir really laughing at a silly voice? "Do you remember?" he asked Ambrose.

But the old sorcerer didn't have to say anything. Realisation dimmed the smile on Emyr's face, replaced the humour with sadness. Left him staring at the shadow of his old friend. "You laughed for days," he said in a small voice.

Tom couldn't imagine Ambrose laughing.

"It's late," Emyr said. "And an old man gets tired easily. Set a watch." And he closed his eyes, and said no more.

"We can't leave him out here," Tom said, and Draig helped him carry the old king into his tent. It was awkward work, but despite how they jostled Emyr, he didn't wake. Whatever Mennvinn was giving him, it was strong stuff. They left him under a blanket before returning to the fire, and Tom could feel Six's eyes on him the whole time.

"Could you please tell her to stop eating all the food?" Gravinn asked as Tom sat down; Katharine had helped herself to a piece of the bacon from the pan.

"I'm hungry," she said.

"And you've had your full share."

"She's with child," Tom snapped.

"Our supplies won't last if she eats them all."

"She can have mine."

"And mine, if she wants it." Six held out his plate to Katharine.

"I couldn't," she said. But it was an empty protest. Six stepped over, flipped his meat onto her plate, and took his bread back to his place at the fire. "Thank you," she said, before taking an enormous bite.

Tom gave him a nod, and Six returned the gesture as he said, "You're welcome."

"Tom."

Ambrose was still lurking in the shadows beyond the fire, not even looking at them. He was sat on a rock, staring at a space next to him as if someone was sat beside him.

Tom sighed and said to Katharine, "He wants to talk to me."

"Go." She waved him away. "I'm warm and fed."

"Let me know if you need anything," he said. He had a sudden urge to kiss her forehead, almost did it. But he knew Six was watching. And Tom knew he didn't deserve to kiss Katharine. Not after what he'd tried to do.

Katharine grabbed his face with both hands and mashed her lips against his. She tasted of salt and meat and metal. When she let him go, she gave him a shy yet mischievous smile and said, "Don't be too long," before taking another bite of bacon.

Tom tried to say something, but ended up walking away

from the fire without a word, only vaguely aware that everyone was watching. His thoughts were a muddy mess. Was he forgiven? More than that? Did she want him back? Would they have more children? What would Maev think? Why did he care what Maev thought?

He realised Ambrose had spoken but he hadn't heard the words. "I'm sorry," he said.

The old man grunted and took a few slow, unsteady breaths. Was he angry? In pain? Exhausted by travel? But before Tom could ask, Ambrose said, "You have not yet burnt the twig."

Tom took a weary sigh. "I don't think I can."

"Yet I have told you that you succeed."

Yes. Making it real by foreseeing it. Just as Tom had foreseen Katharine's death. Tom shook his head, snorted out his frustration, and realised as he did that he was sat in the space he'd seen Ambrose staring at. The old sorcerer had been waiting for Tom to inhabit it.

As if he'd spoken aloud, Ambrose confirmed, "The future is written. Like the past."

The old man spoke with the weight of that future. The responsibility of seeing it come to pass. "It seems cruel to let us see the future without giving us the power to change it," Tom replied. He tried not to think of Katharine, crying in that dark place. Her grip growing weak in his own. "We should be able to use our foresight to change things."

"A nice idea. But if that were true, we would not be here."

Something let out a low keen in the distance. A wolf, perhaps. It sounded lonely. Would Katharine feel lonely when it happened? She would tell him that she loved him. He wouldn't say anything. How would that make her feel, as the life went out of her? And what would happen to their child? "How do you live with it? When you foresee something terrible, how do you just allow it to come to pass?"

"Accept what has to happen, Tom. Play your part. It is all you can do."

"That isn't very comforting."

Ambrose gave an awkward shrug, like his memory of how to do it was imperfect. "I cannot remember my past, Thomas Rymour. I suspect I once thought as you do. But when all you remember are the things to come, you realise there is no fighting destiny." He turned to him, met his eye. His dark gaze bored into Tom's, and Tom couldn't help but be a little frightened. "Grieve today for the things you will lose tomorrow. Or grief will blind you to what you must do next. "

Tom poked the fire and listened to Ambrose snore, a low, constant buzz. Nothing like the loud, intrusive snores coming from Emyr. But snoring nonetheless. Snoring from a man who said he needed more than sleep.

Emyr thought his old friend wise. Perhaps he was. But Tom couldn't do it. He couldn't give Katharine up for dead. He felt like he was on the precipice of something wonderful, while unseen forces were trying to collapse the cliff beneath his feet.

And those forces would win. He knew they would. The foresight showed her dying. And when she died, he would be alone. There would be no-one to reach out to, to touch and hold in the dark, no-one to share his days with.

Tom uncovered only part of the jar, hunched over it, stared at the sprite within, hugging its knees to its chin.

The light was otherworldly. Magic. Void. But it was a comfort. Tom had thought to speak to the sprite. But what could he say? So he sat there, gazing at the sprite, basking in its light. Drawing a cold comfort from the mere presence of a fay.

He could go. He could give this all up and go back to Faerie. Take his punishment. Absolve his wrongs. Return to the fold. It would be easy. He just had to say the words.

He covered up the jar with shaking hands and sat alone in the dark.

Ambrose's damnable twig was mocking him. Or, at least, that's how it felt. Tom rode with the cold, lifeless, empty thing in his palm. He'd already examined it, felt the smooth bark, peered at the faint lines wrapped around it, stared into the fibrous pith, smelt it, held it up to his ear like a fool. It was a twig. A dead bit of wood. There was no fire, no earth, no air or water in it. Not that he could feel anyway. So he rode with it in his palm and sighed at it.

Gravinn still wound their path between the mountains as best she could. They had long left behind any signs of civilisation. A few days ago there had been smoke in the distance, a goatherd, Gravinn had said. But nothing since. No signs of people or habitation. Just the occasional hare, which Six shot as often as he could, and at night Katharine would tell him how to skin and cook them.

Tom tipped his head back and spotted a bird flapping lazily through the cold, clear sky. Hares and birds, that's all they saw. The black shadow above seemed to float in the air, needing no effort to stay aloft. It seemed so easy.

Gravinn led their party around an enormous boulder, three times as tall as Draig, and back down the mountainside.

Tom missed roads. They were smooth and easy. Not like their current path. He felt he spent the whole day riding back and forth across the same patch of land. He looked up to watch that bird soar away over boulders and mountains.

Except it was still above them. It had turned to follow.

"Six," he called, as softly as he could. The elf was alongside in a moment. "What kind of bird is that?"

Six squinted into the sky. "A magpie?" He grunted. "Big magpie, though."

"Emyr's bones." Melwas. He was healed and he was tracking them. "Can you bring it down?"

Six made an uncertain sound. "I miss as many hares as I hit."

But why else would Ambrose have insisted on iron-tipped arrows? "Do your best. Quickly."

Six looked up again, peering at the shadow. "Why?"

The bird dipped a wing and left them. Iron nails. "On my horse. The fay have found us!"

CHAPTER 9

SIX SCRAMBLED from his mount to Tom's, and Tom kicked his heels and flicked the reins, sending his horse into a gallop. The magpie had turned, flying back south. It had a clear path. Theirs twisted and turned. They stood little hope of catching it. But it was too good an opportunity.

"I'll never hit it like this," Six cried into his ear. He had one arm wrapped around Tom's waist, squeezing hard as they thundered across uneven ground.

"We have to try." To its credit, the horse was doing well, neatly jumping or darting around any obstacles. It seemed to relish the chase, and Tom wondered if their slow pace had left it bored.

He risked a glance upwards. The magpie was watching them.

"What does it matter?" Six asked. "It's seen us. The fay know where we are."

"Trust me," Tom told him.

Six grunted, not exactly a vote of confidence, and Tom quested towards Caledyr, hoping it would guide him.

Fight, was all it had. It was a sword. It knew nothing of riding.

"Cursed stinking iron nails," Tom swore. Calmness of the soul until death. Calmness of the soul until death. A death that was hopefully years from now, and not waiting for them in a rabbit hole or a half-buried rock that would bring down the horse and crack their heads open.

The magpie was teasing them. They had to cut around a huge stone, so the bird slowed, let them catch up. When their path was blocked, forcing them up the mountainside, it slid across the sky, keeping them in sight. But Six didn't draw his bow. "Are we close enough?" Tom asked.

"Still too far."

Melwas was toying with them. And then, when he got bored, he would leave.

"Try!" Tom called out.

They crested the hill and rushed down the other side, so steep that Tom thought they would fall, but they didn't, and they raced across open grassland, hooves pounding the dirt. But the horse was getting tired. The bird was going to get away.

Six released him, and Tom heard the bow draw and ring beside his ear as the arrow loosed, which arced through the air only to fall short.

Tom dug his knees into the horse, spurred it on. A burst of speed, before the terrain dropped, forcing them to slow and half-gallop, half-fall down the hillside.

"Again," he told Six. They had to bring the bird down. They had to.

The bowstring sang, the arrow arced. The magpie didn't flinch, and it didn't need to: the arrow didn't come close.

"It's too far," Six growled.

Down another hillside, this one so steep the horse stumbled and shuddered with the effort of keeping its uneven footing. But at the base of the hill was a huge, open stretch of grass. They could build up a gallop, close the distance. They could do it.

Wait.

The thought from Caledyr turned his head and he caught sight of a narrow crack in the mountainside. All moss and grass and stone, like someone had cut it through the mountain eons ago.

He'd foreseen this.

He tugged the reins and the mountain rushed up and swallowed the world.

"What are we doing?" Six was forced to hunker against Tom's back; there wasn't much room here.

"I'm not sure." Tom let the horse slow to a walk before it stopped, panting and shivering with fatigue. Tom looked up at the sliver of sky above them.

"Have we given up?" Six sounded like he couldn't decide if he was pleased or irritated.

"I don't think so," Tom replied. All he could remember was this, sitting here inside this little crack in the world. Waiting.

"Why is the bird so important?"

"Keep an eye on the sky."

They waited. They watched. Tom began to think they were wasting their time.

A shadow passed above. Nothing more than a flicker. It could have been anything. But Tom grinned. "He's looking for us." He clambered down. The horse seemed content to wait. It nibbled on some weeds. Tom didn't wait for Six, just picked his way through the tiny valley as much as he could while staring up into the sky.

The ground climbed upwards, the going steep. Whenever they disturbed loose rock it seemed to fall forever, the tumbling stone against stone ringing like a thunderclap. Tom's first thought was that the noise would give them away. But they wanted the bird to look for them. So he kicked stones free of the dirt, and Six grumbled behind him.

Their path opened up onto a plateau of rock, pathetic clumps of grass clinging to tiny cracks in the stone. The view was incredible, the mountains rising up on either side, tall green trees clinging to impossible steep slopes, a river wending its way far below. The sky above was grey, a little blue in the south, dark clouds to the north. Despite himself, Tom took a deep breath. Clean, pure air.

"Wait there," he told Six, pointing back into the crack. Six said nothing, slipping back into the shadows. Tom turned back to the tableau. There was no sign of the magpie. Had it given up? Had it returned to Faerie? Perhaps it was just looking in the wrong place?

Tom drew a breath and cried, "Melwas!"

He waited. Listened. Nothing. The silence was almost something tangible. Like you could reach out and touch it.

A flicker of motion. To the right. There, below, the magpie. Definitely one of Melwas'. Twice as big as a normal magpie, with a splash of white around one eye.

"Melwas!"

The bird heard him, banked, flapped its wings and climbed, before fluttering to a landing at the edge of the plateau. Well out of reach. It stood there, tipped its head at him. Didn't make a sound. It was taunting him, by getting so close. It was telling him there was no hurting it.

Tom drew Caledyr. The blade sang. Fight. Kill the enemy.

The bird tossed its head, like a challenge. It knew it could fly away before he could even get close.

Tom hefted the blade. Lifted and lowered the point, a salute to the elf hidden in the rocks.

He jumped as an iron-tipped arrow skewered the bird and knocked it down. It flapped, screamed, tumbled towards the edge. "No!" He dropped the sword, scrabbled after the bird. Caught it by the tail and heaved it away from the fall. He dropped it again, let it flap for a moment longer before it stopped, lay still, glared balefully up at him as it lay prone.

"Good shot."

Six stepped out. "It wasn't moving much."

"No." Tom allowed himself a smile. Nudged the bird with his foot. Midhir or Melwas, the Faerie king's arrogance had always blinded him. And now he was blind indeed: the splash of white was over the left eye.

"What's so special about this bird?" Six asked.

"You saw the swans Midhir had at Calmae?" When Six nodded, Tom continued. "They change to magpies, but their function is the same: Thought and Memory. They embody those traits for Midhir or Melwas."

"Which one is this?"

"Thought."

"So the fay can't think?" Six sounded sceptical. And he was right. It wasn't that simple.

"Just Melwas." Memory had once become trapped in Tir for four days. Midhir had tottered around his realm like a foolish old man, vacant and scared, memories coming to him only in snatches, just long enough for him to remember what he had forgotten. What would he be like without Thought?

"So do we kill it?"

A good question. Dead, it would return to Faerie and take time to reform. Alive, they could keep it from Melwas indefinitely. But the fay would come for it in force.

But would they come anyway? For the effrontery of shooting down Thought?

Tom wanted to keep it. Put it in a cage and hide it from Melwas. Let that smug monster drool like a babe for the rest of time. But Katharine was already in too much danger. "We kill it." He retrieved Caledyr, reversed his grip to aim the point at its neck. The sword sang at the thought of tasting Faerie flesh.

Dead-bane, it sang.

Tom thrust the blade into Thought and watched it twitch in silence. It wanted to scream. But it didn't want to give him the satisfaction. So it just glared at him until it grew still and glared at nothing at all.

The bird's death had been so much quieter than Fenoderee's. It seemed unfair, somehow. Tom tried not to take satisfaction as he cut the head from its neck.

Six pulled his arrow free of the dead fay, slid it back into the quiver on his back. "Do we leave it here?"

"No sense in bringing it with us." Tom spoke with a bravado he didn't feel. It was as if fears had poured out of the dead fay's body and were trying to crawl into his mind. Melwas wouldn't stand for this. The fay would come for them. Still, Mab had told him to kill the fay sent after him. And Tom couldn't argue with the smile on his face at the thought of Melwas without Thought. Would Mab smile, he wondered. Would she delight to see a mortal in contest with her king?

"Well," Six said, staring down at the fay at their feet. "I certainly feel a lot better than I did after the last time we rode on horseback together."

"Yes," Tom agreed. It felt like decades since they'd led that dragon on a merry chase through the streets of Cairnalyr, but his neck still ached at the memory of it. "And this one was far less frightening."

"Why did we do it?" Six lifted his chin in a silent challenge. "What one fay knows, all fay know. That's what you say."

Tom shook his head. "It works differently with Memory and Thought," he told the elf. "Their only link is to Melwas. He has to touch them to share what they've seen and heard."

"So the fay don't know where we are?"

"No." It was reassuring to hear his own answer. "The knowledge died with the bird."

Six nodded. "Fine." He lowered his chin. Tom felt like he'd passed some kind of unspoken test. "But we shouldn't have left her." The elf turned and stepped back into the crevasse. The waiting horse snickered at them as they picked their way down.

"Katharine is with Ambrose," Tom said.

"Can he protect her?"

"I think so."

"It would be better if you knew for sure."

It was patronising and Tom wanted to tell him so. But he couldn't. He felt like he couldn't speak up at all. When Six stopped and turned to him, gazed down at him, he felt small. Chastened by the memory of admitting his weakness to the elf.

"Let's go," Six told him, and they mounted the horse in silence and began to make their way back.

Tom let the horse pick the pace; they had ridden it hard and it deserved to take things easy, so he let it stop to graze on the thin grass or drink from a small pool nestled against a hillside. But without the mad energy of the chase, the cold seemed to have a much stronger hold on Tom's fingers and toes, and fatigue tugged at his eyelids.

"Tell me about the foresight," Six said as they rode a gentle path up a hillside.

Tom didn't want to talk about it. Putting voice to what he'd seen made it too real. "There isn't much to say," he replied.

"Then it won't take you long."

What did it matter? What good would it do? "I try not to think about it."

"We'll never find a way around it if we don't think about it." Six's words were firm but kind, and Tom could tell that elf didn't want to hear the foresight either.

Tom's first instinct was to indulge Six's secret desire. Tell him that there was no way around it, that foresights might as well be written in stone. But this one couldn't be. This one couldn't come to pass. So he said, "It's dark in my foresight, and very cold. Katharine is lying down. Her hands are covered in blood." I love you, she said. But Tom couldn't share that part. Not when he knew he would say nothing to her in return. So all he added was, "And her hand grows weaker in mine."

"Is that it?"

"That's enough."

"So you don't see her die?"

"It feels like she dies."

"But you haven't seen it?"

"No." But that sounded too much like hope. "But I can feel it, Six. She'd need every one of Sir Allyst's Miracles to survive."

"Maybe we only need one." Six sounded thoughtful, but also pleased with himself. "Ambrose should have died centuries ago."

Yes. He should have. "You think maybe he can do the same for Katharine?"

Six snorted. "Ambrose looks like he's a stiff breeze from being a pile of cryptic dust. But he must know something."

"If he hasn't forgotten it."

Six was silent for a moment. "True," he admitted. "But there's a chance, isn't there?"

Yes. There was a chance. "You might be right." Tom pulled the twig from his pocket. Was that why Ambrose had given him this? To teach him magic, so he could save Katharine? "Thank you." And he reached into the twig with a new resolve to make it dance with fire and save Katharine's life.

But the twig refused to burn, and whatever hope Six had given Tom was sputtering like a dying candle by the time they reached the others.

CHAPTER 10

By the time they returned, the others had already set up camp. There was still a little time until nightfall, but everyone seemed too tired to start travelling again. But not too tired to start a barrage of questions about where they had gone and why, so Tom found himself explaining Faerie lore to them all.

Which Jarnstenn found unimpressive. “Fairies and magic.” He snorted and shook his head. “Plenty of marvels in Tir, but not one of them could convince me of that rubbish.”

“What attacked the train,” Draig asked, “if not a fay?”

“Something.” Jarnstenn nodded, ceding the point. “But a fairy?”

“A fay,” Tom corrected.

“I think we’re beyond insulting them now,” Katharine said.

Perhaps. But it felt unwise to antagonise them.

“You don’t have to believe,” Tom told Jarnstenn. “You just have to understand.”

“No, I don’t.” The dwarf pushed another piece of bread into his mouth and talked around it. “Kun wants to help you find a lost city. So I’m helping you. That’s all I need to know.”

Kunnustenn fidgeted.

"We need water," Draig said, evidently tired of the conversation. The elf was right. They were running low.

"We saw a river," Tom told him.

"South," Six said. "Maybe ten miles."

How could he tell? The chase had twisted and turned so much Tom had no idea which way they'd been facing.

"A river?" Katharine seemed shocked and angry, turning to Gravinn and demanding, "Why aren't we following it?"

Gravinn shook her head. "There are no signs of a river."

Tom frowned. "We saw it with our own eyes."

She looked stricken. "I believe you. But there was no way to tell."

"No way to tell?" Katharine spoke as if Gravinn had told the most outrageous lie. "You've been taught to look for river-sign, haven't you?"

Gravinn's face had flushed a bright red. "Well, you didn't see it either."

"I've been riding in the wagon."

"It doesn't matter."

"It does if we've been wasting time," Katharine shot back. "A river could give us an easy path to follow."

"Not all rivers can be followed."

"It's worth a look."

"I grew up in the mountains."

"I've travelled them."

Emyr raised his hands and his voice. "Ladies, please. You are both skilled Pathfinders. We would be fools not to heed your experience." Once the pair of them were looking at him, he told them. "We will find this river. Fill our waterskins at the least. If it can be followed, then we shall follow it."

"There are no guarantees it will take us to Cairnarim," Gravinn said.

"There's no guarantee your path will take us there either." Emyr's words were harsh but his tone was gentle, warm, taking the sting out of it. "We are all stumbling towards a place we don't know how to find."

"There'll be hunting by the river," Jarnstenn said. Thinking with his stomach as usual.

"I think there was some mention of a river in *Rorvinn's Compendium of Lost Tales*," Kunnustenn said, chin in hand and staring into the ground like it was withholding the answers.

"We should change our path anyway," Tom told them. "Even without Thought, the fay might know where we are."

But it seemed Gravinn wasn't quite ready to cede defeat. "The wagon." Said desperately, like she was losing something important. And when everyone looked at her, she said as if it was plain, "Finding a path wide enough for the wagon has been hard enough. You won't find one by a river."

All eyes turned back to Katharine. Exhausted Katharine, her temper fraying, her eyes closed as she held back a sharp retort. "It's worth looking."

"It is." Emyr made it clear that was the final word. "Tom. Six. Good work today." And he took a step away from the fire and lay down. It was strange. Emyr had stormed into the argument, stamped out the fires as he saw them, and then left. He seemed oblivious to Gravinn's hurt feelings. It seemed at odds with the stories of the great king of Tir.

But he was old. Still healing. Perhaps he just needed some help.

So Tom said, "Gravinn and I will take the first watch." In truth he wanted to sleep too. But he felt a duty to resolve this. A duty that should be Emyr's.

Gravinn had turned her back to the fire. But she made a sound of assent. Tom tended to Katharine, made sure she was as comfortable as she could be. Spent some time in quiet conversation with her, talking about nothings, feeling the baby kick. Smoothed her hair, let her doze off, and left the tent.

"You love her." Those were Gravinn's first words to him. She had moved away from the fire, sat cross-legged on a rock higher up the mountainside.

Did he? Perhaps. But it all seemed too complicated for something as simple as love. Besides, if he loved her, he would have saved her by now.

"I've led us safely through these mountains for days," Gravinn said. "I know what I'm doing."

"No-one is questioning that," he said as he sat beside her.

"She does. At every opportunity, she tells everyone I'm wrong." Gravinn wouldn't look at him. Just sat on her rock and glared out into the night.

Gravinn was right, in a way; Katharine did question and contradict her. Almost delighted in it, at times. But Gravinn seemed to crow her superiority too. A rivalry had sprung up between the two Pathfinders, and it was something they could all do without. "She's been doing this for years."

"So have I."

"You were a thrall. An assistant. I don't mean to sound cruel," he said when her head whipped towards him. "I'm just pointing out that Katharine has learnt her trade. You're still learning."

"I got you in and out of a dozen Western cities." Like he was ungrateful.

"You did." How to phrase this? "Katharine has learnt how to read the land. She knows how to find a path where there isn't one."

"I know that too."

"Do you?"

Silence. There wasn't much light to see by, but Tom could see her clenched jaw as she looked down at her feet.

"There's no shame in not knowing a thing," Tom said. "Learn from her. Take all the knowledge you can. Let her help you become a better Pathfinder."

"Better than her."

Tom sighed.

More silence. She was wavering. But her stubborn hurt wasn't quite gone. Not yet.

"We would never have survived the Kingdom without you, Gravinn," he told her. "But there is always someone better than us. A better fighter, a better hunter, a better cook." A better father. "They can be rivals or they can be teachers."

More silence. Then Gravinn huffed. "I will learn from her."

Tom let himself smile. Something going right for once. "Good."

"And I will be better than her."

Tom felt his victory sputter but kept his smile frozen in place. "Fine."

Gravinn gave him a smile too, as if they had shared something, like they were conspirators. He knew if he said anything he would start an argument or worse. But staying silent felt like he was betraying Katharine somehow. "Get some rest," he told her. "You can take the next watch in a few hours."

Gravinn nodded and obediently clambered down from her rock. Tom watched her go, then stared at the tent he shared with Katharine, as if he could see through the canvas and see her sleeping shadow. He waited until Gravinn had been in her tent long enough to have fallen asleep, then he pulled out the jar and peeled back its wrappings.

"Tell me about Melwas," he demanded.

The sprite was sat with its knees under its chin, wings folded, glaring at him. It said nothing.

"Did it work?" he asked. "Is he without Thought?"

She was so bright it was hard to make out her expression.

"Tell me."

But the sprite only smirked at him. So he reached into his pocket and pulled out the shard of black monolith stone, ignoring the sprite's squeals as he opened the jar just enough to push the stone inside. The sprite scrabbled away from it, pressing itself against the glass and spitting hate at him with its eyes.

Tom glared back at it. "Tell me, I said."

The sprite lifted its head, chin jutting out, and spat one, tiny little word. "Run."

"You have not been successful," Ambrose said to him as they rode.

"You'll have to be a bit more specific." Tom had failed to convince Katharine to return to wagon that morning. Instead she had mounted a horse and started issuing instructions as to where they would travel and how. Gravinn perhaps had expected some sort of joint leadership and, finding herself pushed to the sidelines, glowered at Katharine, gave Tom pointedly exasperated looks, and sulked.

At first Tom had thought of speaking to Katharine. But she was impatient that morning, and snapped at anyone who questioned her or was slow in doing as they had been told. Even Six hadn't been immune to her sharp words. And while Tom had been trying to think of what he might say to Gravinn, Mennvinn had come up to him and said, "I believe my usefulness to you is over."

"What?" Her words had pulled him from his thoughts. In truth, he had given Mennvinn little thought in the past few days. She rode in the wagon and said little. She was easy to forget. "What do you mean?"

"My patient is healed." She pointed to Emyr who was stretching delicately. But stretching nonetheless. Standing. Riding.

"Katharine needs you," Tom replied. He knew the complications a pregnancy could bring. In a lower voice he asked, "Should she even be riding?"

Mennvinn was quick to say, "I am not well-versed in the lore of child-bearing." Then she hesitated before adding, "No. She should not be riding. There is a risk of falling, and of jouncing the unborn child."

Katharine was jabbing a finger towards some pots and pans and asking Jarnstenn if he expected them to walk alongside the horses. "We should tell her," Tom said.

Jarnstenn stood firm for a moment, before shrinking under Katharine's withering glare and picking them up with a few muttered words in dwarfish. Even those stopped when Katharine reminded him that she spoke the tongue. "I'm not sure I'm brave enough," Mennvinn had said.

And when Tom had relayed the warning, Katharine wasn't interested. "Do you think I'd put our child in danger?" There was a sharpness in her look and an edge to her words that told Tom to say no and walk away.

Instead he said, "Not deliberately." And as her nostrils flared, he added, "But we aren't healers. We might make a mistake and not realise."

"You've been speaking to Mennvinn?" Katharine cast about for the dwarf, but she had retreated to the wagon. "You can tell her I know my body. If I say I can ride, I can ride."

"She says there's a risk of jouncing." Whatever that was.

Katharine read his expression and explained. "Shaking. As if there isn't as much in the wagon." She stabbed a finger at Tom. "Are you going to bundle me up and put me away like a feeble little girl? Or let me be who I am?"

This time there was no arguing. "Let you be who you are."

She wasn't gracious in victory. "Good." She jerked her chin towards the others. "Get them in the saddle."

She led the way, leaving Tom in the middle of their line, reflecting on how he had failed to convince Mennvinn she was needed, failed to make Katharine feel like she had his support. And, of course, failed to keep the fay placated. Run, the sprite had told him. Run to where? There was nowhere in Tir they could hide.

And now Ambrose was telling him he was a further failure. "You have not brought forth the elements from the stick I gave you," the old man said.

His chance to save Katharine. "No."

"But you have tried."

"Yes." With every spare moment. But no matter how much he wanted the thing to burn, nothing happened.

Ambrose grunted. "You do not see the point."

"Even if I can burn the twig, the magic I want to see done will still be beyond me."

Ambrose let out a sigh, one that seemed too big to have been held in such a fragile, frail body. "You must learn this craft, Tom, because soon I will not be here to do it for you."

"What do you mean?" Tom asked, though he knew exactly what he meant.

"I will not survive this journey." Ambrose's dark gaze stared at something only he could see. "I will die. Soon."

Soon. Tom swallowed. So Ambrose couldn't save Katharine. It was up to him. "Does Emyr know?" The old king rode ahead, alongside Katharine. As Tom watched, he laughed at something she said. She smiled. She liked him.

"No. Do not tell him."

Ambrose was going to die. Emyr's only friend left in the world. "Shouldn't he know?"

"Perhaps." No regret. No fear. No anger. No emotion at all.

"Aren't you scared?"

"I burnt up my fear a long time ago." He finally turned his head, gazing that empty gaze at Tom. "As you will burn that stick."

Tom pulled the twig from his pocket. How could he keep Katharine alive if he couldn't make a piece of wood burn?

"Think of how Gravinn lights a fire," Ambrose said. His voice was soft now, lulling.

"She rubs two sticks together." One between her palms, spinning the tip within a hollow in the other.

"And she makes fire." Ambrose murmured. "If so simple an action can bring forth fire, willing it forth must be easy."

Tom snorted. "If it was easy, wouldn't everyone do it?"

Ambrose smiled. It was such a rare sight, Tom almost didn't know how to react. "There is not much magic in the world." The old sorcerer looked up at his staff, at the black stone nestled in the tip. "Finding it is the hard part."

Tom stared too, remembering the monolith in Cairnagwyn. The monolith outside Cairnabren. And the way the peddle in his pocket had drawn his thoughts as powerfully as those monoliths had. "How do I find magic?."

"You don't. It has already found you." Ambrose hefted his staff, pointed it at Tom. It was an oddly threatening gesture. "The fay left you touched by it when they gave you foresight and truth."

Gave. Not cursed, or inflicted. Was Ambrose angry? Or jealous? Did he wish he had Tom's imperfect foresight and the ability to remember his past?

"Touch this stone," the old man said, "and you would feel it, wouldn't you? The cold. The push against the magic inside you."

Even at a distance, Tom could feel how the air felt too clear and too still around the stone. He nodded.

Ambrose lifted the staff again. "So you have the magic."

"If that stone dulls magic, why do you carry it?"

Another smile. Two in one conversation. It seemed to tax Ambrose. "The memory of pain helps us find pleasure. Closing your eyes helps you appreciate the sunlight." He took a deep breath and sighed it out as if basking in a beautiful summer's day. Then he looked up at his staff. "That stone, which pushes away magic, helps me cheat death. It serves to anchor me."

Cheat death? Tom's heart quickened. "How?" he asked. "Could it help anyone avoid dying?" Could it help Katharine?

"Burn the twig," Ambrose demanded. "Only then can I explain it to you."

That night Tom watched Gravinn start a fire. She did it almost without thinking, her hands moving without the need for thought behind them. Spinning the stick back and forth against the small log. Wisps of smoke, then a glow that flared under her breath. She touched it to kindling, there was more smoke, and then there was fire.

So quick. So easy. The fire must be waiting to come out. Tom looked down at his twig. Reached for it, like he had reached for the monoliths. But it was just wood. Nothing more.

But there needed to be more. If burning this twig was what

Tom had to do in order to save Katharine, then he would burn it. He would find a way.

The twig was dry. So there couldn't be much water in it. Or much air, of course. Just earth and fire then.

Ambrose would die, and all his knowledge would die with him. He would take away any chance of saving Katharine. Unless Emyr knew a way? Tom looked across the camp, watched the old king in quiet conversation with Kunnustenn. The dwarf was pointing to something in a book and Emyr nodded. He seemed so intent, like he was listening to every single syllable. He asked a question and Kunnustenn smiled. Perhaps he would know. Perhaps Tom should ask him instead of wasting time with this stick.

Focus, he told himself and stared at the twig again. Six had said that unbalanced elements lead to sickness. So if the elements were unbalanced in this twig, that should lead to, what? Not sickness. But something. Perhaps he just needed to push the elements out of balance. Somehow.

He was tired. Not just from travelling, but from his fears, too. His fear for Katharine. For their daughter. Fear that they would fail to find the glarn. He glanced at Caledyr, resting in its sheathe beside him. What good was a thinking sword that couldn't offer any advice?

No enemy, the sword thought, before falling silent.

No enemy. Except the fay. Who might reappear at any moment. The sprite had told Tom to run. He glanced over at Dank, sat with Draig. The elf talked. The boy listened. Tom should have made more of an effort with Dank. They had taken his sprite from him, a companion who had been with him every moment of every day for decades. Now the boy was just one person, trapped inside a cage of flesh.

But at least there were no Faerie strings tied to his limbs. Tom could look at him and know that Melwas wasn't staring back at him behind the boy's eyes.

It was all links, wasn't it? Dank linked to Faerie. Tom to the sword. The monoliths had been linked together to form a wall between Tir and Faerie. Without those links, the fay could push their way through. Many bodies with one thought, all linked together.

So the only way to burn this twig was to build a link.

The bark was smooth under his fingertips, with little bumps along the length. At first he stared at it, then he closed his eyes. Quested for it. Tried to feel it with his thoughts as well as with his fingers. Like the monolith. He remembered how it felt to break the links between the monoliths, tried to imagine building one. Tried to imagine spinning a strand of magic and wrapping one end around the twig.

There! The elements, all four of them, buried deep within every fibre of the twig. Tom stared for a moment, half-expecting something to happen. But the twig was still.

He had a sudden memory of Dank in the dungeons of Cairnalyr. "There's magic everywhere, even if it's only a little."

Focus, he told himself. He closed his eyes and reached out, found the elements again, each small and dark and still. He pushed at them and they seemed to stir. Seemed to ask him what he wanted.

Fire.

Fire, they echoed.

And sudden pain, he snatched his hand away and cried out, scrambled to his feet away from the twig that now had merry flames dancing over its length.

It was burning. It was on fire.

He had made fire. He held up his hand, throbbing and painful. He had made fire.

He looked up, found the others watching him. Found Ambrose and told him, "I did it." He grinned. "I did it."

Mennvinn fussed over to him, took his palm, tutted, pulled him away from his success and closer to the larger fire, pushed and prodded at his palm.

"I did it," Tom repeated.

"Yes," Ambrose said. He didn't move. In fact, he didn't seem pleased at all. He looked like a man who had just seen the door to his cell close shut. "You have done it."

"What's going on?" Six asked.

"Your friend just performed magic," Ambrose replied.

"Tom did magic?" Emyr looked up, and Kunnustenn's jaw dropped. "You're teaching him?"

Jarnstenn snorted. "The lad burnt a twig. We calling that magic these days?"

"Stop." Ambrose didn't speak to anyone. But everyone fell silent. "None of you are asking the right questions."

The right questions. The one Ambrose had said he would answer once Tom had burnt the twig. "How are you still alive?"

The old man just nodded. "Yes. That is the right question."

Everyone waited for the answer. And, as they waited, Tom felt something. It was dark and cold and hard and it settled down in his soul. Like a black pebble on a white sandy beach. "Magic," he said.

Ambrose nodded. "You see it now, don't you?"

"It's a trade," Tom replied. "You use up part of yourself to perform magic."

"Yes."

Touching that pebble was like touching darkness itself. It was lonely and empty. Hopeless and dead. Was that why Ambrose was the way he was? "Is that how you kept yourself alive? You've used yourself up?"

"Not quite." Ambrose smiled a wry smile, like he had a secret he'd kept from the world. "There is more to it than magic. The secret lies in the thing we hunt."

Emyr said, "Orlannu."

"What is it?" Six asked.

Ambrose turned to Kunnustenn, who blushed and cast his gaze to the ground. But Tom caught the look in the dwarf's eyes; there was a hunger to be heard there.

So Tom said, "Tell us about Orlannu, Kunnustenn." And the dwarf smiled, even as he refused to meet anyone's eye.

"There isn't much written about it. The texts all agree that it's a cauldron. Some call it a trap or a seal. And there are some ancient children's stories that say the seal is so tight that even death can't open it up."

"Yes," Ambrose said. "A cauldron made of the same stone as the monoliths. Anything inside cannot die, because the elements cannot escape."

Cannot die. Tom kept his gaze away from Katharine even as his heart began to hammer inside his chest.

"We're looking for a cauldron?" Jarnstenn asked. "Adalstenn's balls, I could have made you a dozen cauldrons without getting out of my chair at home."

"But how many could you make from the same stone as the monoliths, master dwarf?" Ambrose asked. "And how many of them could cheat death?"

"There ain't no cheating death," Jarnstenn replied. "We eat, drink, suffer, get our pleasure where we can, and we die. That's life."

"You don't think that," Kunnustenn said.

"You know I do."

"You know I do not."

"That's why I like you."

"But why do we need it?" Katharine spoke like she hadn't even heard the dwarfs' exchange. "Is one of us going to cheat death?"

Cheat death. Tom met Six's eyes. The elf was thinking it too.

"In a manner of speaking," Ambrose replied.

Tom could feel his cheeks rising and fought his grin down. There was a way out. A way for Katharine and their daughter to survive this.

Six looked like he wanted to smile too. But he forced a frown and said, "So this is what we'll find at Cairnarim?"

"We gave it to Rimestenn," Emyr replied. "It was his duty to hide Orlannu where none of the fay could find it."

"Where?"

"We left that to him. He had the finest knowledge of magic other than Ambrose."

"No," Jarnstenn shook his head. "Rimestenn was no sorcerer."

"He studied the monoliths. He knew the stone. And he'd studied Caledyr too." Emyr nodded to the blade at Tom's hip. "All magic."

"Did he perform magic too?"

Emyr shrugged. "He did impossible things all the time."

"He was a dwarf of reason," Jarnstenn said, jabbing a finger toward them as if skewering the point. "He built engines of reason. None of this magic malarkey. None of it."

"I'm sorry if it upsets you, master dwarf," Emyr said.

Ambrose murmured to himself, "I didn't know Rimestenn could do magic."

"It's what I've been telling you, Jarn," Kunnustenn said. "Magic and reason, they are two sides of a coin. Different roads by which to arrive at the same art."

"Keep your philosophies," Jarnstenn snapped. "Rimestenn was the greatest dwarf who ever lived. Don't drag his name through the mud."

"I'm not," Kunnustenn protested. "Don't you see? Think what engines we could build if we opened our minds. Think what marvels we could create with magic."

"Your stories belong in books. Not out here." Jarnstenn slapped a hand against his chest. "Not in the world."

"They're not stories."

"Yes they are. Fairy stories. And I don't want to hear them anymore."

Kunnustenn's expression closed down. "As you will." He picked up his pack and moved it away from Jarnstenn's, who watched with fury burning in his eyes. Kunnustenn dropped his pack in the first clear space he found and sat with his back to the fire. Neither dwarf said another word.

A moment before the silence thickened into awkwardness, Emyr said, "Everything I do now is to stop the fay." In the mouth of another it would have seemed argumentative. Confrontational. But Emyr made it sound like a rallying cry. "I ask each one of you to have faith. Whether or not you believe, in the fay or in our chances, that matters not. Faith will see us through. I ask for your faith, and I give you mine in return."

Faith wasn't enough. They needed strength, weapons, power. The fay had all of them and more. But Tom didn't dare say it. He didn't dare challenge the old king.

And then Draig said, "Do I give you my faith, Angau."

Six gave Draig a grave nod. "I also give you my faith, Oen."

Katharine reached over to lay a hand on Emyr's and said, "I give you my faith." But she looked at Tom as she said it.

He could save her life.

Each of the others echoed the sentiment. And when Kunnustenn got up, knelt beside Emyr and said, "I give you my faith," it looked like Jarnstenn was about to scream.

There was only the dwarf, Dank, and Tom left. Tom looked at Dank, waiting to see what the boy would do. He was sat on a rock, above the camp, arms folded over his bent knees, hiding half of his face. Staring down at them. And they all watching him.

"We thought we'd tricked you," Dank said to Ambrose. "But you tricked us, didn't you?"

Ambrose didn't say anything. Didn't even look up.

So Dank said, "You wanted to get here. To this time. But you needed to be sealed away, inside the stone. And you didn't know how to do it. So you tricked us into doing it for you."

"What do you mean?" Tom asked.

"The cell, beside the Nimuë's lake," Dank replied. "The fay built it. To trap Ambrose. He kept trying to break into Faerie. We tried to kill him, but he was too strong. We knew he'd get into Faerie one day. So we lured him to the Nimuë. Ensnared him. Sealed him away to weaken and wither. We thought we had won. We saw him like this," he pointed at Ambrose, "and thought he was nothing. But you wanted this, didn't you? This was exactly where you wanted to be."

Ambrose looked at no-one, and there was nothing in his voice when he said, "Of all the places I wanted to be, this was none of them. But, yes, this is how things were meant to be."

The boy shook his head. "All this time Maev and Midhir have been so proud of themselves. Melwas and Mab would make cruel toasts about the lovesick sorcerer. How easy you had been to defeat after all." A slow grin spread across the boy's face. "And you tricked them."

Ambrose treated Dank to eye contact and inclined his head in small agreement.

Dank unfolded himself, hopped down from the rock and crossed the camp until he stood over Ambrose. "No-one ever tricked us."

Ambrose said nothing. Just met his gaze. Dank searched his eyes, as if there was a secret behind them. The camp was silent but for the crack and fizz of the fire. Tom closed his hand around Caledyr's grip. There was a strange, almost maniacal energy about the boy. Tom couldn't be sure what he would do next

Ready, the sword told him.

"No-one ever tricked them," Dank whispered again.

Then he turned and said to Emyr, earnest but casual, "You have my faith." And he clambered up onto his rock again and stared out into the night. He didn't move. Didn't say anything. Was he keeping watch? What was he thinking?

Dank had spoken of himself in the singular.

"Does he now stand with us," Draig murmured, nodding to himself as if everything was as it should be. But all Tom could hear was the implication that Dank hadn't stood with them before.

And Tom couldn't help but think that there was something in a jar that might change Dank's mind again.

Still, it was hard to worry about what Dank may or may not think. Tom's thoughts were filled with Orlannu. A way to cheat death. A way to save Katharine. He passed the rest of the evening with a smile on his face, and when she announced that she was tired, he followed her into their tent, lay next to her and asked, "Have you thought about names?"

It was dark and Katharine was facing away from him, so he couldn't see her expression. But he could hear the surprise in her voice when she said, "Names?"

Tom nodded. "My first thought was naming her after one of our mothers. But now I'm not so sure." He touched Katharine's belly and felt a kick in response. It was always a marvel to feel their daughter kick. As if she was here before she was here.

"I don't want to use my mother's name." She spoke like Tom was a rabbit, easy to spook.

"We're making our own family. We should pick our own name." A dozen possibilities passed through his thoughts, all good names. But they all seemed too small. Somehow none of them seemed capable of encompassing his daughter.

"I like 'Rose'." Katharine's voice was small, quiet, tentative.

"Rose." Tom smiled. He imagined calling out to a little girl playing with sticks in a field. Calling 'Rose' and her running in for dinner. "Rose Delham. I like it." He placed a kiss on the back of Katharine's head and took in a deep breath. Everything was going to be okay.

He drifted off to sleep, and he slept well. And when Draig woke him for his watch, Tom didn't uncover the jar.

CHAPTER 11

THEY FOUND the river halfway through the next day, and it was apparent to all that there would be no following it, and no crossing it.

Gravinn had been less than gracious. "This was a waste of time," she said, both angry and satisfied at the same time.

"Water is worth the time," Katharine replied. But it was clear she was annoyed. She'd wanted to be right.

But their little rivalry seemed unimportant; Orlannu could save Katharine's life. What else mattered? Tom smiled as he brought her a flask of cool water. "Drink," he told her.

"Have you got something a little stronger?" She rolled her eyes at his surprise. "I'm joking. Help me." He lifted her into an almost-sitting position while she drained the cup. "Can I have some more?"

They rested by the riverside for a time. It was cold, but there were green trees that shielded them from the worst of the wind and the sun was out. It felt almost pleasant to sit and take an meal before it was scheduled, a stolen treat. Gravinn unrolled maps and began to explain to Emyr why they had made a mistake and how they could rectify it, and the old king sat and listened and nodded while he chewed his dark bread. Katharine sat apart from the others, and Tom sat with her, hand in hand, just enjoying a quiet moment. But Katharine grew more and more agitated until she pushed herself to her feet and joined Emyr and Gravinn.

By the time Tom caught up, Katharine was angrily pointing up the hill and telling them, "That path will take at least two days longer than this one."

Gravinn scowled. "You don't know that."

"I know my trade," Katharine replied. "I'm reading the land."

"My path keeps us from the worst of the cold. And we save no time by climbing even higher into these mountains."

"We'll save plenty of time because we'll stop doubling back on ourselves," Katharine snapped. "How many times have you lost your way on this journey?"

Gravinn's eyes couldn't have spat more fury. "You are questioning my abilities."

"No. I'm saying your abilities aren't good enough."

Emyr stepped between the two, saying nothing but somehow his mere presence was enough to stall the argument. When it was clear he had their attention, he said, "Gravinn, you showed me some maps. You said you knew our path."

"I do."

"Katharine, what makes you think you know better?"

"Her maps are guesswork here." She waved a dismissive hand at Gravinn's stolen papers and tubes and satchels. "Ask her. She'll tell you that no-one has documented the mountains this far north."

"Is this so?" There was no judgement. Emyr hadn't decided who he believed. He simply asked for the facts.

And he received them. "Yes," Gravinn said. She didn't meet his eye. "But there is enough there to make a reasoned guess."

Emyr nodded. "Katharine, why do you disagree with Gravinn's guess?"

"The mountains are getting higher." She nodded up at a peak before them. "The longer we try to avoid climbing them, the longer this journey will take."

And time was something they didn't have. They were hunted. And this was not the road for a newborn.

Emyr nodded. Then he turned to Ambrose. "What say you, old friend?"

"We enter the mountains." The old man looked tired today. More so than usual. He slouched in the saddle, huddled under his robes, his hat pulled down low. Even his voice, normally so dead and lifeless, sounded old and tired.

But if Emyr noticed his friend's discomfort, he said nothing about it. Only, "We follow Katharine's path."

As they began to mount up, Tom took Katharine to one side. "Ride in the wagon," he told her and, as she began to protest, added, "Gravinn can lead us along the path you chose. And it's safest for the child."

Katharine was unconvinced. "She'll lose her way again."

"If she does, she can ask for your help."

"She hates me, Tom."

"She's jealous," he said. "She wants to be as skillful and respected as you are. And she needs a chance to prove herself. Just as you did when you first chose this craft."

Katharine's gaze lost focus, perhaps remembering her struggle to learn her skills, perhaps thinking of how hard she still had to try to be taken seriously as a Pathfinder. "You're getting too good at this," she murmured.

"At what?"

"Persuading people to do what you want."

It didn't feel like he could get anyone to do what he wanted. At all. But he said, "So you'll ride in the wagon?"

"Today," she said, to suggest it would be an exception. But Mennvinn had said she shouldn't ride a horse, and Tom intended to persuade her into the wagon every day from this point on if he had to. That resolve felt cruel as she planted a kiss on his cheek. But he was looking after her, despite herself.

So he helped her inside, placed blankets beneath her head, covered her against the cold, exchanged a few words with Mennvinn before leaving the two inside.

He was conscious of everyone watching him as he walked over to Gravinn, all of them waiting to see what he did next. He tried not to overthink what he was about to say.

"You know the path Katharine has advised." Not a question. He didn't want to question the dwarf in front of everyone.

Gravinn nodded, waiting for something.

Tom nodded too. "Lead on."

She didn't try to hide her smile, almost leaping onto her horse to ride ahead for an advance look at their route. While the others mounted too, Emyr patted Tom's shoulder. "That was well done," he said.

Tom shrugged. "I didn't do much."

"Precisely." Emyr gave him a broad grin. "It's as much about what you don't do as it is what you do. Remember that, son." The old king gave him a strange look as he clambered onto his mount. "Sometimes the difference between changing the world and damning it is whether you stay your hand."

"I can't imagine Tir is turning on my hand."

But Emyr shook his head with a knowing smile. "The hand that bears Caledyr, resurrects Emyr and Ambrose, and assembles a quest for the glarn?" He flicked the reins and his horse bore him away. "You're a lot more than you think you are, son."

Katharine's path was trickier than they were used to. It twisted and undulated as before, but it rose ever upwards. They struggled to find routes wide enough for the wagon, and they were often forced to move boulders or dismount and push the thing when it got stuck. The horses seemed unfazed by any of the terrain, which was a mercy. But it grew colder. By the time they stopped for the night, the air was freezing and the wind was up. There was no chance of lighting a fire, and the tents flapped and shook so much that Tom half-expected them to leap off the mountain and sail away.

Katharine must have sensed his concern. "Don't worry, we'll be safe." Her tone suggested she wasn't in the mood to discuss it further; she was struggling to lay out her bedroll.

"Can I help?"

"I can do it," she snapped. "Give me some space."

He retreated to the entrance, but that wasn't far enough. So he stepped outside. He'd go back in a few moments, once she'd had a chance to settle and relax. It was a hard road, and it must be even harder for her.

He found Kunnustenn outside too, and the dwarf looked embarrassed to have been spotted. "It seems my sleeping arrangements remain uncertain."

"You're still arguing with Jarnstenn?"

The dwarf let out a sad little laugh. "He is arguing with me," he said. "But yes." He hugged himself against the freezing wind. "It is not easy, when the one you love does not value your work."

"Is that what you're arguing about?"

"Isn't it?"

Tom hadn't thought so. But he knew very little about the pair. "You came because of Caledyr."

"Yes."

"And Jarnstenn came because of you."

"Yes."

Tom shrugged. "He believes in what you have. Does he need to believe in anything else?"

The dwarf said nothing and stared into the growing darkness for a long time. He was struggling with something.

Tom remembered the hunger he had seen when he had asked the dwarf to tell him about Orlannu.

He opened the flap to his tent and said to the darkness within, "I'll take first watch."

"Fine." Katharine sounded tired and irritated.

Tom didn't need to see the sword to find it. He could feel it waiting in the dark. "Call for me if you need anything."

"Fine."

His first thought was to leave her alone. But he thought better of it. He stepped carefully into the tent, picked his way to the source of her voice. Bent awkwardly to place a kiss on her head.

She reached up and placed a hand on his cheek. "I'm sorry," she whispered.

"For what?"

But she didn't say anything else, just curled her fingers in his hair. "Your beard is getting long." She was right. There was enough for her to get a handful of it. "I like it."

He took her hand in his, squeezing it. "Sleep," he told her. "I'll be back soon."

The light was almost gone when he emerged, the wind still high, the faint stars blotted by dark clouds in the north. "I don't like the look of that," he said to himself.

"Do you think it's a storm?" Kunnustenn was still stood

outside, now staring at the wagon but making no move to get inside.

"Maybe." Tom glanced about and spotted a hollow in the mountain that offered a good view whilst providing shelter from the wind. "If you're not ready for sleep, I'm always ready to learn more about the glarn."

"From me?"

"Of course."

Kunnustenn nodded and followed Tom up the mountainside, squeezing into the alcove alongside him. It was a tight fit for two, but perhaps warmer for it. "What do you want to know?" the dwarf asked.

"Whatever you can tell me."

Kunnustenn's sigh was almost lost to the wind. "Where to begin?"

With Orlannu, Tom wanted to say. Tell me how it will save Katharine. How it will save my daughter.

But he was here for Kunnustenn. So he said, "Begin wherever you would like to."

"Very well." Kunnustenn cleared his throat, and when he spoke again his voice was a little deeper, a little slower and clearer. His speaking voice. Tom didn't get the feeling it was deliberate. More like a habit formed long ago that he now had little occasion to lean on. "Caledyr's first name was Ymellith." So he wanted to talk about the sword. That was fine. Tom could turn the conversation to Orlannu soon enough. "An old children's story tells that it was forged by the giant Taneto, who dwarfs know as the Smith Before Time, thousands of years before the time of King Taranau, who you call Emyr. That same story also tells that Taneto forged another sword, Hemyleth."

Hemyleth. Emylt. The sister sword borne by Melwas. The sword that gutted Emyr.

"The swords were used in a great war against the invaders, but alas the giants fell and created the land."

"The invaders?" Tom asked.

"The first people." Kunnustenn spoke as if it was plain and carried on. "The children's story ends there. There is mention in *Eystenn's Codex* of two bronze blades displayed by the Drowned Cities in the south. And, of course, we know that Uran bore two bronze swords in his war on the dead."

Tom shook his head. Did everyone know about this Uran except him? "The man who made the monoliths."

The stars shone just brightly enough that Tom could make out the dwarf's frown. "I haven't read that."

"Emyr told me."

"Interesting." But from his tone, it was plain the dwarf didn't believe it. "The swords go separate ways after that. Various lords and leaders claim to bear one or the other, but *Jokuvinn's Incomplete Bestiary of Tir* has an unusual passage in her entry on the fish folk that claims Caledyr, at least, returned to their lands until their queen was kidnapped, along with the sword as well."

Kidnapped. Nimuë. "When did that happen?"

"Not long before King Taranau took the throne."

"The fay. It had to be."

Tom hadn't realised he'd spoken aloud until Kunnustenn replied, "Dead-bane."

"What do you mean?"

"That is the translation of the sword's first name. The name that Malvis sought to purge from mortal memory." The dwarf was quoting something. "No thing did the Black Knight fear save the name of the weapon borne by King Taranu."

"Why?"

"I suppose because it tells you their secret. And a secret known is a weakness shared."

Tom could feel thoughts and words and memories coming

together in his mind, pieces of a puzzle he had never tried to solve. He tried to push it away, but the sword pushed it back at him.

Dead-bane, it told him.

Nothing can die in Faerie. When you walk in Faerie, you see glimpses in the corner of your eye of friends and family long gone. Nothing can die in Faerie. They are made of magic. Magic uses up part of yourself. Everything living must die. "The fay are dead."

"The dead become the fay," Kunnustenn corrected. "Or so *Gellvinn's Memories of a Time in an Undead Realm* would have us believe."

"The dead become the fay." It didn't make sense, yet he believed it. It was true. Well, of course it was. If he could say it, it was true.

"You seem troubled?"

Tom nodded. "I need to speak to Ambrose." He needed answers. He could feel the world around him tipping. The foundations he'd thought unchangeable stone were instead mist and fog. He pushed himself to his feet, clutching Caledyr to his chest. Anchor me, he told the sword. Keep me here.

Ready.

Somehow that made things worse, the sword's quiet patience clashing against the unsteady sensation of slipping beneath these terrible thoughts. He scrambled down the mountainside, staggered to Emyr's tent and pulled the flap aside.

"Ambrose," he said. He was out of breath. He took a gasping gulp of freezing air. Tried to hold onto the sensation of the stinging breath in his chest. "The fay. The fay are the dead."

"Of course." Ambrose's voice came out of the dark, ominous and lacking in comfort.

"You knew."

"At one time."

"My king?" Tom asked. Did Emyr know too?

Emyr grunted, stirred and took a deep breath. "What's the matter?"

"This is the moment Tom learns the nature of the fay." There was no movement from Ambrose's side of the tent. Tom expected he wasn't even blinking. "It is a difficult time for him now."

"Ah." Emyr shifted in the dark. "Yes. It's a difficult thing to come to terms with."

"My king?" He knew. Why hadn't he said anything?

"To know that the energies of those you miss and mourn have become part of the fay. That your loved ones fuel the forces arrayed against you." There was a very great sigh in the dark. "There is a part of my Eirwen somewhere in the fay. Amyr. Ganed and Cei and Lyr. And when I die, I'll become part of them too."

Dizziness twisted Tom to drop to his backside, cold wind tossing the tent flap against his head. Elaine. Degor. They were fay now? No. The fay were unreal creatures. Woodkin and brownies, not dead people.

Except the Cauld Lad was a drowned boy, wasn't he?

Was there a fay that looked and sounded like Siomi? "Are you saying we become fay when we die?"

"No." There was no comfort in Ambrose's voice. "It is all energy. You pulled the fire from the twig. When we die, the fay pull the elements from our bodies. Just as the fire used the twig for fuel, so do the fay use our bodies."

"They feed off us."

"If the analogy helps you."

The fay ate the dead. So they had consumed Siomi. Elaine and Degor.

"It's not like eating a pig," Emyr added. "They consume the

soul, and all that comes with it. Your memories, your knowledge, your heart. They know everything the dead knew."

Tom felt naked, exposed. "They know what the dead know."

"Yes."

The fay were the dead. The fay ate the dead. The dead became the fay.

He had lain with a dead thing.

He felt bile rise in his throat at the memory of the things he had done with Maev. It was like he had done them with a corpse.

Fight.

That was the wrong thought at the wrong time. Tom struggled to his feet, dropped the sword. He wanted no more of it. He had been lied to, deceived. Played for a fool. And it was plain to see, now that he knew. Nothing lived forever. So the fay weren't alive. Obvious, really. He almost laughed as he staggered across the camp.

The tent was warm and so was Katharine. She woke as he pulled back her furs, and if she was surprised by his advances, she quickly became rougher than he did.

When they were spent, she pulled the furs over them and held him as he fell into a dreamless sleep.

If anyone noticed that Emyr rode with Caledyr the next morning, they said nothing. The old king had risen with even more vigour and purpose than ever, giving orders and almost leaping onto his horse. He made no attempt to hide the sword at his hip, and Tom made no attempt to take it back. He had been too busy talking to Katharine, words pouring out his mouth seemingly of their own volition. He'd talked about Rose, where she would be born, he knew Katharine wanted to continue her work as a Pathfinder but shouldn't they stay in one place at least for a little while, maybe one of the cities, she could sell maps, he could find some work, they could make a home, just for a time.

In the end Katharine took him by the shoulders and told him, quite forcefully, that she was happy he was so excited, but that listening to him was exhausting. Then Six had helped her climb into the wagon. Her absence opened a space in his mind, a space which unpleasant thoughts could invade and occupy, a space that couldn't be filled by the tasks of breaking camp.

So he wasn't sure whether to be pleased or dismayed when Emyr asked to ride with him. Conversation would distract Tom from his thoughts, but he was sure Emyr would want to talk about the fay.

He was right.

"It's a hard thing to learn, son," Emyr said. "It took me many years to come to terms with it."

Tom tried to think instead of his life to come, of Katharine and Rose.

"Maev changed when Eirwen died." The old man dropped a hand to Caledyr's pommel. An old habit, one he didn't seem to notice. "Maev tried to seduce me once, when I was still king. Her efforts felt clumsy compared to Eirwen's. My lady had a dark glance and a smile that could suggest worlds. But, after she died, Maev seemed to have learned her art. She looked at me, and smiled with my lady's smile, and my breath quickened the way only Eirwen could quicken it."

Tom felt his stomach tighten. It had been Maev's smile that had ensnared him. A smile stolen from a dead woman.

"They used to say Eirwen bewitched me." Emyr had a fond smile on his face. "Perhaps she did. I always felt I loved her more than she loved me."

"Many of the stories say that Eirwen was devoted to you," Tom said, to make Emyr feel better.

"I know what the stories say about her," Emyr said, the cheer now gone from his voice. "They say that she lay with one of my knights."

Tom didn't want to ask if it was true. So he said, "An Easterner once told me that story was only in the mind of Sir Picell. That he saw Eirwen, imagined a great epic romance between them, and loved her so much he died of it there and then." Siomi's eyes had smiled when she told the story, like it was a balm to hear even if she didn't believe it.

"I didn't knight anyone called Picell."

"So she wasn't unfaithful?"

"Oh, she was unfaithful." Emyr was grinning again, staring into the distance. "Did I never tell you how she came to wear the Tanatei?"

The necklace of the dwarfs, an exquisite piece of jewellery charmed to protect the wearer from magic. "You didn't. But I've heard the story. Is it true?"

"Oh yes."

Tom frowned. If his wife had lain with four dwarfs for a necklace, he wouldn't be grinning about it. "You don't seem to mind."

Emyr bowed his head a moment, his grin growing soft, wistful. "Son, they called me a warrior and a king. But that woman had a fiercer heart than anyone I have ever known." He patted Caledyr like a faithful hound. "I had my weapon. She had hers."

Weapon. Tom felt uncomfortable thinking about it like that. "She used her body to get what she wanted."

The old king lifted his head and frowned. "Is that so different from using a sword?"

The carrot and the stick. Maev and Melwas. The dead played games with the living. "No."

Emyr's brow softened and so did his tone as he said, "Our loved ones become weapons to use against us," he said. "The fay learn our weaknesses. Learn the tricks they need to make us do what they want. It's what makes them so dangerous."

"You could have told me."

Emyr nodded, looked down at his hands. "Would you have listened?"

"All I could do in Faerie was listen," Tom pointed out. He'd had no voice with which to argue.

"But perhaps you wouldn't hear." Emyr fiddled with his reins. "I'm not a fool, Tom. I know why you came back to Faerie."

Tom felt his cheeks redden and a flush despite the cold wind. He looked away, stared at the horizon as if he'd spotted something interesting. But there were only mountains and dark clouds.

Emyr cleared his throat. "Still. Now you know."

"Now I know." He knew he'd been seduced by Eirwen's smile. What else had Maev stolen from the dead? Did pieces of Elaine and Degor look out from behind her eyes? "How?" he managed. "How do they do it?"

"I don't know."

The plod of the horse beneath him, the weight of the packs, the soft sounds of conversation, the creak of the wagon. Everything seemed so small and fragile and mortal. Now the fay had the strength of the dead behind them.

What had happened to Siomi?

"You spent your reign looking for these glarn," Tom said.

"I did."

"You found two."

"Yes."

"The same two we're looking for now."

"You're wondering what has changed. If we couldn't succeed

with a kingdom and nineteen years behind us, what hope do we have now?"

"Exactly."

"We have things we didn't have then." Emyr raised his chin to the people behind them. "Ambrose. Dank. A thousand years of advances. You."

"Me." Tom looked at the clouds again. They were moving fast. He tugged his fur tighter at the throat. Bad weather was on the way. "I don't know what help I can offer."

"You once said you would call me a friend."

Because Emyr had asked him to. And Tom could still feel the pride and responsibility the request had given him. But now they seemed emptier. As if the dark pebble inside him had somehow drawn the colour from them. Just a little. But enough to make Tom grimace.

"I need a friend, Tom," Emyr said. "Mine is lost to me. I am alone amongst strangers."

It was easy to forget that. Emyr always seemed so at ease with everyone, as if he had known them for years. But he had known them for a matter of weeks. He relied on Tom to know them on his behalf. And even though it felt like another responsibility, another burden to bear on top of burdens, Tom said, "I would be honoured to serve as your friend."

"I don't want you to serve," Emyr growled.

And Tom couldn't help but smile. "My king."

"I've changed my mind. You'd make a terrible friend."

"If my king says so."

"A king can take off your head."

"That would make the horse's load lighter."

Emyr roared with laughter, and if it seemed he laughed a little too hard, Tom didn't say anything. With so little to laugh about, the old king could be forgiven for making it count. His laughter ended as pain pinched the corner of his eyes and he put a hand to his gut. “Do you ever look back on your life and wonder how you got to this moment?”

“Often.”

Emyr just nodded. “We’re a long way from where we want to be.”

Where they wanted to be. Tom turned in the saddle, stared back at the wagon and imagined what life would have been like if he’d run away with Katharine.

The wagon blurred and faded, and Tom saw it overturned and burning in the dark.

The mountains echoed with a screech. A cry. Someone was crying.

A woman’s voice said, “Sir Beduir knew that movement clears all paths and unlocks all doors.”

The present returned with a gust of cold wind that made Tom shiver.

“Tom?” Emyr had hold of his arm. Perhaps he had swayed in the saddle.

“The air.” It was thicker. He felt a sudden surge of energy, as if he’d been half-asleep for weeks. Magic. He shook his head, disgusted by the sudden alertness that rushed through him.

“I feel it too.” Of course. Emyr has spent centuries in Faerie. He would know what magic felt like.

“Is it the fay?” Tom couldn’t face them. Not when he knew what they were, and what he had done.

“I don’t know.” Emyr had Caledyr in his hand. “Draw your sword, son.”

Tom reached for an iron blade at his waist, but his hand was stayed by a voice that seemed to bellow from the mountains themselves. “Blades down!”

It wasn’t hard to find the source of the voice. He was stood atop a ridge, no more than a tall, slender shadow with the sun behind him. “Dismount,” he told them.

"Who are you?" Emyr called up to him, gamely refusing to squint at the bright sun.

"Worry more about them." The shadow's gesture pointed out two archers with bows drawn. "Dismount," he said for the second time. His tone suggested there would not be a third.

The archers were in good positions. If they were any good, they could take down anyone who tried to flee. And the wagon was just too slow. Katharine wouldn't escape. So there was no choice but to do as the shadow said.

"We won't make it," Emyr muttered.

"I agree," Tom murmured.

As if that had decided things, Emyr nodded and sheathed Caledyr. "Do as he says," he told the others, but waited until Tom had dismounted before making his own, awkward climb down. The old king hissed as his foot got caught in the stirrup, and his face was screwed up in agony until Tom freed him. He leant heavily on Tom, panting, and Tom took the moment of stillness to watch and try to learn who it was that stopped them.

Not fay. That much was immediately clear. Figures emerged from behind that first shadow and there was something in the way they picked their way down the mountainside that betrayed their mortal origins. As they descended, Tom could see more of them. Two humans, one Easterner. All three dressed in furs and rags, armed with nothing but obvious speed and strength. The archers didn't descend; they kept their bowstrings taut and their arrows aimed at their victims. Whoever these people were, they weren't fools. They wouldn't be easily outwitted, or easily outrun.

The three reached them, and the woman took charge. "Away from the horses," she told them. "Over there, all of you." She had a trace of an accent from the Marches and wore her hair in a traditional braid. She had jewellery on her fingers, at odds with the tattered rags glimpsed beneath the thick wolf fur draped over her shoulders.

"We have people in the wagon," Tom told her. "One of them is with child."

"Speak when I ask you to speak," the woman snapped, but she immediately turned to one of her fellows and said, "Get her out. Carefully."

Tom took some small comfort from that command. If they were to be simply killed for their goods, these bandits would not waste any care on them. So they would be kept alive for at least a short while. And, Tom noticed, no-one made an attempt to disarm them. Either they were supremely confident, or perhaps they weren't as smart as he had first thought. Perhaps if they waited long enough, there'd be a chance to turn the tables.

If Jarnstenn didn't get them killed. "Get your hands off me, you filthy purse-snatcher," he was growling. "Think we're scared of a bleedin' bow and arrow?"

"Hush, Jarnstenn," Tom bade him.

"I'll hush this elf if he touches me again." Jarnstenn waved clenched fists at the Easterner, who looked down at him, bemused.

"Peace, master dwarf," Emyr bade him. He had his hands out at his side, open, unthreatening, and asked the elf, "Do you mean us harm?"

The elf shrugged. It was the woman who answered. "If it were up to me, I'd have shot you all already." She jerked her chin towards the shadow, which hadn't moved. "But it isn't up to me. So do as I tell you, and you won't be harmed."

So. No sympathy there. But someone had given her orders, and she would follow them. That, at least, some small reassurance. "See, Jarnstenn?" Emyr said. "Nothing to worry about."

"Did you hit your head?" Jarnstenn waved a hand at the wagon. "They're robbing us."

"So it seems."

"We outnumber them."

"There might be more archers in these hills."

"Listen to your leader, dwarf," the woman said. "He's wiser than he looks."

"Ain't no-one leads me but me," Jarnstenn grumbled. But he said no more.

One of the men who had followed the woman down the hillside brought Katharine and Mennvinn from the wagon. "Plenty in here," he reported. "We'd better take the whole thing with us."

The woman nodded. "Fine. You drive it." And to Emyr she said, "Your people will follow the wagon. On foot. But for every horse we lose, we'll shoot one of you." Her eyes were as hard as her voice, and the lack of flesh on her face suggested that horse meat was far more valuable than the lives of their captives. Emyr gave a stern nod. A moment later, the wagon began to roll again, and the others began to walk.

"Are you going to be okay?" Tom asked as he slipped his hand into Katharine's.

"I think that's up to them now," she replied as they fell in and followed the strangers to a destination unknown.

Their path meandered around peaks and valleys long after the sun had set, and the clouds meant there was little light from moon or star to illuminate their way. That was why, before they set eyes on their destination, they saw it all the same: the glow of light between two peaks. The stink of magic in the air had grown stronger all day, but it grew thicker as they approached and, as they passed between the peaks, Tom felt almost as if he had dived into an ocean of it.

It was like someone had taken a handful of Faerie and cupped it in mountainous hands. High, snowy peaks on all sides descended into an oasis of warmth and water, a lake surrounded by a halo of mud, in turn surrounded by verdant grass and bushes and even the occasional tree. There were no structures, huts, or homes. Just open fires, and dozens of people sat around them. None of them wore furs, for the air was warm like midsummer.

It was just like Nimuë's place. Was this a Faerie trap after all?

But while the others had marvelled at this impossibility and exchanged awed exclamations, Katharine had been beyond exhausted. She took small, faltering, painful steps, and she was slower even than Ambrose in descending.

Their abductors were clearly anxious to get out of the cold, but one remained behind to escort Katharine and Tom; the shadowy man who commanded the others. Tall, wiry, his bronze skin bare despite the cold, he called himself Tree and offered his help. But Tom was too angry to accept help from a man who would make a woman with child march through the snow, so he said nothing to him. Tree had shrugged and walked beside them in companionable silence, as if they were all old friends on a gentle stroll together. Tom felt a furious urge to push Tree down the hillside, but instead gritted his teeth and let Katharine lean on him as much as she needed to.

There was a crowd ready to greet them when they finally reached the bottom. Human, elf and dwarf crowded around the wagon and the horses, crying out and asking countless questions of Tree and his people. But they were interested only in the spoils of war; their captives were pushed to one side, where Tom found a space for Katharine to lie. Without the wagon or horses, they had no bedrolls for her comfort, nor food or water. But she was happy to lie on her side in the grass, and waved away Tom's efforts to look after her. So he sat beside her, and watched Tree address the throng of people.

"For once we have plenty," he told them. "So let us take plenty of time to savour it." He selected a few to empty the wagon and sort the goods, then said to the woman, "Oversee the work, Hawne, or select someone to do it for you as you see fit. I'll take these to see her."

"I'll come too," Hawne replied, surly and daring the man to argue.

The man shrugged, apparently indifferent. "As you will." He turned to Emyr. "Bring your people. We'll see what the princess makes of you."

The others began to follow the man, but Tom didn't move. "Katharine needs to rest."

Tree looked at her and his eyes softened. "Yes." He inclined his head and said, "I will bring the princess to you." He left without another word, leaving the woman, Hawne, standing awkwardly with them.

"What is this place?" Emyr asked her.

She debated whether to answer for a moment before gruffly saying, "We call it Tirend."

It meant nothing to Tom, but Emyr nodded gravely. "I see."

"You're robbing us," Jarnstenn growled at her as he watched wagon being unloaded.

"If you're asking for an apology, dwarf, save your breath." Hawne lifted her chin, highlighting how much she looked down on him. "We have mouths to feed."

"Yeah? And what about our mouths?"

"You'll get food." But for the first time there was a flicker of doubt in Hawne's eyes, and she looked out across the oasis, up towards the fire that was twice the size of all the others.

"The scraps?" Emyr's voice was soft, compassionate. "Once those at the big fire have enjoyed the choice cuts?"

Hawne shook her head, but she wasn't disagreeing. She said nothing, which said everything.

But then she straightened and her expression settled into a stony mask. Tom followed her gaze and saw Tree returning with a woman by his side. No, it was a Western elf. She wore a curious mix of rags and riches, though even her rags spoke of a finer material. But even without the paint and pomp of royalty, there was no mistaking the obvious air of grace and authority she carried. That, and the resemblance to her father.

Esyllt. The lost princess of the Western Kingdom. Daughter of King Idris. And the reason for the West's war on the rest of Tir.

She gave them a warm smile. "Welcome to Tirend."

CHAPTER 12

"WHAT OF MY DAUGHTER?" King Idris had asked. And Dank had replied, "She lives. In the north. Far from here." Tom had promised Idris he would send any word of her. But he had never imagined they would find her.

And now they stood before her, in this of all places, and Tom was angry. Yes, it was the fay who had seduced her away from her kingdom. But it was Esyllt's feet that had done the walking, and it was her absence that had been the lever the fay could use to move Idris to declare his war. If she had stayed, perhaps Neirin wouldn't have sought Thomas Rymour to find a magic sword. Perhaps Tom's hands would have been clean, instead of bathed in blood. Perhaps the dragons wouldn't have been enslaved.

But that wasn't true, was it? Melwas himself had said that he would have found another mortal to manipulate if Tom had refused. If Esyllt had stayed, the fay would have found another to spark the war.

So Tom pushed aside his anger, and said, "Your Highness." He bowed, and the others followed suit, except for Emyr who simply echoed his greeting. But Six pushed past them all without ceremony or decorum. “What are you doing here?” he asked.

Her eyes grew wide and she lifted a hand to her mouth. “Yemdarro.”

Yemdarro? Tom frowned. He’d always known that Six wasn’t the elf’s true name. But he’d never given any real thought to what it might be.

“Esyllt,” he said, and rushed to kneel at her feet.

Tree moved to step between the elfs, but she waved him away. “It’s fine. This is a very dear friend of mine from Before.”

Before what? Before Six was exiled?

“I never thought I would see you again,” Esyllt murmured, placing a hand on Six’s head. He took a deep, satisfied breath. As if that small gesture had lifted a burden he’d carried for many years.

“I feared for you.” His voice was little more than a murmur.

“As I feared for you.” She lifted her head and her voice. “But we can discuss the journeys that brought us here in due course. First, who are these companions of yours?”

Six rose and swept to a position at her side, hands behind his back, stooped ever so slightly so that his words better reached her ear. It was the position of a loyal advisor, and it was a position assumed out of habit. What was Six to this princess? “My lady, I have travelled with some of these people for many moons now. Though you may marvel to hear their names, I can vouch for them.”

Esyllt wore a polite smile, but there was a genuine pleasure in her eyes. “I cannot wait to meet the people who have brought you back to me.”

“Katharine Delham, my lady, a Pathfinder of extraordinary ability.”

Esyllt smiled and exclaimed, “And with child, how wonderful.”

Tom wondered if anyone else noticed Six's smile dim as he said, "And the father, Thomas Rymour."

"A name we know from stories," Esyllt said.

"Likely exaggerated, Your Highness." Tom smiled and bowed again.

Six pointed out the others. "Draig, a warrior of principle. Dank, a man of the Faerie realm. Jarnstenn, a smith from Cairnakor, and his partner Kunnustenn, a dwarf of learning. Gravinn is a Pathfinder too, and Mennvinn is a healer of great skill." Six paused, before saying, "You will think me deluded or dreaming, Your Highness, but the truth of these last two is beyond reproach."

"You have never before lied to me, Yemdarro."

Six nodded, took a breath, and said, "Your Highness, I present King Oen of Tir, and his loyal servant, Ambrose."

Whoever had taught Esyllt had taught her well; although her demeanour slipped, her eyes widening for the briefest moment, she gathered herself quickly. Collected once more, she quirked a single eyebrow and tilted her head towards Six, inviting further explanation.

"We but recently retrieved Oen from the Faerie realm, Your Highness, and Mennvinn has been nursing him to health from the wound that felled him at Camlann. Ambrose has used mighty magics to preserve himself, and joined our party when we brought Oen back to Tir."

Tree snorted. "This is nonsense, Your Highness," he rumbled.

"Yemdarro was a member of my father's court," Esyllt said, though Tom could hear that she was unconvinced by Six's claims. "I trust him."

"Do you believe him?"

She took a breath, taking a moment before admitting, "It is quite a claim."

"Princess Esyllt." Emyr stepped forward, his bow made stiff and awkward by his healing gut. "Who I am is almost irrelevant at this moment."

"On the contrary," Tree replied. "Who you are determines what we do with you."

"Everyone here is lost, Tree, which is why we welcome everyone." Esyllt's tone suggested the matter was settled.

"We can't feed the mouths we have," Hawne argued, adding after a long moment, "Princess." Said to mock Esyllt, not honour her. Tom watched Hawne, the way she stood, the way she lifted her chin in a challenge to the princess. She had a definite air of someone used to authority. Maybe even nobility. Was there a hidden contest between her and Esyllt at play? Did Hawne see herself as more fit to rule this place?

But Tree shrugged, folded his arms and said, "As you will, Your Highness." Emphasising the term of address for Hawne's benefit. And when Hawne dropped her gaze, Esyllt said, "All are welcome here."

"And what is this place?" Emyr asked. "And how did you come to be here?"

It was Tree that responded. "We have been brought here from all across Tir," he said. "And if you are going to ask me why, well, there are as many ideas about that as there are stars in the night sky."

Tom looked up. Though the sky had been unfamiliar for many nights now, tonight he couldn't see a single constellation that matched what he knew. He had an idea as to where they were.

"Brought here?" Emyr asked.

Esyllt nodded. "Taken. Tree was snatched from his home in Tanabawr. Hawne went to sleep in her hall in the Marches and woke up here."

"And you?" Six asked. He leant closer, lifted a hand as if he might touch her elbow then thought better of it. "How did you come to be here, Esyllt?"

She painted a smile onto her face that didn't touch her eyes. "I fear I made a very silly mistake. I allowed myself to be fooled, and in doing so I brought myself here."

"None of you travelled by foot or horseback, did you?" Tom asked.

"No," Hawne replied. "We were brought here in an instant."

Tom nodded. Faerie Circles. The fay had snatched these people and brought them here. But why?

"Your father has been distraught since you left," Six said to Esyllt. "He is searching all of Tir for you."

The princess' lip quivered for just a moment, before her forced smile grew even wider. "Tell me he is well, Yemdarro, please. It would do me good."

Six glanced at Tom with a question in his eyes and Tom nodded. "Your Highness, we had no idea that Yemdarro was so known to you." It felt odd to use that name. "Perhaps you would like some time alone?"

Esyllt nodded. "You are most kind." Her eyes were wet as she said, "Tree, find our new friends a place. See that they are fed."

"From our own supplies," Jarnstenn grumbled as the two Westerners turned and walked away. Did their heads lean a little closer than was proper? Esyllt certainly thought of Six as more than another subject.

But if Esyllt was in charge of these people, and Six had her ear, perhaps he could encourage her to return the wagon. And their supplies. Tom turned to see if Katharine was warm enough, but she was sound asleep.

"You say you were all taken," Emyr said to Tree. "Has anyone tried to make the journey back?"

"Back?" Tree had his arms folded, frowning down at them as if they were a puzzle to solve. "There is nothing beyond this place. Plenty of the young and foolish try to leave. They return, or their bodies are discovered by the next fools to try."

Tom looked at the crowds around the wagon. These people had no idea in which direction to travel, and what few supplies they could gather wouldn't last the long road to Cairnoher. With so little, it was no surprise they couldn't escape this place. The fay had very neatly imprisoned them all. But why?

"We could help you," Tom found himself saying. "We could offer you some supplies, enough for the journey. We can draw you a map. We could help you go home."

He'd expected surprise, suspicion, a joyous grin, hope, anything. But Tree was entirely unmoved. He was so still that Tom began to wonder if he had, in fact, spoken at all.

It was Hawne who said, "Home?" With layers of suspicion to hide her curiosity.

Tom turned to her and said, "We travelled here from Tir with two Pathfinders. We could show you the path we took."

Hawne's eyes shone with desire and Tom could see her mind's eye picturing her return to whatever place she called home. Her lips quirked into the beginnings of a smile, and Tom could see that, despite her brusque attitude, she would be an ally here. They would help her and she would help them.

"Hawne." Tree's voice was low, soft, and all the more threatening for it. "See to the distribution of the food."

"Didn't you hear them, Tree?" Now she did smile, a brilliant smile that transformed her sharp, angry face. "They can show us the way home."

"I won't repeat myself."

The smile faded, and the angry young woman returned. "And I won't be given orders by a money counter."

"We are no longer what we were," he chided her. "Prince and pauper are all one here. Now." He bent at the waist, arms still folded, bringing his face down to her level. It was an oddly intimidating gesture, designed to highlight his height over her. "Go."

She stared right back at him for a moment. Then something in her resolve seemed to crack, and through the crack shone a flicker of realisation and sorrow and loss. Her shoulders slumped and she walked away with the trudge of someone who has lost everything and knew there was no getting it back. Tom brushed a finger against Katharine's hand and she stirred but didn't wake.

"And you, Thomas Rymour, should be careful who you say such things to." Tree had straightened, looming over Tom as if his height was more intimidating than dragons and fay.

Emyr placed himself between Tom and Tree, equally undaunted by the other man's height. He placed a hand on Caledyr's pommel and said, "You will speak courteously to my people."

But Tree just snorted. "Will I indeed?"

Emyr said nothing, his answer lying in his planted feet and his ready sword arm. It gave Tom a thrill to see Emyr, King Emyr of Tir, stood before a foe and defending his people. It was what Tom had been waiting to see since they'd rescued the old king from Faerie.

Tree took a breath, let it out through his nose. Like an animal. It was so deliberate a gesture that it was almost comical. "Tell your people not to excite mine. You don't know how much better you have it here."

Better? Was he serious? The people here lived like beasts, without a roof over their heads, scratching for scraps. They were eking out an existence, not a life. "Your people?" Emyr nodded towards Esyllt. "Do you rule here?"

"Royalty?" Tree's lips quirked. "They don't always have the clearest heads." He placed his hands on his hips, displaying himself and his strength. "We are all better off here. In time, you might come to agree with me. If," he added, "nothing happens to you."

"I won't let you keep us here," Emyr told him. "We deserve to be free. As do the people living here."

Tree smiled. "You set yourself in opposition to me?" There was both amusement and danger in that rumbling question.

But if Emyr recognised the threat, he didn't acknowledge it. Just said, "These people deserve to go home."

Tree was fast. One moment he was nodding. The next, he threw a cracking blow to the side of Emyr's head that sent the old king to the ground and Tom was shocked, frozen, aghast that someone would dare strike Emyr, then he surged to his feet, but there were others, a sudden mob of humans, elfs and dwarfs ready to fight for Tree and Emyr was shouting, "No, stay back, stop," even as Tree lifted him by the belt, no, he was taking the sword, stop him, retrieve the sword, but Draig was holding Tom back, no, let me go, let me go.

Tree dropped Emyr back to the ground and held Caledyr across his shoulders. "You are in my place now," Tree told them. "You do as I say. Or you will suffer."

Emyr was on his hands and knees, head bowed, holding up a hand to stay Tom and the others. But Tree couldn't be permitted to strike Emyr, and he couldn't be allowed to take the sword. Retrieve the sword. Retrieve it. Tom struggled against Draig's grip, but the elf was too strong. And Tree just smiled, laughing at Tom's weakness, at his own ability to knock down a king and steal a sword. "I'll kill you," Tom growled.

But Tree just shrugged, as if such threats were commonplace. "Make yourselves a fire," he said. "Eat what you are given. Do not give me cause to hurt you again, and you will be happy." Then he turned his back, without concern or fear of retribution, and walked away.

The others lit a fire, presumably for comfort as the air was already warm. Tom didn't help. He was filled with a restless rage, pacing between Katharine and Emyr and failing to offer comfort to either.

Tree had struck Emyr and taken the sword. As if he was king. As if he deserved it.

Retrieve the sword. His hands twitched at the thought of taking it from Tree right now.

Emyr hadn't moved, still on his hands and knees, but Mennvinn waved him towards the little fire. "I need him sitting," she said.

"I might vomit." Emyr looked pale and unsteady.

"Then face away from me."

Tom helped Emyr crawl over to a rock and sit, and the old king let his head hang between his knees. He let out a low groan as Mennvinn parted his hair and examined his scalp. "A nasty gash," she proclaimed, pulling needle and thread from her set of tools. "No more than that."

"Did you see his hand?" Kunnustenn said.

"Is it hurt?" Tom demanded, snatching at Emyr's hands.

"He means Tree's hand," Mennvinn replied. "He broke his knuckles."

"Needs a one-way ticket to the madhouse, that one," Jarnstenn said.

Mennvinn patted Emyr's back. "Don't sleep," she told him. "Not yet."

Emyr didn't move, just nodded. His hands were trembling. Tom felt sick to see him like this. To know he hadn't done anything to stop it. He spoke his thought aloud: "We outnumber him."

"He's right," Jarnstenn growled. "We could have had him."

"No," said Emyr.

Tom couldn't help himself. "No?"

Emyr pointed a shaking finger up to the largest fire. "Look," he told them. "We could not have won that way. You saw the crowd ready to back Tree. And we are few that can fight. Plenty of us have neither the training nor the bodies for combat."

"So he gets away with it?" Tom growled. He knelt beside Emyr, searching his face for a secret, a plan. How could he give up so easily?

But he hadn't. "No," he said, clear and angry and ready for a fight. He opened his eyes and met Tom's glare with a fire of his own. "Six has Esyllt's ear. Hawne knows we can show everyone here the way back."

"So we wait until everyone else comes to us?" Gravinn nodded. "They won't follow him when they know the way home."

"They'll follow him." But Emyr held Tom's gaze as he spoke. Pointed again and said, "Look."

Tom followed the old king's finger, taking in fire after fire and the people who sat around them. "Do you see it, son?" Emyr asked him.

Tom saw it. The big fire wasn't in the centre of the clearing. It was at the far end. Those who sat around it, and around the fires nearest, were young and strong. They strutted, confident of their place in things. But as the fires grew farther away from the head, the people around them grew older, or weaker, or bore the bruises and the limps of a fight gone badly.

"It's a hierarchy," Tom muttered. "Based on strength. Tree rules this place because he fought his way to the top. And anyone who depends on Tree for their own position will support him. Otherwise they'll end up here." He looked at their tiny fire. "At the bottom of the pile."

"So someone has to best Tree?" Katharine asked.

There was a surprising ferocity in Emyr's voice as he corrected her. "Someone has to beat him."

"Who?"

The old king simply reached up and clapped Tom on the shoulder.

Tom wanted to. His limbs twitched with the urge to beat Tree, to take back the sword. But, "Draig is the better fighter."

"Is he?"

"He bested me in Cairnagwyn."

"Ah." Emyr nodded. "Which is why the dragons aren't free."

"That's different."

"No, it isn't." Emyr lifted his head and took a steadying breath. Blood was drying in his greying hair. "Winning a fight only means achieving the goal you set out with." It sounded like he was quoting someone, and he smiled a wistful smile.

Tom shook his head. I can't fight him, he wanted to say. But he couldn't. Because he knew he could fight Tree. He just couldn't win. "He has Caledyr."

"He'll find it less of an advantage than you might think." Emyr's smile grew broader. "Trust me."

"So what do we do about that?" Jarnstenn waved towards the wagon, which the people of Tirend were unloading, handing out blankets and food and weapons.

Emyr watched for a moment. "We can't stop them until Tom has beaten Tree," he mused.

"He's in no shape to beat anyone," Jarnstenn replied.

"Could I train him," Draig suggested.

"They'll have eaten everything by the time he's ready."

Tom ignored the insult. A far more frightening thought had

occurred to him. "And I don't think it's safe for us here." He turned to Dank and added, "Am I right?"

The boy just nodded. "We shouldn't stay."

"Why not?" Katharine asked, dread running through her words.

"It's linked to Faerie, isn't it?" Tom asked. He peered at the boy, and saw he was right. "A part of Faerie that sits within Tir. Like Nimuë's place."

It was Ambrose who said, "Just so," with a bitterness that surprised Tom. Did the old sorcerer regret coming here? Or leaving his merrow gaoler? "While we are here, the fay know where we are."

Dank was hiding his fear well. But Tom could see it in his eyes all the same. "They could come for us at any time," the boy said.

As if this journey hadn't been difficult enough. "Then we need to leave now." Tom pushed himself to his feet, trying to fuel himself with the rage he'd felt moments ago. But it was sapped and weakened by fear. "Draig, you're the best fighter; you'll have to fight Tree." But that wasn't enough; the fay could snatch Katharine away in a heartbeat. "I'll speak to the fay and convince them to leave us be."

"How will you do that?" Katharine's voice was heavy with reproach.

"I'll point out how interesting it will be to watch us try to escape." Entertainment. It was the weak point of any fay.

"They'll only come for us after we leave," Gravinn pointed out.

She was right. They all knew she was. But what else could they do? "We'll deal with that if it happens," was all he could say. It was an answer that made no-one happy. But there were no easy answers here. No simple paths.

Katharine touched his arm, squeezed it. "I don't want you to talk to them," she said. Barely more than a murmur, as if she didn't want the others to hear.

But they did. "Could I talk to them," Draig said. "They owe me a boon."

Yes. They could use Draig's boon to demand their safety from a Faerie attack. In fact, why not extort from them an oath to leave Tir forever?

Because a Faerie boon was a sword with two edges. But no blade could seriously harm a fay save Caledyr, whereas a mortal cut was a mortal wounded. "A boon is a dangerous thing," Tom said. "We should only use it if we have no other choice."

The others seemed unconvinced. But Tom knew he was right. They had so few weapons to use against the fay. There was no sense in wasting one when there was an alternative available.

"You should fight Tree, Tom," Emyr said, voice low and encouraging.

Why? Because he saw in Tom the same potential he'd seen in his son? "I'm not Amyr," Tom replied. "I won't see my friends hurt for putting their faith in the wrong person."

The words came out harder than he'd intended. But it was true. Amyr had made poor choices. And Emyr was making one too, if he thought Tom was the man for this task. It was for the legendary king to battle the evil. Not a simple man like Thomas Rymour. So Tom let his words hang in the air and began walking towards the wagon. Tried not to feel the eyes on his back. The disappointment he'd seen in them. Well, let Emyr be disappointed. He needed to realise that Thomas Rymour wasn't a great warrior or a respected leader. He was just Tom. All that mattered to him was keeping Katharine alive.

"They look to you." Dank had followed him, unnoticed until he spoke. The boy was thoughtful, but there was an air of anticipation about him, too.

"I don't know why," Tom replied.

"Neither do we." Dank didn't seem to realise that his words were offensive, and Tom couldn't help but smile. "But you make difficult choices. And you fight for those choices."

What was it Six had said? When was the last time you took the hard road? "Not everyone would agree with you."

Dank shrugged. "It's easy to agree with me. I don't make any choices."

But that wasn't true; Tom could see that Dank was building to a decision, finding the courage to speak its name. So Tom said nothing and let silence pull the words from Dank.

"You're going to talk to my sprite."

There was an unspoken question beneath Dank's words, and Tom wasn't surprised by it. "I'm not sure it's a good idea for you to see it." Tom picked his words carefully. Despite travelling together for months, there was so much he didn't know about Dank. How would he react to this refusal?

But, although the boy seemed to have turned his back on the fay, it was harder to pry free talons that had been so long embedded in your heart; too often, they remained ready to squeeze when you least expected it.

Perhaps he shouldn't be talking to the sprite either.

But Dank nodded. "I'm not sure, either." He caught Tom's eye and added, "Will you tell her that I miss her?" And, as Tom was wondering if that wasn't also a bad idea, he added, "You understand."

It felt like Dank saw him all too well in that moment, and Tom felt naked and raw under his gaze. He opened his mouth to speak, to say anything that would send the boy away, but what?

And before he could decide, Hawne was stood in their path. "The wagon is ours," she told them. "You'll be given a share."

Tom ignored the spark of anger that wrapped itself around his chest. "We just want a jar."

"And I want to go home." Her expression was hard. But Tom

thought he could see hope buried beneath the mask. "We don't always get what we want."

"I want to see everyone here returned to their homes," he told her. "But Tree has threatened us."

Hawne searched his face for signs of deception. He might have been taller than her, but she seemed to look down on him. Definitely nobility of some kind. "Tree isn't easily bridled." Her tone said she spoke from experience.

"So I gathered," Tom replied. "He doesn't seem to respect Esyllt."

"Or anyone else." Hawne cast a glance about her, as if concerned about eavesdroppers. "Esyllt is nothing more than a figurehead. Tree ruled this place with fist and fear before she arrived. He rules that way still." Her jaw grew tight and her eyes hard as she spoke. "He's nothing but a minter from Tanabawr. He pours metal into moulds to make coins." She rubbed her fingers together with disdain. "But here, he is a king. He won't leave, or allow anyone else to. He'd rather sit on a throne of our rotting limbs than see us prosper without him."

There was righteous anger in her words, and it was clear Hawne thought she should be ruling this place. Not Tree. Not Esyllt. But perhaps her ambition could be ally enough to earn their freedom. "Would you stand with us against Tree?" Tom asked, voice low.

Her lips quirked into a cruel smile and she nodded towards the others. "You think you'll fare better a second time?"

Tom couldn't help but glance back at Emyr, visibly beaten if not grievously injured. "Not me," he said. "I'm no warrior."

Hawne tipped her head. "You have the bearing of one."

"Perhaps it was you that hit your head."

"I saw you astride your horse. You ride tall and ready. And you have the stride of a man ready to fight."

Fight. It was an echo of Caledyr's mantra, a memory of it in his mind. "I have had to fight," he admitted. "More than I'd like."

Her expression warmed, as if he'd passed some kind of test. "Such is the refrain of every true warrior." She gestured to the wagon. "Find your jar and some food for your friends."

Tom nodded. "And will you stand with us?"

"Do you need me to?"

The twilight faded, and Tom saw an old woman behind bars and wreathed in shadows. It was almost too dark to see the tattoo on her wrinkled cheek, a line swirling in an ever-decreasing circle. "Only a fool spurns an ally," she said.

The foresight faded and Hawne was watching him with a slight frown, waiting her response.

"Only a fool spurns an ally," Tom parroted, but in his mind he still saw the old woman. He recognised her from Cairnalyr. She'd been amongst those they'd freed from the rat pits.

"Then you shall have one in me," Hawne said, and he was almost too distracted to smile and nod, and too slow to shy away when her hand darted out and snatched at his wrist. He barely had the wit to clasp her wrist too before she released him and waved him away. "Find your jar," she said, then raised her voice for the benefit of others and added, "Just don't bother me again."

People were clambering all over the wagon, talking about using it for firewood or making tents from the canvas. Tom and Dank had to push past those helping themselves to weapons, food, and Jarnstenn's beer. But the jar was just where Tom had left it, tucked amongst crates that hadn't been reached yet. Tom slipped some food to Dank and sent him back to the others, then slipped away amongst the few remaining trees and pulled the rags free of the jar.

The sprite was cowering from the touch of the stone he'd put in there with it. It wouldn't even look at him. "I just want to talk," Tom said. "Please." He turned the jar around and around, but the sprite turned again and again to keep its back to him. What did that mean? It was angry, upset, hurt? Did that mean the fay would come or not? “Just tell me if we’re in danger.”

He jumped as a voice murmured in his ear, “More than you know.”

One hand grasped for a sword that wasn’t there, the other stretched out to keep the intruder at bay as he stepped away and turned, gaining space and finding his footing.

Glastyn stood there with a grin on his face. The fay had come for them already.

CHAPTER 13

Glastyn. Tall, beautiful, his dark hair bound back into a simple tail, making his pointed ears more prominent, Glastyn was certainly the fairer counterpart to Fenoderee. But while Fenoderee had been foul of appearance, he had been an ally; Melwas and Mab had unmade him for telling Tom their secrets. Now, Tom supposed, Calmae had come and gone, and Fenoderee was changed to Glastyn once again. And he was here. Now. Why?

"The girl was right." Glastyn's grin grew even wider. "You at least have the feet of a warrior."

"What are you doing here?" Tom asked.

The fay had taken to dancing, graceful steps that both mimicked and mocked Tom's footwork. "We have the grace of a warrior, but no spirit for the violence." He stopped, lifting an arm and awaiting adulation. "Still, we did a fair turn as good Sir Robert, did we not?"

The distraction that had enabled Tom to escape Duke Regent and join Neirin's quest for Faerie in the first place. "A good turn indeed." Slowly, the shock and the fear was seeping from Tom's muscles; Glastyn was no assassin, and nothing about the fay's manner suggested violence. "I asked you why you are here."

"You didn't." Glastyn grinned, still holding his turned hand aloft as if receiving silent applause from the bushes. "To be exact, you asked what we were doing here. Right now, we are wondering how it is we have received so little thanks for our help in setting you free."

"I don't feel very free."

"We imagine not." Glastyn lowered his arm and abruptly folded himself into a seated position on the damp grass, hugging his knees to his chin. "We had not thought to see you a father-to-be."

The abrupt change of subject was nothing new for Glastyn, and habit made Tom go along with it. "Nor had I," he said. "But I am glad of it."

"You are, aren't you?" Glastyn grinned, wide and genuine. "We can't wait to see what a little Tom looks like."

If his foresight didn't come to pass. If Glastyn could be trusted. Here they were, talking like friends. But were they? Fenoderee had suggested that Glastyn was naive to the games Maev played. But what if Fenoderee was wrong? "Why are you here, Glastyn?"

The fay heard the suspicion in those words; it was clear by the way the joy left his eyes and left him sombre, serious. So unlike himself. "You spoke to the sprite. You wanted to know if we were going to come for you and your friends, like thieves in the night."

"I did."

Glastyn wagged a finger at him, as if Tom was a naughty child. "You have done a thing not done since the days of your resurrected king, Tom." Just like that, he was grinning and fey again. "Melwas and Mab are at war with each other. Our king would see you in Faerie, dismembered, burned, torn and beaten, reassembled and then tortured all over again. He is nothing but rage and hurt and confusion."

So. They had succeeded. Melwas was without Thought, and so was without thought.

"And our queen is just as eager to get her hands on you. But for a different reason." Glastyn waggled his eyebrows. "Never have we heard her speak with such admiration or ardour."

Tom cursed his body for quickening, for warming, for letting his imagination wander. "So they will come?" he asked. "Our concern is only who reaches us first?"

"That *was* your concern." Glastyn opened his arms. "But we spoke to them. We told Mab that you should have to fight your way to her. To prove yourself. And to Melwas, we turned his attention to his own healing. Suggested he should punish you with his own hands. Better to part your flesh himself, feel your bones break in his own grip. Better to take you when Thought returns."

Tom couldn't say he cared for the imagery. But it seemed like Glastyn had stayed their execution. "You spoke on our behalf?"

Glastyn's smile was small and pained. "We are feckless, Tom, 'tis true. But, for our part, we always considered you a friend."

He was waiting for Tom to say the same. So Tom nodded and said what he could. "I thought you a friend, too."

Glastyn heard the past tense. "We understand." He nodded. "We hate how these events have sundered you from us. But we understand why. Our king and queen were cruel to treat you so."

"Is that why you spoke for me?"

"Partly." Glastyn shrugged. "They swore to leave you be, Tom, but only if you fight the one named Tree."

Always a condition. Always a price to pay. "Why?" he asked, but he already knew the answer.

"They want to see if you can win."

Entertainment. Why snatch them now, when they could be entertained first?

"If I win," Tom said, "will they let us leave?"

Glastyn nodded. "They will. But this amnesty will not last."

Tom had known it was the case. But the knowledge settled heavy on his shoulders. "Will you stand with us?"

Glastyn shook his head. "As we said, Tom, we are no warrior." He rose with a grace that suggested he could be, if he so chose. "Fight Tree, and no fay will stop you leaving this place."

Ally or not, Glastyn had helped them. Kept Katharine and their child safe a little longer. "Thank you."

Glastyn's smile failed to wipe the sadness from his eyes. "We would have been her favourite uncle, wouldn't we?"

Impossible to say, and impossible to hesitate without hurting him. And upsetting a potential ally. So Tom simply smiled.

Glastyn faded like smoke dissipating into a gentle breeze, and Tom stood alone.

"So we do what the fay tell us to," Katharine said. "Again." She was sat beside Emyr, who was the only one who looked pleased by Tom's news.

But Tom spoke only to Katharine when he said, "I don't like it either. But I'll do whatever it takes to keep you safe."

His words didn't do much to mollify her. And they didn't stop Jarnstenn from asking, "And what do we do when you lose?"

"Jarn," Kunnustenn chided. But spoiled it by adding, "He

might win," in a tone that could be used to suggest that trees might talk and Emyr's knights might rise again.

It didn't matter. Only Katharine mattered. Tom took her hands, held them. But what could he say? I'll be fine? He can't separate me from you? Comforting lies, but lies all the same. So he said the only thing he could. "I fight for our daughter. And for you."

It sounded weak to his ears, a simple statement of fact with no reassurance. But, somehow, it was what Katharine built her resolve upon, and she nodded, matching his stare with hers. "I believe in you," she said, and Tom felt his own resolve grow strong. He would beat this little tyrant. For her. For Rose. So they could be safe.

"Were I a betting dwarf, and I am," Jarnstenn interrupted, "I would place my coin on the elf." He nodded to Draig.

Tom drew a breath and said, "So would I." It wasn't what they expected to hear. But it was the truth. "But if Draig fights, the fay come. It is as it must be." He turned to Draig. "But if you have any advice for me, I'm listening."

Draig wore a strange smile on his face, and somehow it reminded Tom of their journey through Tir, with Siomi and Neirin and Brega. Before any treachery or mistrust, when Draig taught Tom the basics of swordplay. "Are Tree's knuckles broken," Draig told him. "Will he favour the other hand. Remember you the weak points of a man." He pointed them out, the nose, behind the ear, the neck, beneath the ribs. "Has he hurt us before without reprisal. Will he be arrogant. Strike fast and hard."

Far easier to say than to do. For a moment Tom considered delaying. This wasn't the dark place in which Katharine died; she would live as long as they were here. But Glastyn had told him that Melwas and Mab wouldn't wait forever. Better to make the most of their temporary stay of execution.

So they all strode towards the head of Tirend's little community, drawing glances and murmurs. When Hawne caught Tom's eye, she nodded and began to whisper in people's ears, causing even greater excitement. Tom wasn't sure what she was telling them, but it was causing a lot of agitation. Perhaps some of them would help in the fight. Or perhaps they were just excited to see Tree beat down his latest opponent.

Tree was sat at the main fire, feeding himself some of the biscuits from the wagon. He didn't rise, barely spared them a glance as they approached. It was Esyllt and Six that watched them with concern and confusion.

"We're leaving," Tom announced. He managed to keep his voice steady. "We have a journey to finish."

Tree gave him a lazy, indifferent look. "I told you, there is no leaving Tirend." But he waved a hand without waiting for argument. "Go, and good luck to you. If any of you die in the cold, there will be fewer mouths to feed."

It wasn't the answer Tom had expected. Would there be no fight? Could they just leave? "We will be taking our supplies."

Tree shook his head. "You have no supplies. But the people of Tirend now have food and blankets."

"Our food. Our blankets."

There it was. The dangerous look that Tom had expected. "Which have been shared amongst those who needed them." Tree broke off a piece of biscuit and placed it in his mouth, chewing it slowly, deliberately. Challenging Tom to challenge him.

Well. There was no sense in delaying it. "We will, of course, donate some of our supplies, as well as maps, so that everyone here can make their own journey home."

Tree's eyes blazed but, before he could say anything, Esyllt rose to her feet. "Pardon me for interrupting. Are you suggesting you would be willing to show us the way home?"

"Of course, Your Highness." Tom bowed his head, deeply enough to show respect, shallow enough not to lose sight of Tree. "I can only imagine how much everyone here would like to escape this place."

There was a riot of emotions on the princess' face. But her words remained regal and stoic. "We would be in your debt."

"He's lying, princess," Tree growled. "There is no way back to Tir." Six murmured something in Esyllt's ear, earning another growl from Tree. "Speak up, damn you!"

Six's eyes flared but he said nothing. It was Esyllt who said, "He was telling me that they travelled from a dwarfish village. On horseback."

"Lies."

"Yemdarro has never lied to me."

"He brings you a man, calls him King Emyr, and you think him honest and true?" Tree shook his head.

The question brought doubt to her eyes and she glanced, just for a moment, at the exile's tattoo on Six's face.

It was Hawne who spoke next. "We were all brought here with only the clothes on our backs." She was stood a distance from the fire, but with a crowd behind her. "But we found them travelling out there with plenty. Why?"

Tree had spotted the crowd too, could see the challenge ahead of him. "Why were any of us chosen?" He rose, stretched, showing off his muscle and his strength. He caught Tom's eye as he did.

"I can tell you why you were chosen," Tom said. He pitched his voice to be heard across the whole clearing. "You were sent here because you somehow posed a threat to the fay. But distanced, lost, and unable to find your way home, you could not help to stop the fay from fusing Tir and Faerie into a single playground, putting an end to our way of life. You represented resistance. Alliance. Your Highness, the care you show for these people demonstrates your dedication to everyone in Tir. And Hawne's strong spirit would never have yielded to Faerie dominion."

"And I, soothsayer?" Tree grinned. "What did I represent?"

Tom smiled too. "A way to keep them all here."

Tree rested his hands on his hips. "It's a remarkable story."

"A true story," Six said. "Tom cannot lie."

"Then perhaps he can tell us why we should go back." Tree was pitching his voice to be heard, too. "If things are as bad as he says, perhaps we are all better off here."

Murmured assent rippled through the crowd. Tom hadn't expected that. He looked about, saw people nodding to each other. His eyes landed on Kunnustenn, and he realised he might have made a mistake. Not everyone here was royalty or nobility. Some of them might have been living in alleys, or earning coin barely sufficient to put food on the table. But here, where there was no coin, no rich or poor, perhaps they had a better life. Perhaps Tom was wrong to try to send them back to Tir, where the fay were already breaking through the barrier between realms and making sport of the mortals they found.

But they had the right to choose that for themselves.

"The fay are dangerous," he admitted. "And difficult to fight. But if you think you are safe here, you are mistaken. They will come for you, sooner or later. If you are forced to defend yourself, where do you take your stand? Do you fight for the prison they gave you, or do you fight for the home they took you from?"

The murmurs weren't as loud or as certain. But they were there. Yes. Let them choose. If they wanted to stay, so be it.

"Tom is right." Esyllt stepped forward. "All those who wish to remain may do so. But I am Esyllt of the Western Kingdom. That is my home."

Hawne stepped forward too. "I am Hawne Swiftrider of the

Marches." Swiftrider. The duke's daughter. That explained much. "That is my home."

There was a moment of silence as people waited to see what the rest of the crowd would do. If no-one else spoke, then this was over. Even if Tom could beat Tree in a fight, he couldn't fight all of them. But then a dwarf stepped out of the ranks, and said, "I am Kaervinn of the Provinces. That is my home."

"I am Samuel of the Heel. That is my home."

One by one, they stepped forward, emboldened by each other, calling out their names and their homes. Until Tree shook his head and barked, "Enough!" He stared at all who had stepped forward and sneered. "You think the world waiting for you is better than this one?" He gestured. "Is the weather so temperate? Is the living so easy? Here we hunt for our flesh and grow our own fruits. We have no concerns for coin or gossip. We have no betters. We *are* better."

Tom stayed silent. This wasn't a moment for outside voices to be heard.

It was Hawne who replied. "Perhaps there is plenty up here, at the big fire. But down there?" She pointed to the smallest, weakest fires, around which sat those too old or weak to join the crowd. "The people down there scrape for scraps."

"Only the strongest survive," Tree replied. "It is the natural way of things."

"I stand against nature." Esyllt lifted her chin ever so slightly for a quiet air of defiance. "It is our duty to make life better for everyone."

"And weaken us all in the doing."

Six murmured something in Esyllt's ear and she nodded. "You may feel so," she said, defiance gone, replaced with a sad certainty. "But it is our will that everyone is cared for. I have always trusted you, Tree, to see to the distribution of food and resources. If it is as Hawne says, that some lack while others do not, then that is something that you have overseen. And it is something that cannot continue."

Tree grinned. It shocked Esyllt, to see her reprimand dismissed so readily. "It is as it has always been here," he said. "It cannot be changed."

"I will change it."

"You change nothing."

Six's eyes blazed. "You will not speak to Her Highness Princess Esyllt so."

"I will speak to her however I please!" Tree roared, pounding a fist against his chest. "She is no princess here. She has only the standing that we allow her. I am the first among us here. Me!"

"Be silent!" Six demanded, stepping past Esyllt. Hands behind his back. Like a good courtier, not someone ready to fight. Tom held his breath. Six hadn't seen how swiftly Tree had knocked Emyr down.

But Tree didn't strike Six. Just grinned at him. The two were of a height, but somehow the man seemed to loom over the elf. "By strength and will did I put myself here, at the head of these people." Tree opened his arms, fingers flexed like claws, muscles and tendons standing out all over him. "Do you have the strength and will to challenge me?"

Six remained calm. Kept his courtier's demeanour. But it was obvious he had finally realised that he wasn't at court. This place was more feral, more violent. Tree had made it that way. So it was time to undo Tree.

"I do." Tom put no bravado into his words, no drama or excitement. Keep it plain, keep it simple. "I challenge you."

The bigger man turned, his grin even wider. "You?"

"People of Tirend!" Emyr's bellow caught everyone by surprise, and they watched the old king stride out to stand before the crowd, arms aloft. His injury apparently forgotten, the old king spoke with an energy and an excitement Tom had never seen in him. "Thomas Rymour hereby challenges Tree. Thomas Rymour, who travelled through the Whispering Woods and lived to tell the tale. Who escaped the dungeons of Cairnalyr and the prisons of the heartless merrow. Who freed dwarfs, freed dragons, and ended the war with the Western Kingdom. Who bearded the King of Faerie in his own den." Tom could feel his face warming at this effusive praise, this bizarre litany of deeds that made him sound like a hero rather than a man caught in a series of strange circumstances. "Thomas Rymour, the liberator, the bearder of kings, the prophet who cannot lie. The champion of Tir challenges Tree of Tirend."

Emyr held the moment, and a strange silence descended on them all. The crowd began to shift. Whisper to each other. Tom could see that they weren't impressed. He was no-one to them. Those deeds meant nothing to them.

Emyr lowered his arms and stepped back to his place amongst the others, making no attempt to hide his smile. He winked at Tom as he passed, looking terribly pleased with himself. What he had achieved, Tom couldn't tell. Tree seemed only bemused.

But Tom knew he had to be the one to break the silence. So he said, "I challenge you, Tree. These people deserve to be free."

"They are free." Tree began to stalk towards Tom.

"No-one is free under a tyrant."

"No-one can be free without someone to tell them what's best for them." Tree was close now, and Tom saw he already placed his feet as if expecting to dodge a blow. Or land one. No formality to this fight, then. Tree would strike whenever he saw fit.

"Is this a debate, or a challenge?"

Tree answered by swinging a fist at Tom's head. But Tom was ready, ducking and dancing to the side. Tree nodded. "Good. You learn from your leader's mistakes."

Tom didn't feel like he had learnt anything. It felt like he was back in Cairnagwyn again. Facing a much bigger, more skillful opponent. Picking a fight he couldn't win. Except he didn't have Caledyr to help him.

Fight.

The thought was distant and unclear. Like a murmur that wasn't directed at him.

Tree lunged and Tom stepped away.

Fight.

Another lunge.

Fight.

Another. And Tom began to see that Tree's lunges were clumsy, unbalanced. As if he wasn't ready for his own attacks.

Kick.

The blow caught Tom in the chest and sent him staggering. But Tree was off-balance too. Tom rushed forward, trying to press an advantage.

Swing.

Tom almost failed to duck the blow, and it left his charge blunted, weak. He collided with Tree but failed to bring him to the ground. Great arms wrapped around Tom, crushing him to the other man's chest, trapping his arms, lifting him from his feet, which flailed and kicked but had no effect. Tree tightened his grip, crushing Tom, forcing the air from his lungs, he'd lost already.

Headbutt.

Tom obeyed without thought, rearing back his head. But Tree had clearly come to the same idea, and Tom had just enough time to duck before Tree's face came hurtling at him, crashing into the top of his skull. Tom fell, dazed, staggering to keep his balance. It took him long moments to realise he was standing, free, and that Tree was staggering too, clutching his face, blood streaming from it. His nose. Tree had broken his nose.

Charge.

Tree was running before the thought was finished, a stumbling, unready rush. Tom dropped to the ground and rolled into the other man's feet, sending him sprawling. Tom didn't need the sword to tell him what to do: press the advantage. He was on the other man's back in a moment, landing blows to the kidneys, wrapping his fingers in Tree's hair, slamming his bleeding face into the ground.

"Yield," Tom demanded.

But Tree wasn't listening, jabbing at Tom with his elbows. So Tom threw a blow to the point Draig had mentioned, just behind the ear. It stunned Tree, but he kept moving, so Tom hit it again.

Tree roared in pain, surged to his feet before Tom could react, sending him spilling to the ground. The other man whirled, and there was an almost silent hiss as he drew Caledyr and pointed it at Tom's throat.

The fight was over.

Tree's face was smeared with blood and mud, his hair matted across his features but failing to obscure his burning, furious gaze. His breath came heavy and snorting, like an animal. He seemed little more than a beast, and Tom almost expected the other man to fall upon him with teeth and claws. Why hadn't he landed the final blow?

Hold hold hold hold hold hold.

It was the sword. Telling, not Tom, but Tree to stay his hand. Issuing a barrage of thoughts to override the man's own.

But it was a tactic that wouldn't work for long.

So Tom kicked. It wasn't an artful blow, but it caught Tree's wrist, knocked aside the blade just long enough for Tom to roll away and scramble to his feet. He was alive. But he had no weapon. And Caledyr couldn't make Tree surrender.

Chop.

Tree swung the blade in a massive arc over his head, Tom stepped aside.

Swing.

Another huge arc, taking too long and giving Tom time to jump away.

Stab.

Tree was overreached but obeyed nonetheless, an ineffective jab that gave Tom plenty of room to step within his reach. A reach that couldn't crush him while it held a blade. Giving Tom a chance to jab at Tree's bleeding nose, cartilage and bone crunching beneath his fists, Tree staggered, Tom landed a blow to the ribs, two blows, one to the neck. "Yield, damn you," Tom panted, but the other man refused to go down. Tom was running out of ideas.

Steal.

Ah. Of course. Tree held Caledyr with just one hand, the other blindly flailing to ward off Tom's attacks. It wasn't difficult to snatch Tree's arm and drive his fist into the other man's wrist once, twice, Tree's other hand scrabbled for a hold in Tom's hair, a third blow and Tom had the sword, once again he wielded the blade, and he pulled himself free from Tree's grip, hair tearing from his scalp but it didn't matter, he had the sword.

"Yield, Tree." He pointed the sword at the other man's chest. "I don't want to kill you."

"Kill me?" Was it a question? A request? The eyes that stared out at him were wounded, hurt, angry but frightened. Tree's face was already beginning to swell under the muck that covered it. "You think I will yield, take my place amongst these cattle? A calf to suck at another's teat? I am an aurochs, Rymour. I am the wild beast that cannot be tamed."

He was right. He wouldn't be tamed. He would heal and raise another challenge. Esyllt and Hawne would never get these people home if Tree was with them.

Cripple. Kill.

No. Tom shook his head. Tree did not deserve to die. And no-one deserved to be permanently wounded.

Tree stumbled at him, waving his fists wildly, driving Tom back, back again. The man was tenacious. It was impossible not to respect that. That kind of tenacity would be needed to fight the fay. "I am not your enemy," Tom told him, retreating from the other man's swings. "The fay threaten everything. You could help us stop them."

But Tree just spat blood and snarled. "I will eat your cursed bones."

Tom felt the heat of the fire at his back; Tree meant to drive him into it. Tom flicked his wrist, opened a cut in the other man's flesh, blood dribbling down his chest. When it didn't stop him, Tom opened up another cut, and another. When that didn't work, he sliced the man's thigh, dropping him to his knees.

"Enough," Tom told him. Tree's head was bowed, his breath ragged and hard, his body shaking. The fight was over. He just didn't know it. "They won't follow you anymore."

Tree lifted his head, staring at the crowd with one eye. They gazed back at him in awe, devouring the sight of his broken body as if it was a fine meal. "Cattle," Tree muttered.

Beware.

But Tom didn't need the sword to warn him. He fully expected Tree's ugly stumble to his feet, had already stepped aside from his clumsy charge, and was well clear when Tree slipped and fell into the fire.

Tree didn't scream. He roared. In defiance of the flames, of pain, of existence itself. He tried to stand, slipped and fell amongst the wood, the bone, the debris that burned. His hair flicked with merry flame, his flesh and clothes danced in the heat. The fire collapsed under his weight and he tumbled free. Voices called for water and blankets. But Tom glanced at Mennvinn and saw in the tiny shake of her head what he knew in his heart: it was over. Tree might have healed from his wounds. He might have healed from those burns. But both?

"I'm sorry," he said. And he was. He drove Caledyr into the man's chest and held it there as the life fled from his limbs. Pulled it free and stepped away from the burning corpse. Tree had been a petty little tyrant. But he hadn't deserved that. "You have done wrong in this life, Tree. As have we all. I take your wrongs and bear them on my shoulders. Enter the West in innocence and goodness. Go in peace." He had no offering to make to the body, no chunk of bread to eat. But he knew where Tree would go now. He would go to Faerie. "The father and the prayers, and fasting and charities, and calmness of the soul until death."

What would become of Tree? Perhaps he'd become part of Herne, or Melwas. Tom didn't like the idea of either of those fay taking on Tree's stubborn refusal to yield. Perhaps they would be lucky, and Tree would simply be consumed. But that was no end to any life. No end at all.

The crowd began to mutter, watching him wide-eyed. "He grieves." Voices called him bearder of kings. Prophet. Liberator. So. That was what Emyr had been doing. Building a legend so that, when that legend bent his knee to Esyllt, their admiration would pass to her.

Always a task to do. Never his own life to live. His steps felt heavy as he crossed the space between Tree's body and the princess. He didn't meet her eye. Just knelt on one knee, and lifted the sword. "Princess Esyllt, daughter of King Idris of the Western Kingdom." He had to make her a pledge, but he couldn't promise her anything. His sword, his loyalty. What could he say?

"If I may?" Tom lifted his head to see Emyr approach Esyllt and, at her nod, murmur something in her ear. She was visibly shaken, her eyes drifting to Tree's body. Perhaps she had never seen something so horrific. But when Emyr was done, she nodded, straightened, and settled a mask of regal calm over her features.

She took the sword, and Tom hated how his fingers twitched to snatch it back. "For your services to the people of Tirend, and to all the people of Tir, I hereby bestow upon you the honour of knight." She laid the blade on one shoulder. "Such an honour has not been bestowed in many a decade," she said. Forgetting the knights of the Heel? Or ignoring them? "But I find you worthy of such a burden: to fight for what is good in this world." She lifted the blade and placed it on the other shoulder. "To protect those who need protecting."

"I am King Emyr of Tir." Somehow Emyr didn't snatch the moment from Esyllt, but simply added his voice in support of hers. "Long separated from my realm, now returned to it by this man's hand. What Princess Esyllt here grants, so shall I uphold."

"I name you Sir Thomas of Tir," Esyllt said. "Rise, Sir Thomas."

Was it the rush of energy following the fight that made his limbs tremble? Or was it this strange occurrence, that he was named a Knight of Tir? No. He rose and bowed to Esyllt, then to Emyr. This was for show. For the crowd, so they would see how he bowed to Esyllt and how he allowed her to grant him honours. Nevertheless, when he saw how proud Emyr looked, he couldn't help but smile. The same potential as his son, the old king had said.

Someone coughed, and Tom realised everyone was waiting for him to say something. He tried to conjure something suitably solemn. "Your Highness, I am almost without words." He touched a hand to his chest. "I swear to you, I will bear this duty, and uphold what is right and good in this world." And though he knew this was just a performance, that he was no true Knight of Tir, he felt a moment of weight and resolve that would accompany such a title.

Esyllt smiled and turned the sword, presenting the pommel to him. "I know you will make us all proud, Sir Thomas."

Tom took and the sword and, in a heady moment of ceremony, turned to the people of Tirend and lifted the blade above his head. "Your Princess!" he cried.

The crowd cheered.

CHAPTER 14

IT SEEMED like days before Tom could sit down again. He shook hands and listened to stories and allowed nearly everyone to have their moment, to tell him how they'd been rooting for him, how much they admired him. Stories were spreading and growing, it seemed, until one boy asked him how he alone had stormed the fortress of Cairnagwyn all by himself.

The boy was enjoying the tale so much, Tom didn't have the heart to disillusion him. But he did tell him, "No-one is alone. I travel with very good friends."

Tom suspected it fell on deaf ears. But, it seemed, someone was listening. "And where is it you travel to, Sir Thomas?" Once the crowds had grown tired of him, and rushed instead to ready themselves for the journey home, only Hawne was left. "You were travelling north when we found you. What are you looking for in the Northern Wastes?"

"An artefact." All Tom wanted to do was lie down and sleep. Instead he placed a hand on Caledyr, now strapped to his hip again. He would need to give it back to Emyr. Right now he leant on it for strength. "An ancient tool that will help us stop the fay."

Hawne's expression darkened. "The things that brought us here."

Tom nodded. "They plan to invade Tir and turn it into their playground."

"Good." Hawne offered him a grim smile. "I'd like the chance to run a few spears through them."

"It wouldn't do you much good." Tom patted Caledyr. "Only this sword can truly hurt them. And, hopefully, the hidden artefact we seek."

"Hidden? Where?"

"We're not sure."

Hawne looked unconvinced, and her gaze fell on the sword. Tom could guess her thoughts: if the fay were coming to Tir, why leave the only thing that could hurt them with someone who might die on a fool's quest? He tensed, ready to fight for it. But Hawne said, "Plenty of us tried to find our way home." She lifted her gaze away from the sword. "Few returned. But those that came back from the north told stories of a split in the mountains. Full of terrible voices. They called it the Doubtful Chasm."

An appropriately dramatic name. "What was at the end of it?"

She shook her head and looked aside. "No-one ever reached the end." She looked like she was remembering something. Had she heard these voices herself? "If I was going to hide something, I'd put it at the end of a chasm that everyone was too scared to traverse."

She was right. "Is it far from here?"

She gave him a grim smile, devoid of humour. "I'll show you."

Hawne led Tom out of Tirend on horseback, up the mountainside, out of the eternal twilight and back into the freezing winds and the perpetual gloom of the mountains. Emyr's bones, it was cold. A few days in temperate weather and Tom had forgotten how cold it was out here.

"There." Hawne pointed. "That peak that looks like a knife. There's a pass that leads into a clearing, and a narrow path up the hill. That's where the Chasm starts."

It didn't look far, maybe a day's ride. Not that he was a good judge of distance. But he could see where they needed to go.

"Prepare yourself," Hawne said, and tugged her fur around her in a manner that suggested it was nothing to do with the cold. "The Chasm can make even the sternest Windrider turn back."

"Did you try to travel it?" he asked.

"I did." She grimaced as if she had swallowed something bitter. "You seem to accept hardships without flinching, Sir Tom. I admire that. But the Chasm might be too much even for you."

Part of Tom doubted that voices could be more terrible than dragons and fay. But Hawne did not seem like a woman who was easily cowed. "I flinch more than you suspect," he told her. But he had no choice but to go. "I do what needs to be done."

Hawne nodded and took a deep breath, squaring her shoulders and forcing a smile. "I shall tell my father about everything that happened here."

Tom wasn't sure what to say to that. "Please give my best to Duke Swiftrider."

"I'm sure he'll be grateful to see me safely returned." Though she didn't seem too certain herself. "And, if you wanted to go back to the Heel once you've found your artefact, I'm sure he would plead your case to Duke Regent."

Duke Regent, to whom he'd sworn his service and abandoned in order to help Neirin find Faerie. "Plead my case?"

She nodded. "You'd escaped him months before I found myself here, but Regent was still furious." She gave him a wry smile. "If you stood on his doorstep today, you'd be in his dungeons tomorrow."

Well. It was to be expected. Regent didn't easily forget a slight. It was partly why the Heel and the Eastern Angles had been, ostensibly, at war for decades. "Perhaps I should avoid the Heel if I return to Tir."

"And anywhere that seeks to curry Regent's favour," she added. "Or wants leverage over him."

"That could describe most of Tir."

"It could. Which is why I shall talk to my father." She reached out and clasped his wrist, squeezed it when he clasped hers in return. "Thank you."

"Thank *you*."

She shook her head, with wet eyes and an embarrassed smile. "I may see the Marches yet, because of you."

"I can't take all the credit."

A wistful smile took over her face. "Modesty tamed no horse," she told him.

Tom wasn't sure he agreed. But crunching snow announced a visitor and Hawne withdrew, wiping at her eyes and muttering about things to do. She flicked her reins and passed their visitor as she rode back. Huddled against the wind, hunched under so many furs that he almost disappeared under his wide-brimmed hat, Ambrose looked like he would collapse in the saddle.

"What are you doing here?" Tom asked him.

"What I must," the old man muttered. "Working my way down the list."

Tom wanted to sigh, to growl out his impatience with Ambrose's cryptic mutterings. But the man looked so old and tired and pathetic he couldn't do anything but say, "We should get you out of the cold."

"I don't feel the warmth anymore, Tom." He lifted his head, just enough for Tom to see his dark, empty eyes. "I can't remember what it feels like." He took a rattling breath.

"You shouldn't be out here." Tom pulled his horse around and reached for Ambrose's reins. "Come. Perhaps Mennvinn has something for you."

Ambrose tugged his reins from Tom's reach. "You know she doesn't," he snapped. A flicker of a smile, and he seemed to sit straighter in the saddle. "I have so little left," he explained. "So little fuel to burn on the fire of my life."

Tom nodded, the cold pebble like a dead itch in the back of his mind. He tried to imagine feeling nothing but that, and shuddered.

"We are close, Tom."

He nodded. "I think so too."

"And yet you will ask the others if they want to turn back."

"I've never made any demands of them."

"Haven't you?" Ambrose shook his head.

"Six will want to go back with Esyllt. He's loyal to her. And he deserves a chance to go home."

"You think you should let him go?"

"I do."

"You mustn't. No matter what either of you have said or done, you must keep Six close. Everything depends on it."

Ah. Yes. This moment had been a long time coming. When had he first foreseen this conversation? Was it in the Whispering Woods? It seemed like a lifetime ago. Tom nodded. "I've kept Six close," he told Ambrose. "Because of what you told me. But isn't it time he be allowed to follow his own path?"

"He already follows a path of his own making," Ambrose replied. "All you need do is remind him of where it is."

Tom sighed. "He could be happy."

"Don't speak to me of happiness, Tom."

Ambrose was right. He'd sacrificed such feelings. It was hardly fair to complain to him. "What of the others?" Tom asked. "Do I need to keep them all close too?"

"None of the others will ask to leave yet." Yet. Not a comforting notion. They'd have no better opportunity. But Ambrose had turned his horse and begun to ride back to Tirend. Apparently he had done what he must. Tom tugged his reins and fell in beside him. The poor man was simply following footsteps his future self had laid out for him, going through the motions until he had no motions left. "Do you fear the end?" It felt cruel to ask. But he had to know.

"You only fear what you don't understand," Ambrose replied. "And I know exactly what is coming."

So he knew what it would feel like when the fay absorbed him, devoured him? That sounded worse than not knowing. "So you remember that too?"

"I remember nothing beyond my last breath. I shall cease to be at that point." He turned his head, like twisting a great boulder across craggy ground. "It is a small comfort. But a comfort, nonetheless."

To take comfort in something as dark as that. That was no way to live.

"Do not pity me, Tom." Ambrose smirked. The fact he could do so made it clear how amusing he found himself. "My trials are almost over."

"And mine are not?"

"Barely begun."

Barely begun. Everything he'd done, and Ambrose thought his journey barely begun? "Do you think we'll find the glarn?"

Tom asked. "I know you don't know. I just want to know what you think."

"I have little experience left to me on which to base an opinion." Ambrose tugged his reins and they stopped at the cusp of Tirend, the unnatural light bathing them from below, throwing odd shadows across the sorcerer's face. "But I've seen how you fight. That gives me hope."

"So there's a fight coming."

Ambrose didn't meet his eye. Didn't offer a comfort or a reassurance. Just said, "Keep Six close," before flicking his reins and descending again into the warmth he said he couldn't feel.

Tom knew he needed to talk to Six. But he also needed a moment to himself. Just one. He rode to the arbitrary space their party had claimed, dismounted, and lay down. No blankets, nothing but his arm for a pillow. And he slept.

Their wagon was overturned. Burning.

He lay in a cot. It was painful to breathe. He stank, unwashed for days. One eye was swollen shut.

He walked down a long, dark corridor that echoed with his haggard breath. His arm was wet and warm. He could smell blood. He was dragging something heavy.

"To Malvis' door the tunnel did wend," Glastyn told him. "And by Malvis' hand would be the knight's end."

Tom woke, groggy and aching and bleak of spirit. Someone was shaking him. "Tom."

Katharine. She was nudging him with her foot. Too big to reach down and use her hand. She looked tired and miserable. How many days did she have left?

"What is it?" he asked.

"We're almost ready."

Wake me when we leave, he wanted to say. But he couldn't. He reached for the sword to draw strength from it. Remembered his oath to her and stopped himself. He rolled onto his knees.

"You're exhausted," she said.

"I am."

She put her hands in his hair, stroked his head. He leant lightly against her belly.

"She's almost here," she said.

"Almost here." He ran a hand across, felt something push back. A foot, perhaps. Their daughter's foot. If she was almost ready to be born, perhaps she could survive?

He waited for the surge of resolve to tell him that Katharine would survive too. But it didn't come. Not every day could be fought.

"I'm sorry," he told her.

"What for?"

For dragging you halfway across Tir. For treating you so badly. For failing to find a way to keep you alive. Instead, he said, "They could do with a guide. Someone to help them find their way home."

She tapped his head with her fingers once, a tiny reprimand.

"It's just an idea."

"It's a bad idea." She was stern. But not angry. "Send Gravinn."

"I'm not sending anyone. I'm just suggesting."

"Suggest Gravinn."

Tom nodded. "I thought you would say that. But I had to ask."

"Did you?"

Yes. Because it might be my last chance to save you. "It's only going to get more dangerous from here." He placed his arms around her. "I don't want either of you to get hurt."

"Nor do I. But we'll be safe with Sir Thomas of Tir."

Tom smiled. "Don't make fun."

"I'm not." When he looked up at her, she was smiling down at him. Kind. Proud. Beautiful. "Do you remember what I said to you in your room in Cairnagan?"

When he'd first had the foresight in which she died. "You said a lot."

She brushed hair from his face. What did she see? Cuts, bruises? A liar and a coward? The father of her daughter? Or something more? "You stopped sitting by the fire," she murmured. "And it's made you alive."

Alive. The pressure crashed against his insides like a great wave, unseen, unexpected. No. Don't say anything. Don't tell her. Tears pricked the backs of his eyes as he tried to swallow down the truth. He took a haggard breath and hid his face against her belly.

She stroked his hair and hushed him. "It's okay. I'm scared too."

He had his hands and face against her, but she felt so far away.

"Hey. Lovebirds." Jarnstenn's call punctured the moment and Tom wiped his eyes before anyone could see him. "We're ready to go."

Tom sniffed and pushed himself to his feet. "Back into the wagon?" He forced a smile.

She sighed. "At least being here gave me a break from being in there."

Tom nodded. "I have to convince Six to come with us."

"Do you need help?" She didn't ask why. Didn't tell him no. She wanted him to come with them. And she deserved her friend.

"Probably." But he patted her hand and added, "Get comfortable. I'll try not to be long."

She nodded and kissed his cheek. Somehow it gave him the strength he needed.

Six wasn't hard to find. He shadowed Esyllt at every step, and she was at the heart of every throng. At first Tom expected to have to push his way through the crowds, but people made way for him, giving him a nod, or a bow, and the bravest reached out and brushed him with their fingertips as he passed by. He wanted to tell them to stop, he was just Tom, he wasn't anyone special. But they had faith in the man Emyr had crafted. A knight, a hero, a liberator. He couldn't take that away from them.

"Sir Thomas." Esyllt begged leave from the old woman she'd been speaking to and led Tom away from the throng. "I am glad of the chance to speak to you. I wanted to thank you." Her whole manner was too earnest, too grateful. It made Tom uncomfortable.

"You don't have to thank me, Your Highness."

"I do." She cast a glance over the crowd, gathered in knots, talking, sharing stories of home. Excited to be leaving. Scared to be leaving. Happy to have the chance to be leaving. "They would have followed you. And you gave that to me."

"I never wanted anyone to follow me," he admitted. "I just want to keep my friends safe."

Esyllt nodded and bowed her head. Disappointed that he hadn't said something more altruistic? That he hadn't sworn to protect all of Tir? Well, he'd played his part. "Will you leave straightaway?" he asked her.

She shrugged, a gesture oddly lacking in royal grace. "We have little to gather. What food we had. What supplies you allow us." Her eyebrows jumped and she hurried to add, "Which we gratefully thank you for."

Tom waved the moment away. "I only wish we could spare

more." Even though Jarnsten had originally provisioned food enough for an army marching across all of Tir, it still felt like there was precious little to go around. "I was hoping to beg a moment of Six's time." At her confused look, he added, "Of Yemdarro's time."

"You need not beg from me, Sir Thomas. You may have anything that is within my power to grant you."

In the face of such generosity, it felt rude to change Six's mind behind her back. "In that case, Your Highness, I was hoping to persuade him to come with us."

Her eyebrows leapt up her forehead for the briefest moments before settling back into practiced calm. "Oh?"

"It would take much time to explain," Tom told her. "But our journey is of the utmost importance. I fear we will need him."

Esyllt frowned, stared at the ground. "I see." Tom watched her weighing her own desire against another's need. It was endearing to see such honesty in someone of such high birth. "And why is your journey so important?"

"We seek an artefact that we believe will help us stop the fay, Your Highness."

She nodded. "The creatures that brought us all here." She took a deep breath, as if steadying herself. "And who encroach on our lands and harass our people." She saw the need, and saw it was greater than her own. "I grant you permission only to ask him, for it must be his decision. He is not mine to command."

The way Six stood dutifully at her side belied her words. But Tom said only, "Thank you, Your Highness."

She reached out and took Tom's hands in her own, her skin cool and smooth. It was far too intimate a gesture for royalty. "Look after him," she told him, before retreating into the crowd to hide her sorrow.

Six was looking at him with a bemused smile, as if Tom had

asked for something strange and senseless. "Why?" was all he asked.

"Many reasons," Tom answered. "Ambrose foresaw it."

"I'm not interested in foresights." Six kept his courtier's posture, back straight, hands behind his back, but his voice slipped into the tones Tom was familiar with. Dressed in his dwarfish clothing, exile's tattoo on his face, his golden skin dirty from his travels, he looked prim, proper, and unusual. "I swore my loyalty to Esyllt a long time ago."

"She'll release you from your oath."

"But should she?"

Tom didn't want to say it. But he knew it would help weaken Six's resolve to go. So he said, "You gave your oath before you were exiled, didn't you?"

Anger flared in Six's eyes. "She shouldn't pay for her father's mistake," he snapped. "She needs me."

"Does she?" Tom looked at her, walking amongst people that weren't her subjects but followed her nonetheless.

"That isn't the point."

"What is the point?"

Six drew breath to snap an answer, stopped himself. Drew a deep breath. And when he exhaled, a different Six emerged. This one lifted his hands in front of him, twisted the ring he'd worn after first meeting Emyr. His posture wasn't as stiff, and his voice was softer, with some of the accent his brother, Athra, had spoken with. "I want to go home, Tom."

Then go, Tom wanted to say. Leave the fay and all this madness behind and go back to where you want to be.

But would it be so easy? His king had exiled him. He'd turned his brother over to the watch. Where would he go?

So Tom sighed and pointed at the ring Six was playing with. "You told me the engraving says 'lamb' in elfish." Six nodded.

Waited for the cruel blow Tom was going to land. "You started wearing it after you met Emyr. Oen."

"I did." Did Six sound defensive? Or was he challenging Tom to question him?

Tom did neither. "When Neirin took you prisoner, you didn't put up a fight. You didn't care about finding Faerie, stopping the war, or freeing dragons. You even told me you'd never go home."

There was a refusal in the elf's eyes. But there was also an acknowledgement of the truth.

"You're not that elf anymore," Tom continued. "Meeting Emyr woke something inside you. Whatever it is, I don't think it will let you allow Emyr to go on without your help."

Six wanted to argue. Instead he dropped his gaze to his ring, which he twisted around his finger. Tom felt an urge to say more, to push the argument further. But no. Wait. Let silence do its work.

"Emyr doesn't need my help," Six murmured. Tom drew breath to argue, but Six lifted his gaze and a smile blossomed on his lips. "You, on the other hand, need all the help you can get. Sir Thomas."

"I can't deny it."

"Of course you can't." Six gave him a meaningful glance up and down. "You look like you've been dragged through the aurochs paddock. Twice."

This was more like the old Six, ready with a smile and a joke. The two of them grinned at each other for a moment, then Six turned back to his ring. "Do you really need my help?"

They'd left behind Six's knowledge of locale and of dragons when they'd left the Western Kingdom. For weeks, the elf's biggest contribution had been shooting rabbits.. And yet, "Who else will tell me that I'm doing everything wrong?"

"I'm being serious."

"So am I. I'm trying to find my way here, Six. I need someone who will help me."

"By questioning you."

"Feel free to find a different way of doing it." Tom grinned and Six smiled back. "Ambrose told me to make sure you accompanied us. But I'd be glad if you did. I need your help. And knowing you'd be there to take care of Katharine would help me sleep at night."

Six nodded. "Very well." But things didn't sound well. They sounded heavy with duty and responsibility.

"Hawne seems capable," Tom offered.

"She does," Six agreed with a sigh. "She'll get my princess home." Then he straightened, tucked his hands behind his back, smoothed out his accent and gave Tom a sideways glance. "I won't call you 'Sir Thomas'."

Tom nodded. "And I won't call you Yemdarro."

Six dismissed the name with an easy shrug. "An old nickname," he said. "It means 'changer' in our tongue."

Appropriate, for an elf who had worn so many faces in just the time Tom had known him. "So it isn't your real name?"

Six gave Tom a shake of his head.

"How do you wear so many faces?"

Six looked up at the foreign sky. "Says the man who has been a liar who couldn't lie, a furious avenger, a champion of dragons and dwarfs, a protective father-to-be, and a Knight of Tir." He gave Tom a sad smile. "Perhaps I learned from watching my friends."

Tom wasn't sure if he'd been insulted but, as he watched Six go to tell his princess he wouldn't be travelling with her, he was just glad the elf was still calling him a friend.

In an oasis amongst the mountains, dressed in rags and furs, they had the most formal of goodbyes.

"We have no gifts to present to you, Sir Thomas." Esyllt was stood in the most regal outfit she could muster, fabrics draped about her almost making a dress. "But know that I speak for everyone here when I say that we cannot begin to express our gratitude. You have given us the chance to go home, to see our loved ones again. It is a kingly gift, and I thank you for it."

She gave him sole credit, but it had been Emyr who had orchestrated the challenge that unseated Tree, Gravinn and Katharine who had drawn the maps, Jarnstenn who had handed out supplies with surprising generosity. What had Thomas Rymour contributed? Violence and empty words. He felt like a sham. So he knelt before her and said the truest thing he could say. "You bestow great honours on me, Princess Esyllt. Knowing that you lead these people home with help give me strength to face the trials ahead."

She placed both of her hands on his head. A benediction. A blessing. "You carry all our hopes with you. They could not be in better hands."

It was all for show. Tom knew that. But his throat was unexpectedly thick when he said, "Thank you, Your Highness."

She lifted her hands and he stood, bowed his head to her, stepped back. What now?

"We should go," Emyr murmured.

Tom hadn't heard the old king's footsteps, and in that moment realised how much Emyr had healed. He no longer walked with a careful step or a bent back, and hadn't in some time. Perhaps now he was ready to lead them?

"They're nervous," Emyr continued. "If we leave, it will give them the courage to leave themselves."

Tom nodded and climbed into the saddle. The others followed his lead, and then Tom faced dozens and dozens of faces, all watching him, waiting for something. "Say something to them," Emyr told him.

He tried to think of something appropriately heroic and inspirational. What would inspire him? "We ride to stop the very fiends that brought you here." He met as many eyes as he could. "The thought of you returning to your homes in Tir will warm our hearts on cold nights and steel our resolve in the face of our enemies. Go home. Live your lives. Be happy and free."

Happy and free. How true would that be for these people? But he saw nodding heads and smiling faces, and it seemed enough. So Tom flicked his reins and led their party up and out into the cold.

Gravinn took charge of their path once Tom pointed out their destination, and he was happy to let her do so. Dark clouds left the mountains in a deep gloom, but Gravinn's Pathfinder eye found a way to penetrate the thick snow underfoot and pick out the safe paths. She rode ahead, seemingly oblivious to the icy wind that wormed its way beneath furs and beneath scarves and left Tom's fingers numb. He found himself riding alongside Kunnustenn, the dwarf huddled in what furs remained to them, and Tom could tell it wasn't enough.

The dwarf caught him watching and said, "This weather is hideous."

"We're close now," Tom assured him. "I think."

"I hope you're right. To be truthful with you, Master Rymour, I hadn't appreciated how arduous this journey would be."

Tom thought back to his days in Cairnagan and how readily he had given them up. "Nor did I."

"It's harder for Jarnstenn. He isn't accustomed to hard living."

Tom cast a glance over his shoulder, watched Jarnstenn and Six riding in hushed conversation. Both of them carried something on their shoulders, a regret and a loss. They seemed of a sort, the same enquiring mind, the same quick wit. The same focus that drew their gazes inward, picturing with their minds eye whatever they were discussing. "He followed you without a second thought," Tom said.

"That makes it worse."

Tom nodded. Six had readily followed Tom when he'd asked, and the guilt was a heavy burden to add to his others.

"He has offered me every comfort it was within his power to give," Kunnustenn continued. "I offer hard travel and frozen wastelands in return."

Something in Kunnustenn's voice turned Tom's thoughts to Katharine. Hard travel and frozen wastelands. When she deserved rest, soft pillows, good food. "At least you are together," he said.

"Yes." Kunnustenn was smiling a shy smile. "We do not have to hide here."

Tom opened his mouth, closed it, then braved the question. "Have the two of you made your peace?"

Kunnustenn's smile vanished. "He will not speak of it. He is stubborn, that dwarf. There are some things he just will not let his mind see."

"Don't hold onto your anger," Tom said, unsure where the words were coming from. "It will rob you of your days together." As it had robbed days from him and Katharine. He could have been there for her as soon as she'd discovered the pregnancy. Instead Six had stepped into his shoes. Now he could never get that time back.

"You are right. It is nothing in the grand tapestry of all matters." But it didn't seem to comfort Kunnustenn. If anything, the silence that fell upon the two of them felt melancholy. So Tom fell back on a habit that had proven effective with the dwarf: he asked a question.

"What can you tell me about Cairnarim?"

Kunnustenn said nothing for a long moment, before taking a deep breath as if waking. "What would you like to know?"

Tom didn't know what he needed to know. So he said, "Everything."

"That will not take very long." The dwarf hugged himself tighter against a gust of wind. "Most of what I have read is rumours, myths and legends. The usual fare: a citadel full of treasure; a lost paradise; a dark home to a foul monster. Only one fact is known: Rimestenn disappeared, and he left behind no city."

"But you know more than that," Tom replied. "You know he was building something in the north."

"We suspect it," Kunnustenn corrected.

"If we only suspect it, why are we trying to find it?"

Kunnustenn shrugged, a gesture hard to see beneath the layers he was swaddled in. "The last known and verified fact about Rimestenn is that he was working on locking mechanisms. In secret. But all of that work vanished when he did."

Locking mechanisms. Perhaps to lock away Orlannu in his hidden city? "So we would need a key when we get to Cairnarim?"

Kunnustenn frowned, catching up with Tom's thoughts. He shrugged again. "If the city is locked."

Gravinn's horse slipped on something in the snow and whinnied in protest. She gave a savage yank on the reins, and Tom realised how much pressure she must be feeling. One wrong footing and she could send them all tumbling down the mountainside.

And even if they made it to the gates of Cairnarim, it could all be for nothing if they didn't have the key.

But Ambrose would know. He'd be prepared. Wouldn't he?

"Thank you, Kunnustenn," Tom said. "You've been very helpful."

"You're welcome, Master Rymour."

Tom thought to tug his reins, fall back and ride alongside Ambrose and Emyr. But something in his gut made him stop and ask, "Is there anything else that we might need to know?"

But the dwarf shook his head. "I could consult my books?"

Tom nodded, though the offer felt somehow futile. In fact, when he looked at Kunnustenn he felt the beginnings of a deep despair. "Go to Jarnstenn first," he said.

"He's busy."

Jarnstenn laughed at something Six said.

"He won't be too busy for you."

The dwarf's forehead creased into a deep, pensive frown.

"Trust me," Tom said. "Don't delay it."

"No time like the present?"

The dread uncoiled, settled again. Something was coming. "No time at all."

The sky grew dark long before the sun was due to set, but Gravinn pressed on until they reached the clearing Hawne had mentioned. It was nothing but a space surrounded by sharp rock on all sides, a few tiny trees trying to eke out an existence in what crevices they could find. Something about that place felt too familiar, and Tom felt an urge to dig his heels into his horse and flee.

"We'll stop here," Gravinn called. The wind was strong now, bringing with it the first flakes. "We need to get the tents up before the storm hits."

Tom had no desire to ride in a storm. But he couldn't shake the dread in his belly.

"You're pale as Ankou," Emyr murmured.

Did his hands shake from the cold? "We should unload the wagon," he told the old king.

"Unload it?"

"Into the tents." Although the tents could burn as easily as the wagon.

"Why?" But Emyr wasn't really asking; he already knew why. So he pointed at Draig and Dank. "Tom wants the wagon unloaded," he called. "Food and clothes first."

"Here." Tom watched himself press Caledyr into Emyr's hands. "Take it."

Emyr shook his head, but didn't say anything. Even the sword's protests were muted. "Everyone needs a weapon." Was the old king giving orders to the group? Or talking to him?

It didn't feel like it mattered either way. "Iron hurts them," Tom replied. The cold seemed to reach right into him, like the black pebble in his heart had drawn a frozen fault line that joined with the falling snow. "But nothing can kill them."

"On the contrary." Ambrose was stood alone in the clearing, leaning on his staff like he was ready to collapse. "That's why I'm here."

If Gravinn had hoped they would find shelter from the storm, she had been mistaken. The wind howled around them, sleep impossible. All they could do was lie in the cramped black of their tents, stare at nothing and listen to the wail of the wind. At times it almost sounded like it was speaking, a voice that could be understood if only they knew the dialect. But it didn't sound like it had anything pleasant to say.

And the snow fell. It would settle on the tents, only to slip off when the weight got too much. Tom wondered if they would be buried in it, if they had erected themselves little silk tombs. What if the snow crushed them? What if they were to die, freezing and choking in this forsaken mountain range?

Then Katharine would shift. Take a deep breath. Squeeze his hand or place it on her belly, and he would feel Rose kick or twist underneath it. And, despite that dark pebble, Tom could smile. He was still worried, still scared, he still wondered how in Emyr's name they would survive this journey. But he smiled.

They began to talk. Katharine told him stories from all over Tir. Some were old tales that he knew from when he was a boy. Some were newer, and Katharine wouldn't say if they were true or not. So Tom heard How The Eagle Lost His Voice, a funny story about a dwarf who was turned to stone by the sun, and the sad tale of an Easterner who accidentally broke the death mask of his father and was scared to go back home.

Tom told her stories too. He couldn't tell her the tales, because they hadn't happened, and he felt a pang of guilt that he would never tell his daughter Why The Tortoise Wears His Shell or What The Bee Whispers To All Flowers. So Tom told Katharine stories he had heard from Emyr, when he had sat beside the bleeding king and listened to stories of his life, stories of brave knights and foolish courtiers and how Emyr came to be king.

"He just wanted to go home," Katharine said into the dark.

"Yes."

"He had so much waiting for him. He left it all behind."

"He told me it would have all been lost if he hadn't taken the crown." Tom squeezed her hand. "He gave it up so he could keep it safe."

For a moment all he could hear was the wind. Then she squeezed his hand, hard. "Don't do that," she whispered. "Don't give us up. Not for anything."

Tom waited for the wind to die before he tried to leave the tent. He had to force his way out, the snowfall reaching almost his knees, a few errant flakes still falling from the cloud-covered sky. The air was sharp and clear and still, and once he had struggled free of the tent he stopped and drew a few deep breaths that stung the back of his throat.

No. The air wasn't still. There was a thick humming to it. Magic. Oozing into the clearing from the north. Was that what birthed the aching dread in his gut? The tension in his chest? He reached for a sword he wasn't carrying and a ghost of a foresight flickered at the edge of his vision. A shadow draped over the world. A whisper of suggestion. "A fire," he muttered. Though he couldn't imagine how they could light a fire in such deep snow.

It was impossible to tell one tent from another in the dark, so he was forced to wait for a break in the clouds in order to find

Emyr's. Just a few dozen steps away, but the depth of the snow meant it took him some minutes to cross the camp before he could lean towards the flaps, clear his throat and say, "My king?"

For a moment there was only silence. Perhaps he was asleep? Then a voice replied, "I thought you weren't going to call me that?"

Despite the cold and his fatigue, Tom couldn't help but grin. "May I enter?"

"Yes."

Tom stepped into a space darker and only slightly warmer. He didn't dare take another step for fear of treading on someone.

"It's dark, Tom." Ambrose, somewhere in the darkness.

"It is."

"And you come to countenance that we stay."

"Do I?"

"We all stay a time." Ambrose sighed. It wasn't a pleasant sound. It was like he had resigned himself to something. "Time. I've had so much and yet have so little," he muttered.

"What is it?" Emyr asked.

"The culmination of my life's work. I think."

It was clear that Emyr didn't understand Ambrose's cryptic mutterings either. "What do we do?"

"Let the boy set up camp." Boy? But before Tom could say anything, Ambrose added, "When you're as old as I am, Tom, everyone is 'boy' or 'girl'."

Tom nodded, though they probably couldn't see him. "Can I fetch you anything, my king?"

Emyr sounded tired. "I will be out in a moment."

A dismissal. Tom nodded and stepped back outside. Roused Gravinn and Jarnstenn and told them to start a fire. He'd expected protests, but they did as they were asked. Draig helped to clear away snow, Jarnstenn fetched something from his pack, and soon they had somehow started the fire Tom had foreseen.

Emyr stepped out of the tent, stretching gingerly and groaning as he did so. The king had grown old. There was much more grey in his hair and beard, and he seemed slimmer, as if he carried muscle through sheer will rather than any inherent strength. When he gave Tom his hearty smile, there was something of a wince to it, as if something pained him.

"What's worrying you, son?"

Tom shook his head. "I'm not sure. I was hoping Ambrose could counsel me."

Emyr nodded. "He's tired. He said he would come out soon."

"I'll see him now, if you'll permit it?"

"Of course." He stepped aside and said, "I'll speak to Gravinn and Katharine about our path." As Tom moved to enter the tent, Emyr added, "How is Katharine?"

"Tired. Hungry. Cold. She misses riding."

"She said so?"

"No. I just know she does." His chest tightened and he said, "Would you make sure she has a weapon? Iron. She favours a short sword or a long knife."

"Do you think we'll be attacked?"

The dread crystallised. Had he seen this clearing before? Had he seen a dead dwarf lying near that fire? "Possibly."

Emyr's expression turned grim. "Weapons for everyone." But he said it almost as a question, and turned to Tom for confirmation. Still refusing to take the lead. And, Tom noticed, holding out Caledyr to him.

So Tom said, "You are the King of Tir."

"I have no throne."

"We follow you."

"No," Emyr countered. "This is your quest. The quest of Sir

Thomas Rymour, Knight of Tir. Don't shake your head," he said as Tom began to deny it. "You were made so by a princess."

"That was just an act. Something for those people."

But Emyr shook his head. "It was an act. But it was real." He clapped a hand on Tom's shoulder. "If you insist on calling me your king, then you cannot deny me when I call you a Knight of Tir. Or deny that it is a title and a duty bestowed by those around you." He took in their snow-beleaguered camp with a sweep of a sheathed Caledyr. "They are all here because of you. Just like me. They follow your conviction. Your example." He nodded towards the tent behind them with a wry smile. "So go confer with the wise man. And I'll pass on your orders." He pushed Caledyr into Tom's hands and, without waiting a response, bowed his head and stamped his way over to the fire.

Perhaps the old king thought his work was done. But Tom felt more uncertain than ever. Was he truly a knight? Could he possibly live up to that? He looked at the sheathed sword in his hands, and felt guilty for being glad to have it. Ready, it thought. Emyr had seemed happy to drop a heavy duty on his shoulders and walk away. Tom wasn't sure he was ready for it.

A tiny light blinked into existence as Tom stepped into the tent. Dank's sprite? Had it escaped? No, the light was wrong. It was too white and too sharp. As his eyes adjusted, Tom could see it was in the palm of Ambrose's hand. Magic.

"You look tired, Tom." Ambrose's soft words were almost swallowed by the wind outside. Deep, dark circles lay beneath his eyes, and his skin was almost grey.

"You look worse." Tom tried to force a smile, and was surprised when the other man's lips quirked. Not quite a smile. But the ghost of one.

"I suspect that is true." Ambrose took a deep, rattling breath. "But then I am so much older than you are."

There seemed little to say to that. "Kunnustenn thinks we might need a key to get into Cairnarim."

"We do. But do not worry about that."

"You have the key?"

Ambrose's eyes blinked in a slow assent.

Tom hadn't expected that. It seemed almost too easy. In the absence of any struggle or argument, his fear poured forth before he could stop it. "I can't shake this feeling that something bad is going to happen. It's not a foresight. Not really. But it feels like one."

"I have been thinking of a memory," Ambrose replied. "Trying to remember exactly what it is I will do and how I will do it. It is a complex piece of magic."

"Is that what this is?" Tom asked. "Is that what's making me feel this way?"

"No." Blunt and hard, but Ambrose continued, "You are experiencing the nagging feeling you have forgotten something, only your forgetfulness faces forward rather than back."

"I'm forgetting a foresight?"

Ambrose grunted. No. Not that. "Your foresight is like an echo of mine," he said. A flurry of wind made the sides of the tent shake. "You remember the future, just like you remember the past. But memory changes. What you remember today is not what you will remember tomorrow."

Tom felt a cruel leap of hope in his heart. "Does that mean my foresight can be wrong?" Had he misunderstood what he had seen of Katharine? "Can the future change?"

"No." Ambrose made no attempt to hide his bitterness. "Just our understanding of it."

It was a cruel snatching of the foolish hope Tom had built in mere heartbeats, and he felt a rush of despair. No. There was still Orlannu. That could save Katharine. It could.

"What happens now?" he asked.

"I need to rest."

"For this piece of magic?"

"Yes." Ambrose turned his head, met Tom's eyes with his own. "Look after him, Tom."

He knew exactly what the old sorcerer was asking. "I will do everything I can."

And a full, unburdened smile blossomed on Ambrose's lips. "Hearing that has made the last thousand years so much easier to bear." The smile soured. "And now, when I need that comfort more than ever, it is taken from me."

It was cruel, that any fond memory was taken from Ambrose as soon as the event took place. Which meant that, in his final moments, Ambrose wouldn't recognise anyone at his side. All he would remember was death and darkness. Tom made a vow to himself: he would make sure Ambrose would always have something good to remember.

The old man closed his eyes. His smile was gone. And he drew breath like the effort cost him dear. "Do not blame yourself, Tom."

But before Tom could ask what he meant, there was a scream from outside. Katharine? Tom rushed out of the tent, Ambrose's last words following him into the roaring wind: "No more time."

The wind was up, raising flurries of fallen snow. The world was still dark, but there was enough moonlight to see why Gravinn had screamed: Herne and four Faerie hounds were gathered around Katharine's tent.

CHAPTER 15

The summer face of a Faerie hound was that of a man, albeit a scruffy, hairy, mute man that acted more like Midhir's loyal pup, wrestling with his brothers and growling and yapping at his king's feet for scraps. But come Calgraef, they became monstrous, skinless beasts, prowling on all four splayed claws, snapping at anyone and anything with enormous jaws filled with serrated teeth. Their eyes were milky, and the fay whispered that they were blind, led only by their bloodscent. When Melwas led the Wild Hunt, it was these creatures that chased the kill. They were untiring, strong, savage. And they surrounded Katharine's tent, skinless muscles steaming in the cold night air, waiting for Herne to give them the command to attack.

"What are you doing here?" Tom couldn't keep the tremor from his voice. Even Caledyr was silent and still. He wished he hadn't left Katharine by herself. He wished he had never been to Faerie.

Herne tossed his hart-skull head. "It is our turn, Thomas Rymour."

"Your turn to do what?" Keep him talking. If they were talking, they weren't maiming.

"You bite us." Herne snapped his jaws. "We bite you."

"I bit you?"

"You killed Thought." Herne had always been fond of stalking around Tom's heels as he spoke. But now he was still. It was unnerving. As if the time for toying with his prey was over. As if it was time for the kill. "Our king is filled with a mindless rage. We are to bring you back to him. In as few pieces as possible." The fay's jaws gaped wide in his approximation of a smile. "We couldn't promise not to take a limb for ourselves."

Tom tried not to imagine Herne biting through his shoulder. Or tearing through it with his bare hands. "It's a poor hunt," he managed. "Your hounds will run me down before I make three steps."

"You want me to let you flee?" Herne's scorn flooded his echoing words.

"It's a poor hunt." And an even weaker argument.

"Sometimes the hunt and the chase are not the same thing." Herne snapped his jaws. "We have hunted you for years. Now we have you. Thomas Rymour. King Defier. Queen Defiler."

Queen Defiler. What one fay knows, all fay know. Unless they could keep it a secret. Apparently Maev hadn't seen fit to do so. "And what does the Queen have to say about this?"

"Mab would have you in Faerie too. Along with what you stole." Herne jerked his head, and Tom followed the gesture to Emyr. Stood by the fire, with the dwarfs behind him. Kunnustenn and Jarnstenn looked through the fay, still blind to the Second Sight. But Gravinn was very still, and Emyr had an iron blade in his hand. Tom couldn't see Six. But he saw Draig and Dank stood beyond the fire's light, bearing iron. It wouldn't be enough to stop the fay. But it might be enough to discourage any idle interest. So Tom had to keep their interest. Had to make it all about him.

"I stole Emyr," he said. More. What else would irritate them?

"I kept Caledyr. I imprisoned a sprite, killed Mester Stoorworm, killed Thought and attacked Melwas. It was my hand that wrought those deeds."

"It was." There was a grin in Herne's terrible voice. "Such quarry you have become."

Quarry. Tom recalled Herne and Melwas whispering about him in Faerie. Had the King and his dog engineered an opportunity to finally avenge themselves on him for lying with Maev?

Movement caught his eye. Tom tried to look without looking, saw something up the cliff face.

"I'll come peacefully." It would be of no interest to Herne. But Tom was running out of things to say. He lifted his hands. "I surrender myself."

Herne coughed, gagged. "That is a poor hunt when the prey does not run." His jaw gaped again. "But there are ways of making them flee." He turned his head to Katharine's tent. One of the hounds snuffed at it.

Before collapsing into the snow with a yelp, an arrow protruding from the back of its head.

The other three hounds screamed. The sound was a jagged blade through the mind and through the heart, sapping the will and severing thoughts. The bay of the Faerie hounds was enough to bring a man to his knees.

But Katharine was in that tent.

So Tom ran. He drove forward, towards Herne, blinded by terror, fighting through knee-deep snow. He almost fell twice. Someone shouted his name, and Caledyr tried to speak to him. He ignored it all, and tried to ignore the urge to empty his bladder at the sound of baying hounds, tried not to wail as one of them knocked him down, driving him onto his back in the snow, crushing him with its paws on his chest.

He stared into milky eyes and hot drool dripped onto his

face. All the hound had to do was put its jaws around his head and bite.

Don't leave us, she had said.

A thud and the hound jerked, howled, danced away and began to chase its tail. An arrow in its flank. An iron arrow.

It was Six, shooting iron arrows from a spot up the mountainside. Tom felt a burst of infinite gratitude towards the elf, though it was a tiny infinity next to the endless void of terror he felt. It would take any of the fay just seconds to take Katharine's life.

Move. He was on his feet. Move. Push through the snow, push through the fear, get to Katharine. But Herne stood by the tent with a smile on his skeletal face, reached with one filthy hand to lift the flap and take away everything that mattered.

"No!" Do anything, say anything, stop him, stop him. "Face me!" Herne hesitated. "Face me!" Tom waved Caledyr, shouted over the wailing hounds, didn't care that his voice cracked as he cried, "Are you a coward, are you scared to fight me, are you scared I'll beat you the way I beat Stoorworm, where's the great hunter, where's the bane of men?" Herne stepped away from the tent and Tom didn't dare let himself relax. "Are you too scared to touch me, are you scared what Mab will do, are you afraid of her, the great hunter afraid?" And Herne was bounding over the snow like it was firm ground, and Tom had no time, Herne knocked him to the ground, Caledyr flew from his hands, the fay pinned him down, clawed at his face, Tom struggled but the fay was strong, unbelievably strong, maw snapping at his throat and Tom braced himself against the fay's neck, get him off me, keep him off me, this is it, this is how I die.

Herne rocked and Tom's flailing hands caught against something in the fay's flank, an arrow, an iron arrow, grab it, twist it, Herne grunted in his ear and the pressure lessened, just for a moment. Pull it, twist it, tear it free, Herne made a sound like he might vomit gravel and Tom pushed, the fay fell away and Tom was free, scrabbling away in the snow. Get to your feet, get to your feet, but his hands and feet were numb with fear or cold or both. But he managed to stand, turned, stood shivering with something and saw Herne hunkered in the snow.

"Do you think that is enough?" There was no blood, no ichor, nothing seeping from Herne's wound, but it was still a ragged tear in his flank and he clutched it all the same. Tom looked down at the arrow in his hand. "Do you think that will stop us?"

No. Nothing would stop Herne. Even wounded, the fay was grinning. This was a hunt, now. And Tom had never heard of a hunt in which Herne hadn't brought down his prey.

He shouldn't have taken his eyes from Herne, but a bellow made him turn. Emyr, an iron blade aloft, running through the snow towards them. Towards Herne. "No," said Tom, but too quiet and too slow. Herne bunched, sprang into the air, batted Emyr's sword aside and fell on him, growling and grunting like an animal. "No!" Tom was moving again, he was on the pair of them, stabbing at Herne's back with the arrow. "No no no no." Pain exploded in his side, he flew, landed face down in snow, don't stop, keep moving, he rolled onto his back and saw he was staining the snow red, and there was a hound stalking towards him.

He felt warmth. The fire. Just within reach. The hound barked and Tom was on his feet, pulling a heavy piece of firewood free in a shower of sparks and ash and waving it over his head with an incoherent cry. It wouldn't do anything. Fire couldn't hurt the fay. But it was better than waiting for the hound to rip out his throat.

But it didn't pounce. It was alone. It was cautious. So it circled. Waited for an opportunity. And Tom's arms were already tired. He was trembling. His footing was uneven. The hound didn't have to fight him. It could wait him out.

A voice, behind him. Jarnstenn. Asking him, "What is it, Tom? What's happening?"

Emyr was on his feet, keeping Herne at bay. Dank and Draig had a hound between them, slashing at it with iron. Another hound was peppered with iron arrows. Where was the other one? Tom couldn't see it. But Katharine's tent was intact. She was safe.

"Faerie hounds," he told Jarnstenn. "Stay back. Stay close to iron." He wished he hadn't lost Caledyr.

"We have iron." Kunnustenn. "Take it."

"No," said Jarnstenn, but something crunched into the snow beside Tom. Iron, colder than anything. The hound saw it too, and Tom watched its muscles bunch, no time to think, he drew back the burning firewood and flung it as the fay charged, the log flipping end over end in a shower of sparks, the hound shied from the flames, gave Tom enough time to pluck the iron sword from the ground, throw himself out of the hound's path, swing blind, the tip of the blade raking against flesh and then Tom was rolling in the snow.

He was on his feet in time to see the hound turn to Jarnstenn and Kunnustenn, the two dwarfs huddling against the cliff face, staring at nothing, blind to the hound. Jarnstenn had an iron pike in his hand, but he was pointing it the wrong way. And the hound was close, too close, its jaws snapping at the blind dwarfs.

"To your left, Jarnstenn!" Tom ran again, forced a path through the snow, waved his sword above his head, cried out, "Here, here!" to draw the hound's attention. Jarnstenn stabbed with his pike, caught nothing but air, but it was enough to push the hound back, and then Tom was close enough to swing at its leg, slice deep into its shin, the blade caught on bone, the hound yelped, jumped back, tore the sword out of his hands.

"The pike," Tom demanded and Jarnstenn threw it to him. Tom's numb hands fumbled the catch, he wasted precious moments picking up the weapon, and the hound was already on him, maw gaping at his head, he stabbed, buried the pike in its neck and it screamed, emptying his mind of thought.

Tom was climbing to his feet before he remembered what was happening. Jarnstenn. Kunnustenn. They were alive. So was he. The hound was whimpering, collapsed in the snow. Katharine. He had to get to Katharine. And Emyr. He was facing Herne alone. Tom had to help him. He reached for the iron blade still stuck in the hound's shin.

A cry from above drew his dull gaze. The firelight didn't extend that high, but he could hear a struggle, the growls of a hound. Six.

Tom pulled the sword free, stumbled to the cliff face, started climbing to where the elf was sat. "Six," he tried to shout, but he was breathless and tired and it was no more than a weak cry. His hands and feet slipped on the rock, his right hand was almost useless with the sword in it. "I'm coming, Six."

There was a yelp from above, and then a rush of air and shadow fell past Tom and crunched into the snow below. Tom looked down to see Six and the hound, two patches of darkness sprawled beneath him. Six was still. Too still. The hound was already getting up, whimpering and shaking itself.

"Six," Tom called. But the elf didn't move. Jarnstenn and Kunnustenn were already running towards the elf. Towards the hound that was on its feet and snarling at them. "Stop!" Tom told them. But the hound was already readying itself to pounce. Tom had no choice but to let go of the cliff and push himself into the dark.

The drop was short, quick, and terrifying, and although Tom raised his sword, he wasn't able to plunge it into the hound. Instead he glanced off the beast's flank and crashed into the snow. But it was enough. It distracted the hound. It sprang around and growled at him, before planting a hot, heavy paw on his chest. A slash of iron was enough to make it yelp and dance away, but it was back before Tom could get on his feet, knocking him face-down with its snout, snuffling at him, dribbling down his neck.

Tom tried to swing the sword, but he couldn't connect. And then he felt hot, fetid breath on his head and the scrape of teeth over his scalp, and it was over, this was it.

"Stay!" The gravelly bellow echoed off cliff walls, as if the mountains themselves couldn't contain their fury. But it wasn't mountains. The stinking breath and serrated teeth were gone, and Tom lifted his head to see Herne pointing a finger at the beast standing over Tom. "That one is mine," the fay said.

Mine. My prey. My kill. It sent a chill through Tom's already cold limbs. And then Emyr swung his iron sword, a chop that would have severed hart's head from shoulders if Herne hadn't twisted away.

A thump on Tom's back sent pain up and down his spine and drove him deeper into the snow. The hound had stamped on him in frustration. Tom scrabbled at the ground, drawing himself up and onto his back, but the hound had already turned around to find prey it was allowed to kill. Like Six. Or the dwarfs.

A voice in Tom's mind asked him how he thought this could end. How could they win this fight? Only Caledyr could stop a fay. And there were too many fay for just the one sword. But what else could he do but get to his feet and stagger towards the hound, swinging iron for all he was worth?

The hound kicked him, claw-tipped paws sending him flying back through the air. He landed hard, and then Herne was on top of him again, clawing at him, Tom barely had time to register the new attack before Emyr was there, slicing up through Herne's chest, and the fay howled pain and frustration before attacking Emyr again.

Tom pushed himself to his feet. Too much going on. Too hard. He groped at his iron sword with numb fingers. Too impossible. He turned back to Six and the dwarfs. The dwarfs huddled behind Six, who had his bow drawn and an iron arrow pointed at the hound menacing them. Run. Tom stumbled towards them, raised an exhausted shout. But it was Six's gaze he drew, not the hound's, and the beast struck, swiped at Six's arm, the arrow sliced up into the night sky and Six fell back. The hound's maw gaped and it darted in for the kill, howled, Six had stabbed it with something, it snatched his leg in its jaws and flung him aside.

Six spun, cartwheeling through the air. He flew over Tom's head, and Tom couldn't help but watch him fly even as he ran. It was almost beautiful, in a way. Almost peaceful, to fly through new snowfall.

Jarnstenn's cry cut through the spell, and in a heartbeat Tom was at the beast's back and plunged the blade deep into its flank. Its scream scoured Tom's mind, left him barely able to stand. It began to lunge at the sword in its flesh, chasing its tail in feeble hops and bounds, whimpering to no-one. Tom let himself drop to one knee.

Jarnstenn was babbling to Kunnustenn, pulling at him, pawing at him, telling him to get up, you're just winded, this is nothing, please, please.

Tom wanted to go to him. Wanted to lie down. But he could hear Emyr crying out. So he pulled himself to his feet and turned his back on the dwarfs.

Emyr was still locked in a battle with Herne that was clearly approaching its end. Emyr was tired, his sword wavering in his grip, one arm clutched to his chest. Herne circled his prey, crawling spider-like and grinning up at the old king. As Tom staggered forward, Emyr thrust, impaled Herne, the iron blade slicing down into Herne's shoulder and out through the fay's chest. But Herne twisted, tore the blade free of Emyr's grasp, and pounced on him.

"Emyr!" Tom cried. He couldn't get there in time. Dank and Draig were keeping a hound at bay. Six hadn't moved since he had been thrown. Herne's laughter seemed to be joined by the dark, evil shadows thrown by the wagon, on its side and burning. Herne wrapped his hands around Emyr's neck and all Tom could do was uselessly shout because he was too far away. The old king's arms slapped at the fay on top of him, scrabbled for his sword, flailed. But Tom knew how strong Herne was. How fruitless the struggle.

But Herne stopped his assault a moment later, tipped his head to one side, let out a curious, questioning growl. Tom felt it a moment later. The air changed. As if it was made of iron. Cold, empty. A match for the cold pebble Tom could still feel inside himself.

Ambrose.

He shuffled out of his tent towards Emyr and Herne, leaning heavily on his staff, clutching it like it was keeping him from being swept out to sea. He didn't look up. He didn't speak. He moved like he was the only man in the whole of Tir. But the air around him was dead, still, every ounce of magic fleeing from his touch.

Herne clambered over Emyr to face the old wizard, but he seemed uncertain. Fearful. "Sorcerer," he croaked.

Emyr took his chance, surged for the sword in Herne's back, gripped it, twisted it. The fay roared and lashed out, catching Emyr in the temple with a fist and sending him to the ground.

Ambrose's voice stayed Herne's hand. "Leave him!" And the old sorcerer began to whisper in a tongue Tom had never heard. In fact, he shouldn't have been able to hear it at all. But

Ambrose's foreign words sounded like they were being spoken into Tom's ear. No, it was more like the whisper was somehow inside his mind. Like Caledyr's voice, but it could never be confused for Tom's own thoughts. And it grew in its insistence, mounting pressure that made Tom want to flee.

And it was working on the fay. The wounded hounds were pawing at the ground in a vain effort to get away. And even Herne, whom Tom had never seen back down, was taking careful steps away from the approaching sorcerer. Letting out a pained whine. Muscles twitching. Caught between the twin impulses to flee and to attack.

The whisper became a voice, and Ambrose straightened, lifted his staff over his head, took certain, even strides. In that moment Tom could see Ambrose as he would have been in his youth. Confident, even cocky. Outraged that someone would try to hurt his king, his friend. His voice was sure, powerful. And the stone on his staff pulled at the world. Tom found himself walking towards it despite himself.

Herne had stopped retreating, fixed like he was pinned in place with iron nails. "We will taste your flesh, sorcerer." He gnashed his bare, hart's teeth. "We will tear you piece from foul piece!"

But it was an empty, frightened threat. Everyone knew it. And Tom knew, too, that Herne wouldn't bear this humiliation; the fay wouldn't stop until they were all dead, even if Melwas himself ordered them left alive.

"I know what is to come, hunter." These words came from Ambrose's lips. They carried the croak of his years, but they were no less powerful for that. He stopped just one step away, well within Herne's reach. Possibly the most dangerous place to be in Tir or Faerie, and yet Tom felt no fear for him. It was clear where the power lay. "Your days of tasting mortal flesh are at an end."

"You are no more mortal than we are," Herne spat back. "You burnt it all away on your fool's quest."

Ambrose smiled. "Not all of it." And he touched the stone in his staff to Herne's forehead.

Herne's scream was made of sound and magic and pain never imagined, a single, constant note that didn't waver even as Ambrose's spell flayed the fay before their eyes. Skin, muscle, fat, flesh, bone, it peeled away into dust and nothing. And yet, even as Herne was undone, he didn't shy from Ambrose's staff. He was defiant, even as his tumbled into a pile of bones, even as those bones turned to dust, and even as the murderous red glow in his eyes winked into darkness.

Silence. Inside and out. Ambrose lowered his staff and allowed himself a satisfied smile.

"One to go," he said, loud and clear.

He dropped his staff. Lowered his arms. And collapsed face-first into the snow.

CHAPTER 16

THEY COULDN'T WAKE AMBROSE. Kunnustenn was dead. Six's leg was a mangled mess. But Katharine was unharmed, and so Tom hated himself for the gladness in his heart as he climbed to Six's perch, where Mennvinn watched him like a rabbit watched a fox.

"We need you," Tom panted. His limbs were burning and he was painfully, selfishly aware of the blood soaking his flank. "Many of us are wounded. Six's leg is crushed."

She blinked, just once. "What happened?" Her tone was flat, empty, dead.

"The fay," Tom said, arms burning from hanging onto the cliff face. "Please, Mennvinn. We don't know what to do."

She blinked again. But of course she was terrified. She'd had to watch the rest of them fighting an invisible foe, watch them be injured and tossed about by something she couldn't see and couldn't fight.

"They're gone now," he told her. The Faerie hounds had vanished moments after Herne had been undone, and Tom was trying not to think of what might be sent in their stead. He reached over the edge of her perch and she shrank from his hand, like it might bite. "Please. We need you."

Her gaze moved, so slowly, from his hand to his face. Tom watched the terror fade from her eyes and reason took its place. Not entirely. But enough that she could ask, "Crushed?"

"Get me a belt. Now. Put your hand here and squeeze. Harder. Harder, damn you! Where's my kit? Fetch it. Boil some water. A lot of it. Quickly, now!"

Mennvinn had taken just one look at Ambrose before turning to Six. The sight of him had stopped her in her tracks and she'd drawn a quick, sharp breath of surprise. Then she'd started barking orders.

Tom pulled off his belt and wrapped it around Six's thigh, pulling it impossibly tight. Six whimpered but said nothing. His skin was deathly pale and sweating, and when Tom spoke to him he didn't seem to hear.

"You can let go now. Go on, out of the way. My kit, thank you, open it up and find me milk of the poppy. No, not that. Let me do it. Where's that water?"

She elbowed Tom aside and he stepped back, watching Six pant and sweat in the snow. He wouldn't survive this.

"I'm sorry." Tom's words tumbled out unbidden. "I should have been faster."

Six met his gaze but said nothing. His breathing was quick, shallow. Topknot's breath had been the same as the life went out of him.

"Come away." Katharine's voice was soft, low, sombre. "Come. Come away."

He let her lead him to Emyr, who sat on a rock, staring at the spot where Ambrose had fallen. Ambrose himself was gone; Emyr must have moved him already. The old king's forehead bore a nasty gash, tiny rivers of blood sliding down his face, smeared across his features where he had wiped it out of his eyes.

My king, Tom opened his mouth to say. But Emyr had never looked so old and alone. His stoic expression was held up by a thread, ready to collapse at the merest pluck. So Tom said, "Are you hurt?"

Katharine answered when he did not. "He needs stitches." She sat Tom on the rock too. "So do you, by the looks of it."

What could he say? Emyr's last friend in the world was, what? Dying? Tom wasn't sure. "Ambrose," he began, but wasn't sure how to phrase his question. Was he dead? Did he live? It seemed too blunt and harsh for Emyr's demeanour to bear.

"He lives." Emyr's voice was deader even than his friend's. "But barely. He breathes like an afterthought. And his blood moves so slowly I can barely feel it in his wrist."

Katharine had threaded her needle and said, "This may hurt," before she began to stitch Emyr's forehead together.

"It does." But he wasn't talking about the needle. "He is one step from death's door. And it is my fault."

"Your fault?" Tom echoed. "It was the spell that did this to him, wasn't it?"

Emyr nodded. "And who placed these demands on him? I took every act and spell as if they were owed to me, and then I told him to bring me more. He has killed himself by degrees with his arts. Because of me."

It didn't sit right. Tom couldn't claim to know Ambrose as well as Emyr did. To know him at all, really; there was so little of him left. But Tom had seen the glint of greed in the old man's eyes when Tom had burnt that twig. As if he hungered to do the same.

"And he wouldn't even have known why he did it," Emyr said. "He doesn't remember our pact. Father's grace, he didn't even have a fond memory to fuel his courage. He had only his will."

He spoke as if his friend was already dead. But, "He still lives, my king."

The rage in Emyr's eyes stilled any more words Tom might have said. "Don't talk to me as if he's only ill," the old king growled. "He told me what he's been teaching you. You know what he's done."

Katharine watched Tom as she asked. "What has he done?"

"He's burnt himself up." Emyr sighed. The fire disappeared from his eyes and his shoulders slumped. "He's gone. His body just doesn't realise it yet."

Tom shook his head. "He would have known. He would have said something."

Emyr gave only a short, sceptical grunt. "Finish your work, Katharine."

He seemed so foreign, slouched, glaring at the world, with none of his usual strength or charisma. Even bleeding from a wound that would never heal and trapped amongst the creatures that had wounded him, Emyr had still managed to seem like a king. Now he was just an angry old man.

Katharine's stitches were done and Emyr stood. "What do we do now?" Tom asked.

But Emyr strode to his tent and disappeared inside without a word. It left Tom feeling lost, bereft. Emyr couldn't ignore them. They needed him.

"Give him time." Katharine beckoned Tom closer and he obeyed, letting her peel pack his furs and shirts until his bloodied left flank was bare. She sucked air through her teeth. "This is deep."

"It doesn't hurt much."

"Probably because you're cold. You'll feel this once you're warmer."

But pain was the least of Tom's worries. Emyr's silence had given strength to a horde of fears and they had breached the gates. Kunnustenn was dead. Six was dying. Ambrose too. And there was no avoiding Katharine's fate. He would lose her, and Rose too. Dank, Draig, Jarnstenn, Mennvinn and Gravinn, they had all put their faith in Thomas Rymour. But he would fail them all; their supplies were broken and burning, they wouldn't make it back. Even the nearest village was too far. And he'd brought Emyr back to Tir only to watch it fall to the fay.

"Just breathe," Katharine told him.

"What do we do?"

"We breathe." Katharine's steady voice matched the even rhythm of the needle through his flesh, tugging with only the slightest pricking. She was right. He was too cold to feel it properly. "We take it one step at a time. Injuries first."

"And then?"

"And then we decide what comes second."

He watched her face, her concentration on her work. The slight pinch at the corner of her eyes. She was afraid too. But she was hiding it. Putting on a brave face for him. And it was working. Not because he believed her. But if she could be brave, so could he. He could try to be like her. If he let himself get overwhelmed, he couldn't look after her. "Thank you for protecting Rose," he said.

That brought a wry smile to her face. "All I did was hide in a tent."

"You kept our daughter safe."

Her smile grew softer and she met his gaze. He couldn't help but smile too. "You're welcome," she said.

And for just a moment, Tom allowed himself to believe that everything would be alright.

And then Six howled.

"Wait," Katharine said, putting a firm hand on his shoulder as he tried to rise. "Just a moment." Her needle flew through his skin.

"I might have saved him, if I'd been faster."

"He's not dead yet."

"Do you think he can survive it?" Tom had seen the splinters of bone piercing Six's flesh, how the elf's foot had laid at the wrong angle. "Mennvinn isn't a cirgeon. She used most of her supplies on Emyr. Can she have much left?"

"I don't know," Katharine replied, cutting him off. She finished her stitching. "We'll have to hope for the best."

The optimism Tom had felt just a moment ago was gone, and he was left again with the bleak feeling that hope was something they couldn't afford. He slipped his arm back into his clothes, redid buttons and tied his furs tight.

"Six is very fond of you," he said. He wasn't sure why. Perhaps because he didn't think Six would have the chance to say it himself.

"I'm fond of him too," she replied as she wiped her needle in some snow and packed it away. "He's a good elf."

How often had Tom been at odds with Six? And how often had Six been right? "He is," Tom realised.

Mennvinn was shaking her head when they arrived at Six's side. "I can't save it," she said.

"So is he going to die?"

The dwarf looked up at him. She was doing her best to appear calm and professional, but there was fear in her eyes. "We might save his life, but we'll have to remove the leg."

"No," Six managed. "No, you can save it. Please."

Tom remembered a knight in Cairnagan who had lost a leg to a bear. While others had danced and mingled and gossiped in Regent's court, the knight had been left to sit and watch. He had been ostracised, deliberately by some, accidentally by many. After three weeks he left with no word or warning. Left for home, to live his days in an exile imposed by that missing leg.

But it was better than dying.

"There's no way to save it?" Tom asked.

Mennvinn stood, her hands bloodied, a smear of it on her face. "Even if we were in Cairnakor, in Dorstenn's cirgery, we could not save it."

Six swore in elfish.

"Can't you give him something?" Katharine asked.

"I have only a little milk of the poppy," Mennvinn replied. "And he will need it shortly." She turned to Tom and said, "I did not bring the tools needed for this procedure. Please ask Master Jarnstenn if he provisioned us with any saws, preferably ones with fine teeth."

Iron nails. She was going to saw off Six's leg. Tom felt his stomach clench and he couldn't help but look at Six's pale, sweaty face. The elf shook his head. But there was no other choice. So Tom said, "I'll speak to Jarnstenn."

The dwarf hadn't moved since the attack. He was lain across Kunnustenn's body, his back to the rest of the camp. He didn't stir as Tom crunched through the snow towards him; the dwarf was so still it would be easy to think he was dead too.

"Jarnstenn." Nothing. Tom stepped closer. "Jarnstenn, we need a saw. We have to remove Six's leg." His stomach clenched again and he tried not to imagine it.

"I don't care." Jarnstenn's voice was muffled.

"He'll die if we don't."

"He's dead already. You've killed us all."

"I'm sorry about Kunnustenn."

Jarnstenn lifted his face and bellowed, "Don't you say his name!" to the cliff face. The echoes seemed to go on forever, but Tom was more concerned with Jarnstenn's ragged breathing. Was he hurt too?

Of course he was hurt.

What could Tom say? Could anyone have said anything to him if he was hunkered over Katharine's body?

What would Emyr do? "We'll give our respects, every respect, in due course," he said, repeating the words and tones he heard from an imaginary Emyr in his mind. "Right now we need to attend to the living."

"I don't care about the living."

"I understand that. But you have something we need to save Six's life. Right now, in this moment, we have to prove we were the people Kunnustenn thought we were. We have to be better than we want to be."

Jarnstenn wiped his face. "You're using him against me."

Don't say anything. Let silence do its work. But every moment felt like an age. How much closer did Six come to death while they waited for Jarnstenn to do something?

Panic and urgency drew a breath and opened Tom's mouth to cajole Jarnstenn, but the dwarf stood before he could speak. "Damn your eyes." He turned away from Kunnustenn and pushed his way through the snow towards the wagon. Towards Draig, who was rescuing what he could from the wreck. The interior was cocooned in flames, but some of the spilled contents were beyond the reach of the fire. "Have you found my tools?" Jarnstenn asked without ceremony or manners.

Draig looked up. He was stood amongst bags and boxes and piles of individual items. He was visibly exhausted. His shoulders slumped, his arms hung by his sides and he drew rapid, shallow breaths. His right eye was swelling shut. "Lie there some tools." Tom followed his finger to an assortment of hammers and pliers and other instruments Tom didn't recognise. And a saw. Small, its shining surface dancing with reflected firelight. Waiting to bite into Six's bones.

Jarnstenn pulled it free and held it up. "It's meant for wood, not bodies." He thrust it toward Tom. "But it's all I have."

The handle was smooth, dark, beautiful wood. Tom tried not to touch the blade. Tried not to imagine it buried in Six's flesh. "Thank you, Jarnstenn," he said, and tried to inject as much gratitude into his words as possible.

Jarnstenn said nothing, didn't even nod. He stepped away and sat next to a collection of books and bags. Kunnustenn's. Say nothing. Let him be.

"Can I save little more." Draig winced and touched his ribs. They must have been broken. But he didn't complain, didn't rest. No-one had asked him to salvage the burning wagon. He had simply accepted it as a thing that had to be done.

"Thank you, Draig," Tom said, and tried to sound as grateful as he had a moment ago. And finally put aside the memory of how Draig had delighted in battling him in that Western tower. Put aside how the elf had betrayed them. they were beyond such old hurts now. "Would you like to rest a moment? I could take over."

Draig shook his head. "Tend you to Six." But he smiled. He appreciated the offer. And he gave Tom a nod that told him he knew what the offer represented.

Mennvinn tutted at the saw. "Is there nothing more?" She barely waited for Tom to shake his head. "So be it. Hold him down. I've given him something for the pain, but it won't be enough."

"Please, don't." Fear sharpened the slur out of Six's voice and made it something brittle and foreign.

"No choice. I'll be quick. Bite this." Mennvinn pushed a

wooden cylinder between Six's teeth. Tom tried to pretend he didn't see deep marks already bitten into the wood. "I need you all to hold him as best you can. No, that's not enough," she said to Dank, who was pinning Six's wrist to the ground with one hand. He clutched the other hand to his chest. A broken arm? "Kneel on this arm. Tom, you too. Katharine, sit on his other leg. You there, Draig, come here and hold his thigh for me." Mennvinn's brisk efficiency was frightening, Tom needed a moment to gather himself, to ready himself, but she was already bracing herself against Six's thigh.

"Wait," Tom said, but she ignored him and said to Six, "Try not to move," and then she was slicing through flesh and Six was panting and whimpering, and Mennvinn started sawing through bone and Six was thrashing and screaming and Tom could only concentrate on holding down the elf's arm, he was stronger than Tom had imagined, the howling and screaming was constant, the sound of the saw seemed to vibrate his own bones and his stomach clenched and roiled, iron nails, iron nails, don't throw up, Tom, don't throw up, and then the sawing was done and Mennvinn was slicing and slicing and then she was done and Six was still and he was crying, his entire body shaking.

"Iron nails." Tom's voice shook and he realised his face was wet with tears.

"Hold him a little longer. I need to finish."

Tom barely heard her. It was so quick. One moment Six had two legs. Then he didn't. It had been so quick.

Six was bawling without shame, staring into the sky.

"It's over," Katharine was saying. "It's over, Six, it's over."

She was wrong. It wasn't over. Not by a long stretch.

"Will he live?"

They'd moved Six into a tent and wrapped him in furs, leaving what was left of his leg under fewer layers as per Mennvinn's instructions while she cleaned blood from her skin with handfuls of snow.

She looked exhausted. "I hope so."

Hope. They had cut through flesh and bone and Six had screamed and writhed and shed shameless tears while his bloody stump was stitched up. And all they had given him was hope. It seemed such a slender thread on which to hang his life.

"What do we do now?" Tom asked. The others were huddled around the wreckage of the wagon. Despite his warning, they'd lost a lot to the flames.

"I've done all I can," Mennvinn replied. She wiped her hands down her fur before slipping them back into her mittens and rubbing them together. "I can do nothing for Master Draig's ribs. Master Dank needs stitches, nothing more. I understand Lady Katharine has seen to the minor injuries."

That wasn't what he'd meant. "Can we move Six?" He was sure they couldn't. That meant they would stay here.

"Should we? No." She reached into a pocket and pulled out another of her little cigars. "But I don't think we have much of a choice."

"No?"

She had the cigar halfway to her lips and stopped, eyebrows raised. "Can we stay here after what has happened?"

Perhaps not. He nodded and watched her walk to the fire, use the end of a glowing plank to light her cigar, and sit with the others. The sky was still dark. There was no telling how long until the moon birthed the sun again.

He wanted to sit with the others. He wanted to sleep. But he knew he should speak to Emyr. He took a step, stopped, fetched Caledyr first, lying uselessly in the snow.

Dropped me, it reprimanded him.

But Tom felt like he had no feelings left. He'd been too scared, too hurt and tired, to feel the sword's recriminations. So he ignored it and trudged across their little campsite to stand outside his king's tent.

"May I enter?" he asked, swaying on his feet. He should have slept. "My king?"

"Enter." Quiet. Flat. Disinterested. Tom pulled aside a flap and stepped inside.

His gaze was drawn to Ambrose first, curled around his staff like a child, hugging it to him. His brow was slightly furrowed, like he was having a bad dream. But Tom couldn't hear his breathing. He couldn't see the old man's chest move.

That stillness extended to Emyr too. He sat on a pack, slouched, wrists resting on his knees, hands limp. Like a puppet with its strings cut, he didn't move, didn't even glance at Tom. Just stared at Ambrose. "What is it?" he said with a voice that betrayed how little he cared.

The truth was that Tom wasn't sure why he was there. "No change?"

"None."

Tom waited. For direction, for comfort, for something. But nothing came. So he said, "Mennvinn had to remove Six's leg."

"So I surmised."

Another stretch of silence. Tom longed to sit. "We still have a few hours to dawn, I suspect."

Emyr said nothing.

"Do we strike the camp?"

"As you like."

"We act at your command."

"Act on your own."

"My king?"

"No." Emyr lifted his gaze and Tom was faced with wet eyes filled with regret and anger and apathy. "I am no-one's king. Not anymore."

Tom felt like a monster, to barge in here and demand that Emyr lead in the midst of his grief. But he had reminded Jarnstenn of his duty. Emyr needed to be reminded of his. "You are my king." And he began to lower himself to the ground.

"Bend your knee and lose it."

Tom stopped, unbalanced, forced to half-stand again or fall. Emyr's words had been so calm, so reasonable, but the threat seemed so sincere. But he hadn't meant it. Had he? Of course he hadn't.

"Get out."

It felt right to leave him in peace. But Emyr had to see that, "We need you more than ever." Tom rested Caledyr's point on the ground and proffered the pommel to Emyr.

But he gave the sword only a brief, baleful glance. "And what do I need, Tom?"

Time. Peace. And hadn't he earnt those things? "I am sorry," he said.

"You came in here looking for someone to tell you what to do." Tom had to stop himself nodding at Emyr's accusation. "You didn't find him." And he swatted at the sword, knocking it to the ground. "Go away."

"My king," he began, but Emyr reached over to the sole candle and snuffed the flame between his fingers. A rustle and then stillness. Had he laid down? Laid down to sleep while everyone sat bereft around their burning wagon?

Leave him.

Tom picked up the sword. I told you not to do that anymore.

Rest.

Caledyr was right. Tom stepped out of the tent. Stared down at the sheathed blade in his hands. Felt for a ridiculous moment that this was all the sword's fault, really. If they hadn't gone looking for it, none of this would have happened.

Rest.

Tom nodded. Took heavy steps towards the others. "Sleep, everyone."

"I don't think I can." Gravinn still held her iron pick-axe on her lap, hunched over it as if she was worried someone would try to take it from her.

He wanted to say something comforting to her. They're gone. You're safe. It will be alright. But the words wouldn't pass his lips. Instead he said, "I'll take first watch." It felt cruel to nominate someone else. They were all terrified and exhausted, all because of him. All because he had dragged them on this quest to find something that they might never find. "Draig, I'll wake you in an hour."

"Let me," Katharine said, and when Tom shook his head she held up her hands to be pulled to her feet. It was impossible not to groan as his aching limbs pulled against her weight, and he regretted it immediately. But she didn't give voice to the hurt in her eyes, just murmured, "They have to see me carry my fair share. I won't be a burden on you all."

He couldn't help but smile. Carrying a child, visibly exhausted, she was determined to be independent and useful. He touched his fingertips to her cheek.

"And put some gloves on, for Emyr's sake."

"Yes, Katharine."

He fetched them from where he had cast them aside, and they all spent a few minutes righting tents and persuading Jarnstenn to sleep. Soon enough only Tom and Katharine were left.

"Get some rest," he told her.

"I want to take a watch."

Tom was too tired to argue. She would win in the end anyway. "Agreed," he said. "Later."

She gave him a tired, wary smile. "Will it always be like this? Will they always come for us?"

He gave her the only answer he could. "I don't know. But I'll die to protect you."

"You can't." Her smile was broader now. "I have your word. You won't leave us. You said so."

And she felt comforted by that. It felt like the worst kind of lie, a horrible, fatal inevitability lurking just behind a truth.

Should he tell her?

But she was already climbing into the tent, and he was left with the burning wagon. He sat on an empty crate, unwrapped the jar, and held it up to his eyes. The light was weak and watery, and the sprite's wings drooped.

"You and I are going to have a conversation," he said.

CHAPTER 17

"THAT STONE HURTS YOU."

The sprite nodded.

"And it severs your connection to the fay, doesn't it?"

Another nod, but Tom wasn't sure he believed the answer.

"But that doesn't protect us, does it? Herne knew exactly where to find us."

The sprite shrugged. In the face of the violence and the death, it shrugged. But Tom was too tired to be angry.

"I have some questions that need answering," he said. "If you promise to answer them, I'll take that stone out of there. It isn't doing us any good anyway."

The sprite nodded as enthusiastically as it could, and Tom loosened the lid just enough that he could tip the jar and slide out the stone.

It landed in his palm and he closed the jar. Even through his glove, he could feel the stone's otherworldly coldness. How it tugged at his thoughts. More disturbing was how it echoed with the dark pebble inside himself. He tucked the stone into a pocket and turned to the sprite. It already looked stronger.

"Tell me the truth," he said. "Are the fay following us?"

It nodded.

"How?"

The reply was too quiet and weak. Tom lifted the jar to his ear. "Gwyllion," it said.

It shouldn't have been a surprise. She was an immortal fay; a fall down a mountainside was nothing. But Tom felt a stab of fear all the same and looked out into the darkness around them. "For how long?"

"Since you cut off her finger."

"Why hasn't she attacked us?"

"She would not dare disobey our queen."

Mab. Was she protecting them? "Why would Mab tell her not to attack?"

"We are not privy to our queen's thoughts."

"I took away the stone. Ask her."

"Let us see Dank." The request caught Tom off-guard and he blinked, took the jar from his ear to look at the sprite. It was kneeling, hands on the glass. Pleading. "We miss him."

There was a true longing in the sprite's tiny voice. But did it really miss Dank? Or did it simply want its puppet returned?

"Tell me what the fay are up to," he whispered into the night. "Why would Mab order Gwyllion to leave us be, but let Herne and his hounds tear us to pieces?"

Nothing. Was the sprite sulking? Should he threaten to put the stone back in? Or promise it could see Dank? No. Dank might have sworn himself to Emyr, but there was no guarantee that he wouldn't be tempted to rejoin his sprite. Tom couldn't let the boy enslave himself again.

Besides. He knew too much.

"The king and queen are at war," the sprite said at last. "Herne has sided with our king, and the hounds are loyal to their master; they obey his order to attack you."

"And Gwyllion?"

"She cannot choose between her king and queen."

Which was why she had not attacked again; her indecision stayed her hand. For now. But who else was a threat? "Have other fay chosen a side?" he asked.

"Many. Many have not."

"Are we safe from the fay that have chosen Mab?"

"They will not disobey her."

"And who has chosen Melwas?"

"Many. Please. Let me see Dank."

"Tell me who have chosen Melwas."

"There are many."

"Tell me which fay are most dangerous to us."

"Herne. Mester Stoorworm. Nuckelave, the Grindylow, and Black Annis. The hounds are loyal to their master."

It hurt to hear Stoorworm's name in that list. But Tom had driven Caledyr into his maw. it wasn't unreasonable to bear a grudge. "What about Glastyn?"

"Mab believes Glastyn has chosen her," the sprite replied. "Though some suspect he is playing his own game."

His own game. Tom wasn't sure he liked the sound of that. But Glastyn wasn't a threat right now, and Tom knew who and what to fear. "Thank you," he said.

"Can I see him?"

Such a longing. It missed something, whether it was the boy or the connection itself. He surprised himself by asking, "How is Mab?"

A tiny sigh. "She is enjoying the entertainment."

Of course. That was why she protected him. Not out of fondness. She liked using Tom to aggravate her king. He was no more than a good way of creating drama.

"She wonders why you are talking to us," the sprite added. "She asks if you miss her, Thomas Rymour."

He felt a stab of guilt, shame, remorse. “Of course,” he mumbled.

“Would you like her to come to you?” Was he imagining a seductive lilt to the sprite’s words?

“It would be unwise,” he managed.

“But pleasurable.”

He looked over at the tent he shared with Katharine. At the tent in which Six lay, the tent in which Ambrose lay. The dark bundle of Kunnustenn’s body lying in the snow. “Some of my friends are hurt or dead because of the fay.”

“That is another matter,” the sprite replied. “Entirely separate to what we are proposing.”

Tom knew exactly what Mab was proposing: something beyond loyalty and loss. Comfort, pleasure, nothing more than a passing moment.

But that was temptation talking. He put a hand on Caledyr’s hilt and felt that sword’s familiar warning. Fight.

“I don’t want to see her right now.”

And before the sprite could say anything else, he wrapped it up and set it down in the snow. Planted Caledyr between his feet and rested heavily on the hilt. Fight, it said, fight fight fight.

And it was a battle to sit there and stay true and wait to see if any other threats emerged from the darkness.

He was cold and tired and hurt and lonely. He’d been hoping Katharine would offer him some sort of comfort. But she only mumbled, “You’re cold,” when he lay down in the tent.

“Sorry.” He burrowed under the blankets and tried not to let in too much cold air. But rather than sleep, he found he could only lie and stare at the dark, mind too full of thoughts even as his body ached to rest.

Fingertips brushed his arm, felt their way down, and Katharine's hand slipped into his. "Thank you," she whispered.

A rush of gratitude stilled his racing mind. "For what?"

"You protect us," she replied.

Six. Ambrose. Kunnustenn. "I'm not sure I do it well."

"Our daughter is safe."

For now. But he was still able to smile and squeeze her hand. "She is."

Katharine squeezed back. And the darkness of the tent faded into bright daylight.

"Your women will suffer, little Tom," Melwas said. His black armour shone in the sun. "Twice as much as you will."

But before Tom could despair, he fell into a deep, dreamless sleep.

When he woke he was sweaty, sore, hungry. Still tired. But the world outside was light. He allowed himself to lie there a moment longer, to stare at the back of Katharine's head and pretend everything beyond the tent was a bad dream. That there was only her, and him, and their baby. That they were all safe and happy and home.

Home. Not his little hut in the Heel. Hawne had already made it clear that Regent wouldn't allow him to return to the Heel. And that any of his allies would turn over Thomas Rymour to curry favour. So if not the Heel, or any of the Heel's allies, where was home?

It was a simple question, but it shattered Tom's warm,

comforting illusion. They weren't home, or happy, or safe. They were lost, in peril, hunted. He freed himself from the blankets and clambered out of the tent without waking Katharine.

Cold. His side hurt, throbbed. Only Dank was visible, sat by the glowing heap of the wagon and tending a pot over a small fire. Tom lifted a hand in greeting and staggered away from the camp to relieve himself. When he returned, Dank offered him a metal cup of water with his good hand. It was warm and smelt of something fragrant.

"White willow bark tea," Dank explained. "Mennvinn gave it to me. It helps with the pain." He gestured as best he could with his other arm, splinted and bound and resting in makeshift sling.

It tasted exactly how Tom had imagined it would: tree bark. But it helped push back the cold; Tom's old sweat already felt like it was freezing on his skin. "Thank you," he said. "But should you be sharing it? Don't you need it?"

"I got used to pain a long time ago." The boy shrugged. "A broken arm doesn't really compare to a fay pushing through your skin."

Tom nodded. He'd noticed Dank was speaking about himself in the singular, but it didn't feel right to say anything. So he just said, "I'm sorry about your arm."

"I'm sorry for your wounds too."

"It's not your fault."

"It's not yours, either."

"It's my fault we're all here."

"It's my fault the fay are hunting us."

Why did Dank think that? He hadn't stabbed Melwas. He hadn't stolen Emyr out of Faerie. Dank must have seen the confusion on his face because he added, "If I hadn't taken you all into Faerie, none of this would have happened."

"You did it because I asked you."

"I could have said no."

That was true. But, "You shouldn't feel responsible. This is too big for one person to take the blame for all of it."

Dank gave him a wry smile. "Then why did you apologise?"

"Because," he began, stopped, realised what Dank was saying. Smiled despite himself.

"I'm older than I look." Dank stood up and he seemed taller than before. "And wiser too." He looked at nothing, staring into the distance. "Perhaps it's time for me to be more."

But Tom could see now that he already was. The boy – no, the man, – was no Faerie puppet. He was scared of the fay, but any sane person would be. But the fay were no longer the masters of him, and neither was his fear. It was almost unsettling, to see Dank so different, and yet it was heartening.

Movement drew Tom's gaze and he saw Jarnstenn emerge from a tent. The dwarf said nothing. Didn't look at Tom or Dank. Didn't look like he'd slept at all. He just fetched a spade, picked a spot in the snow and began to dig.

Tom didn't want to dig. He didn't want to do anything. But he had promised Jarnstenn that they would pay Kunnustenn every respect. So he found a spade of his own and joined Jarnstenn without a word.

The ground was hard beneath the snow, each strike sending a jolt through his worn limbs. The digging tugged at the stitches in his side. The spade was short, forcing him to bend double to reach the ground, and soon his back was aching. It wasn't long before he was sweating again, and he shed gloves and hat and layers until he was topless. Jarnstenn didn't say a word, but Tom felt the dwarf's own frostiness thaw. They went deeper and deeper, and despite his aches and pains and fatigue, Tom didn't stop. It was only right that he dug until Jarnstenn told him to stop. Despite what Dank said, Kunnustenn had only joined them at Tom's request. Another death on Tom's conscience.

Finally Jarnstenn put a hand on Tom's shoulder. Enough. Tom nodded and looked up, realised the grave they had dug was deeper than a dwarf was tall. Tom's limbs were tired and weak, and he felt a stitch pop as he hauled himself out of the new grave. He heard a gasp, and looked up to see Draig, Dank, Mennvinn, and Katharine watching them. Katharine sat on a crate, staring at his chest with a hand to her mouth. He looked down and saw what she saw: scars, stitches, and a mottling of bruises all over his pale skin. She went to rise but he shook her head and she sank back down.

There was silence as Jarnstenn unwrapped Kunnustenn's body. The dwarf's features were frozen, his eyes open and staring, his jaw slack, his skin pale and covered in ugly bruises. Jarnstenn stroked his cheek and muttered something Tom couldn't understand. Then he turned to Tom and said, "Help me."

Tom carried him by the shoulders, Jarnstenn by the feet. Kunnustenn's stiffness felt unnatural, like they were carrying a rock, not a body. Before they lowered him into the ground, Jarnstenn took a handful of dirt and forced it between Kunnustenn's lips.

"We are of the dirt." It sounded like an explanation and a prayer. "We return to it." He looked up at Tom, waiting for him to say something.

But it was Mennvinn who said, "Who returns to the dirt?"

"Kunnustenn." Jarnstenn looked away. "Who was to me my one true love." He glared at everyone, daring them to argue with him.

No-one did. "Kunnustenn," Mennvinn echoed. "Who was to me a friend I wish I had known better."

"Kunnustenn," Gravinn said. "Who was to me an inspiration and a warning."

"Kunnustenn," Katharine said. "Who was to me a friend, and a source of wisdom I envied."

There was a pause. Then Dank said, “Kunnustenn, who was to me a travelling companion.”

“Kunnustenn,” Draig said. “Who was to me a friend who offered comfort when felt I loneliness.”

“Kunnustenn,” Tom said. Who was to me a victim of my fight with Faerie. “Who was to me an ally, a guide, and a friend.”

“Kunnustenn,” Jarnstenn said. “Who has been taken from our world, and whom we envy the world for taking back for itself.”

The dwarf reached for Kunnustenn’s feet but Tom stopped him. “May I?”

Jarnstenn paused for a moment, rage boiling behind his gaze for a brief moment before he nodded. Tom strode to the salvage Draig had rescued from the wagon, casting his gaze over what they had left. An iron knife? No, it would have been better in his living hand than his grave. A book? It was valuable, but it felt wrong. There. He picked up a small roll of scorched paper. Perfect. He returned to the grave, where Katharine already had a scrap of bread ready. He thanked her with a smile, touched it to Kunnustenn’s chest and placed the paper in his hands as best he could.

“Take this offering, Kunnustenn,” he said. “Take it with you to the Isles of the Dead and let it buy your passing into that place, where the sun never sets and it is always summer.” Sun never sets. Summer. Iron nails he was describing Faerie. He lifted the bread to his lips without thinking. All these times, he had been happily commending the dead to Faerie. He put the bread in his mouth, chewed, swallowed. “You have done wrong in this life, as have we all. I take your wrongs and bear them on my shoulders now, so that you may enter the West in innocence and goodness. Go in peace.”

Except there would be no peace for Kunnustenn. Just a

strange afterlife with the fay. They would feed on his energies, consume him. And now they knew what he knew.

Jarnstenn snatched the offering out of Kunnustenn's hand. "We're not burying good paper," he muttered. "Besides, he doesn't need to buy his way into anywhere."

His words stung, but Tom was too distracted by thoughts of Kunnustenn joining with the fay. He lowered the body into the grave in a daze, covered it with dirt without thinking. Emyr said that Mab wore Eirwen's smile when she died. Would a fay wear Kunnustenn's smile? Or speak with his soft voice? Or would the fay simply consume him and leave nothing left?

They stood over the grave after they had filled it. "I always imagined I'd bury you in the Hallowed Gardens, or maybe the Knightly Grounds," Jarnstenn said. "Course, I imagined I'd bury you in another decade or so, didn't I?" He sniffed, grinned at his own joke and wiped his eyes. "Or maybe you'd have buried me, eh? Still, that don't matter no more. I'm here. You're in there." He got down onto his knees, put his hands on the dug earth. "But I'm in there too, Kun. Always will be. So don't you be thinking I'm leaving you. I'm not going nowhere." He hung his head. "Taranau's spit, I miss you already."

His shoulders began to shake, and Tom left the dwarf to weep in silence. The dead were buried. It was time to break camp and do what they could for the living.

"Fine." Emyr didn't even look up when Tom told him they'd buried Kunnustenn. Just sat there, still staring at Ambrose. Ambrose who hadn't moved an inch. Even his expression was the same.

Tom had expected even a little remorse or sadness. But Emyr didn't seem to care. "Mennvinn tells me that Ambrose and Six can be moved if needs be. And I suspect we should leave this place."

"Very well." He straightened, took a deep breath. At last. Tom offered him Caledyr. But he ignored the sword. "Are we breaking camp straightaway?"

Why was Emyr asking him? "As you will it."

"No," he was quick to reply. "I don't will anything. Let someone else will it."

"You are Emyr."

"My friend is dying."

Tom let his hand fall to his side. "What do I tell them?"

"Can you tell them anything other than the truth?"

It was hard not to take those words as a slight. "As you say."

Emyr nodded. "You once said you felt the time that passed in Tir while you were in Faerie. I never understood that. I've always felt like I was younger than my years. But seeing him lie there? He's smaller somehow. How did he get so old?" Emyr rubbed his hands over his face, then back through his hair. "I'm tired, Tom. In my bones. I'm so tired."

Tom nodded. He knew that feeling. For many mornings he'd woken up with the aches and pains of a much older man. But no longer, he realised. Somewhere along the way, on this journey, his joints had stopped bothering him. He didn't feel the weight of the years he had missed. When he'd brought Neirin and the others to Faerie, he'd mentioned that perhaps his body was older than Emyr's. But now it seemed like time had caught up with the old king.

So Tom just nodded. "If there is anything I can do, my king."

"You can stop calling me your king." But he didn't smile when he said it.

No-one questioned Tom's decision to leave. They simply nodded and set to work in the same hushed tone that had fallen over them when they buried Kunnustenn. Mennvinn and Jarnstenn started taking apart the tents. Katharine and Dank bundled together their rescued possessions as best they could. And Draig and Tom went looking for the horses.

Hoofprints made their way north, though one horse hadn't made it beyond their campsite, torn apart by a hound before it could escape. Tom had little hope of finding the others, but they had no choice. Katharine certainly couldn't walk far, and they had too much to carry between them.

Their path was not that steep but the deep snowfall turned it into a climb, and Draig had to pull Tom up more than once. But the ground levelled soon enough and it became clear that there was only one way to go: a straight, narrow valley with vertical sides.

"The Doubtful Chasm," Tom muttered. It had to be.

"What is this name?" Draig asked.

"It's what Hawne called this place." A split in the mountains, as if it had been chopped out of the world with an enormous axe. It reminded him of the story of the world told to every child, that Tir had been built on the corpses of four ancient giants. Perhaps this was the remnant of a blow that had felled one of them.

"Then with us is luck," Draig said. "Is it likely the horses found shelter in here."

Perhaps. But the Chasm didn't look like a place to go for shelter. It felt unnatural and unpleasant. The rock was filled with ripples and ridges, swirling and whorling in strange patterns. And there was something else too. Tom stepped closer, slipped his hand from its glove and touched the rock.

Duke Regent sat on Emyr's throne and demanded of a Westerner, "We held up our end of the bargain. We do not expect your king to shirk his responsibilities."

In Cairnagwyn, Neirin said to Idris, "Duke Ria is fierce, strong, and intelligent. She was never going to surrender."

"She might if the Eastern Angles threaten to invade Erhenned."

"I am your prisoner, not your puppet."

And a storm rumbled over the Lannad Sea as Duke Ria watched Western elfs load their final ship, and said to the departing Proctor, "I hope this has been an appropriately humiliating defeat for your people."

"We are leaving at our king's request."

"You are leaving because we are forcing you to."

Unseen to either of them, Nuckelave hauled itself out of the water, fins flapping over its skinless, horse-like body, the head replaced by an equally skinless human torso. The fay's single red eye glowed with malevolent glee as it poisoned the ship's water.

"Tom."

He blinked. Draig's hand was wrapped around his wrist, tugging his hand from the surface of the rock.

"Were you gone."

Tom nodded, taking back his wrist and sliding his hand into its glove. "It was like touching the monolith in Cairnagwyn. But not as strong." Snow settled into the strange patterns carved into the rock.

"Here." Draig pointed, revealing a patch of rock that had worn away to reveal the secret beneath: black stone with silver veins. Monolith stone. Did it hide beneath the entire mountain? "Must you not touch the stone," Draig said.

"But we have to walk this path."

"Watch I over you, as when we travelled through the woods."

When Tom's mind had wandered into foresight so regularly, so easily, that he could barely stay a heartbeat in the current moment. He stared down the valley, trying to see an end and failing. The thought of making another such journey made his stomach clench.

But he said, "Thank you," to Draig. Drew a deep, steadying breath and added, "We should fetch the others. We'll have to hope we find the horses on the way."

Draig made no move to leave. "Carry you the sword again." There was disapproval in his voice.

Tom pretended not to hear it. "Emyr doesn't want to carry it."

"And you are forced to bear it instead?"

No. He wasn't forced to. He'd been hungry to lean on it again. Even now he rested his hand on the pommel, letting its strength push back his fatigue. "Emyr needs time to grieve. And Caledyr is our best weapon against the fay."

"If have those words truth, should not another carry it?"

Do not give up the sword.

Quiet, Tom hushed the blade. But he could tell that Draig had seen his grip tighten on the pommel. "You are the only swordsman we have."

Draig only nodded. And why shouldn't the Easterner carry the sword? It would probably be more effective in his hands.

But that wasn't the question. "You still don't trust me, do you?" Tom asked.

"Say it once," Draig said. Almost pleading. "Only once." The Easterner stared down at him. He was thinner than he once was. Still broad and strong. But hard living had burned away the fat. "Say the queen of Faerie does not have your heart."

She didn't. Surely she didn't, not after everything she had done. Tom loved his unborn daughter, without having met her. And perhaps he loved Katharine; that was still confused, bound up with the terror of losing both of them. But Mab? He didn't love Mab. He didn't.

And yet he still felt the familiar tug in his chest when he thought of her. Of Maev. Was that love? Obsession? Lust? Or was it just a memory? Did he yearn for an idea of her?

Draig shook his head. "Am I not sure you should be the one who carries that sword." And the elf turned and walked down the hill.

They found Jarnstenn building sleds out of the wreckage of the wagon, in order to carry both provisions and wounded. Draig volunteered to pull Six's sled, and everyone assumed that Emyr, who wouldn't speak unless he had to, would pull Ambrose. And, despite her protests, Tom insisted that Katharine sit on a sled too, leaving Jarnstenn, Dank, and Mennvinn to haul supplies.

"There's not enough," Jarnstenn said. They had to abandon too much of the weaponry, too much clothing. The food seemed meagre. "I can't see how we'll make it back."

Nor could Tom. But it was Dank who said, "We will find a way." And he said it with such certainty that Tom believed it, just for a moment.

There wasn't room in the Chasm to walk abreast, so they walked single file. Draig and Dank called back and forth to each other for a time, but soon they fell quiet and everyone trudged in gloomy silence, the weak sunlight unable to reach them over the high, close valley walls. The snow wasn't deep, which made the going easier, although it also meant there was less between the sled and the ground below, and Six cried and groaned with each jolt. Mennvinn had given him what she could for the pain, but she'd admitted she didn't have anywhere near what was needed to treat him. So he suffered. And his pain wore everyone down, their shoulders slumping and their backs hunching under sympathy and empathy and guilt. Perhaps that was why they didn't hear the voices at first.

It was Draig, at the head of their caravan, that stopped and raised a hand. His entire manner suggested danger, and Tom dropped the ropes and drew Caledyr in a heartbeat.

"Please, Six, be you quiet," Draig hissed.

The Westerner's breathing was still haggard. But everything else was still. What had Draig seen or heard?

The Easterner pointed up. Tom looked, but there was nothing, just the same strip of cloudy sky that had loomed over them all day. He could see nothing lurking in the rock. Just the same strange patterns and carvings.

But Draig wasn't pointing out a sight. It was a sound. At the edge of Tom's hearing.

"Voices," Draig whispered.

He was right. It was the voices Hawne had warned him of, though the increasing breeze whipped away the words before Tom could make them out.

"They're behind us," Jarnstenn said, an iron axe in his hands.

But Draig was shaking his head. "Ahead." He had drawn his own iron blade and stood, ready.

"Sounds like they're coming from above," said Katharine, a knife in her hand.

They didn't seem to come from any direction. It was like the voices were in the very air itself. What were they saying? Tom strained to hear.

"She will die."

It was no more than a whisper amongst the chaos of noise, but it was clear. She will die. Katharine? He raised Caledyr, stepped closer to her.

Fight.

I will, he promised the sword. I'll defend her.

Fight.

"You cannot save her."

"I can hear them," Tom whispered to the others, and they replied, "So can I," and "I do too." And Emyr added, "They're talking about Ambrose."

Katharine said, "They're talking about Rose."

Jarnstenn said, "They're laughing about Kun."

Mennvinn said, "They say we're going to die here."

Gravinn said, "They're saying we're lost."

Six grunted, "They say I'm going to die."

Draig said, "They say I'll never go home."

His words hung heavy in the air, everyone's fear given voice.

"The air rings with magic." Dank stepped up to the wall, held a gloved hand an inch from the rock. "These walls are riddled with the same stone as the monoliths."

"Wouldn't that protect us from magic?" Katharine asked.

"No," Tom said. "The stone repels magic, so it can also channel it."

Dank nodded. "Someone built this valley." He pointed at the carvings in the rock. "These channels guide the wind to make noise. The stone guides the magic to give voice to the sound."

"And it whispers our fears to us," Tom added. "That's why we each hear something different." It was clever. It was cruel. It was the perfect way to dissuade the unwary from continuing. He turned to Emyr and asked, "Rimestenn's handiwork?"

Emyr nodded, a wistful smile playing about his lips. "It feels like him." Then a gust of wind blew away his smile and replaced it with worry. There was no knowing what it had whispered to the old king; to Tom it had said, "You will fail him."

And Caledyr said, Fight.

"We're on the right path." Tom tried to inject hope and

certainty into his voice. But it sounded weak in his own ears. He slid Caledyr back into its scabbard, and pulled the ropes of Katharine's sled over his shoulders again. "We can take heart from that."

"You will be the death of them all," whispered the wind.

But whatever the others heard, they sheathed weapons, picked up their burdens and they walked. With even less enthusiasm than before. With bowed heads. With heavier steps. But they walked. And the wind continued to whisper.

"You've seen her die. You cannot prevent it. And when she dies, Rose dies too. You'll lose them both."

But Tom knew it was nothing more than magic. Just a trick. Ignore it. Just keep walking. They're only words.

"Turn back. There's no point in fighting any more. You've already lost Maev. Soon you will lose Katharine and Rose, too. What will you have then? Not these others. They aren't your friends. They don't trust you. They know you're a liar and a coward. All you do is make them suffer and die. You've already killed Kunnustenn. Ambrose is dying. And how long does Six have left to live? It would be kinder to slit his throat than let him suffer this way. But you're a coward. You'd rather let him suffer for days than do what must be done."

Mennvinn said she could save Six. But could she? She wasn't a cirgeon. Just an assistant. Perhaps she was wrong. Perhaps they were just prolonging Six's pain.

"And then how many will you have killed? Topknot, Siomi, countless Western elfs. Athra and Storrstenn were surely executed. And how many innocent men and women died when you freed the dragons?"

So much blood on his hands.

"And everyone who travels with you. None of them will survive this journey. And what will happen to you? Centuries of torture in Faerie. If Emyr couldn't outwit Melwas, what hope do you have?"

It was only magic. Clever, cruel magic, designed to unearth his fears and his weaknesses. Nothing more.

"It can be both magic and true."

Tom bowed his head and tried to ignore the torrent of whispers.

"I'm going back."

Tom was working so hard to block out the whispering wind that it took him a moment to realise Jarnstenn had spoken. The dwarf had stopped, eyes closed, shoulders slumped, face tipped to the sky.

"Keep going," Gravinn told him. "We can't listen to the wind."

"It's not the wind," Jarnstenn replied, but Tom didn't believe that. "I don't belong here anymore. I only came for Kun. I don't have a reason to be here."

Gravinn said nothing. What reason did she have to be here?

"We need your help, Jarnstenn," Katharine said.

"What use do you have for a blacksmith, eh?"

"You made these sleds."

"A child could have made them."

"I couldn't have made them," Tom said.

"What *can* you do?"

It was said without malice, without anger. Just a sadness. It caught Tom off-guard. "Excuse me?"

"You seem to be leading us, but you're not very good at it. You got yourself a nice fancy sword, but you only carry it when he don't want to." Jarnstenn jerked a thumb at Emyr behind him. "Kun is dead." He waved a finger between Six and Ambrose. "He's dying, and he don't look much better. You tell me you're doing a good job, and I'll tell you the one about the honest Elect."

He was right. There was no denying it. Not when the evidence lay before their eyes. But Gravinn said, "If you knew half of the things Tom has done, you would be singing a different tune."

"What did he do, exactly?" He turned on her. "Helped you run away from your elf-master? Know how many runaways there are in the streets of Cairnakor? Ain't hard to run away."

"He freed me."

"Didn't he say he'd free all the dwarfs in the Kingdom? When are they all coming home, eh?"

That hit home, and Gravinn fell silent.

"You won't make it back," Katharine said, voice quiet, subdued. "It's too long a journey."

"Maybe. But if I stay here, it's a sun-cursed certainty I'll leave my bones here."

"Rest us here for a time?" Draig asked. He was looking at Tom. Waiting for confirmation. Perhaps he was right. If they couldn't get Jarnstenn to continue, they'd stop, rest. Gain some time to convince him.

"But what will you say?" asked the wind. "What can you say, when the dwarf he loved is dead because of you?"

Draig dropped the ropes for his sled. "Eat. Talk. But rest is more important." He stepped past the others, fetching cooking supplies from Jarnstenn's sled, and muttered, "Before driven I to madness by this wind."

They set up camp, started a fire, huddled around it as if the flames could protect them. It didn't stop the whispering. And it didn't stop Jarnstenn from wanting to leave. He sat in hushed conversation with Gravinn and, by the doubt creeping onto her face, it looked like he was enjoying the better end of the discussion.

"Should we let him go?" Tom whispered to Katharine.

"Don't whisper." She lay on one side, cushioned by as many blankets as they could spare. She added, "I don't know." She had both gloved hands on her belly. It wasn't hard to imagine what the wind said to her.

"He'll die here."

"He'll die trying to get back," she replied.

"Shouldn't we let him choose how he dies?"

"It will be your fault either way," the wind said.

"What if we need him?" Katharine asked. "What if we let him go, and then we die because he wasn't with us?"

It was a good point. He had already proved invaluable. They couldn't let him leave for the good of the group.

"You only delay the inevitable," countered the wind.

"Perhaps," Tom muttered, but he got to his feet and walked around the fire to Jarnstenn. Gravinn stopped speaking and wouldn't look Tom in the eye. "Please stay," Tom said. "Both of you. We don't know what we'll encounter. It could be dangerous. It could kill us. But we might overcome it all, and make it back safely, if we have the two of you."

"Or all our bones could be sitting in a nice little pile before the sun sets."

"Perhaps."

"You're not much for inspiration, are you?"

Tom ignored the barb and turned to Gravinn. "We need your help to find our way back."

"You don't need me." Gravinn spoke to the ground. "Katharine is a Pathfinder." She took a deep breath, marshalled herself, looked him in the eye. "I'm not needed here. But there are dwarfs in the Kingdom that need help."

"We need your help."

"I can't ignore their plight."

"They'll suffer a worse fate if we don't stop the fay. You saw what happened last night. Imagine that happening every night, all across Tir."

"Maybe that's not our responsibility," Jarnstenn said. "I didn't sign up to no heroic quests. Neither did she."

"You think I left my warm bed in Cairnagan for heroic quests?" Tom asked.

"I heard what you left for," Jarnstenn muttered darkly.

"The dwarf is right," said the wind. "You're not a leader. You can't do this."

He wasn't a leader. But Emyr was. Yes, he was grieving. But he had to pull his weight. So Tom walked away from the fire to where Emyr had erected his tent.

"My king?" Tom asked and, when he didn't receive an answer, "Emyr?"

"Come in."

It was as if the tent had never been moved. Ambrose lay in the same spot, in almost the same position. Emyr sat on a rolled up blanket, and the candle burned between them.

"Are we moving on?" Emyr asked. He didn't seem annoyed to have set up the tent only to leave minutes later.

"Not yet, my king. We're still trying to convince Jarnstenn and Gravinn to stay."

"Yes," Emyr said, almost to himself. "It was a matter of time until we lost her."

Had he seen this coming? Why hadn't he said anything? "You have to talk to them. You have to convince them to stay."

"You talk to them, Tom."

"I tried."

"Try again."

"I'm not as good at this as you are."

"Perhaps not. But right now, I'm not good at it either."

"I need you to be better."

"I would say the same to you."

"Because you're not good enough," said the wind. "Because you'll never be good enough."

He had to make Emyr see. "This is your strength," Tom said. "Rallying people to your cause. Leading them. That's why he's lying there." He pointed at Ambrose. "He knew what would happen, but he followed you anyway."

Emyr pushed past him and out of the tent without saying a word.

The wind taunted him. "You can't even persuade Emyr to help you."

Tom stared at Ambrose. "Part of me wishes I could do whatever it is you're doing," he said to the sorcerer.

"So you can hide from the whispers?" asked the wind. "Coward."

"Maybe." But would a coward follow Emyr?

"Maybe," said the wind as he pushed his way outside.

Emyr stood alone, away from the fire and rubbing his arms against the cold. Cloud gathered overhead, blocking even the strip of light they had been able to see above. The old king didn't move when Tom took a position beside him, hand on Caledyr.

Fight.

I'm trying.

"I wish I hadn't taken you out of Faerie," Tom told him. "I didn't want to leave you there. But when you told me all those stories of when you were King of Tir, I always thought that, if anyone deserved some peace, it was you."

"You're right." Emyr sounded bitter. It was a strange thing to hear. "I gave my life to the people of Tir. They took up all my thoughts, all my feelings. There was never room in my life for the people that mattered, because the people of Tir took up all I had. Every heartbeat belonged to someone else."

"And I asked you to give even more."

"You didn't ask. You just took me." It was a rebuke and it stung. But Emyr followed it with, "But I wouldn't go back. At least here I can stand and walk and fight. I can live."

There was a hunger for those things in his voice, as if he felt they would be taken away from him again.

"I am grateful for what you've given me," Emyr said, tone softer, conciliatory.

He was coming around. He knew what he had to do. So Tom just said, "You're welcome, my king."

Emyr's face hardened. "But, right now, I don't want to be a king. Let me sit by my friend's side, in his last moments."

"Emyr."

"No, Tom." Emyr lifted a stern hand. "When Ambrose is dead, I will fight with you. But this quest is yours. You lead it."

That wasn't right. That wasn't fair. "You started this. All of it. A thousand years ago." Tom shook his head. "No. I'm not you, Emyr. I'm trying to help. But I'm here to protect Katharine and Rose. I'm not here to be a hero. I'm just Tom. You're the king of Tir, not me."

There was a long, empty moment, when even the wind died down, as if waiting to see what Emyr said next.

"So that's it?" Emyr stared off down the canyon, over the

footprints and sled tracks they had made in the shallow snow. Looking back on all they had done. "I had higher hopes for you, Tom." His face twisted into bitter disappointment. "There's a reason I asked you to carry that sword."

Fight.

"You killed people because of that sword," said the wind. "You hurt Katharine."

"Was there a reason you didn't warn me about it?"

"I had to learn about that sword. It was an important lesson."

"One you could have passed on instead of letting me slaughter my way across the Kingdom."

"What we learn makes us who we are, son." Emyr shook his head. "First Amyr, now you. I thought you were different. But you're just like him."

Tom was surprised to feel the threat of hot tears behind his eyes. "Maybe the fault is in the thing that links us," he said before he realised he had anything to say. "Did you ever think that you're the reason Amyr failed?"

Emyr blinked a blink as slow as a glacier. "Yes."

Tom knew he had hurt him. He'd found the place Emyr was most vulnerable and put a dagger in it. It was a hurt beyond an apology. But why should he be the first to apologise?

"Because you need him to think well of you," said the wind. "And now he never will."

He touched Caledyr, but the sword was quiet. Silent. Like a child watching its parents fight.

"Responsibility isn't something you pick up and put down when you tire of it, Tom."

"I know."

"I need you to deal with this."

"I don't think I can."

"You need to find a way."

Emyr looked so lost. So sad. So alone. But fatigue and fear kept up Tom's attack. "This is your strength. This is what you do. You're the legendary King of Tir."

Emyr just shook his head.

"Maybe he isn't who you always thought he was," suggested the wind.

"I rescued you from Faerie so you could do this," Tom said. "Not watch an old man die."

Emyr closed his eyes and whispered, "Stop." He took a breath. And another. Like he was remembering how to do so each time. Then he said, "Make it work." And he walked away and disappeared back into the tent.

The others were quiet when Tom returned to the fire. How much had they heard? It didn't matter. He stopped behind Jarnstenn and Gravinn.

"You're not leaving," he said.

Jarnstenn snorted. "You can't stop us."

"I can," Tom replied. He didn't rest his hand on the sword. He didn't stoop, or crouch, or sit beside them. "The group needs you. Katharine will have a child to worry about soon, so she may rely on you to help her, Gravinn. Jarnstenn, I suspect you might have a few ideas on how Six might walk when he feels up to it."

"I'm leaving," he replied.

"You can try, if you like." Tom touched the sword. Not to draw strength from it, but to draw Jarnstenn's eye towards it. "But I'll bring you back."

He waited, daring Jarnstenn to argue. But the dwarf just

looked away. "Suppose it makes no odds whether I die out there or with you lot."

"Thank you." And he turned his gaze to Gravinn.

She was more gracious, bowing her head and murmuring, "I will stay by your side, Tom."

Tom softened his tone. A little. "Thank you." He lifted his eyes to the others, nodded to Draig who was cooking something on the fire. "Is there enough for everyone?"

The elf wore a strange expression. "Yes."

"Good. Everyone needs to eat. Then we'll press on." And he marched across the camp and knelt by Six. The elf was sleeping, it seemed. Mennvinn was sat nearby and Tom asked her, "How is he?"

"Weak," she replied. "He lost a lot of blood. But his leg shows no sign of corruption. He could live."

He was so pale. Was he thinner? "What can we do for him?"

She seemed afraid to answer. "I'm doing the best I can."

"I don't doubt it." She had looked after Emyr, and he seemed well enough.

"But a cirgeon did the hard work," said the wind. "She just tended to him while he healed. It isn't the same."

Tom refused to listen. "If you need anything for him, just ask."

She nodded, looked like she might speak and thought better of it.

"Ask, Mennvinn."

"I have some herbs to prevent corruption. But I'll run out of pain relief by nightfall."

Tom nodded. "Gravinn," he called. He tried not to notice how quickly she scurried over. "Mennvinn needs a Pathfinder's skills."

"However I can assist," she said. Tom left the two dwarfs to talk and crossed the camp to sit by Katharine. Draig had already given her a mug of tea and some dried meat. Tom nodded his approval to the elf.

"Are you warm enough?" he asked Katharine. "Do you need anything?"

She was giving him a strange look too. "I'm fine."

Dank brought tea and food to Tom. He took the tea, but waved the meat away. "Give it to her."

"No," she said.

"Yes."

"You need to eat."

"You need it more."

"Tom, please."

"I won't argue about this."

Something in his tone ended the discussion and Dank tipped the meat onto Katharine's plate and walked away. The camp was quiet. Tom held his mug close to his face, closed his eyes, enjoyed the heat.

"What did Emyr say to you?" Katharine murmured.

But he didn't want to talk about it. "I'm just tired of people not doing what they should."

"She'll think you're talking about her," said the wind. "She'll hate you, and you'll be alone."

But a moment later he felt a hand on his shoulder. It was tentative, uncertain. No doubt the wind was making her doubt everything too. So he reached up and put his hand on hers, squeezed it through gloves.

"Thank you," she said.

"You're welcome."

"I'm sorry."

"What for?"

When she didn't answer, he opened his eyes and looked into her smile. "I don't give you enough credit," she said.

That gave him more strength than Caledyr ever could.

Jarnstenn tried to leave in the night.

CHAPTER 18

THEY HAD TRUDGED through the canyon until long after the sun had set. Draig had suggested camping before it was full dark. "Need we some rest." But Tom had refused. Walking into the whispering wind was exhausting. It crushed the spirit. It made stopping all too appealing. But they had to escape this trap. So he told Draig to keep walking, and he did.

And then it was Dank who said, "We can't see where we're going anymore."

"We know where we're going," Tom replied.

"Please, Tom," asked Gravinn.

"A little farther."

"They'll ignore you," said the wind. "They don't respect you."

But they kept walking and finally, when the darkness was almost complete, Tom said, "Stop."

They made camp without urgency. A day of listening to their fears had made them listless.

"You'll all fall prey to me," said the wind. "Everyone does."

Tom touched Caledyr.

Fight.

He helped Mennvinn wash Six's stump, running warm water

over it and patting it dry. She brewed the last of her pain relief into a tea and Six slurped it down greedily. "How do you feel?" Tom asked him.

"Like a Faerie hound tried to bite my leg off and she finished the job with a hacksaw."

Mennvinn looked stricken, but Tom said, "Mennvinn saved your life."

Six grunted. "I know." He took a deep breath through gritted teeth. "Sorry. It's the pain talking."

"Bad, is it?"

"That's what I like about you, Tom," Six replied. "Your incisive insight. You see things others don't."

Tom smiled despite himself. He hadn't realised how much he'd missed Six's sarcasm and biting barbs until that moment. This was the Six he'd met in that tavern in Aeryie.

"Is there anything you need?"

"I rather fancy a leg. Got one you're not using?"

It was a mask. He used it to hide his fear. So Tom said, "Mennvinn says the signs are good. And I've tasked Jarnstenn with engineering something to keep you walking."

"I heard you say the fay are made of the dead? Is that where I'll go?"

You're not going to die. That's what he wanted to say. But he couldn't. So he said, "You don't look dead to me."

"Give me a chance." Six forced a grin, but it didn't touch his eyes. "It's my first time dying."

Tom uttered silent thanks when Mennvinn interjected with, "You're going to be fine." She was wrapping his stump in rags. "I've seen dwarfs with worse live long and healthy lives."

But Six ignored her. "Tell me I'll live, Tom," he whispered. He reached out, placed a hand on his shoulder. All enmity forgotten. Just pleading. Just begging Tom to give him hope. "Say it, and I'll believe it."

Such as simple thing to ask. Tom wracked his memory for a foresight, anything that suggested Six would live. Nothing. So he closed his eyes, and tried to clear his thoughts. The father and the prayers, and fasting and charities, and calmness of the soul until death. Calmness of the soul until death. Calmness of the soul. Please, show me something of Six.

"I wasn't able to lie for many years," he said to an old woman. "The truth is a hard habit to break."

"The truth is a dangerous habit to have." Her smile creased the tattoos on her face, all swirling lines in decreasing circles.

He stood before a door that towered over him, easily ten times his height, maybe more. "It's a spell," he muttered.

He saw Jarnstenn stealing away from their camp in the dead of the night, only for Tom to step out of the dark and say, "We still have a ways to go before we turn back south."

And finally, he saw Six.

"You took her to Faerie," the elf said.

"I did what had to be done," Tom replied.

"She'll hate you for that."

"Perhaps."

"I think I hate you for it, a little."

The foresights faded, and the cold and the whispers of the wind returned. Resignation was creeping into Six's eyes, smothering his last embers of hope.

"I see you." Tom couldn't help but smile. "We're arguing."

The resignation didn't vanish. But the hope remained. "Careful, Tom. Such a surprise might kill me yet."

Tom laughed. When had he last laughed? "I think you'll live, Westerner."

"I'd better. Who else is going to keep you in check?"

Tom patted the elf's hand. "Rest." And then he stood, arranged the watch, and waited for Jarnstenn to leave.

The dwarf didn't creep out of his tent until Gravinn took her watch. And when she asked him what he was doing, he said, "Leaving. Call out, if you like. But would you hold a fellow dwarf against his will?"

Tom couldn't see them. He was sat behind Emyr's tent, farthest from the fire and furthest south, huddled against the cold. He couldn't feel his fingers or his toes, and he'd nodded off once or twice. He wanted to get this over with, so he could get into his tent and go to sleep.

"They need us," Gravinn said.

"Kunnustenn's dead." Footsteps crunched towards Tom. "I don't care about anything else."

And why would he? Tom recognised the anger in Jarnstenn's voice. It was the same wordless, directionless fury he felt when he thought of Katharine dying. The desire to blame someone, to hurt them, to make them pay. Except there was no-one to blame for her death. No-one but himself.

He almost let Jarnstenn walk past. Let him be alone with that anger. Let him grieve. Let him be. He'd already lost everything. Wasn't it a torture to make him stay? To demand more from him?

But Tom had lost Elaine and Degor, his wife and son. He'd lost his world, he'd lost Faerie, and he might lose Katharine and Rose too.

We do what must be done.

Tom stood and said, quietly, but loud enough that Gravinn would hear, "Go back to sleep, Jarnstenn. We still have a ways to go before we turn back south."

"You might." Jarnstenn didn't stop walking. He pulled no sled, and carried what looked like a lightly-packed bag. He couldn't possibly have enough to make it back to Cairnakor on foot.

"You won't survive the journey back," Tom said, and stepped into Jarnstenn's path. The dwarf stopped, but didn't look up.

The firelight was weak here. They were all shadows and darkness.

"Kunnustenn's dead," he spat.

"I know. And I am sorry. So sorry."

"I don't want you to be sorry, I want you dead and him standing here instead."

There was a cold silence. Even the wind was quiet. But Tom knew that Jarnstenn wasn't threatening violence. He knew exactly how the dwarf felt.

Fight.

No. Now is not the time to fight. "I didn't kill Kunnustenn," Tom said.

"It's your fault he's dead."

Tom replied to the dwarf's unspoken words. "It's not your fault."

Jarnstenn said nothing. Then he sniffed. His shoulders slumped a little, and he was no longer challenging Tom. When he spoke, his voice was shakey. "He lived in his books and his learnings. Real things were a different world to him. He needed me to bring him to that world."

Say nothing. Let silence do the talking.

"And when you came along with your damn stupid quest, it was like you made his books real. You gave him something I couldn't. And I didn't give him what I should've." The bag slid to the ground. Jarnstenn stood there like he was being kept up by a single, unsteady thought. "He'd thank you, you know. The way he went, looking for Cairnarim, taken by invisible Faerie creatures. He'd say he couldn't ask for more." Jarnstenn drew ragged breaths. He wasn't far now. "I couldn't see them. Couldn't hear them. Couldn't do nothing to stop them." Finally he looked up at Tom, and said, "Tell me what I could have done."

"Nothing." It was the kindest, cruellest thing to say. "You did everything you could."

Jarnstenn sagged until his forehead rested against Tom's belly, and the dam broke. Tom placed one hand on the back of the dwarf's head, one on his back. Said nothing, and let the dwarf cry in the cold.

Gravinn was still at the fire when they returned to camp. Tom made a point of saying to Jarnstenn, gently, before he stepped inside his tent, "So you'll stay?"

Jarnstenn nodded. "I want to tell Kun what Cairnarim looks like when I return to the ground. Whenever that might be."

Tom just nodded, bid him goodnight, and turned to Gravinn. She didn't meet his eye. She was expecting anger, for letting Jarnstenn leave. He was angry. But not for that reason.

"You didn't know I was there," he said to her.

She shook her head.

"Why not?"

She looked surprised. Offended? "You concealed yourself."

"An attacker would do the same."

She looked annoyed, but also aware she was on the back foot. "I was distracted by Jarnstenn."

"Then we can all sleep easy, as long as you aren't distracted." Before she could say anything, he added, "Go and wake Dank for his watch."

"It's not yet time."

"Go and wake him."

She scowled, stamped her way across the camp and gave Dank a brusque awakening before retreating to her own tent.

"Is it so late already?" Dank asked with a yawn. He stood by the fire, stretched, rubbed his arms. "I never feel like I'm sleeping enough lately."

Tom's eyes were drooping, so he just nodded and yawned himself.

"What are you doing up?" Dank asked. "You've taken your watch already, haven't you?"

Tom nodded. He'd had first watch, then slipped off to his hiding place. "Jarnstenn needed convincing to stay," he replied.

"I see." Dank tipped his head to one side. "Why is Gravinn upset?"

"I told her she needed to keep a better watch."

Dank nodded. Watched Tom as if appraising him, weighing him up. It made Tom uncomfortable. His discomfort only increased when he said, "I can't decide if Maev would find you more interesting these days, or less."

It was the open, honest way he spoke of Maev's interest in him, and inferred Tom's own interest in her. He cleared his throat, asked, "What do you mean?" Because, despite himself, he still wanted Maev to desire him.

"A lot of her interest stemmed from how she could manipulate you." Dank didn't couch his response in a soft tone or an apologetic expression. He didn't even look at Tom, just poked at the fire instead. "I suspect it wouldn't be so easy now. So would she be bored of you? Or would you represent a challenge?"

Tom hated how his heart still leapt for her approval. Perhaps that was why he said, "Her interest in us is all that keeps us safe."

Dank's silence gave him time to realise what he had said. What he had let slip; that he had been speaking to the sprite. Iron nails. He'd been thinking of Maev instead of thinking of what he was saying. Distracted, he'd let an enemy thought slip through his mind and out across his tongue.

"And now he knows," whispered the wind.

"How would you know that, Tom?" Dank asked. Watching him carefully.

Cover it up. Lie. "I stabbed Melwas. I cannot believe he wishes me anything but dead."

Dank offered only a considered, "Yes."

"Someone must be speaking for us."

Dank stared at him. Rose to his feet. And finally asked, "Have you been speaking to our sprite?"

Our sprite. "Glastyn." As if that was an answer. "He told me that Melwas and Mab are at war with each other."

But Dank shook his head. "Tell me, Tom." He started taking slow, steady steps, and Tom resisted the urge to back away. "Have you been speaking to our sprite?"

Dank's words told Tom one thing: don't tell the truth. So he stood strong, refused to look guilty, and dropped a hand to Caledyr. "You gave your faith to Emyr."

Dank stopped one step away, and Tom could see the hunger in the other man's eyes. He wanted his sprite. And he didn't want it. "I did," Dank managed.

"You want to be more than what the fay made you."

"I do." Dank looked aside, licked his lips. Nodded. "I do," he repeated, trying to convince himself. And Tom wished he had sent Dank back with Esyllt and Hawne, sent him away from the temptation and let him make a life for himself without the fay. "I could see her once," Dank muttered. "Just to say goodbye?"

Silence. Dank needed to fight this battle alone. Or did he? Tom had been fighting his own battle against Maev by himself for years. Perhaps it would have been easier if someone had helped him?

And the wind whispered, "You will never be free of them."

So Tom reached out and gripped Dank's upper arm. The other man started and met his eye. "You don't need to see the sprite, Dank. You don't need to talk to it. The fay are not your friends. I'm your friend, Dank. So I won't tell you what to do. You can see the sprite, if you want. But I don't think you should. Because you're already more than they will ever let you be."

Dank didn't believe him. Not at first. But Tom could see the other man persuading himself. Pushing aside his urges. Rebuilding his sense of self, squaring his shoulders, straightening his back. And when he nodded, he was firm and certain. "You're right."

Tom relaxed muscles he hadn't realised were tensed.

"Thank you, Tom."

"You're welcome." He clapped Dank's arm. "I can leave you to take this watch, can't I?"

Dank answered the question Tom hadn't asked. "I won't go near it."

"Good." Tom unstrapped Caledyr and the sword began to protest, and the wind told him he was a fool. But the gesture would give Dank more confidence than anything else he could do. So he handed it to the other man. "Watch over us while we sleep."

He was just a few steps from his tent when Dank said, "I was angry with you." Tom stopped. "For talking to my sprite. I was jealous."

And the wind whispered, "He's changed his mind. He's picked them over you."

Tom was unarmed. He'd just given the sword to Dank. So he didn't move. Didn't even turn. Just listened for the soft hiss Caledyr made when it was pulled from its scabbard. Please don't draw it, he begged. Please, Dank.

"I was jealous," the other man said again. "Is that how you feel when you see Maev with Midhir?"

It was something Tom didn't want to think of, didn't want to admit. "Yes."

"Hmm." There was no other sound, no drawn sword, and Tom allowed himself to look over his shoulder and watch Dank consider the apple pommel on Caledyr. "We aren't the first people to try to seal away the fay. No-one has succeeded. But I think you're right; if we stay true to each other, we can do it, can't we?"

Tom gave the boy a grave nod, said, "I hope so," and tried not to think of how he had let Maev embrace him outside Cairnakor.

That night, he dreamt disturbing dreams. Everyone knew he spoke to the fay. They cursed him for loving Maev. They shunned him and laughed at him, took away Caledyr, took away his hands and left him alone in the cold.

He stood with Brega in a small, dark room. "Which side do you fight on?" she asked.

Tom was exhausted the next morning, yet it seemed there was never any rest to be had. Mennvinn was reminding him she had no pain relief for Six. Gravinn was complaining there were no herbs to be found in this hideous canyon, Draig was moaning that another day with this wind might drive him to madness. Katharine was grumpy and uncomfortable. Six was in very obvious pain. Only Emyr and Jarnstenn gave Tom any peace; the old king remained withdrawn, and the dwarf was silent in his grief.

But all of them seemed to look to him to coax them into breaking fast, breaking camp, and moving on through the Chasm. He knew he was short with them. That he snapped and berated. But none of them seemed willing to be helpful.

They acted as if moaning about their lot would somehow improve it.

"How do you improve the prospect of a cold, certain death?" whispered the wind.

They trudged, bellies carrying more water than food, and tried to ignore the wind. But it grew stronger, and louder, until it was like a bellow. You will fail, you will fall, turn back, give in, give up. Constant, unending, without even pause for breath. You lead them to their deaths. You lead them to their doom. You've seen it. You see her die. Your daughter will die too. And what do you do to prevent it? Secret conversations with your bottled fay, secret desires to lie with the Faerie Queen. Weak, foolish, liar, coward, traitor, fay-lover, untrue, disloyal, oath breaker, death maker.

Fight.

But Tom didn't need the sword to tell him to push back against the whispers. Seeing Jarnstenn's grieving anger had woken Tom's own fury. Yes, he had squandered his youth. He'd been a poor husband and a terrible father. He'd suffered years of silent degradation at the hands of the fay. He'd endured years of alienation in a Tir he didn't recognise. He'd let himself be pushed and pulled and given orders by the fay, by Neirin, by Storrstenn, by Caledyr, even by Emyr.

"Yes," said the wind, "because you are weak, and nothing, and little more than a lost little man who has no strength of his own."

But he'd fought in merrow and Erhenni arenas. He'd been the scourge of the Kingdom. He'd brought back the legendary King Emyr and he'd pushed Melwas to his knees in Faerie. And he wouldn't be turned back by a few nasty little whispers. No. This foul little magic was nothing, a hedge magician's trick. He would stop the fay. Not because other people told him he had to. Not because he had anything to prove. Because he was protecting the people he cared about. Do you hear that, Rimestenn? Your cheap little magics are nothing. You won't stop me. You won't. You won't.

And the whispers stopped. He took a few more steps before he realised there was no more wind. He looked up. There was no more Chasm, just an enormous set of doors.

They were easily three times as tall as Tom, set deep into the side of the mountain, and covered with sculptures and carvings. Gargoyles leapt from the surface of the stone, and dwarfs and elfs and men spoke and fought and displayed their strength of arms with faces so lifelike that Tom half-expected them to turn and speak. It seemed the longer he stared, the more detail appeared. The spaces between figures were filled with constellations of suns and stars and moons, the dragon that spanned both doors was covered in tiny, individually carved scales. And the gargoyles were not generic monsters: they were fay.

There was Puck, crawling down the door towards them, each hair of his fur individually carved. There was Melwas in the shape of the Black Knight Malvis, fighting an army of men and dwarfs and elfs yet looking out at his new, living audience. There was Fenoderee, looking like a malevolent swamp given limbs. There was Knocker, who haunted tunnels and mines, ready to strike his little anvil with his little hammer and lead travellers astray. Not one of the fay looked friendly or carefree. Each of them was openly hostile, each of them looking down at the exact spot they had stopped.

Only one figure looked aside: Morwen of Rhomer. Sat in a corner, faced away from her fellow decorations and her living audience, looking entirely unlike every other depiction of her that Tom had seen. Her curly hair was unbound and fell across her face; only her sharp nose was visible, and thin, sad, downturned lips. She wore billowing robes, not the beautiful dresses she was so often given in art and sculpture, making her formless save for one foot, bare and unadorned, toes pointed downwards. She wore none of her usual jewellery, displayed none of her usual confidence or bravado. The only reason Tom recognised her at all was her staff. Unlike Ambrose's rude instrument, hers was artful, bearing the symbol of the crescent moon atop its clean, smooth length.

"Magnificent," Dank breathed. His eyes were wide as if he was trying to see it all before it disappeared. "Just magnificent."

He was right, of course. These creations were an incredible sight to behold. How many weeks had it taken to make just one? It was a shame they were hidden so far from sight; although they were somewhat frightening, with the fay looking ready to spring to life and cut down anyone within reach, these doors were a work of art. Katharine and Gravinn were already scribbling notes and rough sketches. Everyone else stared in wonder and appreciation. Except one.

"Pretty fakes," Jarnstenn said.

"What do you mean?" Tom asked.

"They're not real doors." The dwarf waved a hand. "Just look at those hinges."

Tom looked, saw that, yes, there were elaborate hinges, each topped with a miniature fay. "What about them?"

"Hinges on this side means they'd open outwards."

"Right."

"Ain't no room to open outwards."

He was right. Although the Chasm had widened on either side, there wasn't space for these doors to fully open.

"Could we squeeze through enough space," Draig offered.

"Probably. But what fool would put all this effort into doors that don't open properly?" Jarnstenn shook his head. "Not Rimestenn."

"He's right." Emyr was almost squinting at the great doors, as if trying to see through them. "This isn't Rimestenn's style."

"Are you saying this isn't the entrance to Cairnarim?" Katharine made no effort to hide her disappointment.

"Ain't no entrance to anywhere," Jarnstenn said.

"It's a ruse." Emyr's lips quirked in a humourless smile. "Rimestenn's engines and contraptions were always half wonder, half illusion."

Illusion. "Is that why Morwen is there?" Tom asked.

"Possibly." Emyr cast a glance at Ambrose, still unwaking on his sled. What would he have to say about Rimestenn raising an effigy to his rival? How many statues of Ambrose stood in all of Tir? "But Rimestenn held no love for Morwen. I can't imagine why he would put her here."

"And she looks wrong," Tom added. "Not like you described her."

"She does," Emyr agreed.

"It's a marker," Katharine said. When everyone turned to look at her, she gestured at the paper in her hands. "When you create a path, you leave markers along its length so travellers know whether they should take a turn or carry on straight." She pointed at Morwen. "She's a marker. She's telling you which turn to take." She grunted the last and winced.

"What's wrong?" Tom asked her.

"I'm fine." She shook her head, denying her own words.

"Is it the child?"

She shook her head and pointed at the doors. "Look for the door," she ordered him, but screwed up her face again and hissed.

This was it. "Rose is coming," he told her. "This is the beginning."

"You can't give birth out here!" Mennvinn sounded almost scandalised.

"She's not coming," Katharine said. "Not yet."

But she was wrong. Tom had seen the beginning of Degor's

birth. Elaine's face had looked just like Katharine's. This was it. His daughter was coming. "Mennvinn, do what you need to do. Make Katharine as comfortable as possible."

"Out here?"

Yes, she had a point. They needed to get inside. So Tom turned to the doors and said, "Morwen is telling us where to look." He followed the statue's gaze, but it rested only on an empty crevice of rock. Nothing.

"Not her face." Katharine pointed. "Her foot."

Her bare foot, pointed away and down. To a snow-covered boulder sat a few feet from the doors themselves. Tom stepped over to it, placed his hand against it.

It felt wrong.

He tapped it and almost jumped when it rang hollow; the boulder was so light he could pick it up and lift it over his head. And while the others cried out in surprise, he found something hidden behind it.

Another door. Much smaller, just enough for a dwarf to step through. Plain stone, with no decoration save an inscription in an old tongue. The same tongue he had seen on Sir Dolorio's tomb in Cairnidol.

A tongue that Emyr spoke. "The father and the prayers," he read, "and fasting and charities, and calmness of the soul until death."

"Your prayer."

"Not mine." He reached out and ran his fingertips over the script. "What does it mean?"

"Look." Tom pointed at the rock around the door. Thin strips of black stone, veined with silver, ran from where a lock might be, down to the ground and across to a shallow, round indentation in the ground.

"It's a channel," Emyr said. "It directs magic into the lock."

Tom nodded. "It's a spell." He looked up at the script. "Your prayer is a spell."

Emyr shook his head. "I said it but nothing happened."

"Not an incantation. Instructions." Tom smiled despite the dread growing in his belly. "Your prayer is telling us how to open the door."

CHAPTER 19

THERE WASN'T time to make camp, but they couldn't leave Katharine exposed to the elements. Or Ambrose and Six. So Tom told Draig and Dank to raise two tents, one for Six and Ambrose, one for Katharine. While Mennvinn tended to her, the rest of them huddled around the tiny door.

Everyone was agreed that Emyr must be the father. "No other fathers here," Jarnstenn said, and then everyone looked at Tom.

"Must the prayer be words," Draig said, and everyone agreed with that too.

That's where the agreement ended. "Fasting means not eating," Gravinn said.

"So we sit here and starve until it opens?" Jarnstenn didn't sound convinced.

"Maybe we put some food in the hollow?" Katharine called from within her tent.

"Childbirth first, puzzles second," Six called from his.

"What about the charities?" Gravinn asked. "Do we have to give it something?"

"As well as the food?"

"Perhaps instead of."

"Dinner and a gift? We ain't wooing this door, are we?"

"What about the calmness?"

"Meditation?"

"And death? Must one of us be made dead?"

"We're not killing anyone to get in there, Draig."

"What if we have to?"

Only Dank had nothing to add. He sat there as if he was alone, staring up at the enormous fake doors.

"I'm surprised you don't already know the answer," Tom murmured to him.

"What? Oh, the riddle? No."

"But Rimestenn is long dead. The fay must know all his secrets."

But Dank shook his head. "Whatever Rimestenn built here, the fay never knew of it." Dank grinned. "Look at it, Tom. We must be the first to see it in centuries. Not even the fay have laid eyes on it."

Tom frowned. How had Rimestenn kept his secrets? Fenoderee had said that one fay could keep a secret from the rest of them. But could the dead?

"So the fay don't know how to open this door."

Dank gave Tom a smile, one you might give to a child who has asked an innocently daft question. "It's closed, Tom."

Of course. If the fay knew, they would have opened it long ago. Tom sighed. Perhaps he was wrong. Perhaps there was no spell. Perhaps the hollow was meant for some magical artefact they forgot to bring with them.

No. Ambrose would have said something.

Wouldn't he?

He looked over at the tent Ambrose lay in. He should have been awake for this. He'd have opened the door already. How long would he lie like that, barely breathing, barely living? If this was all he had to look forward to, why was he clinging on like this?

Because he knew what was waiting for him. He knew, when he died, the fay would take him. And they would know everything he knew.

So he must know something they didn't already. Not where they were. Not what they were doing. Something he had said and done.

"The father and the prayers," Tom muttered. "And fasting and charities, and calmness of the soul until death."

"It isn't meant to be an instruction," Emyr said. "It's advice. It's something to live by."

Tom shook his head. "It's all there. Calmness of the soul until death. Fasting. Charities. Sacrifice. It's all talking about magic."

"We already knew it was magic," Emyr grumbled.

Tom touched the hollow, shallow, round, the perfect size for coin. "Charities. Alms. A coin." A foresight came back to him, and he knew exactly which coin was meant to sit there.

Emyr let out a tiny gasp. "The coin Rimestenn gave me. He told me never to spend it. It must be that one." And then a mix of fury and despair passed over his face. "And it's lost," he growled.

"No." Tom shook his head. "I took it."

"You took it?"

"It fell from your pockets when you were lying in Faerie. I thought it nothing but an old coin. Worthless. I buried it with a dead man."

"One-eyed father," Emyr cursed. "Do you think another coin will do?"

Tom shook his head. "We have to retrieve that coin." He gave Emyr a small smile. "I've foreseen it."

"So we have to turn back?" Restrained anger burned behind Emyr's eyes. He looked ready to hit something.

"I don't think so." He turned to Dank. "You said the barriers between Tir and Faerie were weakened. Does that mean the Circles aren't needed to cross over anymore?"

Dank nodded. "The fay can enter Tir anywhere they please." Tom gave Dank an apologetic smile, and the boy's shoulders sagged. "You want me to take you somewhere again?"

"Again?" Emyr asked.

"Dank took us in and out of Faerie when we rescued you," Tom explained. And to Dank he said, "I know it's asking a lot of you. But I need to retrieve something from Cairnacei. It's our only hope of getting inside, and you're the only hope I have of getting there."

"You could walk." Dank's smile was weak, but he didn't argue as Tom thought he would. He squared his shoulders, took a breath, and said, "It will be harder. I haven't been linked to the fay for weeks."

"I'm just asking you to try." Tom put a hand on his shoulder and added, "That will be enough for me."

Tom had hoped his words would lift some of the pressure Dank must be feeling but, If anything, they seemed to add to it. The other man's smile wavered but he gave a brave nod and said, "When?"

"Katharine needs to be inside now." He waved Gravinn forward. "You too, Gravinn. You can find the herbs Mennvinn needs." Gravinn looked like she might say no. "I know it's not pleasant. But Six is suffering far more than we will."

"I can attest to that," the elf called from his tent.

Gravinn nodded and stepped forward. "Thank you," Tom said and she just nodded. He slipped into Katharine's tent. She was lying down, her head propped up by blankets and one draped over her legs. A fine sheen of sweat slicked her face, and Mennvinn gave Tom a fearful look.

"Before you ask, I don't know how long it will be," the dwarf said. "It could be hours, it could be a day."

Tom just nodded. "I know she's in safe hands," he said, and watched Mennvinn take strength from that. He awkwardly manoeuvred his way through the tent and placed a kiss on Katharine's head.

"Don't go," she whispered.

"I'll come back," he promised.

"You had better."

Tom grinned. "I wouldn't dare cross you." He looked at her belly and said, "Look after your mother for me," he told the bump.

Katharine found his hand and gripped it tight. "Be safe."

"You too."

He slipped out from under her touch, felt her eyes on his back as he stepped out of the tent. Why did he feel like he was abandoning her? Why did he feel like he was running away? He unstrapped Caledyr and pushed it into Emyr's hands. The old king drew breath to argue, but Tom shook his head. "Protect her," he commanded. And Emyr's protests died on his lips and he took the sword without a word.

Tom glanced across the camp, all eyes on him. He felt like he should say something to buoy their spirits. What would a Knight of Tir say? What would Emyr say? But the king of legend was silent, and Sir Tom didn't have time to waste on pretty words. So he placed a hand on Dank's shoulder, Gravinn took his hand, and Tom stared at the tent where his daughter was being born as Dank ripped him from the world.

It was worse than before.

It was like his mind was being scoured with handfuls of coarse sand even as it was poured into a vessel with Dank and Gravinn and allowed to mix.

He felt Dank's steely determination that he would do this, that he would do this for the man who had freed him from the fay.

He felt Gravinn's dread, the fear that her deepest fears would be revealed, her shame that they would all know how she wished she had never left her elfish masters.

What did they feel from him? Did they feel his fear, that Katharine might die, that Rose might be born without him? Did they feel his uncertainty, his anger, did they feel the cold little pebble that sat inside him, that little nugget of nothing he'd put there?

The maelstrom wailed all around him, and he felt a grip that he hadn't felt before weaken around him. He felt himself begin to tatter. Thoughts slipped away. He watched without eyes as they left him, little scraps on a wind, like ash drifting up from a bonfire. Who was he? What was he trying to achieve?

Stay here, someone thought, but he couldn't.

Fight.

But it wasn't like before. There was nothing to cling to, just an endless sea of formless magic and he was drifting away on it. And he knew he was leaving someone behind, but he couldn't remember who or why he cared.

Then something squeezed his very self together in a crushing grip and he felt himself pulled, dragged through something that didn't want to let him pass, and a thousand voices cried out in uncertainty before there was silence.

Not silence. The sound of his breath. He was breathing. Lying face down on a field of poppies, warm breeze blowing over him.

He was going to vomit. He raised himself on his elbows, let it come up. He held himself on trembling arms, eyes watering, and all he could think of was how he had wasted food.

Gravinn was still retching. What about Dank? Tom forced himself to his feet, staggered a few steps before he regained his balance. Emyr's black bones, he wanted to lie down. He wiped his mouth on his sleeve.

And saw Dank twitching on his back, eyes wide and staring, choking on his own vomit.

"Dank!" Tom dropped to his knees, hauled Dank onto his side, and the other man retched, coughed and threw up over the poppies. His entire body was stiff; holding him was like holding a plank of twitching wood. Was he breathing? Tom slapped his back. "Breathe, Dank, breathe."

Dank retched, straining to empty himself of anything and everything, but nothing would come. And he didn't blink. He just stared at nothing.

"What's wrong with him?" Gravinn was on her hands and knees, staring with dull eyes.

"I don't know." What else could he say? He wanted to say Dank would be fine, tell Dank the same, reassure them both. But he couldn't. So he said, "See if you can't find what Mennvinn needs. I'll wait with Dank."

Gravinn just nodded, staggered away. She didn't meet his eye, not now that he knew she regretted leaving the Kingdom. Perhaps she thought he judged her for that. But given what sort of life she had these days, he could hardly blame her for missing an easier existence. A miserable freedom was probably a cold comfort on freezing nights.

Not that it was freezing here. In fact, he was sweating. Tom shrugged off his furs, enjoyed the warm breeze. It was a nice day. It seemed wrong that it was. The others were shivering hundreds of miles to the north. Katharine was giving birth, alone, just as Elaine had. Dank was having some sort of fit. The fay were already preying on innocent people. But the sun shone like everything was fine, and the breeze idled through the air as if there were no cares in Tir.

The worst of it was that, even if they got into Cairnarim, they would still only have two of the four glarn. And there was no-one to tell them where the others were. So did that mean this was all for nothing? Would they be better off finding a quiet corner of Tir and hoping the fay would overlook them?

"I don't think they'd ever stop trying to find you," Dank said.

Tom blinked, realised that Dank's limbs had relaxed and he was breathing normally. Had he read his mind? No. He'd been talking aloud. "Are you well?"

"Well enough."

"You gave us a scare."

"Think how I felt," Dank replied. And then he said, in a quiet voice, "I don't think I can do that again, Tom."

They both knew he would have to. So Tom just said, "Get some rest." He stood. "Gravinn is fetching supplies for Mennvinn. We'll be back soon."

Dank didn't move. Just nodded. Pulled his knees up to his chest.

"I'll be back soon," Tom repeated.

There was no telling where in Cairnacei Dank had taken them. Katharine would probably have known in moments. But Tom had to rush to the river and follow it back towards the Whispering Woods. By the time he found Topknot's grave, the sun was already beginning to set.

If he hadn't recognised the spot in the river where he had tried to wash off the man's blood, Tom could have easily missed the grave. Blood-red poppies were already beginning to grow over the ground they had disturbed. Their stems snapped and their roots ripped as Tom clawed up handfuls of dirt. He knew he should take a moment to remember the man he'd killed, to mourn his passing, to feel guilt and regret and all the other appropriate emotions. But Katharine needed him. So appropriate emotions could wait.

The coin wasn't buried deep, just a few inches under the surface. He pulled it out, brushed away the dirt, hefted it. It seemed unremarkable. The stylised sun on one side, a profile of Emyr on the other. He expected it to feel different. To be heavier, or to feel like magic somehow. But there was nothing. What if this wasn't the right coin? What if this was nothing more than a piece of metal?

Then they were lost. No sense in worrying about possibilities.

"So that's the key."

"Not now, Glastyn." Tom got to his feet and began to hurry back to the river. Tried not to worry that Dank wouldn't be able to take them back. Tried not to worry that Rose had already been born. Or that something had gone wrong.

"Isn't a walk on a beautiful spring evening more pleasant with a friend?"

Hard to think that it was spring after weeks of riding through snowy mountains. Time was slipping away from them. "I'm in a hurry."

"Of course." Glastyn seemed to have no problem keeping pace, and somehow made it seem like he was in no rush at all. His fine silk shirts and trouser added to the illusion of an evening's stroll. "So much is happening."

"Why are you here?"

"You seem to often ask us that question of late." Glastyn grinned, basking in the sunset. "You know, one of the things we love about Tir is the sunsets. And the sunrises. We wish we had those in Faerie."

The fay, it seemed, wouldn't be hurried, so Tom saved his breath. The march to the grave, the digging, and the march back were taking its toll. He was out of breath, and his shins burned.

"You know, it's quicker this way." Glastyn jerked a thumb over to his left.

"Should I trust you?"

"Didn't we deliver at Tirend?"

Yes. He had. They had gone unmolested by the fay. But, "It's important I get back to them, Glastyn."

"We wouldn't make you miss the birth of your daughter."

How did he know? But there was sincerity in Glastyn's eyes, or the closest thing the fay could approximate.

"You trusted Fenoderee," Glastyn murmured. "He is just a part of us. As the man who loves our queen is part of the man who opposes her."

"Those parts would be in opposition to each other."

"You're right." Glastyn grinned. "A bad analogy."

Tom shook his head. He had no idea what Glastyn wanted. Playing his own game, the sprite had said. But the fay had helped them in Tirend. Hopefully he was helping them again. So Tom gestured. "Lead on, Glastyn."

The fay made no attempt to hide his pleasure. "Follow me, Sir Thomas."

Glastyn seemed perfectly pleased to be walking in silence, so

Tom did the same. But while he tried to puzzle out Glastyn's motivations, his thoughts kept sliding back to Katharine. Was she alright? What if something went wrong? No, it wouldn't. He knew he'd be by her side when she died.

It was a small comfort.

"Would you mind if someone joined us, Tom?"

Someone? Tom shook away his fears and found new ones. "A fay?"

"Yes. But a friend."

A friend. Was that what Glastyn was? "Will they harm me? Or Dank or Gravinn?"

"No."

"Will they stop us returning to the others?"

"No." Glastyn grinned as if Tom was guessing a great riddle.

"Do I have a choice?"

"Of course." But Glastyn shook his head, brushed his long locks away from his face. "You can always make the wrong choice."

Caledyr was hundreds of miles away. All Tom had was an iron knife. It would be madness to agree. "I think I would prefer it if we walked alone."

"Unfortunately, Glastyn is teasing you." The voice came from his right, her features hidden by the glare of the sunset behind her. "We are already here."

Tom didn't recognise her voice. On the back foot, his only weapon was his tongue. "Glastyn is rude that way."

She laughed, a deep, throaty laugh. "We have often chastised him for being so."

"Rude?" Glastyn folded his arms. "I am the epitome of charm."

"You can be both rude and charming, Glastyn dear." The fay stepped closer, revealing snake scale skin covered in a simple white dress. She was short and lithe, her slitted eyes glowing in the dark.

"Melusine?" he guessed. Mester Stoorworm's other face.

She nodded. "But don't worry; we don't hold the same grudges." She smiled. Tom had expected fangs, but she had perfect, normal teeth. "Stoorworm was the aggressor. You were protecting your family."

She didn't seem like a threat. But Tom had heard the stories about her. And there was no trusting appearances. "Why are you here?"

"He asks that question a lot." Glastyn was visibly pleased with himself as he turned to Tom. "We brought Melusine to speak with you."

"Why?"

"There is much debate in Faerie about you," Melusine said. "You've managed to do what no-one has since King Emyr. And even he never sparked such disagreement."

"So I understand." Everything he said would be known by both Melwas and Mab. He had to tread carefully.

As if to illustrate the point, he stumbled over a stone in the dark. Before he could fall, Melusine was beside him, strong fingers wrapped around his arm, sharp nails pricking his skin. He wanted to push her away, but that might be more dangerous than not. So he stopped, waited.

She slipped an arm around him, turned her hold into an embrace. "You know us, do you not?"

"By reputation only." Her embrace reminded him too much of how Mab had held him outside Cairnakor.

"Then you know of our search?"

"I do." How many mortal men had she taken to husband only to be disappointed? How many men had sworn oaths not to look upon her between Calgraef and Calmae, when she was Mester Stoorworm? Each of those men had succumbed to curiosity, dying by Stoorworm's hand, and Melusine had remained childless.

"You are a remarkable man, Thomas Rymour," she breathed into his neck. "Perhaps you would have made a fine husband."

Say nothing. Do nothing. She could bite his neck out as soon as kiss it.

"But we understand you are promised to another." She released him and resumed her walk. "And you are to be a father yourself." Her voice boiled with envy. "Which is why we are here."

Every thought froze into a painful dread in the pit of his belly. "I won't let you take her."

A small smile played around her lips; she knew he couldn't stop her. "This is the point of no return, you know." But her smile was gentle. Maternal. It made no sense. She gestured to Tom's pocket, the one holding the coin, and said, "You could give that to our queen and all would be forgiven."

Tom touched the coin, reassured himself with its presence, and shook his head. "Melwas will never forgive me."

"We cannot speak for our king. But we imagine, should Maev bring you back into the fold, he will at the least seek your end in less overt ways."

And would Katharine be safe? Would Rose?

"What of my friends?" he asked.

"Our queen has often spoken of your silver tongue."

So Melusine thought they could be bargained for. He knew all the reasons he shouldn't. He knew they wouldn't thank him for it.

But he saw a path where there wasn't one before.

"What would I have to do?"

The sun had set. The moon, a slender crescent, unburdened by child, rose in the east. A thousand stars glittered overhead, and Tom realised he hadn't seen a clear sky in months. It was beautiful. He could have lain back and stared at it for hours. He took a deep breath. The cold in his bones had already been chased away; the freezing misery was already a memory, the edge of it softened by spring in Tir.

Melusine smiled. "We have always thought highly of a man who would do anything for his family. And if any of the fay knows about family, it is us." It was harder to see her scales in the dark. It was possible to think of her as a mortal woman. To allow himself to think there was no Faerie motive or agenda behind her words. "You don't need to share blood to be family. You only need to care for each other, so fiercely that you will do anything to have them be safe."

He would have them all be safe. Katharine and Rose, Emyr and Ambrose, Six and Draig, Jarnstenn and Mennvinn, Gravinn and Dank.

"We put family before ourselves, always, without fail, because they are everything," Melusine said, "More than happiness, more than loyalty, more than hope and heart and home." She was right. There wasn't anything more important than keeping them safe. "We would wound a man for family. We would kill him. We would maim and blind and butcher, we would slaughter innocents, we would watch all things burnt to ash and bone, just so our family might enjoy a few more moments of peace."

He had wounded. And killed. And maimed and blinded and butchered. To protect his family.

But could he slaughter innocents? Could he watch Tir burn?

Katharine would hate him. Rose would hate him. He would have no family.

"If we do those things, we lose them," he said to Melusine.

"But they live."

"They might wish differently."

"We make difficult choices for family."

"You're right." He took his hand from his pocket. Did Melusine's eyes light up? "Glastyn, why did you bring Melusine here?"

"As we said." Glastyn was a shadow in the dark. "To talk."

"I don't believe you."

"We don't need you to."

If this was a Faerie trap, it was an elaborate one. Either of them could have overpowered him and taken the coin, kept Orlannu from his reach forever. Spirited him off to Faerie, never to see Katharine again. Never to see Rose at all.

But he could see firelight ahead. The fay had brought him back to Dank and Gravinn, quicker than if he had walked his own path.

"Thank you for your help," he said to them. "But being part of a family means living up to them. I need to be the man they deserve." He stopped walking, turned to Melusine. Tried to read her expression in the dark. "It would be an easy choice to surrender to the fay. It's a choice my family doesn't deserve."

"Do you think you can succeed?" she asked.

"Our chances are slight," he admitted. "I don't know if we can find what we're looking for. And even then, I don't know if it will be enough. You cannot die. Does that mean you cannot be stopped?"

Melusine made an amused sound. "You think that is our strength? That we cannot die?"

"Isn't it?"

"He has a point." Glastyn stretched, as if waking from a nap. "Being unending does rather have its advantages."

"And its disadvantages, no?"

"Quite so." Glastyn grinned. "You know us too well, my dear."

"We do." Melusine turned to Tom. "You, on the other hand, know us so well, and yet so little." Melusine pointed towards the fire. "How often do you disagree with each other as to where to go, what to do, who can be trusted, what will succeed?"

"More times than I can count."

"You are many, and that made you weak. Whereas we were many that were one. Even while we held different thoughts, we acted as one. And that made us strong."

She was right. How do you defeat an enemy like the fay if you're divided?

"This is something that not even the fay understand," she said. "We walk Tir and think ourselves mighty because the mortals cannot see us and cannot hurt us. Not realising that our strength lay in our unity."

And the fay weren't united anymore. "Now you are at war with each other."

"Good boy." Her teeth shone in the moonlight. "That's why we can have this conversation. Because we forgot how to pay attention to all of our parts."

Tom tried to process the different pronouns. "So the fay don't know we are talking?"

"Just as in Tirend," Glastyn said. "We brokered that deal, Tom. But our king and queen did not know that you knew about it."

Glastyn had come to him in secret? Knowing what had happened to Fenoderee? "You risk a lot."

The fay grinned that charming grin that won so many hearts to his own. "What is life without a little risk?"

"What are you up to, Glastyn?"

"Recruiting Melusine to our cause." He nodded to the other fay.

"How?"

Melusine said, "He gave us the opportunity to offer you the easy choice."

"Why?"

"To see if you will take it."

Tom felt a flare of anger and held it. Calmness of the soul until death. "I've made a lot of mistakes on this journey. And a lot of people have been quick to tell me I take the easy path. The truth is there are no easy paths." He looked up at the stars, took a deep breath and let out his anger with a sigh. "Giving you the coin would put me on a dangerous path. So would trying to stop the fay from terrorising Tir. All I can do is imagine the kind of man my family deserves, and do what he would do." He met her eye, and saw she understood.

"That is what we hoped you would say," she said. "Goodbye, Thomas."

"What does that mean?" he asked. "What will you do now?"

The edges of her shadow were already softening. "What little I can," she replied, as she faded away. "When the time comes."

"We need help now."

"Do you?" Glastyn was vanishing too. "Not the kind of help Melusine can provide. Not yet." He gave Tom a gallant wave.

"Wait," Tom said, and Glastyn stopped disappearing, his form translucent, like fog. He watched Tom, waiting, and Tom realised he wasn't sure what to say. "Fenoderee was unmade for helping us."

Glastyn wagged a finger. "You assume we're helping you."

And then he was gone. Leaving a question in the air; if Glastyn wasn't helping them, what else was he doing?

Tom shook his head. It didn't matter right now. All that mattered was getting back to Katharine. He marched back to the fire, putting Glastyn and Faerie and puzzles out of his mind. But when Tom stood by the fire and said, "I have the coin," Dank replied, "I don't know if I can do it, Tom."

And Tom almost didn't have the heart to ask him. So he said,

"I need to get back to Katharine," as a gentle reminder, rather than a demand.

"I know." Dank dropped his gaze. "But I'm worried I'll lose you in there."

Tom wondered what would happen if he did. Would they fall out of the maelstrom into Tir, or Faerie, or the Between? Or would they be trapped in it forever? "Is there anything we can do to help you?"

Dank shrugged. "I don't know what I need."

Tom bent his knees and crouched beside Dank. "This would be the fourth time you travelled as the fay do," he said. "You can do it. You have done it. I don't think you need anything but you."

Neither of them was convinced. Dank might not need anything else, but the second trip had been worse than the first, and the third worse than the second. Perhaps time was like a hot sun baking dry the river that linked Dank to whatever magic the fay used to travel between realms. What if there was no river left? Or, worse, what if there was enough to get them into the maelstrom, and not enough to get out?

But what was the alternative? Trek thousands of miles north by foot? It would be a trip worth making only to dig their friends' frozen bodies out of the snow.

And Dank knew it too. He nodded, stood.

"Don't you need time to prepare?" Gravinn asked, failing to hide the fear in her voice.

"I'm not sure I'll ever be prepared," he said, countering his dour words with a smile that was too broad and failed to touch the fear in his eyes. He placed a hand on Tom's shoulder.

"You can do this," Tom said, and gave Dank a nod.

Dank nodded too. Took Gravinn's hand. And then he dragged them through the veil.

Agony.

Like someone was shredding him, dragging him through a sea of broken glass, inch by ponderous inch, and scattering the tatters left behind into the wind.

Like someone was placing a hot cinder in every part of his body and mind, in places he didn't even know he had.

It hurt to think. It hurt to not think.

I can't I can't iron nails I can't I'll lose them I'll lose them I've killed us all I've killed us all.

Those weren't his thoughts. It was Dank, panicking. A fresh jolt of pain ripped through all of them, like a bolt of lightning that tore through them head to toe and out of every finger and toe, cleansing every thought as it went.

The end the end this is the end this is how it all ends.

No, Dank. You can do this. You can.

Dead dead dead dead dead.

Forming a thought was like putting his hand into flame, like drawing a knife across his flesh, like pushing his entire body against a bed of nails, but he summoned three words and roared into the void: Do it, Dank!

And it was all gone, in a rush, and he felt nothing because the absence of pain felt like the absence of everything. It took time for his senses to adjust. To remember something other than agony. Air. He was gasping. Cold. He was so cold. He lay on his back, snow falling on his face. The sky was a starless black. Sound. Voices. Faces above his. He knew he should recognise them. He wanted to reach for them, ask for their help, but he was scared to move in case the pain returned.

Fight.

Tom dismissed the thought. Caledyr was just a sword. It didn't know pain. It couldn't understand what he'd just been through.

Know pain.

The thought was a jolt, a shock. It came with a wave of sadness and bitter regret. He lifted his head, looked for the sword, as if he half-expected it to have become a person. But there it was, resting up against a sled, still a sword.

And he realised he understood the voices, and recognised the faces. He was back. Dank had brought them back.

"I'm fine," he told them. He sat up, blinked, found Emyr's face, and offered him a smile. "All in one piece." He took a shaky breath. "How's Katharine?"

"It doesn't go well," Emyr said, and the fear in his voice washed all other thoughts away on a torrent of terror.

"What's happening?" He tried to stand, found his limbs were shaky and numb. "Where is she?"

"Tom?" Katharine's voice was pained. Weak. Scared.

"I'm here," he called back. "Gravinn, give Mennvinn the herbs you gathered. Emyr, see to Dank."

"They're not here, Tom." Emyr pulled him to his feet, held him steady. "You're the only one to come back."

CHAPTER 20

"FIND THEM," Tom ordered his king. Pushed him aside and stumbled into to the tent. "Tell me what's happening," he demanded. But he could already see it for himself.

Blood. Too much blood. And Katharine was pale.

"She's bleeding," Mennvinn said, her voice hard from the effort of keeping any emotion from it. She was holding her fear away from Katharine, like a hot iron that could burn her patient. But the dwarf's eyes betrayed her.

"Make it stop," he told her.

"I'm not sure I can."

"We need to cut her open." Jarnstenn stood near the tent, building a fire.

"Cut her open?" Tom asked. "Why?"

"To save the child."

"I don't have the equipment for that," Mennvinn replied. "Or the training."

"Is Rose safe?" Katharine voice was hoarse, her skin pale and clammy, her breathing ragged as if she had run the length of Tir. She reached for him with bloody hands. "Rose is safe, isn't she?"

The tent was cramped, but Tom found space beside her, took her sticky hands in his. "Mennvinn will look after you."

"Someone boil water and get me some rags. I can't see what I'm doing."

"Jarnstenn, rags," Tom ordered. "Draig, water. Do it now." To Mennvinn he said, "What's happening?"

"We need to get this baby out now." Mennvinn wouldn't look at him.

"Will they live?"

"I need you to keep her calm," she replied. But panic of her own crept into her voice when Katharine grimaced. "Don't push, Katharine."

"I have to."

"Don't push."

Katharine tensed, screwed her face against the pain, strained.

"Don't push!"

"Don't push, Katharine, don't push," Tom babbled.

Mennvinn said something in dwarfish and Jarnstenn stopped and stared.

"What did you say?" Tom asked.

"Hurry," was all Mennvinn said and Jarnstenn threw the rags he'd created to Draig and started pulling weapons from one of the sleds.

"What's happening?" Tom asked.

"We need to get the baby out," Mennvinn replied. She was pale, but Tom had never seen her so determined. "Katharine, I'm sorry, but we don't have anything for the pain. You're just going to have to be really brave."

Katharine babbled, "Wait wait wait what are you doing?" and cried out as Mennvinn brandished a small, long knife and cut her without warning. "Tom don't look, don't look, hold my hand, hold my hand." But he had to know what Mennvinn was doing, he had to make sure Katharine was safe, "What are you doing?" he asked, but Mennvinn didn't reply, just asked Draig for rags that she used to mop up the blood, there was so much, iron nails, this was it, this was the end, this was it.

"Jarnstenn, I need them now," Mennvinn waved a bloody hand and cursed in dwarfish. Jarnstenn hurried over with a pair of tongs.

"What are they for?" Katharine asked.

"I need more room." Mennvinn stood, stepped out of the tent, and took the tongs from Jarnstenn. "Get her outside."

"You escaped from the madhouse of something? She'll freeze."

"Do it." Her voice was still cold and dead, and if anything it was more terrifying for it.

"Draig, help me," Tom ordered, and the elf stepped into the tent, lifted the blankets Katharine was lying on and helped Tom move her out into the snow.

"Lift your legs," Mennvinn told her. "Tom, hold that one. Draig, hold the other."

"What's happening?" Tom asked her as he hooked his arm under Katharine's knee. "Will you give me an iron-cursed answer?"

"I think the afterbirth has torn. The baby will die if we don't deliver it quickly. So that's what we're going to do." Mennvinn looked at Katharine. "Do you hear me? We're going to deliver your baby. All of us, together."

"Together." Katharine squeezed Tom's hand and stared at him with wide eyes.

"Together," he told her, and squeezed back.

And Mennvinn lifted the tongs.

"Wait, you're pulling her out with those?" Tom asked. "Won't that hurt her?"

"It's all we have."

Mennvinn gave herself a moment. Tom watched her take a breath through the nose, out through pursed lips. She murmured something in dwarfish. And then she reached for the baby.

Katharine screamed. She glared into the sky, face clenched with fury and fear, screaming through gritted teeth, tears rolling down her face and into her hair, sweat beading on her forehead only to roll back and join her tears. Emyr's black bones, what was Mennvinn doing? She wasn't even looking at her work, her eyes half-closed as she shifted and twisted and tensed and tugged and Katharine screamed again and it was Six that cried out, "For Oen's sake, you're killing her!"

"You're welcome to try saving their lives if you prefer, master elf," the dwarf replied, voice soft, almost distracted, she twisted the other way.

"They're not designed for this," Jarnstenn said. "I use them to hold hot metal."

"Almost there," she murmured.

"You'll crush the skull."

"Be silent."

"Don't hurt her," Tom told Mennvinn, and he wasn't sure if he meant Katharine, Rose, both, and then Mennvinn pulled and Katharine screamed again and Mennvinn said, "Push, if you can," and Katharine crushed Tom's hand in hers and strained and grunted and cried and then it was done.

She was covered in blood. Her face was covered in marks. And she was wailing like the world itself was ending.

But she was here. Rose. She was alive. She was here.

His daughter.

He laughed. He couldn't help it.

"Is she alright? Is she well?" Katharine's voice was tight with fear.

"She's beautiful." She was. And she felt too far away. He wanted to hold her and never let her go.

Mennvinn obliged. "Take her," she said, still brusque and business-like. She pushed Rose into his arms, where she wailed and flailed, bloodied and beautiful. Tom shushed and crooned at her while Mennvinn took a strip of leather, tied the cord that bound Rose to Katharine, and cut it.

"Wrap her up," she told Tom. "She'll be cold."

"Here." Draig offered some of the leftover rags. Putting Rose into them wasn't easy. Tom felt a stab of fear every time her head lolled, worried his thighs were too cold when he laid her on them to wrap her, didn't relax until he had her wrapped up and cradled in his arms again.

He looked at Katharine and grinned. "We made a baby."

Katharine offered him a tired, pained smile. "Let me hold her."

He passed her to Katharine, and happy new tears joined the old as she grinned down at the tiny person resting on her chest. Rose stopped crying after a moment and just lay there while Katharine whispered to her. Her little face was screwed into a gentle frown, as if she was confused by a curious puzzle.

"Take her back." Mennvinn told Tom, voice soft, unwilling to break the spell.

Tom didn't want to look away. But her voice carried too much concern for him to ignore. "What is it?" he asked her.

"We need to get the afterbirth out." Mennvinn gave Katharine a grim smile. "It's not over yet."

It didn't take long for the afterbirth to emerge, and Tom sighed when it did. "So is it over?" he asked. "Is everyone safe?"

But Katharine was pale and shivering and Mennvinn was still probing and pushing. "She's still bleeding."

"Bleeding for a time, is not that normal?" Draig asked.

"I don't think this much blood is normal," Mennvinn replied. But she didn't sound sure. She kept looking, poking, and Katharine's breathing seemed too heavy.

"Why don't you say hello to Mama?" Tom said to Rose, and holding her seemed to bring some focus back to Katharine's dazed expression.

"Hello," she said to Rose. "Hello, little one."

"You did so well," he said to Katharine, and kissed her on the forehead. "I'm so proud of you."

"She's here," she replied. "Our little girl. Our little Rose."

"Yes, she is."

"I'm cold," Katharine whispered.

"Let's get you back into a tent." Even inside, it was still too cold, and he covered them in every blanket he could find. But they were sheltered, at least. He grinned as Rose began to make little o-shapes with her mouth, searching for her first meal. "I think she's hungry."

"Right." There was apprehension in Katharine's eyes.

"Just let her find it," he told her. "I'll see if there are any more blankets. I'll be right back."

But when he stepped outside, Mennvinn's face stopped him in his tracks.

"She's lost a lot of blood." She sighed, and Tom realised how tired she was. Dark rings sat under her eyes. "And the afterbirth wasn't intact. I think there might still be some inside. I've done what I can. But I can do no more." She looked to the ground at their feet, as if she feared rebuke. "I don't have the supplies. Or the skills."

"Is it enough?" Tom asked. "Will she live?"

Mennvinn stared at the ground, steeling herself for her answer. But Katharine had to live. She couldn't go now. And if she went, she would take Rose with her. A baby couldn't survive in the wilderness without her mother.

"No." Mennvinn made it as gentle as possible. But it was still like a knife to the gut. Tom felt his eyes grow hot, the tears threaten to break over his cheeks.

"What do we do?" He failed to keep his voice steady. There must be something. Anything.

"We need to get her to a cirgeon."

There was no chance of that. Not since they'd lost Dank.

"Tom," Katharine called. His feet moved without thought, taking him back into the tent, back to her side. Where he belonged. He knelt and she reached out with one hand, the other cradling Rose to her chest. "It's too late for that," she said. "Just hold my hand."

He took her hand in his, saw how they were both caked in dry, flaking blood. "This isn't it," he said.

"I can feel it." She was pale, tired. She was cold to the touch. "It isn't fair." Pain made her eyes ugly, pain at the loss, the injustice. She was forced to say goodbye to Rose just moments after meeting her. She was angry. But she didn't have the strength to hold onto that anger.

But Tom did. Rose should have been born in a civilised place, with cirgeons and medicine and the tools to keep her alive. And why was she here? Because of the fay. The cruel, manipulative, callous fay. And now she would die.

No. He wouldn't let it happen. He would change it. He had to. He was a Knight of Tir. He was a father.

And fathers don't give up on their daughters.

"Take her." Katharine's eyelids were heavy. "Please. I can't."

"You can." But he took Rose. She squirmed within her swaddling, made a small noise of protest before settling again. He felt a smile blooming just looking at her, but it was torn from his face by Katharine's deep breath. As if she wasn't getting enough air. He took her hand again. "Don't give up. Please. We need you."

She smiled. "You do." Her eyelids drifted downwards. "You'll have to be both of us," she said. "Be a good father. And a good mother."

"No. I won't." He knew it was cruel to say it. But he knew he'd say anything to keep her fighting. "You have to stay."

"I want to." Her smile faded and her brow furrowed. "It isn't fair. I was so close."

"We're right here. Stay with us. I can keep you safe, if you stay."

She opened her eyes again. Met his gaze, held it, gripped his hand, as if trying to push her words into him with force of will. "I love you." And then her grip grew weak and she closed her eyes.

"No." She couldn't go. He squeezed her hand, almost crushed it to get a reaction, shook it, "No," he told her, held the back of her hand against Rose's swaddled form. "Fight, Katharine, be strong, just for a little while, come back, please."

Her hand was cold.

It came to pass.

The fear of this moment, the tension he'd felt for months bubbled forth. He wanted to roar, to rage, to tear down the world. But he held his daughter in his arms and whimpered, "Don't leave us."

The wind howled and Rose began to cry. "I'm sorry," he whispered to her. "I'm sorry."

"There was nothing you could have done," Mennvinn said.

Tom sniffed, wiped his eyes. "Hush," he told Rose. "Mama's resting, she's just resting, hush now." He pushed himself off his knees, stepped out of the tent. He couldn't face them. He couldn't let them see his shame.

"I'm sorry, Tom," Emyr said. "I truly am."

Six had pulled himself out of his own tent, and was staring into the fire. "I'm sorry," he said.

Their sympathy was like a permission, and Tom let himself sob. She'd deserved so much more. Now she'd never finish her map to Cairnarim, never find her fame, never see Rose grow up. He'd never get to see her smile again. He'd never get to tell her that he loved her. "I'm sorry," he whispered. "I love you." Too late. He'd let her down again. Why couldn't he have left all this behind and just gone with her like she'd asked him, like he'd wanted to?

Voices, hushed, arguing, he looked up and saw Six and Mennvinn whispering at each other, "Eirwen's grace, show some respect," Tom spat at them. Katharine's dead, he wanted to say. But he couldn't.

He couldn't say the words.

"Just do it," Six snapped, and Mennvinn knelt by Katharine's body and touched her wrist with her fingers.

Tom couldn't say she was dead.

He sniffed, wiped his eyes. "She isn't dead," he said. He could say it.

Mennvinn said something in dwarfish, but Tom was already marching towards the supplies, searching for the jar. Don't think, don't fear, don't feel. Just do it. There was still time. Rose was crying, and he was bouncing her in one arm, "Hush, soon, Papa will take care of you soon, I'm sorry, we need to be brave and strong for Mama, hush now." There, there was the jar, he pulled it free with one hand, pulled the rags away from it until the sprite was revealed and the light shone bright in his eyes. He snatched up Caledyr, carried both the sword and the jar over to the tent, pushed Mennvinn aside. A moment of clarity made him stop, pull the coin from his pocket and push it into Mennvinn's hands, before he told the sprite, "Take me, Rose, and Katharine into Faerie. Now."

He pulled the cork free, felt a tug, and the world was gone.

CHAPTER 21

Rose was quiet. Shocked into silence, just for a moment. He held her close to his chest. A warm, midsummer's breeze blew across them, and the air was thick with magic. "Don't be afraid," he told her. "Papa's here."

He lifted his head and gazed up at the whole of Faerie arrayed around him.

This was new.

The fay had built a replica of the arena in the merrow city, only this one was as the original had once been, shining and new and sharp and perfect. A legion of Faerie creatures stared down at him from dozens and dozens of concentric rings of seats, while he stood in the arena's centre, in a great circle of fine white sand. Katharine lay beside him, without her blankets, without her dignity; the sprite had left her bloodied thighs bare and her chest exposed. It was a cheap, nasty move, and Tom immediately lowered himself to one knee and rearranged Katharine's clothes to protect her modesty.

"Do you give us the knee, Thomas Rymour?" A voice called. "Is that why you are here?"

He wanted to stay kneeling. No, he wanted to sit. To lie down. But he wouldn't kneel to the fay. So he pushed himself to his feet, failing to keep in a groan at the effort. Lifted his chin and found the speaker. The fay known as Grim stood on a podium amongst the seats, but he was much changed since Tom had last seen him.

He was still short and stocky, still covered in thick, black hair. His eyes still glowed an unnatural red, and his enormous mouth was still filled with long, needle-like teeth. But now much of him was covered in bright armour that twisted and whorled into patterns that were painful to the eye, and much of his face was hidden behind a tall helm. A golden trident topped off the new look.

The fay looked ready for battle, and this arena was made for violence, not for talk. So Tom tried to appeal to the crowd's desire for entertainment. "I have come here to treat with the King and the Queen of Faerie," he said for all to hear.

Melwas and Mab were sat on either side of Grim's podium, encased in tall thrones that sat black against the white stone. Melwas was clad in his armour save his helm, glaring at Tom like he hoped he would burst into flames. And Mab, wearing a simple black gown, gazed at him with greedy desire.

"In this place, we are both king and queen." Grim grinned, and Tom couldn't help but notice how the fay's teeth flexed and shifted, like they had breath of their own.

He dragged his gaze from Grim's disturbing visage and looked directly at Mab. "I have a proposition for you," he said.

Mab's greedy smile faltered; she'd noticed he hadn't called her his queen. But she said nothing. Instead it was Grim who replied. "There are no propositions in this place," he said.

Very well. He'd play the game. While Katharine and Rose were here, they could not die. Just as Emyr had lived with a mortal wound for a thousand years, so Katharine and Rose could live without dying. "And what is this place?" he said, fulfilling his part.

"The grand arena," Grim replied, lifting his trident to a roar of approval from the crowd.

"And who fights here?"

"The mortals."

Mortals. They were bringing mortals here to fight for their amusement. "And who do they fight?" Tom asked, knowing the answer but needing to hear it from Grim's fat lips.

"Us." He touched fingertips to his armoured chest. Armour that was purely for show, for the flesh beneath could not be harmed by mortal hands. And there was no chance the fay were giving iron blades to their prey.

The fay were bringing mortals here to fight a fight they could not possibly win. It was cruel. Monstrous. Evil. "I fail to see the entertainment in an unfair fight."

"Long have we called you the seer that cannot see," Grim replied.

Tom ignored the jibe. "I am not here to fight."

"Mortals have no voice here. Though you are permitted to wail and moan, for our pleasure."

Fight.

Tom's fingers itched to draw Caledyr and strike Grim down. But his hands, his actions were no longer his alone. Rose and Katharine came first. "I came here to offer the fay something more than a mere fight."

But Grim shook his head. "We have fought many mortals, Thomas Rymour. Their bones built a path that leads to you. You will fight. You will fall. You will heal, and fight, and fall again. I will cut you down from now until the end of days. This is your fate: unending death, by my hand!" He lifted that hand over his head and the fay cheered and applauded, laughed and taunted Tom. Only Melwas and Mab were quiet. Melwas glared at him from his throne. And Mab frowned her concern while Puck whispered in her ear.

"That sounds like it might grow rather dull," Tom replied. "Wouldn't you rather see how our quest ends first?"

"We long to hear your bones crack, see your flesh split, taste your blood on our tongue." Grim's teeth unfolded like a flower under morning sunlight and a long, pointed tongue snaked from between his fat lips. "We want to see how long it takes for you to beg for mercy."

Tom's skin tightened at the thought. "Yet I came here willingly," he said, and managed to keep his voice steady. "If we fought now, until the end of time, you would always know I came here of my own will. That I endured this by choice."

"You did not know this was the fate that awaited you."

"Didn't I?" He forced his own grin. "I've seen first-hand how the fay treats those who have wronged them. This is nothing to the horrors I imagined awaited me here. Fighting you for eternity at least gives me the chance to hurt you in return."

Grim's smile faltered. "Then you came to your doom of your own accord?"

"No." He lifted his voice, to ensure that every fay could hear him. "I came here to ask for a boon."

There was a rush of whispered shock. Scoffing. Disbelief. Distrust. Why would Thomas Rymour ask for a boon, when he knew what such a thing entailed?

Even Grim was at a loss. He turned to Melwas, ceded his authority, and the Faerie King glowered, his lip twitched, preparing to give the order, ignore him, cut him down, take the woman and child.

But it was Mab who spoke. "What boon is this you speak of?"

Tom fought his grin. He had them now. Curiosity. It killed many cats. "You know the woman with me." He nodded to Rose in his arms. "And this is our daughter. I love them both. More than anything." He could see the hurt in Mab's eyes, the anger, and he spoke quickly. "They won't survive in Tir, and so I ask you to keep them here, until I can return and take them back to a place where they can be healed and where they can be safe."

Mab's lips curled in disgust. "And why would we do this thing?"

"Because you want to see if I can get them back." Tom tried not to smile as he realised it was true.

But Melwas shook his head. "You demand a sunset and offer the sunrise that is sure to follow." He tapped two fingers to the point in his chest where Tom had stabbed him with Caledyr. "We already know that you would try to rescue your women. You must offer us something we want."

Sudden, certain knowledge coiled in Tom's gut. He knew what he had to do. And he hated himself for how ready he was to do it. "Dank is missing," he said. "Lost in the maelstrom. If I find him, I will deliver him to you."

A gross betrayal. But he had no choice. The lives of Katharine and Rose depended on staying here. And Tom would do anything to keep them safe.

Mab smirked at the pain in his eyes, before dismissing it with a flick of her hand. "We can find Dank ourselves." She lifted her chin towards Grim. "Begin."

No. He couldn't fight, not with Rose. But he moved her into his left arm, just in case. "Wait."

Grim bowed to Mab. "We will dedicate this first kill to you, our lady queen."

"Wait!"

Grim dropped from the podium and into the circle of sand, and the crowd roared as he pumped his trident in the air. Iron nails, this was getting out of hand. Tom drew Caledyr with his free hand, turned to put himself between Grim and Rose.

"Ask Mester Stoorworm how this tasted," he cried, hefting the sword so all could see it. "If I have to fight you, Grim, I will. I'll skewer you like a pig. I'll get what I want, and you'll have suffered for nothing."

"For an immortal, Thomas Rymour, pain is just another way to pass the time." Grim spoke for the audience, earning another cheer. He twirled his trident like a baton, and adopted a pose intended to provoke another cheer. Was he all show? No. Grim had always been savage, a beast sent to prey on mortal cheer. Performing for a crowd was new. So was the trident. Tom would have to assume he was as adept with the latter as the former.

Which meant violence and peril. So he turned his back, dropped Caledyr, and tucked Rose into Katharine's tunic, "Give Mama a cuddle," he told her, more to distract himself from the tightness in his limbs, the readiness to feel Grim's trident in his back. But he settled Rose, snatched up Caledyr, and turned to see Grim hadn't advanced.

"That was honourable of you," Tom said. "Thank you."

The fay grinned. "We want to see you at your best."

"I'm afraid my best might be far behind me," Tom replied, brought Caledyr to his forehead in salute. "I claim my boon in return for felling Grim," he called.

Laughter in the audience, but not the raucous hilarity Tom had expected. Instead he felt apprehension, uncertainty, excitement. They didn't know who was going to win.

Grim made his claim to his audience. "I claim time with the woman, in return for felling Thomas Rymour."

Tom didn't need the sword to lend him strength or anger. Strike him down.

"Last chance, Grim," he said, and waited for the fay to turn his face to the crowd to deliver his response.

That's when Tom charged.

Grim was quick, but he was caught off-guard. He tried to parry the blow with the haft of the trident, and Caledyr sliced through it like it was gossamer, the blade sweeping up and across Grim's helm. The fay staggered back under the blow, and Tom twisted his feet, shifted his grip, and drove Caledyr up and into Grim's chest.

He released the sword and let Grim fall to the ground. The arena was silent.

Tom kicked aside one half of Grim's trident and planted a foot on the fay's chest. "Now, shall we talk about my boon?"

The audience was sent away, to their disappointment, and Melwas and Mab descended into the arena to stand before Tom. Mab was attended by Puck, who avoided Tom's eye. Melwas was without an attendant; it would be some time before Herne returned, if he ever did. The Faerie King glared at Tom, and his eye frequently drifted to Grim's prone, still form. Or to Caledyr, planted in Grim's chest like a violent flag pole.

"That was an impressive performance, our Tom." There was a hint of pride in Mab's voice. She cast a disapproving glance at Grim's body. "Perhaps we put our faith in the wrong champion."

Melwas towered over Tom. "What do you want?" he growled.

Tom had to crane his neck to meet Melwas' eye. "My boon: I want you to keep Katharine and Rose safe."

"You are beyond boons," Melwas snapped. "You raised a hand to our royal person, unleashed violence upon our people, and used that foul little sorcerer's magics to undo Herne. We have named you an enemy of Faerie, and any effort we expend on you will be only to see you punished."

Tom looked to Mab, who gave him the tiniest of nods. It hurt. And he hated that it hurt. But hearing those words, seeing them confirmed by Mab, pricked at a vulnerable spot inside of him.

Don't show it. Stand tall.

He looked back to Melwas and said, "We have been collecting the glarn in order to seal the way between Faerie and Tir. If we succeed, you would be trapped here, and you would no longer be able to sustain yourself on the magic of the world. You would diminish." He looked at Mab. "Until you were no more."

"You would see us ended?" She wrinkled her nose at Tom.

"I just want to see those I care about safe and well."

Melwas' voice was cold as he said, "And we want to see you holding your own entrails, flayed and burned and begging for the end, knowing that you will not die, that Ankou will stitch you back together so we can pull you apart again, and again, and again, until the sun grows cold and the nights grow long and all is nothing more than dust. And still we will watch you suffer." His anger wasn't a hot, burning thing, ready to burn out when enough time had passed. This was a cold, frozen hatred. Unending. Unyielding. There would be no song in Melwas' heart when he had Tom tortured. And that made it far more frightening.

"I won my boon in combat," Tom replied with a confidence he didn't feel. "You cannot deny me."

"Cannot?" Melwas' nostrils flared. "You come to our realm and dictate to us as if Thomas Rymour were king and Melwas his subject."

"You told me to face you." His boon rested on a knife's edge, and he felt off-balance. "I do only as you commanded."

And Mab smiled her dark smile. The one Emyr said she had stolen from Eirwen. "Be careful what you wish for, my king."

Melwas smiled too. It wasn't the reaction Tom had expected.

"Do you challenge us, little Tom?" he asked, his rich baritone rolling around the shadow of his amusement. "Would you fight for our queen's hand?"

The sight of Melwas with his hand resting on his sword faded, and Tom found himself hot, sweating, tired, ducking as that same sword carved through the air above him.

Step. Step. Duck. Parry.

Emylt and Caledyr clashed, the impact ringing down Tom's arms, making his muscles rubbery, already Melwas was shifting, sliding Emylt free of the parry.

Step. Duck.

Melwas spun and the air almost hummed as Emylt cut through it and passed overhead. Too close, he'd barely ducked in time, already Caledyr was moving his feet, but he was too slow, and Melwas was too fast, and he couldn't win this.

The present moment came back and Tom's heart was hammering. He took a deep, calming breath. Was that how he would meet death? At Melwas' hand?

"I suppose it was always going to end that way, wasn't it?" He sighed. It made sense. Who else had such an interest in seeing him dead? But he'd rather have died at someone else's hand. Anyone else's. "But not today."

"But someday." Melwas smirked as if he had won a great prize. "These are the terms for keeping your woman and your child safe."

"They are not to be fed Faerie food," Tom told them. That would trap them in Faerie forever. "And they will be cared for by Melusine. No-one else."

"Why Melusine?" Mab's eyes were slits, as if she were squinting against a bright light.

In truth, Tom couldn't say why. But she understood family, and Tom sensed she would respect the bond of family more than oaths and boons. Besides, she had offered to help. But all he said to Mab was, "She is a mother at heart."

"What of Lull?" Mab asked. Lull, the Faerie nursemaid. But Tom wasn't going to leave Rose in the care of someone charged with looking after the mortal children kidnapped by the fay; it would feel too much like he was giving Rose up. Like he was helping Mab steal his daughter.

So he said, "I am not certain if they will be safe with Lull."

"But they will be safe with Melusine?"

"I believe so."

"And if we believe otherwise?"

"These are my terms."

"Indeed?" Mab pursed her lips, somewhere between amusement and irritation. "Then you will take the sprite back with you." She glanced upwards and Tom followed her gaze to see Dank's sprite hovering above them.

"Very well." Even though he didn't want a Faerie spy in their midst. "It can help us find Dank."

"Indeed."

"Do you know where he is?"

"The traitor and his companion are adrift," Mab told him with relish. "Grains of sand that would be a beach if they could find the shore."

Tom had felt that tattering, the way the maelstrom tugged and shredded the edges of the mind and the heart. They hadn't deserved such an end. Gravinn could have been safe and sound in the Western Kingdom. Dank could have remained here. Not safe. But sound, at least. "Do they suffer?"

"Not anymore."

"They would have done," Melwas added with a cruel smile. "They would have known nothing but pain, and then the hurt of watching their souls unravel and being unable to recall the very thing they have lost."

Tom tried not to imagine how Dank and Gravinn had felt as they were torn apart. Did they feel abandoned? Did they feel like he had left them to pain and death?

Fight.

The thought surprised him, tugged his gaze to Grim, to the sword that rested in the fay's unmoving chest. Fight? How?

Find the shore. That's what Mab had said. "So we have an agreement?" he asked. "You will keep Katharine and Rose safe. In return, you enjoy watching me attempt to rescue them."

"And you bring us Dank," Mab reminded him.

"And you fight us," Melwas added. "For our lady queen's affections. Once and for all, we will settle this."

"And I will fight you." Tom cast an eye over Mab. Emyr had said she'd taken Eirwen's smile. Where had she taken the eager look in her eyes? Where had she taken her throaty laugh? Where had she taken the way she talked, walked, smelt?

It was revolting to think that she was a collection of dead things. But when she smiled at him, his body still reacted.

"And when I win," Melwas said, "you will bend the knee."

Tom blinked. "What?"

"You heard us." Melwas lifted a gauntleted hand, curled it into a fist. "Once I have defeated you, you will swear your loyalty to us. You will declare King Melwas of Faerie your true king, and you will agree to obey all of our commands."

No. He couldn't. He couldn't lie, and so swearing such an oath would bind him to it. Wouldn't it? He had sworn an oath to Duke Regent and fled. Could he swear an oath that left him enough room to disobey?

As if Tom had spoken aloud, Melwas added, "We know how slippery you are, little man. We will make you swear such an unbreakable oath that you cannot sneeze without our permission."

It was too much. Melwas could make him do anything. Hand over the glarn. Kill Six, Emyr, and the others. Hurt Katharine.

Hurt Rose.

He only had to kneel if he lost this fight. But the Faerie King had bested King Emyr. He would best Thomas Rymour too.

But he had no choices, so he took a breath and said, "Yes. I will bend the knee, if I lose." And he would just have to find a way to win.

Melwas grinned, a proud, arrogant, victorious grin. "It is done," he said, and waved a hand. Melusine stepped forward. Tom hadn't seen her arrive. Seeing her approach with her arms out replaced his dread with a different kind of fear; the reality of handing his daughter to the fay. He was gripped by a sudden panic and clutched Rose to his chest. He couldn't do it. He would take her back. He would take care of Rose.

But whatever place Cairnarim was, it would be no place for a newborn babe.

"We will keep her as our own," Melusine promised.

"Keep her as mine," he replied. "Don't feed her any Faerie food," he repeated.

"We won't." Her smile was understanding.

"Or let her out of your sight."

"Not for a moment."

"And neither Ankou nor Angau is to tend to Katharine. Leave her be."

"Understood."

Tom lifted Rose's head to his lips, kissed her, smelled her. She began to fuss and squirm. How long would it be before he saw her again? "Tell her about me," he murmured. "Every day. Tell her that her papa loves her."

"We will."

"I love you," he whispered into Rose's hair. "Papa loves you. Never forget that. Never."

And then he handed her over, and she started to cry, and it was all he could do to keep from snatching her back and running as far as he could. She didn't belong in another's care. She needed him. He knew he was doing the right thing. But it felt like he was abandoning her. Like he'd abandoned Degor. "I'll come back for you," he told her, and took consolation in being able to say it.

"We'll take care of her until you do," Melusine told him.

"Thank you," he managed, and turned to Katharine before his resolve broke. "I'll come back for you too," he whispered. He ran a hand through her hair. She was still cold. Still pale. It shouldn't have happened like this.

"Enough," Melwas said. Tom felt the weight of the sprite land on his shoulder, the light almost painful at the edge of his vision. "You have your bargain, little Tom. Be gone from our sight."

Tom felt a familiar tug, and opened his mouth to say goodbye to Katharine, to say, "I love you."

But Faerie was already gone.

There was no sight or sound within the maelstrom, but the sprite's voice was a roar, its light was a storm that seared the thoughts, and Tom was an ant next to the inferno.

"Dank is scattered." The words rattled through every corner of his mind, shaking loose his own thoughts. "We must collect him."

And Gravinn. But he had no mouth to say the words. And the maelstrom was already pulling at him. Already he could feel little snags of his self catching on the brambles of the storm.

But there was a cold, black pebble within him that was unmoved.

"That will keep you safe," boomed the sprite. "Cling to it." And the light turned away from Tom and shone across the nothingness. Like an incandescent beast. Like a gargantuan will of the wisp, luring the lost and the prey. Ready to consume.

"We call to him," the sprite said.

What do I do? Tom wondered. He could feel his edges fraying. Why was he here?

"He might not trust us." The hurt was impossibly big, like a black ocean of loss. "You must call too."

How? I have no voice.

"This place is magic," it replied. "And you have magic."

Would the pebble grow larger?

"You would rather leave him here?"

No. So Tom reached out, the way he reached into the twig and into the coin and into the monolith at Cairnagwyn. It felt too easy now, as if he could extend his entire mind and let it be whisked away, and the maelstrom urged him to do it, throw himself into the chaos and find the calmness of nothing.

A single wisp of the sprite encircled Tom, a heatless tendril of bright flame that would burn him if it got too close. "Call. Do not chase him, or you will be scattered too."

The storm was less within the sprite's embrace, the worst of it kept at bay. It made it easier to hold himself together. Iron nails, he had to get out of this place. He reached out past the sprite's defences with a single thought: here. Here.

Nothing. Each thought he sent out was swept away. Did a part of him go with it? Was he forgetting himself? He couldn't remember Degor's first birthday. What colour were Katharine's eyes?

"You're panicking." The sprite's disdain washed through him. But it was right. Had he breath, he would have taken a deep one.

But the thought of it felt the same as doing it, and he felt calmer. He reached out again.

There. He felt something. Not even a thought. Like a fish brushing your ankle in the shallows. He reached for it but it swam away.

"Gently." The sprite's voice was like a slap. So Tom kept reaching out. Here. Here. Here.

Here? Where? Here?

The thoughts weren't Dank's. Tom could tell immediately. He didn't recognise them. Who were they?

"Wayward travellers."

We should help them.

"They are too long lost. They can't remember how to be together."

They would remember. But the sprite ushered them away and held Tom back. He reached past as best he could. Come back. Stay, we can help. But the furious light of the sprite was too much to bear, and they fled into eternal nothing.

Tom?

There! That was Dank. He reached for it, but found nothing more than that same thought over and over. Tom? Tom? Tom?

Where was the rest of him?

"He will gather himself to himself."

That didn't make much sense, so Tom kept calling into the maelstrom. But nothing else seemed to come forward. He tried to ape what the sprite was doing, reaching around Dank's single thought and keeping it from the scattering winds, but it wasn't easy when that same wind was buffeting his own mind.

"No. Let it be free. Let him hear himself."

Tom let Dank's thought go, watched it drift away. Tom? Tom? Tom? He wanted to snatch it back, hold on to at least this part of Dank. But the sprite placed a tendril of burning light between the thought and Tom's own. All he could do was watch it go and call after it: here. Here. Here.

We'll lose him, he thought.

"Have faith," the sprite replied.

In what?

"In your friend."

That shamed Tom, but not enough to quash his fear. If he lost Dank after having hold of him, even a small part of him, it would be his fault. He would have failed them, Dank and Gravinn. He would have abandoned them to this place.

"You're panicking again."

No. He was afraid. And angry. He was losing too many people. He wouldn't lose more. So he called out, with all his fear and rage and desperation.

DANK! GRAVINN!

And the little black pebble grew a little more, and the sprite shied away.

But the little thought wavered. Held. Tom. It sounded less hesitant. More certain. Yes, Tom.

Yes, it's me. Come back to us, both of you. Come back.

There, another thought. One of Dank's, saying to itself safe, safe, safe over and over. And with it came another, a different shape and texture. One of Gravinn's. This one had no words, just fear. But Dank's thought embraced it and held it against the maelstrom. And there was another, and another. Dank's thoughts came together, and each came with a fragment of Gravinn.

"He heard you." The sprite approved, even as it shied from the black emptiness of spent magic that Tom carried like a lodestone around his neck.

The thoughts gathered together, swirled into one, and the more there were, the faster they came. But they were all tangled.

Gravinn's thoughts were mixed in with Dank's, and they didn't separate.

What's wrong? Why are they like that?

"They can't remember who they are." The sprite's terror shook Tom and he felt a thought scatter away into the storm, never to return. The fay reached out with a brilliant tendril, to touch the cloud of thoughts, but they danced away from the painful light. "Remember us," it told the thoughts. "Remember us?"

They remembered the sprite, and they didn't. But the more thoughts that joined the swirling mass, the more confused it became, and in a moment the thoughts began to scatter and flee the confusion and the fear. The sprite reached out and tried to herd them back, but they fought its embrace, desperate to escape.

"Help me," the sprite demanded.

How?

Remind them who they are.

How?

But the sprite was too busy catching stray thoughts. So Tom reached out. Gravinn? Gravinn, come to me. Leave Dank. Come to me.

But that was no use. None of the thoughts knew if they belonged to Gravinn anymore. So Tom drifted closer, reached out to the nearest thought, a simple mantra of free, free, free.

You're Gravinn, he told it, and held it to one side. Reached to another that sang a few notes of a melody over and over. It sounded like Dank, so Tom told it who it was and held it to another side. He listened to each stray thought and tried to figure out which was which. Sometimes he wasn't sure, so he let it go and it would drift to one side or the other. Because it knew who it was? Or was it guessing?

"Faster," the sprite boomed. The cloud of thoughts were

dissipating, zipping this way and that, trying to escape the sprite's prison. "We cannot hold them forever."

Tom snatched thoughts from the maelstrom as quickly as he could.

"If they escape, we won't catch them again."

There wasn't time to examine them all; all Tom could do was try to get the flavour of them and push them to the cloud that felt right. What if he was wrong?

"Hurry." The sprite was closing its grip, pressing the thoughts together, trying to contain them, and suddenly they were a dark cloud surrounding him, a storm within a storm, and he pushed and ordered them as best he could but the terror in them was infecting him too and he felt like he was beginning to lose himself in the chaos, he caught a thought, was that his, iron nails this one felt like his, he kept it, the sprite's grip was tightening, the maelstrom was thick with thoughts, was this Gravinn or Dank, Gravinn, must be her, this one Dank, one slipped past him and sped off into the maelstrom and the sprite said, "No more time," before crushing them all together in its blinding embrace and pulling them from one storm to another.

His first thought was, am I me?

He turned to find Katharine, and she wasn't there.

Then he felt the ache in his heart, to know that his daughter was trapped in Faerie, and he knew who he was. I must be me. This is my pain.

Tom lifted his head and a furious wind blew snow into his eyes. He had eyes to be stung. Skin to be frozen. He was free of the maelstrom. This was Tir.

He knew he should stand. That there was more to do. He had to see if Dank and Gravinn were here. If they were safe.

Please. Just a moment.

Was that his thought?

A cry. Rose? No, not Rose. But it was a cry of shock and fear. His limbs moved before his thoughts could catch up, pushing him to his feet and towards the sound. Cries and shouts and the sound of breaking glass. He reached for the sword, to see off this new threat, to fight another fight.

But Caledyr was gone.

CHAPTER 22

THE SCABBARD at his waist was empty. Had he dropped the sword? Had he lost it in the maelstrom?

No. He knew where it was: Faerie. When Melwas had sent him back, the Faerie King had kept the sword. Of course he had. Why let Tom keep it? Why risk his success? And why allow him a weapon that could stop a fay in its tracks?

It was over. There was no hope without Caledyr. They couldn't seal away Faerie without all the glarn. He let despair and fatigue drop him to his knees.

Fight.

It wasn't Caledyr. Just the memory of the sword. That's what it would say. And it was right. Katharine and Rose needed him. So did the others.

He bowed his head. Just a moment. He just needed a moment to rest.

One moment here was another moment Katharine and Rose had to spend in Faerie. A moment spent with creatures that wanted to hurt them.

Curse you.

I *am* you.

Curse me, then. And he pushed himself to his feet, which felt more difficult than lifting the world itself, and looked around.

The sprite was causing havoc, upending sleds, breaking jars, flying through the fire and sending sparks everywhere. One of the tents had caught alight.

It was taking its revenge. How had he failed to see this coming?

Iron blades were waved through the air, but the sprite was small and hard to hit. Chaos. And what could Tom do? Nothing. The despair rose up in him again for a moment. No. Fight.

So he strode towards the camp, and roared, "Enough!"

The sprite stopped for a moment, hovered out of reach.

"You're angry. I understand that. But we are Dank's friends. Hurting us will hurt him. I know you don't want that."

The sprite was too small and its light too bright to make out its features. But something changed. And Tom got the feeling he had said just the wrong thing.

It darted towards him, he lunged for it, missed, it passed him, raced for Dank's prone form and dove into his forehead.

The man screamed.

The sprite burrowed beneath his skin, climbing in against Dank's will, forcing its way into his body. The tattoos in his skin writhed, lashing across his features, and Dank clawed at his own face, trying to stop the sprite or stop the pain.

"Help him!" Tom rushed to Dank's side and tried to get a grip on the sprite's legs, but Dank's flailing hands caught him in the side of the head and he stumbled back. Draig snatched Dank's wrist, tried to get a hold of the other one, Dank's back arched and he screamed again, the sprite was almost inside, Tom reached for the sprite but Emyr was already there, pressing the flat of an iron knife against Dank's forehead, and Dank roared and writhed and the blade drew blood and then Dank was still.

He hung limp from Draig's grip. The elf let go and Dank fell to the ground. His eyes had rolled up into his head. His mouth hung open. He didn't close either against the driving snow.

The tattoos stilled.

"Is he dead?" Draig asked.

Dank blinked. The eyes that stared out of his head were not his own.

"We warned you." Dank grinned. Melwas' grin. "This one is ours."

Dank cracked his head against Draig's nose, leapt to his feet, faced Emyr.

"The king of Tir," he sneered with Melwas' mocking tone.

"Fight them, Dank," Emyr told him.

Dank laughed, and Emyr tried to lunge while Dank's guard was down, but the boy was too quick, he slapped Emyr's knife from his hand and drove an elbow into his face, a foot into his belly.

Tom charged, but he was tired, weak, slow. Dank blocked his swing with ease and a gut punch made Tom gag before a blow to the head sent him to the ground.

"Stop him!" Jarnstenn swung a hammer into the back of Dank's knees, bringing the man to the ground with a roar while Mennvinn leapt onto his back.

But Dank rolled, crushing Mennvinn under his weight, kicked Jarnstenn in the jaw, and came to his feet, free of dwarfs. And he began to kick them.

"Filthy little smoke-lovers," he spat.

"Leave them alone." Tom's words were hoarse, the snow biting into his eyes, he could barely hear himself over the wind.

But Dank heard him. Turned and glared at him, wild grin revealing a madness within.

"Will you stop us, little Tom?" he asked. Turned and spread his arms, as if for an embrace. "Challenge us now. Don't let your friends fight your battles."

"Don't let Dank fight yours." Getting to his feet was a struggle. As if he had grown heavier.

"This body is ours."

The casual, possessive air with which Melwas wore Dank was sickening. Like he was no more than an outfit. A novelty. "Nothing in Tir belongs to you."

"Tir is nothing more than a delivery room, little Tom." He spoke as if explaining something simple to a small child. "Your time here is nothing more than a birthing pain. Your mortal forms are larvae. Crawling maggots on the face of the world. Until you die, and blossom as just a small part of Faerie. That's all you're good for, little Tom. You and your ilk. You are food. We can hunt you as we will. Who will stop us? You?"

"I will try."

"You will fail."

"Perhaps."

"And what then, we wonder? What will your friends think, when we best you and you fulfil your oath to us? To bend the knee?" Dank grinned as expressions around him turned to disbelief, to horror, to revulsion. "Such a price you bargained for your woman's life."

Tom ignored everyone else. Put out one fire at a time. "If you expect me to fail, why not release Dank?"

"Because he betrayed us," Dank-as-Melwas replied. "We want him to feel his body hurt those around him before we take him back to Faerie. Where we'll hurt him." And Dank's lips grinned, despite what those words meant for him.

"Let him go."

"Never."

Dank launched himself at Tom, who swung a fist, blocked a counter-blow, Dank got hold of his hair, headbutted Tom and stopped every thought cold. Tom was dimly aware of falling onto his back, of the storm whirling around them, a faint voice told him to fight, a ghost of a memory, and then Dank was on top of him, hands wrapped around his throat, crushing his windpipe, he clawed at Dank's fingers, tried to prise them free, kicked, flailed, clawed at Dank's face, Melwas was speaking, taunting him, air, breathe, breathe, air, shadows were creeping into the edge of his vision, blood roared in his ears, his head felt like it would burst, like Dank would twist it right off, air, breathe, save me anyone, please, they'd abandoned him, they would let the fay kill him, please, I didn't mean it, air, air, air, blood dripped from Dank's face onto his and the storm died down and the light faded from the world.

But a voice kept him from slipping away. A voice that spoke words he didn't understand, that struck the dark stone in his self and set it vibrating.

The pressure on his throat was gone. He sucked in a snowy breath, coughed, got an arm over his mouth and tried again, and again, each breath filling his throat with needles, but he had air, he had breath. Dank was gone. On his feet. Tom pushed himself upright and saw the other man had his back to him. Facing the voice.

Facing Ambrose.

The sorcerer walked out of his tent, staff aloft, dark eyes burning and voice ringing clear. The storm didn't dare touch him, swirling and dancing to stay away from him. And Dank growled as he approached, fingers clawed, ready to attack.

Tom tried to call to him, to warn him. But his voice was gone, his throat unable to make the sounds. But Emyr saw it. He rushed towards Dank, knife in his hand, and Dank grappled him to the ground. Draig was a step behind, wrapping an arm around Dank's neck. But Melwas had the advantage; he threw Dank into the fight without a care for his mortal body, whilst Draig and Emyr tried to save their eyes from clawed fingers, their skin from gnashing teeth. So Dank broke free and leapt onto Ambrose, bringing him down to the ground.

The old sorcerer's head cracked against a rock.

Tom stumbled towards the pair, saw Dank wrap his hands around Ambrose's throat, choking him, cracking his head against that rock again and again.

"We have you now, little magic man," Melwas crowed.

But Ambrose showed no fear. Didn't fight back. He just kept speaking his dark words and reaching for his staff. Would he unmake Dank? No time to guess. Tom snatched up the staff and pushed it into Ambrose's outreached hand.

And Ambrose lifted the staff and touched the tip to Dank's head.

Dank's scream was the sound Melwas had made when Tom stabbed him with Caledyr: like the world itself was falling apart. Dank released Ambrose, but he was frozen, unable to move, unable to do anything as Ambrose's muttered incantation held him fast. But his tattoos writhed, lashing and thrashing like they were flaying Dank alive. They slipped across his skin, flailing their way towards Dank's face, towards Ambrose's staff, where they gathered, boiling over the boy's features, ready, waiting for something.

Ambrose drew his staff back, and drew with it the sprite, like a splinter. The tiny fay tried desperately to cling to Dank, but it couldn't resist whatever magic Ambrose was using. And, as it came free, the tattoos came with it. They leapt from Dank's skin like they were creatures in their own right. Like the thoughts in the maelstrom, they danced through the air, swirling around the sprite.

Not swirling. Wrapping. They were embalming the sprite. Curling around and around and crushing the sprite, until the last dot of ink was free, the sprite and the tattoos were no more than a spinning black ball, and the air vibrated with so much magic it made Tom's teeth ache.

Then Ambrose stopped speaking.

Dank fell back, collapsing to the ground. Ambrose's arm fell to his side like a dead weight, his staff rolled from his hand, and the tiny ball fell at Tom's feet, a speck of black against the endless white snow.

Silence. The storm was still at bay, as if it was afraid to roll back into the hush. Everyone stared at whatever sat at Tom's feet. Was the sprite inside? Was it alive?

He reached for it.

"Don't touch it." Ambrose was still. He could be thought dead if his mouth wasn't moving. "The jar."

It took them a moment to react, and it was Mennvinn that brought the jar forward.

"Put it inside. Do not touch it," he said again. "Place it into Orlannu, if you find it."

Mennvinn used the lid to scoop the little ball into the sprite's former prison, fastened it tight, and set it on the ground. She stepped away quickly, as if it might hurt her.

Ambrose stared at nothing. His skin was grey, and his dark eyes seemed empty somehow. Mennvinn rushed to his side, but he said, "No." His fingers twitched. The tiniest gesture, towards Dank, who was sprawled in the snow, his lips moving soundlessly, his eyes wide and unseeing. "Care for him," Ambrose said. "I am beyond your help."

Mennvinn stepped back, silent, reverential. As if Ambrose was ill. No. As if he was dying. Which he was, Tom realised. He was spent. He'd been holding onto his last reserves, just for this moment. Just to release Dank, and save Tom's life. Emyr knelt beside his friend, and took his hand in his own.

"I didn't expect it to hurt so much." Tears slipped from Ambrose's sightless eyes. "I thought I was beyond such things."

"Mennvinn, bring him something for the pain," Emyr ordered.

"It would be a waste." But Ambrose's brow tremored and his breath hitched. His hair was matted with blood. "You'll have to finish this without me now, old friend."

"I won't know what to do without you," Emyr replied. He made no attempt to hide his grief, his regret or his anger.

"That's why he's here." His fingers twitched again. Towards Tom. "Look after him."

Tom nodded, but wasn't sure if Ambrose could see him. "I will," he managed, no more than a whisper, but somehow he knew that Ambrose had heard him.

"I'm so sorry," Emyr said.

"Why?"

"I put you through this. You did this for me."

"And what did you do for me?" Ambrose's lips twitched into a smile. "I don't remember any of my life. It feels like it has not been easy. But there is one last memory that makes it a little easier to bear."

Tom remembered the silent promise he had made himself: to make sure that Ambrose always had something good to remember. So he placed a hand on Emyr's shoulder. The old king looked up at Tom with a desperate hope that near broke Tom's heart. "Tell him," Tom managed in a hoarse whisper.

Emyr's hope died and shrank under the loss and the responsibility. But he lifted his friend's hand to his lips and said, without hesitation, "You have always been my dearest friend."

Ambrose sighed. "That was it." A trace of a smile played

about his lips. "That was my last memory." He'd never seemed so peaceful. So human.

"I wish I could remember her face," he said.

His last breath rattled from his frame, and his face went slack.

Ambrose was dead.

CHAPTER 23

EMYR CRIED the sobs of a man who has learned to keep his grief restrained and proper. He covered Tom's hand on his shoulder with his own, held it, squeezed it. It didn't feel right to embrace Emyr or talk to him, to interfere with his grief. Even the storm kept its distance, the wind and the driving snow battering against invisible walls, just as the waters in the merrow city had been held back by an unseen magical force.

But the magic was gone. Ambrose was dead. So Tom stood and let Emyr squeeze his hand, and watched Mennvinn tend to Dank. She peered into his eyes, felt his neck, his wrist, poked and prodded. Straightened his limbs and made him comfortable. Draig gave her a questioning look, and Mennvinn gave him a shrug in return. She found Tom's eyes, and Tom nodded to Gravinn.

Gravinn had slumped to the ground, curled into a ball. Deep dark circles surrounded her eyes, and she looked like she hadn't eaten in months. She didn't resist when Mennvinn tried to examine her. She was docile and obedient, if distracted; she would touch her face and move her fingers like they were new to her. But Mennvinn finished her examinations and gave Tom another shrug.

Emyr's sobs grew quieter, then silent, and finally his shoulders stopped shaking. His grip on Tom's hand weakened, and then he patted it and released it. Drew a deep breath and wiped his nose and face on his sleeve. But he didn't move. Just knelt by Ambrose's form. So Tom let him be, and stepped over to Mennvinn. He didn't have to ask.

"They're both well, as far as I can see," she told him. "He's in some form of shock. Although I think we all are."

"And Gravinn?" She was scooping up handfuls of snow and tipped it back onto the ground, watching with an expression devoid of interest. Had he done this? He had been so rushed to put Dank and Gravinn back together. Perhaps he had done it wrong? The responsibility was like another weight around his neck and he couldn't stand a moment longer. He sank to the ground, sat, let his head hang.

"There was an accident in the mines near Cairnakor," Mennvinn said. "An explosion. There were dozens of wounded. Dozens more were trapped down there for days while we dug them out. Some of the dwarfs were like Gravinn. Detached. Empty. They didn't recognise anyone. They didn't speak. None of them ate unless they were fed. Some would soil themselves. One cirgeon called it a trauma of the mind."

"Will she get better?" He dreaded the answer.

"Some of them did."

"Some of them didn't."

"Some of them didn't," Mennvinn agreed.

And they were far from any help. In fact, he had no idea where they were. And anyone who might know was dead, trapped in Faerie, or suffering trauma of the mind.

The world faded, replaced by a warm morning, his body a cacophony of aches and pains and hurts. An old woman said,

"Only a fool spurns an ally." And he said to her, "All of my allies are lost."

The foresight faded and he felt even more alone than before. His foresight was right. Ambrose was dead. Dank's mind might never return. The sprite was gone. He had no way into Faerie. No way back to Katharine and Rose. And even if he found his way to them, he'd lost Caledyr. He had nothing to fight the fay with.

The glarn.

He didn't understand the thought at first. But then he looked up at the mighty, fake doors Rimestenn had built, and remembered the chasm, the door, the lock. All to keep Orlannu hidden from the fay. So perhaps it could hurt them. Perhaps it could save Katharine and Rose.

"We need to get inside," he said, but it was nothing more than a whisper. He winced at the pain and Mennvinn lifted his chin, turned his head this way and that.

"There's nothing I can do for that," she told him. But with sympathy. "How do you feel?"

"I've been better." He gave her a smile that he didn't feel inside. "I need the coin."

She sighed and looked aside. She didn't want to say what she said next. "You're always moving. Sometimes the body needs to stop. To rest and recover."

Yes. Rest. He could almost hear Caledyr in his mind, telling him to rest. His eyelids drooped at the mere thought of sleep.

But every moment here was a moment his daughter was in Faerie.

"Later," he promised. He could sleep later.

Mennvinn pressed her lips together and made a dissatisfied sound in the back of her throat. She'd been making it a lot lately. Tom couldn't help but smile. "We must be terrible patients," he said.

Her expression softened. "I've had worse," she said. She even smiled, just a little. Then she pulled the coin from her pocket, gave it to him, and went to check on the rest of her terrible patients.

Standing felt like lifting the whole of Tir on his back. Mennvinn was right. He did need rest. After they were inside, he promised himself. He stepped over to the door, placed the coin in the hollow. A perfect fit.

"What now?" Jarnstenn appeared at his shoulder.

"Now I have to perform some kind of magic."

"Magic."

Tom nodded. "Ambrose showed me how." He didn't add how difficult it had been. "The magic burns a part of you away. A sacrifice." He pulled his right hand from its glove and placed his fingers on the old coin. Tried to feel it, the way he'd felt the twig. The old surface. The old metal. A trace of that silver-grey-veined black stone at its core. Could he find fire within? Ambrose had only taught him what to do with one of the elements. What if there wasn't enough fire to work with? What would he do then?

But the cold, hard pebble of magic inside him stirred as he reached into the coin, and it felt like it asked him what he was looking for.

Fire, he told it.

Fire, it echoed.

And the thought seemed to echo between the stone in the coin and the pebble within. But this echo grew as it bounced from man to coin and back again. And Tom realised the pebble was growing too. The thought was feeding on him, burning him away to create the fire he wanted.

And the coin was getting warm.

What if he couldn't control it? What if it burnt him away, until he was like Ambrose? Was he going to have to sacrifice himself just to open this door?

"Father and the prayers, and fasting and charities, and calmness of the soul until death," he said. Because he had to, and because he hoped it would calm him.

There was a click, and the sound of rock grinding against rock, and stale air washed over him as the door inched open. Distracted, he dropped the connection with the coin, and the magic stopped.

And the pebble inside was now a stone.

"You did it." Jarnstenn's voice was flat and cold, as if he despised Tom's success. Was he thinking of his argument with Kunnustenn? Did he regret not believing in magic?

"Thanks to Ambrose," Tom said. Jarnstenn pushed the door further open. There was no light at all inside. And Tom could feel that familiar deadness to the air. Monolith stone. What had Rimestenn left inside? "It's dark," he said.

"It's an abandoned city," Jarnstenn said. "Not going to have left the lights on, are they?" And he took a piece of burning wood from the fire and walked through the open doorway before anyone could stop him.

It was embarrassing and shameful to watch Jarnstenn walk in alone, but if the dwarf was afraid, he didn't show it. He walked as if he stepped into abandoned cities every day, his torch illuminating a tunnel made of black stone veined with silver-grey. Small wonder the air felt so dead.

And then Jarnstenn's shadow and his tiny torch stepped beyond the tunnel and they heard him take a breath. "Adalstenn's light," he said and, as if summoned by his words, a soft, white light shone upon his face.

Tom knew he should go inside. It was what they had been travelling for all this time. But all he could think was that Katharine should be here. She was the one who would appreciate an abandoned city. Her absence made Tom feel lonely and tired.

Jarnstenn stepped further into the city and out of sight.

"Jarnstenn," Tom croaked. When the dwarf didn't return, he forced himself up, squeezed through the doorway and down the tunnel in a crouch. The walls tugged at his mind when he brushed against them, giving him glimpses of other places, the people of Tir, laughing, working, drinking, fighting. Stay away from the walls, he told himself. The tunnel ended and he stood upright.

The cavern was huge. Enormous. Bigger than Cairnagwyn? Certainly bigger than Cairnagan, stretching for miles away from them. The ground below them, also made of the black, silver-grey veined stone, sloped downwards until it met a wall, easily twenty times their height, the beginnings of a maze that stretched the entire length of the cavern. Their vantage point gave them a perfect view of the enormity of the task ahead of them, paths splitting and splitting and splitting, full of dead ends, a geometric nightmare between them and their assumed goal: the source of the light at the end of the maze.

"That must be it," said Jarnstenn.

"Must it?" It seemed too obvious to Tom. Like the enormous fake door outside. "Couldn't it be a another ruse?"

"No." Jarnstenn shook his head. "Don't you see? It's part of the challenge. He's showing us how far away the end is. He's trying to put us off before we start. Very clever."

And, as if in answer, the cavern echoed with a hideous scream.

"If he's trying to put us off," Tom said. "It's working."

"It'll take weeks to cross that maze."

"Will our supplies last?"

"We're assuming that monster doesn't get us first."

"We don't know there is a monster."

"That scream weren't me serenading you, sweetheart."

"Stop," Tom told them. They'd all gathered on the vantage point, illuminated by the unearthly glow, enjoying the cold breeze because it was better than the stuffy, stale air around them. "We can gather as much water as we can carry," he said, pointing back down the tunnel. "The door is still open. So Rimestenn is clearly giving us a chance."

"What do you mean?" Mennvinn asked.

"He could have rigged the door to close behind us." Trapping them in here with whatever made that scream. "So we gather water. We take stock of our food. Jarnstenn will study the maze. Can you figure out a path from up here?"

The dwarf nodded. "Maybe."

"Good. Let's do those things first, and then we can figure out our next move."

Everyone moved to the sleds or the world outside except for Mennvinn, who stepped closer and whispered to Tom, "I still don't have anything for Six's pain."

Unfortunately, Six's hearing was unimpaired. "I'm happy to drink my pain away," he said. "You've got something in your supplies, no?" His sled was amongst the others, as if he was nothing more than baggage. It didn't seem right.

"That alcohol is for cleaning wounds," Mennvinn replied. "It's not suitable for consumption."

"I'm willing to compromise on taste."

"It's more than the taste," she began, but Tom raised a hand.

"He's joking," he murmured. "I think it helps him." She nodded, and he added, "Help the others take stock of our supplies. Maybe there's something hidden away that might help."

There was little chance of that, and she knew it too. But she nodded and went to help the others. But Draig wasn't helping. He was stood, fists clenched, his expression like stone as he said to Tom,

"Explain you what Dank said."

Time to put this fire out. And there was little point in denying any of it. So Tom met Draig's glare with as much honesty as he could muster. "Melwas demanded I fight him, in return for keeping Katharine and Rose safe. If I lose, I have to swear my loyalty to him."

His words sent a hush over the others. But Tom didn't look at them. He just watched the disbelief, anger, and cold certainty warring on Draig's face. "Swore you to him loyalty?" the elf growled.

"No," Tom replied. "But I will have to, if I lose the fight."

"So what?" Jarnstenn scoffed. "Swear your oath and stab the blighter in the eye."

"No." Six's voice was cold. "Tom can't lie. If he swears to obey Melwas, he'll be be bound to it."

The chill in the air didn't come from the wind blowing through the open door. No-one moved. But Tom could feel everyone recoiling from him.

"I did what had to be done," Tom told them.

"Did we lead you to this Orlannu," Draig said, "And will you turn and give it to the fay."

"If I lose."

"Are you no swordsman."

"He beat Tree," Mennvinn offered.

Jarnstenn nodded, and even Six seemed to relax. But Draig just said, "Where is Caledyr?"

And Tom knew that was the last handful of dirt over his grave. "The fay kept it," he said. "When they sent me back, they kept Caledyr."

Draig said nothing, but his body tensed and Tom felt his own body tense in response. Was the elf going to hit him? But before he could do anything, Emyr spoke up. “Did you trade it for their lives?”

Draig didn’t want to step aside. But, after a long moment, he turned. Just enough that Tom could see the old king. Haggard. Angry. Hurt. “No,” Tom said. It stung that he had to say it. Did Emyr really have to ask?

But if Melwas had demanded it, would Tom have handed it over? Possibly.

Emyr stepped forward until he stood before Tom, looking up at him, Draig looming over both of them. “My friend is dead. Kunnustenn is dead. Six crippled. Katharine a captive in Faerie. Gravinn and Dank mindless. And you’ve lost the sword and sworn yourself to Melwas.”

Emyr was blaming him. And part of Tom told him that the old king was right to. Who else was to blame if not Thomas Rymour?

But a spark of anger raged that Emyr had left Rose off his litany of losses. As if she wasn’t the greatest loss of all. “They have my daughter,” Tom growled.

“Because you took her to Faerie.” There was no accusation in Six’s tone, though it seemed like there ought to be.

“I did what had to be done.”

“She’ll hate you for that.”

“Perhaps.”

“I think I hate you for it, a little.”

“She can’t die there.”

“I know.” It wasn’t that Six accepted the way things were; it was that he couldn’t see an alternative.

But Emyr shook his head. As if Katharine and Rose were of no consequence. “I’m so disappointed in you.”

It was a surprising blow, and Tom wasn’t ready for it. It left him breathless, eyes hot with suppressed emotion, jaw tight with inarticulate fury. He didn't trust himself to speak, but Emyr turned, and Tom would be hoisted by iron nails if he was going to let the other man walk away from him. "I did what had to be done," he snapped. "To protect my family. Or should I have let them die?"

Emyr didn't turn back. "My family is dead."

"I gave mine to the watch," Six said.

"I watched mine die," Jarnstenn said.

"And wouldn't you have done anything to save them?" No-one replied and Tom nodded. "I do what has to be done," he repeated. "I fought Draig so we could free the dragons. I killed Tree so we could escape from Tirend. I almost lost myself trying to rescue Dank and Gravinn. And now the fay have Katharine." His voice hitched as he added, "They have my daughter. If I have to challenge Melwas, and swear my loyalty to him to keep them safe, I'll do it." They understood. Tom could see it in their eyes. They just didn't want to admit it. "You can judge me if you it makes you feel better. You don't have to trust me. You just have to help me find Orlannu, get back to Faerie, and to stop the fay."

"Why should we give you help?" Draig was angry, disappointed, resigned and incensed. He wandered over to their sleds, picked up an iron blade, and Tom tensed, ready to leap away from any strike as Draig stormed towards him, teeth gritted. "Have we lost so much, and still you give yourself to the fay. Are not you a knight. Are not you a leader." He stopped, his chest an inch from Tom's face. But Tom refused to back away. He just stared up into Draig's scowl. "Are you a traitor," the elf said.

Tom didn't need Caledyr's help to fend off this attack. Perhaps it was because a liar knows a liar. But he could see in Draig's eyes the lie the elf was telling himself. So he just said, "I suppose that's something we have in common."

Tom hadn't been sure if those words would provoke Draig

into an attack. But instead they doused the flames of the Easterner's anger. His shoulders sagged, his scowl saddened. "Did I betray my oaths for the good of Tir." But there were no teeth in his argument, and he knew it.

"We have so few weapons against the fay," Tom said. "We have to use the ones we have." Draig took a step back, and Tom spoke to everyone. "We all have our reasons. But we all want to stop the fay." One by one, they looked aside. It wasn't hearty agreement. He hadn't roused the troops. But there was no challenge anymore. So he said, "Jarnstenn, get to work on that map. Six, you can help him. Draig and Mennvinn can assess our supplies."

"And what should I do?" The old king still had his back to Tom, and there was a dead bitterness to his voice.

"You can tell us how we should honour Ambrose."

The ground was frozen; there was no burying him. But they could still perform the ceremony. So they gathered in a circle around the mound of snow that had almost covered Ambrose, and Tom said, "We are of the dirt and we return to it."

And Mennvinn said, "Who returns to the dirt?"

"Ambrose," Tom replied. "Who helped me find my king."

"Ambrose," said Mennvinn. "Who I did not understand, but who saved our lives."

"Ambrose," said Jarnstenn. "Who smiled at my jokes."

"Ambrose," said Draig. "Who was to me a man who deserved to be better known."

"Ambrose," said Six. "Who I found frightening and inspirational in the same breath."

"Ambrose," said Emyr. "Who was to me a true friend, an example to follow, and who sacrificed everything for the people of Tir."

Yes. That was why they stood here, outside Cairnarim. For the people of Tir.

Tom found he couldn't remember the end of the ritual, but didn't want to ask Jarnstenn. Thankfully, Mennvinn said, "Ambrose, who has been taken from our world, and whom we envy the world for taking back into itself."

Tom waited a moment, before adding, "Ambrose. Take this offering." Nothing seemed more appropriate than the coin that had opened the door to Cairnarim. It was now warped by heat, the sun a smear, Emyr's face a horrible, warped vision. Tom pushed it down into the snow. "Take it with you to the Isles of the Dead and let it buy your passing into that place, where the sun never sets and it is always summer." He touched a morsel of bread to the ground, no bigger than the nail on his smallest finger. It didn't seem big enough, but it was all they could spare. He put it in his mouth, chewed it, swallowed it. "You have done wrong in this life, as have we all. I take your wrongs and bear them on my shoulders now, so that you may enter the West in innocence and goodness. Go in peace."

He had said those words too many times on this journey.

"The father and the prayers," Emyr intoned. "And fasting and charities. And calmness of the soul until death."

The silence that followed was long and uncomfortable. Was it because Ambrose had had such a chilling presence that few felt they would honestly miss him? Or was it because they were all questioning this journey, questioning Tom? Let them question. As long as they did what they needed to do, they could be as silent and awkward as they needed to be. So Tom was the first to step out of the circle and enter the abandoned city again. Mennvinn was close behind. "I've been assessing the supplies we have remaining," she told him. She fished a cigar from her pocket. "We only have enough food for five days."

Five days? "Is that all?"

"We lost a lot in the fire."

The news spread a chill in his heart, like he'd been swimming in ice water for hours and was starting to succumb to the cold. But he had to keep going. His family needed him. "We'll have to make do."

"And we still have the journey back to think of," Mennvinn said.

It was depressingly easy to think there would be no journey back. "We'll have to worry about that once we have Orlannu," Tom said. He hated to say it. He wanted to have all the answers.

"We could turn back now," she said. She was trying and failing to make a spark with a piece of flint. "Gravinn and Six would be better served in Cairnakor."

"Scared?" Jarnstenn asked. He offered his own flint and they had her cigar lit in a moment.

"If you're talking about the monster in that maze, yes, I'm scared," she admitted, taking a deep drag on her little smoke. The pale blue smoke stank, but Tom found it somehow comforting. It seemed real. Mundane. A piece of a world long left behind. "But I'm also scared for them. If either of them worsen, there is little I can do here."

It was terrifying to think they could worsen. Gravinn sat where she had been placed, dull, tapping the stone in front of her in a constant, unending rhythm. Dank was up, but he sat apart from everyone else and said nothing. He just stared. "Then we'll have to hope they don't worsen," Tom said. Mennvinn made her dissatisfied sound, and Tom shrugged. "I wish I had better answers for you, Mennvinn. I know I'm asking too much of you. You do an admirable job of keeping us in one piece. I appreciate it."

"We're not all in one piece," Six growled as Jarnstenn pulled his sled past them, and Tom felt his cheeks warm as guilt clenched at his stomach.

"I'm sorry, Six."

But the elf shook his head. "Katharine was right. You say those words, but I'm not sure you know what they mean."

It was cruel, to speak of Katharine that way. And Six knew it. Tom could tell by the way the elf wouldn't meet his eye. But Six didn't apologise or take it back; he left those words to hang in the air, until the silence became thick and angry, and Tom found himself drawing deep, shaky breaths in an attempt to hold back his anger. "Help Jarnstenn with his map," he managed. And Six said nothing, just did as he was told.

"Tom." Emyr's voice was heavy but soft, his eyes filled with regret laced with resentment that hadn't quite faded. It made everyone else drift away, leaving the two men stood alone. "You lost Caledyr." Tom's anger was blunted by confusion; he could almost hear apology in the old king's tone of voice. "Because I failed you."

What to make of that? "How so?" he said, careful, waiting for a blow to fall.

"You think me a great man, Tom." Emyr's words were low. Empty. Tired. "But I'm a farmer's son. A second son, at that. So I surrounded myself with those I thought wise. They orchestrated my victories. I engineered my failures." Emyr sighed. "Now you treat me as your wise man. That makes your failings my own."

Was this the great King Emyr? The Emyr that Tom had seen recruit Mennvinn to their cause with a few well-chosen words, now speaking patronising nonsense? "And why do my failures belong to you, and your failures to yourself?" Tom growled.

"Because I am a king." He said it like he would rather be anything else.

And he was. "That's not what you keep telling me."

"You're right. I'm no-one's king." He turned his baleful eye onto Tom. "But you keep trying to follow me."

"It's why I brought you back. To lead us. To tell us how to defeat the fay."

"I thought we had that someone."

Tom had never heard Emyr so disappointed. It hurt. And the pain threw kindling onto the smouldering anger. "So did I." But if Emyr had ever been the man the legends spoke of, he wasn't anymore. "I was wrong."

Emyr winced. "I'm trying to apologise."

"Well, according to Six, apologies aren't enough." Tom knew how petty he sounded. But his patience was spent. He didn't need everyone to find fault with his actions; he could do that alone. "Are you going to lead us?"

The old king thought about it. He looked into Tom's eyes, weighing the man he found there, considering. Then he took a deep breath, and said, "No." But he didn't sound sure about it.

"Then do as I say." Tom flicked his head towards the others.

"But Tom-"

Tom held up a hand. Didn't move. Didn't blink. Just glared at Emyr until he walked away, the weight of Tir on his shoulders. Well, if he wanted to bear everyone's mistakes, let him. Tom would bear his own. And he would do it alone, it seemed.

His anger ebbed a moment later. He was being foolish. Only a fool spurns an ally. And were the others so wrong? Losing Caledyr, promising to bend the knee to Melwas, were these the actions of a great leader? No. But no-one else was willing to offer any better solutions. No. He did what had to be done.

"Jarnstenn," he barked, and the dwarf flinched. "How is that map coming?"

"Surprisingly well." Jarnstenn almost sounded afraid to say so. He held up his paper. Katharine's paper. Tom clenched his jaw against an unexpected wave of emotion. "Nearly done."

"Really?" It was cruel to ask. But it felt like the dwarf had barely spent any time on it.

"Six is checking it too." Jarnstenn hid his hurt well.

Six nodded. "It's good work." Tom stepped closer and the dwarf held out his map. Tom looked without taking it. Jarnstenn hadn't attempted to draw the entire maze, tracing instead paths from their goal, some culminating in dead ends, some simply abandoned. But one path traced its twisted, angular way all the way to where they stood.

"Good work indeed." Though Tom couldn't muster the warmth needed for such words, the dwarf stood a little taller all the same.

"Got to be thorough." Jarnstenn smiled. "Kunnustenn always says you have to read something backwards and upside down to understand it." And, after a pause in which no-one knew what to say, he added, "Said. He said that."

He was still greeted with silence, so Tom said again, "Good work." And felt like a cold fool when Six provided far more comfort by simply placing a hand on the dwarf's shoulder.

"Break camp," Tom told everyone. "We're leaving."

Whether their expressions were angry or uncertain, everyone gave Tom a wide berth, unwilling to do or say anything until he said it needed doing. So he was even more impatient by the time they reached the maze and they all turned to him, expecting him to take the lead.

"It's your map, Jarnstenn," he said. So the dwarf stepped forward, pleased to be given the responsibility Tom had shirked. But the dwarf's smile faded within moments; the maze was suffocatingly close. The path was narrow, the walls towered over them, and their sky was nothing but more black stone. But worse was the effect of the stone itself. It made the air feel cold, dead, brittle. Leeched of all life, like the morning after a night of heavy drinking.

But Tom also felt a constant, insistent tug at his thoughts. Even without touching the stone, he could feel the current beneath, a murmured conversation that was maddeningly just beyond hearing. The desire to reach out and resolve the murmur into clear speech was an itch that made it difficult to focus on anything else.

And there were no distractions. The claustrophobic maze added an oppressive air to the sullen silence, so the only sound was that of the sleds sliding across the smooth stone, and their own footsteps. Here, in the maze itself, the walls were close enough to create an echo, so it sounded like an army was marching alongside them.

So they didn't realise that they weren't alone until it was too late.

CHAPTER 24

THERE WAS NO WARNING. No sound. One moment they were following Jarnstenn, the next the creature had stepped out from around a corner. The walls echoed with gasps and cries of surprise, but Tom could only stare.

The thing had once been a dwarf, but that had been a long time ago. Now its flesh was grey and thin, stretched and torn by the yellowed bone beneath. Its jaw hung slack, held on only by tattered skin. It wore old, cracked iron armour, and skeletal hands dragged an enormous, heavy, ornate hammer. The empty eye sockets seemed to glare at them. The thin lips seemed to curl into a grimace. Even its rattling breath seemed filled with fury, like it resented each one. There was a palpable air of hate that radiated from it like heat from the fire.

"Rimestenn?" Emyr said.

And in reply, the creature screamed and lunged at Jarnstenn.

"Look out!" Tom pushed the dwarf aside, drew his iron blade and plunged it through the cracked armour and straight into the creature's chest.

The thing stopped still. The head drooped. Tom let himself take a breath and sigh out his relief.

Then the head lifted again and the eye sockets stared right at him.

Tom hesitated, waiting for his sword to advise him. But the cold iron was silent and the creature hit him across the face, the bony hands surprisingly strong, sending him staggering into a wall, his cheek against the cold stone.

A great hall of the Marches was all panic and screams in the night as three Faerie hounds, unseen by everyone, mauled and butchered the horses, along with anyone who stood in their way.

Tom shook his head, dragging his thoughts back to the moment. The creature. Rimestenn. It was coming at him, his sword still impaled in its chest, it was swinging its hammer towards him. He jumped back and the hammer struck the ground with a great ring. Tom couldn't help but notice how the stone cracked under the impact. Monolith stone. Impervious, unbreakable monolith stone. Cracked.

What was that hammer made of?

Draig appeared at his side, bearing another sword, but there was chaos and panic behind him. "Emyr, get everyone to safety," Tom ordered.

"Rimestenn, it's me," the other man called. "It's Emyr. Please remember me, my friend."

"Go!" Tom told him. If this was truly Rimestenn, there was nothing left of the dwarf in there. That much was plain. "Protect them!"

The creature swung its hammer again and Draig hopped back, chopped downwards, his blade ringing off the old armour. Tom tried to jump in and retrieve his sword but the hammer was already swinging back, forcing Tom to retreat and retreat once more. The swings never stopped, across, up, over, again and again. Tom fell back, felt the rush of air as the hammer swept through the spot where his head had been. Jumped back again to avoid a swing at his ankles. And, as the thing took a swing at Draig, Tom ran, leapt, and tackled the creature to the ground.

They landed in a heap, it stank of dried leather, the hammer was gone and bony fingers were scrabbling at Tom, it screamed in his ear and then Tom felt old teeth chewing at his neck, tearing through flesh that grew sticky and warm with blood, he cried out, pushed a hand into its mouth, pulled, and the jaw tore away from the creature's face. Tom pried the scrap of bone and skin from his flesh, tossed it aside, took hold of his sword and dragged it free from Rimestenn's chest.

There was no relief at having retrieved it. No rush of strength or thought to help save him. He staggered to his feet, disorientated by his dead sword.

But the creature was reaching for its hammer and Tom lifted his blade without thinking, brought it down and severed the skeletal hand.

"Tom!" Six, his voice distant. Tom chanced a look over his shoulder and saw the others were fleeing.

"Go," he said to Draig. "We can't be separated."

The pair followed, but Tom could hear the creature behind them too. He spared a glance over his shoulder and saw it, running, screaming from a jawless maw, dragging its hammer in one hand.

"Faster!" Tom cried to the others.

"Should we take another path," Draig said. "Draw it away."

"No." If they were separated, they'd never find each other. And what if the creature got away and attacked the others? He looked back again. It was closer. How was it so fast? Don't stop. Don't stop.

But Draig did stop, stepped around a corner and said, "Attack we from both sides."

He was right. Tom turned, raised his sword, and the creature screamed again as it swung its hammer in a mighty overhead swing that Tom barely dodged. Draig swung his blade, slicing through armour, pieces falling to the ground. Tom dodged another swing of the hammer and allowing himself a grim smile as he hacked away a chunk of armour.

The creature stabbed at his face with the stump of its arm, striking his forehead and sending him reeling back against the maze wall.

Villagers in Tanabawr ran screaming as Faerie woodkin tore up their homes, faces of bark twisted in rage to see their inert cousins turned into walls and floors and furniture.

Tom stumbled away from the wall, wiped blood out of his eyes. It felt like the stone had kept some of his thoughts, like tatters of clothing torn free by brambles.

A cry cut through the fog, and Tom looked up to see Draig fending off the creature alone.

Tom drew breath without thinking and bellowed without meaning. But it was too late. Draig was a moment too slow in dodging a swing, and the hammer sent the elf to the ground.

Rage and fear and uncertainty guided Tom through a flurry of attacks, slicing iron through the air in a fury. It was enough to push the creature back, retreating again and again, until it lifted the hammer for a clumsy parry.

What would Caledyr tell him to do? Step into the creature's reach, turn, drive the pommel back and onto the creature's head.

Without the sword's guidance, Tom was off balance and his blow was weak. But it was enough to crush the creature's eye socket, and it wailed and fell, a handless wrist held to its ruined face, glaring at Tom as it pushed feebly at the floor, trying to get away from him.

It was oddly humanising. In that moment, it wasn't a creature. It was Rimestenn. Emyr's friend, who had protected Orlannu for centuries. And something awful had happened to him. Didn't he deserve a better fate than this?

Rimestenn pushed himself to his feet, glaring out of one good eye socket, and Tom found himself moved to speak. "We come with Emyr," he said. "We came to save Tir."

Rimestenn let out a blood-curdling scream and fled. Whatever he had become, it clearly had no time for sentimentality or reason.

Draig groaned. He was sat against the wall, sword discarded, staring at the ceiling, his right arm resting on his lap and very still. "Know I not the word in your tongue," Draig told him through clenched teeth. "My arm, it is not in its place."

"Dislocated," Tom guessed. "You were lucky." Draig gave him a baleful look, but he knew Tom was right. That hammer had cracked unbreakable stone. Dislocated was better than pulverised.

"Are you hurt too." Draig's concern was grudging, but he nodded to Tom's neck, still warm and wet.

But this wasn't the time for comparing injuries. "Mennvinn can take a look at both of us," Tom told him. "Let's go."

Draig couldn't carry his sword, so Tom wielded both blades as they walked through the maze, casting his gaze left and right for signs of Rimestenn, signs of the others. He didn't call out; he didn't want to face Rimestenn alone, not without help. Not with the flow of warm, wet blood from his neck. So they walked in silence, for just long enough to think they were lost when Draig said, "Light."

Tom allowed himself a tired smile; there was firelight reflected on the stone. They turned towards it without comment, and rounded a corner to find the others sat with their backs to a small fire and a tight grip on their weapons.

Emyr sighed relief. "It's them."

"We thought you were dead." Six lowered his bow. His forehead gleamed with sweat and his voice was tight with pain.

"Not yet." Tom turned to Mennvinn and said, "Draig might have dislocated his shoulder."

"Never mind his shoulder, what happened to you?" she asked, her eyes wide and staring.

"Oh." Tom waved a hand. "It bit me."

She waved him to the ground and unbuttoned his shirt, peeled it away and peered at his neck. "Adalstenn's light," she cursed. She tugged something and held it up for him to see. "There are still teeth in there."

Tom grimaced. "A grim souvenir."

She shuddered. "The wounds will need cleaning. No knowing what disease that thing is carrying."

"That thing is my friend," Emyr said.

Mennvinn had the courtesy to look embarrassed, but Draig was not so tactful. "Cannot that thing be your friend."

"How can it be him at all?" Six asked. "He should be dead a thousand years."

"It's this place," Tom replied. "It's kept him alive."

"How?"

"This stone directs magic. That's what Ambrose said. Anything trapped inside cannot die because the elements can't get out. They're trapped. That's how Ambrose kept himself alive. He made a cave of this stone. His elements had nowhere to go, and so he just kept living."

Mennvinn was wiping his neck with a wet cloth that stung. "You can't cheat death," she said, then muttered, "You're bleeding a lot."

"Ambrose lived a thousand years because of this stone."

"But he didn't look like Rimestenn," Six said.

"There must be something wrong with this place," Tom said. Mennvinn finished wiping his skin and started threading a needle. More stitches. "Rimestenn didn't do it right."

"So we're going to end up looking like that?" Jarnstenn asked. "Walking corpses, the lot of us?"

"No." Tom shook his head, stopped when Mennvinn told him to be still. "We get to the end of this maze. Find Orlannu and leave." Leave and go back to Faerie, for Katharine and Rose.

"Won't be easy. That thing ripped my map." Jarnstenn held up the tattered remains. "And I don't know where we are now."

Lost. In a maze the size of a city. With food and water for five days. And Rimestenn was still out there.

"What do we do?" Mennvinn asked. She sounded calm, matter-of-fact. Her hand didn't shake as she drew thread through the flesh of his neck, but Tom could tell she was terrified.

"Die, most likely," Six said.

"We face one problem at a time," Tom told her. "Take a look at Draig's shoulder."

"I'm more concerned by this wound." She tied her thread and snipped off the excess. But Tom's neck still felt wrong somehow, and Mennvinn's expression told him this was more serious than a simple cut or gash.

"Can you heal it?"

She was silent for a long moment. "No." She said it like an apology.

So now it was a race against time. "Then face a problem you can solve." And when she stared at him with pity in her eyes, he waved her away. He didn't need pity. He needed Draig fit and able to hold a sword. He needed Jarnstenn to find a new way through this maze. He needed to find Orlannu, and get back to Faerie.

"You're right," Mennvinn told him, feeling Draig's shoulder while the elf winced. "Dislocated." While Emyr wrapped his arms around Draig, she planted a foot against the elf's flank and pulled his arm until he cried out and it visibly popped back into place. Draig covered his face with his other arm and whimpered.

Mennvinn lowered his arm like it was made of glass. "Well done," she told him. "Rest. We'll put your arm in a sling. Try not to move it for a time. Definitely no fighting." She said that last to Tom.

"That depends on Rimestenn," Tom replied.

"Can I fight," Draig assured them all. "Have I still one good arm." He lifted it over his head as proof, but winced; his ribs remained broken, after all.

Mennvinn shook her head, though she seemed resigned to the risk of violence. "So what do we do now?" she asked.

Now Tom had to think of a way to escape this place without a map. He looked at the walls, the skittering silver-grey veins on the surface drawing his gaze up towards the glow above that illuminated the entire cave. The wall had to be the height of twenty men. But if they could climb it? "Jarnstenn, could you make a new map from up there?"

Jarnstenn looked at Tom, up at the wall, back at Tom. "You're joking."

"I'm not."

The dwarf scratched the top of his head and let out a big breath. "Maybe." The dwarf looked up again. "If I don't fall and break my neck."

"There's no way up there," Six said.

"Not yet." Tom agreed. "But what if we could make handholds?"

"Only Caledyr can cut monolith stone," Six said. "And we don't have it." He didn't try to hide the blame in his voice.

But Tom ignored it. "Rimestenn's hammer cracked the stone. We could take it from him."

Six shook his head, a humourless grin on his face. And Draig said, "Did that thing almost kill us."

"But we hurt him. And we outnumber him."

"We?" Mennvinn asked.

Tom tried to sound reassuring. Confident. To push away her fear. "We stand a better chance if we stand together."

"Not all of us can stand." Six pointed at Gravinn, who was entranced by the fire. But most gazes fell on his missing leg.

"He's right." Jarnstenn waved a small axe and said, "I ain't a fighter. And you can't kill what's already dead."

Tom thought of the legions of immortal fay that were stood against them, and for a brief moment he could have laid down and never risen again.

No, he told himself. Face a problem you can solve. "Rimestenn isn't dead," he told the others. "But he stands between us and Orlannu. So we're going to take his hammer."

"Ain't possible." Jarnstenn seemed afraid to even speak.

"I didn't ask for your permission," Tom told him. "You asked me what we're going to do, and I'm telling you." He looked at each of them, and each of them looked aside, unwilling or unable to argue. The sullen silence returned. But he didn't care. If they were going to ask him what to do, they were going to listen to the answer. "So," he said. "Here's what we'll do."

They walked. Draig pulled Six's sled with his one good arm. The others ranged ahead and down other corridors, calling back and forth to each other, making enough noise to wake Eirwen sleeping. No-one liked the idea of being attacked again, but Rimestenn had been in this place for a thousand years; he had a better chance of finding them than they did of finding him.

So they engaged in loud, reluctant conversation, the subject matter ranging from the meals they wished they could eat to the things they missed from home. Stories from their youths. And plenty of complaints: sore feet; empty bellies; waiting for a murderous undead dwarf to attack them. And Tom's neck grew hot, the warmth spreading to the rest of him as they walked, and he tried not to think of what would happen to Katharine and Rose if he died here.

But, as much noise as they made, they remained alone. When they grew too tired to walk, they stopped. Sipped their water, nibbled at their rations, and then they slept.

Rimestenn found them in the night.

CHAPTER 25

IT WAS Mennvinn that called out, and Tom was up in a heartbeat, a memory of Caledyr in his mind.

Fight. Fight. Fight.

He drew his iron sword, stumbled over sleeping bodies and placed himself between Mennvinn and the oncoming creature.

Rimestenn stopped. Lifted his handless wrist. Lifted his missing chin. Glared at Tom with his one intact eye socket.

"I can't imagine what you've suffered," Tom said. "I don't want to add to it. But I won't let you hurt my friends."

Rimestenn screamed and lifted his hammer.

Tom stepped aside as the blow came down onto the stone where he'd been standing.

Emyr stepped in with a sword of his own, the blade ringing off the hammer.

Tom tried to sever Rimestenn's remaining hand, but the splintered stump came at him again, trying to blind him, he ducked away but his swing missed. He leapt back from a blow that would have crushed his knees, staggered, fell. Draig stepped into the gap, roaring something in elfish and slicing a constant figure-of-eight arc through the air, driving Rimestenn back.

The corridor was too narrow; Tom had to wait for Draig and Emyr to drive Rimestenn into an intersection before there was room to rejoin the fight. The dwarf screamed and jabbed as Tom stepped forward, cracking the hammer against his chest, forcing the air from his lungs, knocking him to the ground.

Mennvinn stepped forward with a knife in her hand.

Rimestenn swept a mighty blow through the air, forcing Draig and Emyr back, and cracked his stump against Mennvinn's head, knocking her to the ground.

Jarnstenn bellowed something in dwarfish, charged with iron in both hands, and Rimestenn's hammer swatted him away like a bug.

Six let loose an arrow that buried itself, unnoticed, in Rimestenn's armour, and Dank dropped his knife and froze.

Draig dashed forward, seeking to slice Rimestenn's head from his neck, but the creature blocked the elf's blow and knocked him down. And when Emyr stepped forward, the old king hesitated, and Rimestenn delivered a crushing blow to his chest.

Tom charged without thought, swung his sword with all the strength he could muster.

The remains of Rimestenn's left arm clattered to the ground. A crushing swing forced Tom back, and then Rimestenn was gone.

They were too hurt and tired to carry on. No-one started a fire. They just sat, nursing their injuries alone and in silence. Even Mennvinn was quiet as she examined each of them, and Tom was happy to leave everyone to her care. There was a chill in the air that had crept under his flesh and settled beside the ache in his muscles. He huddled against both and tipped back his head to rest against the cool stone.

A caravan of merchants and travellers made its way across the Eastern Angles, and the gargantuan, worm-like fay Ahlatrab burrowed its way through the sands behind them, ready to leap from the dunes and devour them whole.

Tom lifted his head and wiped sweat from his brow. He couldn't even rest here.

Mennvinn was knelt beside him, and her touch on his neck was like fire. "That hurts," he told her.

"You opened the wound again," she murmured. "And I think it's corrupted."

"What does that mean?"

"It means it could kill you."

Tom smiled. Of all the ways he'd imagined dying on this journey, a ghoulish dwarf's bite had never been amongst them. "And the others?"

Mennvinn made her dissatisfied sound. "Emyr has broken ribs. Jarnstenn has a few bruises. And Draig's shoulder could become a problem if he doesn't rest. He needs to learn to look after himself." She gave Tom a meaningful look. "A lesson you all need to learn."

She was probably right. But he didn't have time to worry about his well-being. Not while Melwas and Mab had their fingers wrapped around his daughter. "Let's get out of this place first."

Mennvinn's expression betrayed her fear: she didn't expect to see the outside world again. "We barely survived," she told him. "You said we outnumbered that thing. But we couldn't stop it."

"We hurt it."

"And it hurt us."

She was right. They had each stood against Rimestenn and

come away broken or wounded. Except for Dank. The other man's head was bowed and shame rode plain on his face. He caught Tom staring and winced. "I'm sorry," he murmured.

"Don't be."

"I was afraid."

"So was I." Tom shivered, and Mennvinn touched his forehead.

"You have a fever," she told him.

"No." He shook his head and hugged himself tighter, which tugged the wound in his neck and made him wince. "I'm cold."

"You're sick."

Again, she was right. His body was telling him that something was wrong, he should rest, recover. But this wasn't a thing that rest could cure; time would only bring him closer to the Isles of the Dead. So he pushed himself to his feet with aching muscles. "We need to move," he told them all, and they stared at him like he was mad.

"We need to rest," Jarnstenn replied.

"We're low on food and water," Tom reminded him. "They won't last if we delay." And nor would he.

"What if we run into that thing?"

"We fight."

"We'll lose."

"He's right, Tom," Emyr said. "Rimestenn is too quick." He nodded to the others, scared and hurt. "We can't put them in harm's way."

The words sounded odd coming from Emyr, the man who had led armies into battle. Who had sent countless men and women to their deaths. "We move," Tom said, "or we sit here and wait to die."

"They're not fighters, Tom," Emyr snapped.

No. They weren't. And they could get hurt. Or worse. But

what was the alternative? Iron nails, he wanted to lie down. A Knight of Tir should stand tall and shrug off any injury. But he was only Thomas Rymour, so he sagged against the wall of the maze, easing the struggle of standing, only to struggle against the tugging of his thoughts. "Please," he said, and for a moment he didn't know if he was talking to the stone or to Emyr. He looked at the others. "I want to keep everyone safe. But I need your help."

They stared at him, some in disbelief, some with anger, some with fear. But, one by one, they got to their feet, and they followed him.

There was neither day nor night in Rimestenn's iron-cursed labyrinth, just the constant, taunting glow from the goal that they could not find. So there was no telling how much time passed. They slept at one point. But if that meant one day had passed or two, Tom couldn't tell. He knew his wound was getting worse; he was shivering and his head had begun to pound. It angered him, that his body was failing him. Now, when Katharine and Rose needed him most, his body was willing to give up, surrender after all the pain and suffering and misery. No. He wouldn't allow it. He wouldn't.

So when they turned a corner and found Rimestenn waiting for them, Tom didn't wait for the attack. He lifted his sword with a cry made hoarse and weak by exhaustion. To his surprise, Rimestenn turned and fled. But Tom refused to let him escape. So he gave chase. And, had he not been so tired, perhaps he might have caught him. He followed the creature through turn after turn after turn, only dimly aware of the cries at his back.

He had to finish it. He would be terrorised by this dead thing no longer.

But after a few turns, he could no longer see it disappearing around corners. Soon he could not hear its footsteps, could not hear the drag of its hammer against the ground.

"Damn it," he panted. And then the anger and the hate and the despair boiled over and he screamed, "Damn it!" as he swung his sword against the wall, rewarded only with a ringing peal and a duller edge. He let himself drop to his knees and stopped, trying to catch his breath even as the ugly bruise on his chest made it hard to breathe.

Caledyr would tell him to fight. But he'd lost Caledyr.

And he'd lost Katharine. And Rose. And Ambrose and Kunnustenn and Siomi and soon he'd lose Emyr and Six and Dank and the others, because he was failing. They would die in here. Or, rather, they wouldn't die. They'd go on and on. Perhaps they'd join Rimestenn in terrorising visitors too. Or perhaps they would all chop pieces off each other until only their heads remained to glare at each other for the rest of time.

A voice cried out. Called for him. The others were looking for him, because he'd been foolish enough to run off. What kind of leader was he? What Knight of Tir would abandon his friends?

The voice kept calling. With fear. Panic. And it was accompanied by the peal of metal on metal.

Emyr's black bones. They weren't looking for him. They were under attack.

He started running. "Where are you?" Rimestenn had tricked him. Circled back. Now he was killing the few friends he had left. He'd abandoned them. He'd failed them. "Where are you?"

This looked wrong. He'd taken a wrong turn. He ran back, took another. "Emyr! Six! Mennvinn!"

There was a shout, and Rimestenn's scream echoed through the maze. Eirwen's grace, bring me back to them, forgive my mistake, please. Please. "Where are you?" he called.

There! He recognised this junction, didn't he? And he could hear them, he could hear voices and fighting, he dashed down a corridor, turned a corner, another, he was getting closer. And then he dashed through a junction and saw Jarnstenn brandishing a sword, Mennvinn standing over Six with a blade of her own, and Emyr crying, "Get back!" before Rimestenn swept the old king's feet out from under him and raised the hammer to crush Six.

Tom ran. Blade first, bellowing, demanding Rimestenn's attention, ignoring how the hammer began to swing towards him, how his muscles tightened against the imminent blow, focusing only on driving his sword into the thing's chest and knocking it off its feet.

Tom drove Rimestenn to the ground but the sword was torn from his grip. So he used his only remaining weapon. Rimestenn's skull was hard against his fists, and sharp where Tom had crushed it in a previous attack. The bone cut his flesh as his blows landed. He didn't feel it. All he felt was his fear and frustration and impotent rage. He watched Rimestenn's skull shrink under his fists. Saw its leathery flesh tear. Saw pieces of old bone fall away.

Not enough. He picked up the hammer. Short, in his hands. He could feel monolith stone somewhere in the head, too. But all that mattered was that it was heavy. He pulled back and swung, crushed Rimestenn's leg into dust. The creature screamed and Tom readied himself for another blow.

"Don't!" Emyr cried and Tom turned to see the old king wracked with pain and guilt.

"What's wrong?" he asked. But before Emyr could reply,

Rimestenn had dragged himself around a corner and back into the labyrinth.

Tom knew he should pursue. Finish this. But he was tired. And he had the hammer. So he sank to the ground. Made the mistake of leaning against the wall and letting his head rest against it.

The fay called Hobbledy's Lantern leapt from ship to ship, cinders and sparks falling from his burning skin and setting alight sails and decks and men alike. Jenny Greenteeth waited below, beak snapping in anticipation of those who would jump overboard.

Duke Regent sat in his seat beside Emyr's throne in the halls of Cairnagan, Sir Wrothsley stood at his side. "We have few allies left," Regent said. He looked older, his beard grown longer and greyer and more unkempt. While Wrothsley looked younger, stronger. Whatever was happening agreed with one and not the other.

Storrstenn waited for the Western guards to pass his cell, before sliding a stone from the wall and continuing work on his tunnel.

Something shook Tom and his head drooped, freed from the draw of the labyrinth wall. He closed his eyes. "I hate this place."

"I'm not too fond of it either, son."

"Why did you stop me?"

"He was my friend."

"I don't think he's anyone's friend anymore."

"Perhaps not." Emyr sighed. "But I'm not ready to kill the last friend I have left."

Tom was surprised at how much that hurt. He lifted his head, opened his eyes, met Emyr's. Blinked. Waited.

"You know what I mean," the other man said.

And suddenly Tom was too tired to be hurt. "I do." He hefted the hammer, used its weight to help him push himself off the ground.

"Rest," Emyr told him. "Just for a moment."

But he couldn't rest. Not while Katharine and Rose were at Melwas' fickle mercies. Not while death festered in the wound at his neck. Never enough time. "Make sure the others aren't hurt," he told Emyr. And he began to swing.

The hammer was heavy. The stone was hard. Each impact shook its way up his arms, rattled his teeth, left tremors in his muscles. But the wall cracked. And splintered. And pieces began to fall away. Handholds and footholds. Soon Tom was forced to stand in them, awkwardly swinging the hammer in one hand while holding on with the other. It was dangerous and precarious and he expected to fall with each swing. When he grew tired, he dropped the hammer and climbed back down.

He was exhausted. Covered in sweat and dust. Mennvinn picked a few shards of stone from his face and wiped the cuts clean. "You need to rest."

"I can't."

"Let someone else take over."

So Emyr took the hammer without a word and against Mennvinn's protests. He whimpered as he climbed, his broken ribs no doubt an agony. But he attacked the wall all the same, just one small slip from falling and hurting himself. "Be careful," Tom told him.

"I would say the same to you," Mennvinn said. She peeled back his shirt and a foul waft struck Tom's nose. "This bite is getting worse," she muttered. She disappeared and Tom couldn't muster the interest to see where she went.

"You look awful."

Tom lifted his head just enough to see Six had sat himself nearby. "You say the nicest things."

"I'm not the only one who doesn't lie." Six grinned without humour. "When was the last time you ate?"

When they broke camp? Before they'd entered the maze? He couldn't remember. Answering was too much effort, so he just shook his head.

Someone held a flask to his face. "Drink." Mennvinn tipped his head back and poured water into his open mouth. Emyr's teeth, why did he feel so weak?

"He should eat, too," Six said.

"Not hungry," Tom answered, and coughed as he inhaled water. Once he was done, he tried to pull his shirt back on. "Cold."

Mennvinn's hand on his forehead was like a burning coal. "He has a fever." She poured something on his shoulder that stung.

"Will that be enough?" Six asked.

"I don't think so."

"I can't stay," Tom told them. It was getting too cold, and too hard to think. But if they could find the end of the maze, find Orlannu, they could leave. He could gather his thoughts, and rescue Katharine and Rose. "I have to keep moving."

"You need to sleep."

"I can sleep after we get out of this place."

"That could take days."

"Isn't there anything you can give him?" Six asked her.

"I have something that will make him sleep."

Tom reached up and placed a hand on Mennvinn's shoulder. "You are a good healer," he told her. It was hard to put his words in order. "I am very grateful for what you've done for us. For me. But if you make me sleep, I will kill you."

Shock and fear were plain in her eyes. Then she pushed them aside, and she was again calm and in control. "You could die," she told him.

No. He would not abandon Katharine and Rose to Faerie forever. "Then I don't have time to sleep."

Emyr was climbing back down. "I need a moment," he said, his voice tight with pain.

"I'll take over." Tom pushed himself to his feet, tottered, warded Mennvinn away with a wave of his hand. "I can do it." He reached deep, where the dark stone within him sat cold and unmoved by his unsteady legs, his fatigue, his weakness. That's what he needed to be right now: hard and uncaring of every complaint his body levelled at him. He picked up the hammer, not because his body had the strength to do so, but because he willed himself to do so. He climbed the wall and didn't tumble to his doom because he refused to fall. Hammered new handholds and footholds because they would save Katharine and Rose.

But the body was weak. And soon he felt his grip begin to fail, despite his furious demands on his fingers to hold fast. So he stopped. Better to drop the hammer when he willed it, rather than let it slip free and hurt someone below.

By the time he reached the ground his whole body was shaking, and he was happy to let Emyr take over and to let Mennvinn urge him to the cool stone beneath him.

An old woman was being pushed through the Cairnagan dungeons while Glastyn watched with interest.

Kobolds were chewing the bricks in a city wall, giggling at the thought of its collapse.

Idris knelt alone in front of Eirwen's tomb, head bowed, and muttered, "I have been a fool."

Hands lifted his head and placed his folded shirt beneath it. Tom almost protested; while his mind was elsewhere, it wasn't in his body. He closed his eyes and shivered.

"Make him sleep," Six murmured. "I'll bear the consequences."

"He won't," Tom muttered. "I'll make sure of it."

"You asked me to take care of everyone," Mennvinn countered.

"Will sleep cure me?"

Silence.

"Then what good will it do?" But Eirwen's grace did he want to rest. He could already feel sleep claiming him, his thoughts tattering and disordering into blissful dreams. Tom clenched his aching thighs, took a deep breath, tried to order his thoughts. "Tell me how close Emyr is."

"Close." Six sounded resigned. Good. Arguing was a waste of time. "But he's tiring."

Tom readied himself to rise, to climb, but he couldn't. Not yet. "Dank. Can you take a turn?"

Silence. So Tom opened his eyes and lifted them to Dank. The other man stood apart from everyone else, and Tom could see he was still nursing his shame. He stared at Tom like a rabbit spotted by a wolf. "Please," Tom said. He didn't have the energy to reassure the other man. He just needed him to help. "I don't care about what you did. All that matters is what you do now."

Dank looked down as his hands, hands that had killed Ambrose, hands that hadn't been raised against Rimestenn. But now wasn't the time for wallowing in the past. "Help me, Dank," Tom said. And Dank took a deep breath, lifted his eyes, straightened and said, "Yes, Sir Tom," without any hint of mockery or malice. He accepted the hammer from Emyr, took a sure, certain path up the wall, as if he'd climbed it many times.

Emyr sat beside Tom, sweating and in obvious pain. But he was grinning. "Sir Tom," he said. He watched Dank swing the hammer like a young man. He was a young man. And a very old man, too.

Tom's thoughts didn't make sense. "I'm not well," he muttered to himself.

"Just be glad we don't have any mirrors," Six replied.

"How do we get back to Faerie?" Tom asked. Dank couldn't do it; the last effort had trapped him in the maelstrom between realms. So they would need a fay to help them. Would Glastyn do it? No. "He won't risk Melwas' wrath. Not for me."

Something cool and wet was placed on his forehead and it was bliss, a balm, "Thank you," he said.

"We need more than I have here," Mennvinn said.

"Face the problem you can solve," he told her.

"You are my problem."

He shook his head. "No. Katharine and Rose."

"They're not here. You are."

"Yes." Tom sighed. "That's the problem."

"He's delirious."

"I don't think he is."

And before Tom could correct any of them, Dank called out. "I've reached the top." Tom forced himself to open his eyes and smiled to see Dank stood on top of the wall, hands on his knees, panting, hammer resting at his feet. He pointed off to his right and grinned like a maniac. "I can see the centre. It isn't far."

"Don't mean much in a bloody maze, boy," Jarnstenn grumbled. "Can't believe I've got to climb up there."

"Would you rather I went?" Six asked.

But rather than casting an embarrassed glance at Six's missing leg, Jarnstenn instead grinned and said, "Course not. You'd only make a hash of it."

Six smiled too. "Get us out of here, master dwarf," he said, waving Rimestenn up the wall.

Jarnstenn wasn't a natural climber, and some of the craters they'd made in the walls were a stretch for him. He slipped twice, and each time Tom expected him to fall and dash his brains out. But he made it up the wall, pulled out his paper and his inks, and began to sketch like his life depended on it.

Which it did. "We move as soon as they come down," Tom told the others.

"You're no good to them dead," Mennvinn murmured to him.

"That's why I need to hurry."

"Got it!" Jarnstenn waved the paper over his head. He and Dank began to descend, and Tom pushed himself to his feet. He was shaking all over and the world span as he straightened. No. He was going to hang on a little longer. He touched the dark stone within. He was hard and cold and still. Calmness of the soul until death.

Jarnstenn was almost at the bottom when he slipped and fell, landing with a thud and a groan. What now? Mennvinn rushed to his side and Jarnstenn snapped, "It's fine, it's just my wrist."

She had his arm in her hands, squeezing and pressing as he cursed and groaned. "It doesn't feel broken. It might be sprained."

"We need to move," Tom told them.

"Give me a bleeding moment here."

"I don't have a moment, Jarnstenn." His thoughts threatened to wander away. "I'm sorry you're hurt. But you can walk. And we'll be able to look after you once we get out of here." He waved a hand at Emyr. "Take the map, take the lead."

Emyr did as he was told, and soon they were all trudging through the maze again. Rimestenn was less of a threat with only one arm and one leg, but everyone was still tired and uneasy, hungry and thirsty. They kept telling Tom to stop, to rest, and Tom waved them away. Even when they told him they had to sleep, he said, no, not yet, sleep once we've escaped, there isn't time to stop.

Visions intruded on his sight, not foresights, not in this place. Motion at the edges of his vision, glimpses of children running, Degor and Rose, playing hide and seek. He grinned, waved at them, they played so well together, he truly was blessed. He turned to Katharine and said, "She's a good girl."

Elaine said, "Degor's so proud to have a little sister."

"I'm proud of him."

"He's strong and honest and good."

"Nothing like me."

"Nothing like you."

Their laughter seemed distant, far away. "Don't wander off," he told them. "Don't get lost."

"Degor's already missing," Elaine said.

And Katharine added, "And you've lost Rose too."

"At least you're here."

"She went to look for them," Elaine said. "I'm the only one who waited for you."

"I'm sorry," he muttered, hugging himself against a sudden chill. "I'm sorry."

"This is all happening again."

"No." He shook his head. "I won't let it."

"Then don't let it."

They turned a corner and bright light washed Elaine away. The maze opened up into a courtyard, empty save for two figures in its centre, framed by a flower crafted in glass that glowed from within. One figure was a statue of Eirwen, rising from the ground beneath their feet in an effigy of black stone marbled with silver-grey. She was stood, eyes closed, smiling, beautiful, cradling something in her hands. Her features were sharp and precise, unlike the sarcophagus in Cairnagwyn. Here, she seemed almost alive.

The second figure laid at her feet was Rimestenn. Face down. Remaining hand resting on her feet. Still. Silent. Dead?

"My love." Emyr's smile was pleasure and pain in a torturous tangle. Tom almost expected the statue to open its eyes and reply.

But it was Rimestenn who moved. Looked over its shoulder and let out a mournful cry. He began a slow, awful crawl towards them. Still trying to protect Orlannu. It was gut-wrenching to watch. Rimestenn had given up so much. His life, his thoughts and body and mind, to the point that all he could remember was that he needed to stop anyone he saw.

But Tom had no time for pity. He swung the hammer in an overhead blow, and Rimestenn screamed as Tom kicked aside the pulverised arm, dropped the hammer and staggered to the statue.

Up close, Tom could see that Eirwen's smile was playful. Even wicked. As if she had played a great joke on them all. And she had. She held only a small jar made of the monolith stone.

This, Tom knew, was Orlannu. No mighty tool. No great weapon. Just a tiny cauldron. He lifted it from Eirwen's grip with gloved hands. This could never have saved Katharine's life. And it couldn't help him bring her back. Tom felt suddenly old and tired, as if he was ready for a wind to blow him away, but the wind wouldn't come.

"Who has the sprite?" he asked, holding Orlannu out for someone else to take. He had no interest in it. How to leave? That was all that mattered.

There. A door behind the statue. No handles or hollows or signs of magic. Just a doorway. He leant against it and pushed, revealing a long dark tunnel.

"Come on," he said to the others.

"A moment," Emyr replied.

"I don't think I have a moment to spare."

"He was my friend!" Emyr was knelt beside Rimestenn, who gnashed and thrashed at his king. "Look at what he's done to himself. For me."

Tom looked at Emyr, at Draig's arm in a sling, at Dank's now-flawless skin, at Six's missing leg. Emyr was right. These sacrifices deserved honouring. But the world wavered, drifting out of focus. He didn't have time. "Say goodbye," he said.

Emyr gave Tom a nod. "Go." He placed a hand on his friend's ruined head and the remains of Rimestenn stilled. "Be at peace."

"Dank, with me," Tom demanded. He hefted the hammer as best he could. It was heavy, but he didn't dare face Melwas without a weapon of some kind.

The tunnel was long. He kept brushing against the walls, but it was like he had no thoughts left to snatch. He saw things, yes. He saw Regent talking to a shadowy figure, he saw Gwyllion at the gates of Cairnarim. But he also saw Degor and Rose running ahead of him. He heard Elaine's voice muttering something to him that he couldn't make out. He felt someone take his arm, heard Dank's voice but couldn't make out the words.

The only light came from what little could squeeze past them from Eirwen's statue, so they almost walked into the final door. Tom leant against it, but it was Dank that did most of the work, pushing it on ancient hinges that groaned as fresh air rushed over them and they staggered out of the mountain.

The smell of salt in the air. The feel of sun on his face. Sand beneath his feet. And a rush, as if someone had been holding him down, and now he was released.

"Tom?"

He dropped the hammer. He couldn't make his fingers work.

"Tom!"

His legs buckled and hands grabbed at him as he dropped to his knees. "No," he said, his lips numb, his tongue thick. He reached out, help me, but the world was too dark, he couldn't see anyone there, he felt sand on his face, in his mouth, he couldn't catch his breath, please, don't let this be it, please, not yet, not yet, I don't want to go.

But his body rattled and failed him. And Tom died.

CHAPTER 26

THERE WAS NO PAIN. No thirst. No fever nor chill. He opened his eyes and there was light. He wore the simple clothes he'd taken with him when he'd left Cairnagan, but they were soft like silk. He looked down at his bare feet, over which swirled the fog of the Between. For a moment, he didn't understand. Had the fay brought him here?

No. He remembered now. He knew why he was here.

"Hello, Tom." Glastyn wore a simple white robe, his dark hair unbound and spilling over his shoulders. His expression was tight, like he was in pain.

"Hello, Glastyn." Tom looked about, but there was no-one else. "I was expecting torture."

"What is there to torture?" Glastyn waved a hand at him. "This isn't your body. You left that on the beach."

Of course. But then, "What is it?" He looked down at himself, touched his chest, half-expecting his fingers to pass through his skin. But he felt solid. Real.

"The same as all of this." Glastyn encompassed it all in a glance. "It's whatever you think it is."

Tom frowned, but the fog was already clearing, blowing away to reveal grass underfoot, grass richer and greener than any he'd ever seen. He looked up and saw a beautiful blue sky, not bright enough to dazzle, just clear and gorgeous. Glastyn took a place next to him as the hilltop revealed itself beneath them.

"I died," Tom said, and a crushing disappointment almost dropped him to his knees. Thunder rumbled in the distance.

"You did." Glastyn sighed. "It wasn't what we hoped for."

"I'm sure the fay can torture my spirit."

"That isn't what we meant." Glastyn's words were so sombre, his manner so still. It unnerved Tom.

"So what happens now?"

"That is up to you."

"Something tells me that isn't true."

Glastyn smiled and shrugged. "Shall we sit?" He lowered himself into a seat that wasn't there, and a moment later he was encased in a glass chair, almost identical to Emyr's throne in Cairnagan. Glastyn looked it over and nodded. "Interesting." He gestured for Tom to sit in the second throne that had appeared beside his.

It felt like treachery to sit. To accept a comfort from the enemy. But what use was there in fighting now? It was over. He'd lost.

"Winning a fight only means achieving the goal you set out with," Glastyn said. He waved a hand as if there was a glass in it, and one appeared a moment later. Glastyn grinned and raised it in a toast, sipped it, sighed his satisfaction. "And a fight isn't lost if no-one achieved their goals."

"A fight can be lost by all contestants."

"In order to win, someone has to lose. In order to lose, someone has to win." Glastyn raised his glass again. "Shall we toast?"

A glass appeared in Tom's hand too, filled with an amber liquid. "I won't drink Faerie food."

"You're not in Faerie, Tom. Not yet." Glastyn grinned and quaffed his drink. The liquid changed colour every time Tom looked at it.

"Then where are we?"

"You tell me."

A breeze picked up, clear and pure, and Tom let his eyes follow the dirt track down the hill towards where he knew he'd see a hut. His hut. The one he'd lived in with Elaine, before he'd come to Faerie. A small affair, round with a conical roof, a single room inside, befitting a man of his modest means. But the hut he saw had no gaps in the roof, no patched walls. It was perfect, and smoke drifted from a chimney that simply hadn't existed at the time. Children played outside. Degor. Rose. Others. He heard Elaine calling to them.

"I'm home," Tom said.

"Are you?"

Elaine stepped out of the hut, looked up the hill and waved to him. She was dressed in a blue dress of rich cloth, jewels in her hair, and she was heavy with child.

"No." As he said so, he saw Katharine step out of the forest in the distance, and she waved to everyone as she strode towards the hut. "None of this is real." He turned to Glastyn. "Are you real?"

"We are a motley of thoughts and memories and mannerisms of a thousand dead mortals, Tom. Have we ever been real?" Glastyn drained his glass and held it out for more. Tom blinked and it was full again. "This is your final moment, Tom. The thinnest slice of time, before you leave your body entirely and the fay consume you."

"So I'm imagining all of this?"

"Yes."

"And you?"

"Not entirely."

"I don't understand."

"You're not meant to."

"Why are you here?"

"Because you know you need advice."

"And I think you're the person to give it to me?"

Glastyn just shrugged and took a leisurely sip of his wine. "The fay know things long lost to mortal memory. And you suspect I can be trusted after I recruited Melusine to keep Rose safe while she is in Faerie."

Rose. Who he'd failed by dying. Tom's chest grew tight and he dropped his head into his hands. "Is that what happened?" he asked, because it was better than thinking of how his daughter had been abandoned by a useless father.

"For all of our frivolity, Tom, we do have a certain degree of foresight."

Foresight. It hadn't prepared Tom for this. He straightened, took a deep breath, tried to push aside his failure and his pain. "So what is this place?" he asked. "My idea of paradise?"

Glastyn waved his glass in an expansive gesture. "There are worse to imagine."

Katharine and Elaine embraced like old friends. The children danced around them and begged for gifts from lands abroad. "I'm not sure what it says about me," Tom said.

"Really? It seems clear to me." Glastyn gave Tom a smile given to a daft but endearing pet. "The two women in your life, happy and cared for. Your duties fulfilled. It's rather predictable."

"I'm sorry if you find it dull."

Glastyn waved the apology aside. "You can't help it. But I wouldn't be surprised if your dead friends were down there too. Ah." As if on cue, more figures appeared from the treeline.

Siomi, Ambrose, Kunnustenn, all smiling and laughing as if they were all great friends.

But it was a lie.

"As someone so intimately acquainted with the truth, we should think you know how true a lie can be."

It was tempting. Of course it was. He could walk down this hill and into the open arms of this strange, happy little family. "Could I stay here?"

"No. But it could feel like you did."

He could embrace them all, embrace the lie. But, "I couldn't. I couldn't be happy while Katharine and Rose needed me."

"They're down there, aren't they?"

Fakes. Dreams. Lies. "Enough, Glastyn. I don't want to be here."

"So where do you want to go?"

It was a good point. If it was a choice between this pleasant lie, or being consumed by the fay, then it wasn't much choice at all.

"Why not go back?"

Go back. To Tir? "But I'm dead."

"And you can't think of a way around that?" Glastyn's gaze seemed to look right through him to rest on that little black stone within, cold and hard and dead.

Tom shook his head. "If Ambrose couldn't use magic to heal himself, how could I?"

"Ambrose had nothing left."

"I don't want to be like him."

"Why do you think he was like that?" Glastyn looked at his empty glass, sighed and tossed it over his shoulder, rising out of his chair. Both disappeared a moment later. "He knew it was better than the alternative."

Tom watched the figures at the bottom of the hill. Yes. If the alternative was leaving Katharine and Rose in Faerie, then he would burn himself up like Ambrose a hundred times over. "I need to get to Faerie," Tom said, rising out of his own chair. "I need to save my family."

Glastyn clapped him on both shoulders. "Then it's time to go back."

To leave here. To go back to pain, and uncertainty, and failure. "I don't know how to stop the fay," he admitted.

"That is less of a problem than you think it is."

Tom forced a grin that he didn't feel. "You were never one for riddles, Glastyn."

The fay shrugged. "After what happened to Fenoderee, can you blame us?"

No. Perhaps not. Sudden honesty prompted Tom to say, "I'm scared, Glastyn."

"Scared? If we were you, we would be petrified." But the fay's grin took the edge from his words. "Remember what Melusine told you: strength comes from unity."

But Tom felt very alone on that hill.

"We believe we sang a song for you when we parted in the Heel."

"You did."

"Then we shall do so again." The fay opened his arms and, before Tom knew what was happening, pulled him into an embrace. "Fare you well, Thomas Rymour."

It was oddly comforting. The fay was warm, his robes soft, smelling faintly of lavender. It had been too long since he'd been embraced like this. "Fare you well, Glastyn."

The fay stepped back, drew breath, then stopped and cocked his head. "We almost forgot."

"Yes?" Tom asked, ashamed to be glad for the delay.

"You died, Tom."

"I know."

"A Faerie gift does not extend beyond death." And before

Tom could ask, the fay drew a great breath and began to sing, his voice surprisingly soft and gentle. "The tunnel was long and his nerves were sore tested, for a knight with no blade will fear to be tested."

Tom's audience, it seemed, was over. He reached for his body, and was frightened at how quickly his flesh grasped at him.

"To Malvis' door the tunnel did wend, and by Malvis' hand would be the knight's end."

CHAPTER 27

EVERYTHING HURT.

The pain went deeper than muscles and joints, deeper even than his bones. His entire body felt wrong. As if someone had crept in while he was away and reordered everything. It made him want to flee back to the comforting lie.

But he knew he couldn't. As Glastyn said, this was better than the alternative. So he allowed the scrabbling tendrils of his body to pull him under.

There was something foul in his flesh. It festered in his shoulder, where Rimestenn had bitten him, and lurked in his very blood. And his body was already beginning to come apart, like the different parts of him had forgotten their neighbours and just let go.

First things first. Balance the elements. He reached into his body and found it. There was too much fire, the infection burning his body. So he pulled at it. Out. Get out. And his blood began to move. It crawled around his body, pushing the corruption around and around until it passed the wound in his neck. And there Tom pushed it out. Over and over, until the final traces were gone, and his body was clean again.

He'd thought he'd have to make his body remember itself. But he realised he'd been holding himself back for some time. As the elements had balanced, the grip his body had on him had grown stronger and stronger. So he simply let go.

And now he realised his lungs were burning and without thinking he drew breath, a ragged, jagged breath. He opened his eyes, blinked away sand. The pain was unreal. And something stank. But he was alive.

And the stone inside him had become a boulder.

A voice. Then more. And hands touching him, tugging at him, faces staring into his eyes. Emyr's bones he was tired. And hungry.

He tried to speak, but nothing came out but a hoarse squeak. Someone put water to his lips and he drank until it was taken from him again.

The voices and the faces were beginning to take form. He remembered how to move his eyes, focus them. There. Emyr, cradling his head. What was that expression on his face? Shock? Fear? Relief? He pulled Tom into an embrace.

"My boy, my boy," he said. "My boy."

Tom felt his fingers twitch, flex. How did he make his arms move to embrace him in return?

"How?" Jarnstenn asked. "He's been dead and cold for hours."

Hours. Was that all? He tried to speak again, but he couldn't remember the words. Even breathing was something he had to work at, as if he would forget to do it if he didn't concentrate.

"How touching."

He knew that voice. Knew to expect a knot of fear and dread and wariness at the sound of it. But those waters lapped against the dark boulder and fell still. He couldn't remember how to dread Melwas.

Well. Perhaps that was for the best.

Emyr said, “What do you want?” and spat venom and bile with those words.

“It’s time for little Tom to fulfill his end of the bargain.” Melwas’ words dripped with anticipation. “We promised to keep his woman and his child. In return, he promised to fight us.”

“Yes,” Emyr said. “And if loses, he bends the knee.”

“Yes,” Melwas echoed. “And if he bests us, he wins our queen’s hand for himself. This is the bargain we struck.”

Emyr grew very still. It was like being held by a stone. “Is this true?” he whispered.

Tom tried to speak, but his lips still struggled to form the words. He had promised to challenge Melwas, yes. But not to win Maev’s hand. He growled his frustration and shook his head. Pushed himself away from the old king and crawled across sand, forced himself to sit up.

They were on a beach. Beautiful clear waters stretched away to the horizon. Dunes rolled across the base of the mountains, the sand soft and fine. Strange trees offered shade, grass grew in little patches where it could. And Melwas stood amongst the tranquility, fully armoured in his guise as Malvis, the Black Knight. The enemy of all, so the poem named him. He carried the two sister swords, Caledyr and Emylt, both bronze blades shining in the bright sunlight. Tom couldn’t see the fay’s expression beneath his horned helm, but somehow he knew the Faerie King was smiling.

Tom forced words past numb lips and a befuddled tongue. “Time to fight?”

Melwas’ laugh echoed in his helm. “Oh yes, little Tom.”

Tom’s legs shook like a newborn calf. “He can barely stand,” Six said.

“That isn’t our concern,” Melwas replied. “No-one asked him to die.”

Emyr stood, stepped forward. Ignored Tom’s mumbled, “No,”

and stood before Melwas. "Face me instead," the old king demanded.

"We are not here for you."

"I deserve a chance to regain my honour."

"Your cries of honour and morality are like the buzzing of a gnat." Melwas tossed his head like a great beast. "We bested you centuries past."

"You're not done with me yet."

Emyr was unarmed. Melwas could cut him down again in an instant. Tom took a shaky step. And another. He was growing stronger. His body was remembering what to do. But it was taking too long. His knee buckled and he tumbled to the ground.

But Dank hooked an arm under his and helped him to his feet. "I am not done with you either, Faerie King," Dank said.

"Ah. The traitor." Melwas turned his gaze onto the man who had once been his puppet. "You are so much bolder than when we last saw you. Tell me, did you enjoy cracking open the sorcerer's skull like an egg?"

"I am not your slave anymore."

"You are all slaves." Melwas' satisfied sigh seemed to leak from every plate and joint in his armour. "You dance to our tune."

"Well I'm certainly not doing much dancing these days." Six had pulled himself to the sled and propped himself up beside it. His grin was a baring of his teeth.

Melwas grunted his amusement and hefted his swords, taking them all in with a sweep of the blades. "So you refuse to face us alone, little Tom? You let braver mortals fight your battles for you?"

Tom's lips were more certain, his words clearer when he said, "We'll face you together." Though he had no plan. No idea how to win this fight. "I will stand with my friends. They will stand with me." Or he hoped they would. Because it would be the only way he'd win this fight.

Melwas lifted Emylt to point at Dank. "That one belongs to us. He won't stand with you, will you, Dank?"

Tom looked at the other man. Watched him quail, watched the rage boil beneath the surface of icy terror. "Look at yourself," Tom told him. "You're free of them."

"Come and kneel before us, Dank, and all will be forgiven." Melwas' voice was deep with assurance and trust. "You have provided much diversion and amusement. We thank you for that."

The terror didn't subside. Not at all. But the rage found a crack in the ice. Dank stood a little straighter, and when he spoke his voice didn't quaver. "The armour is a part of him," he told them all, loud and clear. "Cut it, and you'll hurt him."

Melwas lowered his sword and growled. "You betray us."

Dank shook his head. "I stand with my friends." And when Draig offered him an iron sword, he accepted it without flinching. "I stand with you, Sir Tom."

Tom couldn't help but smile. "And I with you, Dank." Tom took a blade too, hefted it. It was short, far shorter than Emylt. But perhaps a sword was less important than who you bore it with. Draig stood on his other side, blade in hand. Jarnstenn stood with them too, hefting Rimestenn's hammer. And Mennvinn too, with iron knives in both hands.

"You will all suffer our eternal wrath!"

Tom turned to face Melwas. So imposing in his black armour, but it was just another show. Just another ruse, a trick, a diversion. An entertainment. "You came to us bearing arms," Tom pointed out. "You threaten us."

"We do." Melwas reached up and removed his helm so Tom could see the vicious glee in his eyes. "Your women will suffer, little Tom, twice as much as you will."

Tom imagined Katharine stretched out on a rack, Puck turning the handles, Mab laughing and clapping over the sound of cracking and popping joints. Rose held over a fire. Rose thrown into ice water. Rose cut and sliced and divided, unable to die, unable to escape the pain. "You swore they would go unharmed," he growled.

"We swore such an oath," Melwas agreed with a slow, smug, perfect grin. "But eternity is time enough to learn ways to inflict suffering without causing harm."

A Faerie boon. Always binding, always cutting the hand that shook on it.

Tom's gut tightened, but a strange calm settled over him even as terror made his limbs shake. "They aren't safe, are they? No matter what I do?"

Melwas dipped his head in the smallest of bows. "You are slow to learn, little Tom. But learn you do." And the Faerie King grinned with unbridled joy. He stood in his black armour, with Caledyr in his hand and a grip around the most important people in Tom's world. For a moment, it felt like all Tom could do was surrender. But that wouldn't keep Katharine and Rose safe. There was only one thing to do in the face of a monster like Melwas, and Tom didn't need Caledyr to tell him what it was: fight.

The arrow whistled past Tom's ear, embedded itself in Melwas' eye, and the fay clapped a hand to his face and let out an almighty roar.

Six lifted his bow in salute. "Together," he said.

Tom touched his sword to his forehead. "Together," he agreed.

Those that could charged.

But if Tom had held any secret hope they could win, it died in the first moment. He wasn't just tired; his body felt wrong. His sword was heavy, his step was leaden, his swings were slow and his mind was dull. And Melwas was strong, powered by a royal rage, faster with one eye than any mortal was with two. He seemed to dodge and parry every blow with ease, and Caledyr and Emylt nicked and notched Tom's sword into a misshapen mess, and the Faerie King laughed as he lopped off the tip with a flourish.

Then Jarnstenn swung Rimestenn's hammer and landed a crushing blow on Melwas' knee.

The fay roared, his leg bent in a way it shouldn't be, he lashed out, cutting a nasty gash across Jarnstenn's face and the dwarf fell.

But Melwas was wounded; his knee wasn't healing, and now he was struggling to dodge blows, and Dank sliced away a piece of armour, Emyr stabbed at Melwas' face, Draig's blade cut armour from the fay's arm, and Tom drove his ruined iron blade towards the Faerie King's chest.

"Enough," Melwas growled, dropped Caledyr and caught Tom's blow in his hand. The iron blade buried itself into his palm, all the way to the hilt but no further. Tom looked up into Melwas' grinning eyes before the fay delivered a back-handed blow that send him down onto his back.

Tom blinked, shook his head. A moment later he felt warmth on his lip, his cheeks. He rolled onto his elbows, dumbly watched blood drip from his nose onto the sand.

Melwas pulled Tom's sword free of his palm, twisted his grip on Emylt and flicked the tip of the blade across Draig's leg, splitting flesh and dropping the elf to the ground. Dank and Emyr fought side by side. But they were no match for Melwas. None of them were.

"Tom!"

It was Six. Crawling across the sand towards him, with the bow over his shoulder and a few arrows in his hands. Tom waved him away. "Get back," he told the elf. His voice sounded muffled, as if he was holding his nose. "It isn't safe." But where was? He shook his head and struggled to get to his hands and knees. He had to get back to the fight. But he was so tired. And he couldn't win. He wasn't a fighter. He wasn't a warrior. He wasn't a Knight of Tir.

"The hammer." Six was pointing, excited, urgent. "Rimestenn's hammer. Look what it did to Melwas' knee." There was grim satisfaction in the elf's voice. "That's how we beat him."

The Faerie King's leg was still bent at an awkward angle; the hammer had delivered a grievous wound. But it had fallen at the fay's feet. There was no reaching it. Tom felt a wave of despair threaten to break over him, only for it to be sucked in and swallowed by the dark boulder he'd burned by healing himself.

"Magic," he muttered. Spat blood on the sand and reached into his pocket.

The shard of Ambrose's old stone prison was still there. Still threatened to tug Tom's thoughts elsewhere. But either Tom was too tired to be distracted, or he had learnt to resist the stone's efforts. He pulled it from his pocket and held it out for Six to see.

The elf nodded. "Not all weapons have an edge," he said.

And if Rimestenn's hammer could break Melwas' knee, what would happen if Tom pushed this little stone down Melwas' cursed throat? Tom's lips stretched over bloody teeth in a humourless grin. "Distract him," he told the elf.

"I've got three arrows left," Six replied. "But he won't even notice them in that armour."

Tom shook his head. "He'll feel it."

Six hefted the bow, notched an arrow. Tom shook his head again, spattering the sand with blood. "Not yet," he told the elf.

"They don't have long."

He was right. Dank was on the ground, leaving only Emyr

standing. And Melwas was still too fast. It was just a matter of time.

"Wait," he told Six. "You'll know when." And he pushed himself to his feet. Staggered towards the fight with no sword, no blade with which to defend himself. "I yield!" he cried. "I yield to King Melwas of Faerie!"

The whirl of blades slowed and stopped. Everyone stared at him in disbelief. "No, Tom," Emyr said. Melwas merely grinned. He'd pulled Six's arrow free and his eye was already healed. Immortal. Invulnerable. But, perhaps, not invincible.

"We swore an oath to each other, King Melwas," Tom said. "You would keep Katharine and Rose safe in Faerie. In return, you and I would duel." He dropped to his knees. It was a battle not to keep going, lie down in the sand and close his eyes. "I cannot best you in battle. I yield. I surrender myself to you."

Melwas cocked his head like a hound.

"You have won." Tom gestured at the others. "We fought together, and you kept us all at bay. What else can I do?"

"This is not how we thought we would win." Melwas sounded disappointed. "We thought we would have to drag you into Faerie."

"It is as I was told many years ago," Tom replied. "Once you eat of Faerie food, you will never be free of it." Which was not what he had been told. But it was true all the same.

Melwas nodded. "Swear your allegiance to us." He pointed his blade, like an accusation. "Bind yourself to us, your true king."

Tom glanced to Emyr. The man who had knighted him. Who had named him his champion, his guide, his protector.

Judged nobler in deed than in what we say. Tom hoped that was true.

"I, Thomas Rymour, the last knight of Tir, hereby swear that

King Melwas of Faerie shall command my loyalty until my dying breath."

Melwas sighed, like a satisfied lover. The smile he turned on Emyr was almost dreamy. "It seems we take all of your knights, Emyr." He took a step forward, and Tom palmed the black stone into his hand. "Perhaps we should command him to take up his sword against you?" The stone tugged at his thoughts, tried to pull his mind into the maelstrom. Melwas took another step. "To kill you all, perhaps?" Tom held himself back from it, as the sprite had shown him, as Melwas took another step. "Even if his loyalty falters, we fancy he would do it. For his women."

For his women. "As you say, my king." Come closer. Just a little closer.

Melwas knelt, brought his face to Tom's. It was a gift. "You belong to us now. Don't you, little Tom?"

The arrow sliced through Tom's ear, across Melwas' cheek, and as the Faerie King cried out in pain, Tom wrapped a hand in his hair and pushed the black stone into his open mouth.

Melwas didn't buck or thrash. He didn't move at all. Instead it seemed like the world shook. The beach, the sea, the sky, the others, Tom lost them all, there was nothing but Melwas' limp form and the effort of keeping a hold on it. Don't let go, don't let go. One moment the body seemed to be nothing but smoke, the next it was solid and real, then it was peeling away, skin from flesh from bone, then wrapping around his hand, then around his wrists and face like tendrils, like tentacles, clawing at his face. Don't let go, don't let go. There was a sound, a painful, constant note that stabbed at him, a scream of pain and rage and treachery. Tom's fingers were on fire, his face was flayed, his body was burnt and he was being pulled piece from piece. Don't let go, don't let go.

Melwas fell to pieces. His skin and flesh dissolved, his bones tumbled from Tom's grip, and they dissolved into ash. But still the world shook, and Melwas' voice echoed all around him, filled with fury and hate and delight. "You and yours will suffer like no mortal ever has."

With nothing to hold onto, Tom was at the mercy of whatever force buffeted him to and fro, and he could do nothing as the black stone tumbled from his grip and the maelstrom tossed him to the winds of magic.

EPILOGUE

When his thoughts came back to him, his mouth was filled with the sour taste of old vomit. Dried blood cracked as he opened his eyes, but the world refused to come into focus. There was light. A thousand smells and sounds, all meaningless. But everything felt solid. Real. He was in Tir. He felt hard stone beneath him. Loose strands of hay. He tried to push himself upright, but he couldn't. He was too weak. He closed his eyes again.

Voices. Footsteps. A shadow fell across his face and he opened his eyes to see two figures standing over him.

"As we promised, Your Grace. Thomas Rymour. In the somewhat battered flesh." Glastyn wore a blue and yellow tunic.

"Eirwen's grace." Duke Regent's satisfaction was grim, his expression cold and hard. He was thinner and greyer since Tom had fled his court. "I had almost given up on seeing you again, Rymour."

Tom knew he had to stand, to run, to escape before Regent could throw him in his dungeons. He tried to rise, but Glastyn put a boot on his chest and it took no force at all to push Tom back down to the ground.

"Very good, Glastyn." Regent nodded. "The Heel owes you a debt."

Tom's mouth was filling with blood. He turned his head, spat. Some of his teeth were loose. "You said you were my friend."

Glastyn gave Regent an easy smile. "All part of the plan, Your Grace."

But Regent didn't seem to be listening. Instead he bent at the waist, looming over Tom. "Welcome back to the Heel, Oathbreaker. We have a cell ready and waiting for you." The duke stepped back so armed guards could pick Tom up and haul him away. "Prepare yourself for a long stay."

The story concludes in the thrilling fourth installment of the Realm Rift Saga; sign up for updates today at jamestkelly.com/readersgroup!

BE THE FIRST TO FIND ABOUT THE FINAL BOOK OF THE REALM RIFT SAGA

Sign up to my readers' group today to get all the updates, sneak peeks, and early access to the last book in Tom's epic journey!

Head to **jamestkelly.com/readersgroup** today!

ACKNOWLEDGMENTS

They say that truth is stranger than fiction. In truth, my life has found strange echoes in the fiction I have written.

If I have been grateful to my wife in the past, then I am now in utter awe of her. Despite everything she has been through, she has unfailing encouraged, cajoled, and bullied me into making time to write. It is no lie to say that these books wouldn't exist if not for her.

The dream of Phoebe inspired much of this book. The reality of her makes it even harder to find the time to write. But she makes me realise what's important.

I could not write these novels without the love and support of my family, and to say that I am grateful is an understatement. I love you guys.

Lindsay Taylor continues to go above and beyond to point out my mistakes.

Ben Jackson continues to explain what I have written.

Annah Wootten puts up with my mistakes and, despite my best efforts, produces stunning cover art for these novels.

Howard Coates took a locale made almost entirely of mountains and somehow created a map that is a joy to look at. I doff my cap to you, sir.

Finally, I'd like to thank and acknowledge you for your support. Knowing that you're reading and enjoying these novels is what keeps me writing. Thank you. You're great.

ABOUT THE AUTHOR

James has studied at the University of East Anglia twice, grown and cut off a ponytail, and builds Warhammer figures but refuses to follow the instructions.

By day, he works as a freelance copywriter, helping you get Your Copy Righter.

By night, he tells the untold. That might be writing fantasy novels, exploring Branwell Brontë's life and work, or interviewing people to tell their stories about making *Dune* games.

James lives in Norwich with his wife, two daughters, and his pet peeves.

jamestkelly.com

instagram.com/realjtk

threads.com/@realjtk

bsky.app/profile/jamestkelly.bsky.social